SHATTERED DESTINIES

SUZANNE NEMEC

Lori,

Thank you for embracing Jennifer & Josh's story. ♡

"Some love stories were never meant to end."

Love,
Suzanne + my spirit guide, Josh

6/2/19

Shattered Destinies
Book 2 of the Destined To Be Lovers Saga
Copyright © 2019 Suzanne Nemec
All rights reserved.

Cover designed by Dane Low of EbookLaunch.com
Interior layout by Standout Books
Editor: Mountains Wanted Indie Author Services & Publishing

This is a work of fiction. Names, characters, organizations, places, events, and incidents are either products of the author's imagination or are used fictitiously. Any similarities to actual persons, living or dead, is purely coincidental.

All rights reserved. No part of this book may be reproduced, distributed, or transmitted in any form or by any means, electronic, mechanical, photocopying, recording, or otherwise, without permission from the author or publisher.

ISBN-978-0-9990417-2-7 (Paperback)
ISBN-978-0-9990417-3-4 (Kindle)

Publisher: Passionately Gluten Free, llc
www.SuzanneNemec.net

This is to all the readers who believe in love stories, soulmates, destiny, and sexy spirit protectors.

MY PARENTS

A special thank you to my parents for giving me such an amazing and adven-turous life. I never realized how much I would miss my crazy childhood, complete with electrical shortages when plugging in the Christmas tree, huge holiday gatherings, chasing our pet duck with my brother and sister making us late to church, playing board games, burnt popcorn, and carsick long scenic drives.

Thanks, Mom, for helping me keep my feet on the ground and live a some-what normal life despite the images I received combined with my vivid imag-ination. As for the voices in my head? I'm happy to say my spirit guide, Josh, is as talkative as ever.

To my Dad in heaven, thank you for instilling in me your love of art and enough of your talent to appreciate how amazingly gifted you were. I will forever treasure our times together displaying and selling your paintings at outdoor art shows, watching you paint for hours, and your love of adventure, which I'm afraid I didn't inherit.

SOME LOVE STORIES WERE NEVER MEANT TO END...

I must have loved you for thousands of lifetimes, for I have never forgotten your touch, your smile, your voice, or your sensual kisses.

Our love knows no beginning, nor will it ever end. Until we are reunited in heaven, I will remain forever yours, my love, until the end of time.

— *ASTRAEA TO DEMETRI, 180 A.D.*

CONTENTS

Chapter 1	1
Chapter 2	8
Chapter 3	19
Chapter 4	33
Chapter 5	41
Chapter 6	49
Chapter 7	59
Chapter 8	72
Chapter 9	81
Chapter 10	89
Chapter 11	100
Chapter 12	107
Chapter 13	116
Chapter 14	123
Chapter 15	131
Chapter 16	139
Chapter 17	149
Chapter 18	161
Chapter 19	170
Chapter 20	182
Chapter 21	188
Chapter 22	194
Chapter 23	202
Chapter 24	211
Chapter 25	220
Chapter 26	226
Chapter 27	234
Chapter 28	243
Chapter 29	255

Connect With Suzanne Nemec	263
Shattered Destinies Playlist	265
Acknowledgments	267
Learn More	269

CHAPTER ONE

It had been hours since Jennifer illegally transported herself to a deserted planet in an unknown dimension. It was a planet where no human life existed, where its three moons cast a silvery stream of light that illuminated the wispy, moss-covered trees outlining the clearing where she and Talos lay cuddled together for warmth.

"Demetri, where are you, my love?" Jennifer called in her sleep, awakening the stealthy panther curled up beside her.

~My lady, to whom are you referring?~ Talos messaged telepathically with a low growl.

"Demetri, please wake up," Jennifer cried out in her dream, her voice full of anguish as tears began to seep from beneath her closed eyelids. "Please wake up, my love; I can't live without you."

~Wake up, princess, we need to figure out where we are.~ Talos gently rocked Jennifer's sleeping figure with his massive paw, claws sheathed so as not to harm his owner.

"Go away! I'll not leave Demetri here alone."

Talos leaned in closer until his snout was mere inches from Jennifer's neck, and he inhaled deeply. ~Please wake up, my lady. We need to find food, water, and shelter in case we're stuck here another night,~ he begged, waiting for any sign from Jennifer that she'd heard him. When none came, Talos swiped his tongue across his muzzle, trying to fight off his growing pangs of hunger. Then he ran his rough tongue across Jennifer's face.

"Eww! Stop!" Jennifer groaned, trying to push the object moistening her cheek away, but it wouldn't budge. Her eyes fluttered open. "Talos!" She stared up at her Christmas gift's copper eyes in confusion. "Where's Josh?"

As soon as she said his name, memories of what happened hit with a vehement force. *I thought he loved me—what a fool I've been.* Her thoughts didn't stop the glimmer of hope rising from deep within her heart. Sitting up, she glanced around for any sign her husband had come after her.

"He hasn't come looking for us, has he?"

~I have no way of knowing that, princess.~

"Why are you calling me princess?" Jennifer asked irritably. "The last thing I want to be is a high priestess or a princess!"

~Yes, my lady.~ Talos tried to appease her, but even his endearment earned him a scowl. ~We need to find something to eat and drink. You must keep up your strength, mistress.~

"You go find something for yourself; I'm not hungry. In case you don't remember, I left my husband," Jennifer sobbed. "I bet if he's out looking for us, it's probably because Gisabella demanded it of him. I'm sure if Josh had his choice, he'd be in Sarnia's arms instead of traipsing around the galaxy searching for the woman he was forced to marry! An eight-year sham of a marriage before he passes me off to someone else, just to placate Gisabella, no doubt."

Jennifer wiped her nose with her sleeve, doing her best to rein in her emotions. *It serves Josh right that he'll be forced to search for me! I hope he has a hard time of it, too! Either way, Josh will need to face me again, and when he does, I have a lot of questions for him!*

~It's okay, princess; you stay here and save your energy while I do a quick search,~ Talos said to his inconsolable mistress before heading toward an opening in the moss-filled trees.

"I'm not a *princess!*" she hollered after the retreating black cat, who disappeared into the grouping of trees and hanging moss. It was light out now, but it didn't help her figure out where they'd landed. Other than a few large rocks and dirt with groupings of sparse grass-like vegetation, there was nothing unusual-looking now that the three moons were no longer visible. In their place was a glowing red object that appeared to be spinning like a gyroscope, casting a soft pinkish hue across the cloudless sky. *I guess that's some sort of sun?*

Now the question is where am I and how do I get back home?! What did I do wrong? I used the exact coordinates that were in the high priestess manual. I bet if Josh or Gisabella were to use the same ones, they'd be able to find us.

Realization of how dire her circumstances were kicked her anxiety into overdrive, making Jennifer wish she hadn't been so quick to transport on her own. Not knowing what dimension she and Talos were in, she had no idea how many hours or days may have passed on earth. *My parents are going to kill me when they notice I'm missing! Have they left to visit their friends in Vermont? Oh, no! Maybe they're searching for me.* The thought of worrying her parents made Jennifer's stomach constrict.

I must try to reach Josh. Surely he cares enough about me and his protector job to help me get back home.

~Josh, it's me, Jennifer.~ *The woman you were forced to marry.* ~I'm sorry to bother you, but I need your help. I have no idea where Talos and I transported to, but there were three moons visible at night. Please tell me you can hear my message.~

Jennifer waited for a response, then tried again to no avail. Breaking down her resistance, she sent a similar message to Gisabella in hope of reaching her, but got no answer. She was still trying to reach them when Talos reappeared with a rabbit dangling from his mouth, swinging back and forth in a sickening way.

"Don't tell me you expect me to eat that! Never mind." Jennifer paled. "Please tell me you found some fruit or nuts in the woods."

~Rabbit's good for you, princess. Don't worry, once I lick away all the blood, it won't look so bad.~

"That's disgusting!" Jennifer's stomach roiled at the sight of the rabbit now lying on the ground with its neck awkwardly twisted. *There must be something I can eat around here.* She hurried away from Talos and his breakfast in search of subsistence as fast has her legs would carry her.

Ten minutes had passed since Josh arrived at Jennifer and his shared bedroom on earth, only to find no sign that his wife had arrived with Talos. With her parents' bedroom at the opposite end of the expansive lake house and the time difference between earth and heaven, it was only 2 a.m., assuring him that his in-laws were asleep.

Fighting off the urge to set out on his own to search the thousands of dimensions and universes in existence, Josh sent off a message to the only person who could help him find his wife. ~Gisabella, have you heard from Jennifer? She hasn't returned home or messaged me.~ Josh kept his tone professional, with no hint of warmth or the slightest trace of their longtime friendship.

~You're just telling me this now?! Have you tried Talos?~

~There's no sign of Talos either.~

~Stay put in case Jennifer returns to earth, and I'll see what I can do from here,~ Gisabella instructed. A quick check in her crystal ball proved useless, and her mystical pond wasn't much help either. *Where are you, Jennifer?* Gisabella fretted before she summoned Merlin.

~I have an emergency and need you to come *here*—~

Before Gisabella finished the message, Merlin was standing before her. "What's wrong?" he asked, pushing back the hood of his black cloak.

"Jennifer's missing," Gisabella blurted through trembling lips.

"Take it easy, lass; I'm sure she couldn't have gone too far. Did she tell Josh where she was going, or did they have a fight? Remember the way we used to argue, and how you wouldn't speak to me for weeks at a time?"

"Oh, there was a fight all right, ending with Jennifer informing Josh she wanted a divorce before she relinquished her high priestess title. After telling Josh and me off, Jennifer transported herself to who knows where."

"Holy hell!" Merlin's jaw dropped.

"Josh transported to earth after Jennifer left, but she never showed up there. That oversized cat you sold to Josh for Jennifer's Christmas present is with her! For all we know, Jennifer and that beast have converged into one—or worse, Talos ate her for breakfast. What the hell were you and Josh thinking—giving our granddaughter a wild animal?"

"How did Jennifer learn to transport? Josh knows it's illegal to teach a visionary to do so on their own."

"Apparently, Jennifer was more clever than he anticipated." Gisabella pursed her lips before adding, "Josh gave her the high priestess manual, probably figuring she'd read each chapter in order, but she must have skipped right to the How to Transport lesson."

"Our granddaughter's a resourceful girl, isn't she? Now all we need to do is figure out where she ended up."

"Merlin, she could be anywhere! The worst part is we can't use my army of protectors to search the galaxies for her because of how risky it'd be if anyone discovered Jennifer's relationship to us. Never mind her future title!"

"I see your point. We mustn't forget about Josh and Jennifer having the first and only interdimensional marriage. That alone is punishable by disintegration if the Council ever found out."

"Exactly." Gisabella laid her perfectly manicured hand on her lover's arm. "If anyone can find Jennifer, I know you can. All I ask is that we find her alive and well, then help Josh patch things up with her."

"Aren't you forgetting that Jennifer is the one who must lead Josh to the dagger? And according to ancient prophesy, Josh will need to defeat and kill the foretold evil entity who's out to destroy every universe but the one he plans to rule."

"Of course I remember. How could I forget that if we fail, every soul on earth and those residing in all other dimensions but the one not destroyed will be disintegrated on the spot?! I sure wish we knew what form this entity will take on, but if we don't locate Jennifer and get the two back together first, when the time comes, Jennifer won't be around to give Josh the weapon," Gisabella tried to reason.

"Okay, let's put our heads together and find the girl. Why don't we start with the High Priestess Manual—maybe we'll find a clue. With any luck Jennifer jotted down some notes that could help locate her."

"Talos, I found some berries!" Jennifer exclaimed, carrying her bounty in the swell of her raised shirt. "Do you think they're safe to eat?"

-I'm not sure, my lady. I could try them first to see if they make me sick.-

"No, Talos. I couldn't bear it if I made you ill." Jennifer popped one of the berries into her mouth, chewed, swallowed, and waited. When nothing happened, she gobbled the rest of her find before sitting down and wrapping her arms around Talos for warmth.

-Princess, we're going to have to find you some water or other kind of liquid to drink.-

Jennifer's hand went instinctively to the locket around her neck. The pain of betrayal clawed at her heart, but, now lost in a land with little chance of anyone finding them, the thought of losing her cheating husband forever was far worse.

"What am I going to do without Josh? He's my everything, and I love him with all my heart and soul," Jennifer softly whispered. *If only Josh had been speaking the truth when he pledged his heart and all his love to me.*

-Please come find me, Josh,- she messaged, pouring all her emotions into the locket she pressed to her heart.

Back on earth, Josh brought his hand to his heart. -Jennifer, is that you?- Closing his eyes, he concentrated with all his might on his heart and the feeling of Jennifer touching him. -Show me where you are, baby,- Josh pleaded in hopes he wasn't imagining his wife's presence.

She must be holding the locket containing my essence.

Soon, he was able to converge with Jennifer's heart, mind, and soul. -Gotcha! Stay put, baby, I'm on my way.-

"Merlin, look—I think this is Jennifer's handwriting," Gisabella said, pointing to the scribble in the margin of the ancient manual.

"Gisabella, if that's where Jennifer went, we'd better hurry! That planet's not inhabitable for humans. I pray she hasn't eaten anything." Merlin grabbed Gisabella's hand and began transporting them both to the coordinates written.

Josh materialized to find Talos standing over Jennifer. "What the hell are you doing? Stand down, Talos, or you'll cease to exist!" he shouted, raising his arm and preparing to fire a fatal energy shot.

"Don't shoot," Jennifer moaned, grasping her stomach.

"Jennifer!" Josh ran to her side just in time to watch Jennifer's eyes roll back into her head.

CHAPTER TWO

Merlin and Gisabella arrived to find Josh performing mouth-to-mouth resuscitation on Jennifer. Without a second to lose, they rushed forward and dropped to their knees to help save their granddaughter.

"Gisabella, help Josh with the chest compressions while I use my powers to bring Jennifer back." Merlin reached into his cloak to retrieve his English Oak wand and waved it over Jennifer several times, creating a foggy healing mist, while Josh and Gisabella worked to revive her.

"Come back to me, Jennifer," Josh begged in between placing his mouth over hers and forcing oxygen into her listless body. "Please come back." He poured another deep breath into his wife. "I can't exist without you." Another breath. "Damn it, Jennifer—wake up now! Do you hear me?" Another mouthful of air forced through her lips. "I love you too much to ever let you go."

"I have a heartbeat!" Gisabella shouted. "Keep talking to her, Josh—it's working."

"Baby, I refuse to go on without you by my side." Josh lowered his mouth to Jennifer's, only this time he felt her kissing him in return. "That's right, baby, stay with me as my wife," he whispered through lips close to hers. Reveling in each of the breaths, she inhaled on her own.

"She's breathing!" He grabbed hold of Jennifer's hand while resting back on his heels.

"Thank god we got here in time," Gisabella cried out with relief. "How did you find her?"

"I felt her energy through the locket I gave her as a wedding gift," Josh explained, leaving out how the locket held his heart and soul's essence.

"I speak for Gisabella and myself when I say how thankful we are that you were here. If not for you, I don't think either of us could have saved her." Merlin patted the younger protector on the back. "Why don't you transport Jennifer back to your honeymoon house? Even though she's breathing on her own, Jennifer will need round-the-clock care until she regains consciousness and we're sure she's stable." Merlin turned to Talos, "Do you know what Jennifer ate?"

~Yes, sir, she ate some berries. I offered to try them first for her, but Jennifer turned me down and ate them all before I could stop her.~

"If you were to see the berries again, would you recognize them?" Gisabella asked.

~Yes, Your Excellency. I can track Jennifer's scent to the exact location.~

"I'll go with Talos and meet you both back at the house after I've located the berries." Merlin took off after the panther, who was already running through the opening in the trees.

"Just relax, baby, while we transport you," Josh reassured her, standing up with his unconscious wife in his arms.

"I'll be right behind you," Gisabella said, bringing up the rear.

It only took a few seconds for Josh to arrive in their honeymoon house in Gisabella's private dimension. "You're safe now, my love." He lowered Jennifer until she was lying on their king-sized bed.

Josh turned to face his former boss with no hint of forgiveness in his eyes. "Thank you for bringing Merlin with you."

"Josh, I know I'm partly responsible for what happened..." Gisabella trailed off when Josh raised his hand, indicating he didn't wish to hear her apology.

"The only reason Jennifer and I are here is because she needs your help—that's all!"

"You of all people know the importance of Jennifer's future role," Gisabella reminded Josh of Jennifer's obligation to take her place as the next high priestess of the Council. "You must help me convince Jennifer to fulfill her destiny."

"I don't give a rat's ass what you want me to do! As far as I'm concerned, you can fuck my wife's obligation! Honestly, Gisabella, don't you give a damn that your granddaughter's lying here half-dead because of the things you said? Surely even you can't be that driven by your title to bring this shit up now! Are you so heartless you don't realize if my wife dies without fulfilling her life-path, Jennifer will be reincarnated—nullifying our forever marriage?! If that happens, she and I will lose any chance of happiness together!" Josh ran a hand through his hair while gazing down at the only woman he'd ever loved.

"I promise Merlin and I will do everything in our power to help her." Gisabella waited for her words to sink in before she continued, "I know you think I'm heartless, but my title doesn't allow me the luxury of forgetting my responsibility to watch over *every* soul in *every* dimension, not just the people closest to me."

"My wife's the only one I care about!" Josh began frantically looking around the room. "Where's Merlin already?"

"He'll be here shortly."

As if Merlin heard Gisabella, he materialized in the room with Talos by his side. "I found the berries, but I fear they might be extremely poisonous," he said bleakly.

"But you have a cure, *right?*" Josh asked in a voice that sounded nothing like his normal tone.

"It'll take some time, but by using the same berries Jennifer digested, I believe Gisabella and I can come up with an antidote."

"Gisabella, don't you have some illegal spell or black magic that'll save her?" Josh didn't bother to hide the anxiety in his voice.

Gisabella held up one of the berries Merlin brought back with him. "I've never seen these before, but I agree with Merlin: if he and I work on a potion, we're bound to find a cure. You stay here with Talos while Merlin and I go to work. If Jennifer starts to have trouble breathing or takes a turn for the worse, message me," she stated before she transported with Merlin to his workshop.

The moment they left, Josh turned his attention back to Jennifer and surrounded her with healing light. "Hang in there, baby; you'll be better soon. Whatever you do, don't you dare give up because you're the only woman I want in my life."

He brought Jennifer's hand to his lips and kissed her icy skin. "Baby, let me warm you like I did when you fell through the ice. Please come back to me as you did then. I don't even care if you yell at me the way you did after finding out I was assigned as your protector. All I want is you in my life forever!"

He lay down and wrapped his arms around his wife, using his body and energy to warm her listless one as the minutes ticked by on the nightstand clock. Nearly an hour and a half had elapsed when Gisabella and Merlin arrived with two jars of reddish-brown liquid.

"We think this might work, but I must warn you, it may cause Jennifer's brain to shut down, or she could slip into a coma," Merlin laid out the facts. "We can't be sure, but it's the only option we have. If we do nothing, she *will* die—if that happens, there's no guarantee she'll go on to live another lifetime. If she does reincarnate, Jennifer may never be the same person."

"Merlin and I decided you should be the one to make the final choice," Gisabella said, placing a hand on Josh's shoulder.

"Please give me a minute alone with my wife," Josh requested. When the bedroom door closed, he brushed a strand of hair from Jennifer's face, doing his best to stay positive. "I wish there was another option, but you heard them, the antidote is the only thing that can save you.

"Baby, it's up to you to fight for your life. Do it for the people who love you. Do it for your family and friends, but most of all, do it for us. Jennifer, I love you with all my heart, and I know you must still love me. How else would I have felt your love for me coming through your locket from so many dimensions away? Please, Mrs. Smith, I promise I'll never ask anything of you again if you do this one thing—live for me."

Though Jennifer didn't answer, he noticed a single tear weep from the corner of her eye to trickle onto the pillow. *She heard me!* His thoughts were interrupted by Gisabella's hand once again upon his shoulder.

"It's time," Gisabella said softly.

"Give Jennifer the tonic," Josh ordered, his eyes never leaving his wife.

"Good man." Merlin patted Josh's shoulder before stepping forward with a syringe. Lifting Jennifer's arm, he used a cotton ball to swab her inner arm with alcohol before inserting the thick needle into her vein. "Josh, be ready to hold Jennifer down if she starts to thrash. Last thing we need is for her to pop a vein and start to bleed out."

Josh placed his hands on Jennifer's shoulders and held his breath as Merlin injected the tonic, watching for any changes in her behavior. When Merlin withdrew the empty syringe, Josh exhaled and wiped his brow.

"We'll need to take turns monitoring her." Merlin's somber voice matched his concerned expression.

"No need to take turns—I'm not leaving my wife's side until she's well."

"Josh, let us help. Jennifer's our responsibility too," Gisabella offered.

"Our responsibility?" Josh shot his ex-boss a dirty look.

"I know you're upset, boy, but that's no way to speak to your boss," Merlin warned with a scowl.

"I guess Gisabella didn't tell you that I quit."

"It's okay, Merlin, there's no reason to get into any of this now. Would you like me to get you anything, Josh? Maybe a glass of wine?"

"I could use a glass of brandy." Josh did his best to summon a softer tone.

"I'll be right back with a bottle of brandy and some glasses." She bustled out of the room.

"What do you mean you quit?" Merlin asked, looking puzzled by the revelation. "You do realize if you give up your position, you'll be sent back to earth to live a series of lifetimes? Surely that wasn't your intention, was it?"

"Oh, I have every intention of staying on as Jennifer's protector, unless..." Josh couldn't bring himself to admit the worst-case scenario. "I don't suppose Gisabella told you why Jennifer ran out on me? If she did, you wouldn't be questioning my motives or attitude."

"I know the gist of what transpired, but I also know Gisabella, and I guarantee she's hurting too. As long as I've known you, she and you have been close friends. Honestly, with Jennifer being so sick, this isn't the time to alienate your closest friend."

"I'll consider what you said." Josh narrowed his eyes at the wizard. "What's the deal between you and Gisabella? The two of you seem rather close."

"On that note, I'd better go see what's keeping her." Merlin winked before heading out of the room.

If I didn't know any better, I'd think that man has a crush on Gisabella. The thought made him smirk. *Heaven forbid if the two of them were to fall in love and have a lover's quarrel—there wouldn't be a safe place in all the universes to escape their fury.*

Four hours and two glasses of brandy later, Josh released Jennifer's hand to stretch. Though her condition hadn't worsened, she showed no improvement, nor had she opened her eyes. Gisabella and Merlin had returned two hours ago, but other than a few whispers between the two, neither said much. Josh wasn't in any mood to start up a conversation.

"Why don't you take a quick walk, lad, before we administer the next dose of tonic?" Merlin suggested.

"Merlin's right, a little fresh air will help to clear your thoughts and your energy. We promise to let you know if anything changes," Gisabella assured. "When Jennifer wakes, you're not going to be much good if your energy's stagnant."

"Fine, I'll be back in ten minutes." Josh leaned over and kissed his wife's forehead before he left. Once outside, he headed toward the pasture with Talos close on his heels, stopping where Jennifer's horse, D'Artagnan, and his horse, Misty, were grazing. At once the horses lifted their heads and galloped over to greet him.

"Sorry, I didn't bring any treats, just sad news. Jennifer's very sick, and I'm not sure if she'll pull through. D'Artagnan, you of all animals might be able to help her by simply thinking of her and talking to her through your mind. I know you can do that because I've watched the way you and she interact."

Josh reached up to scratch the massive Friesian stallion behind his ears, noticing the glimmer in the stallion's eyes. "I'm glad you understand what I'm asking of you. I have to head back now." While Josh prepared to transport back to the house, both horses began pawing the ground, whinnying.

Minutes turned into hours, and hours turned into days in Gisabella's dimension, but there was no sign of improvement in Jennifer's condition.

"Holy hell!" Josh cursed, leaping up, eyes wide. "It's gotta be past six in the morning on earth! Jennifer's parents are going to freak!"

"Calm down; I'll handle them while you and Merlin stay here," Gisabella assured.

"I think I overheard her mom saying something about driving up to visit their friends for the day, or was it overnight?"

"Okay. I'll be back in a little while. If anything changes, message me," Gisabella instructed before she transported down to earth.

Gisabella arrived just in time to dart into the bathroom and lock the door. She turned on the shower as Mrs. Parker came upstairs looking for Jennifer. She didn't have to wait long before a knock sounded at the bathroom door.

"Jennifer, are you in the shower?"

"Yes," Gisabella disguised her voice to mirror Jennifer's. *I sure hope she doesn't come in here.* She quickly remedied the possibly by instilling suggestive thoughts into Mrs. Parker's mind, discouraging her from entering. Heaven forbid what Jennifer's mother would think if she found no one inside the room.

"Your dad and I are leaving for Vermont. We should be back tonight by dinnertime."

"Okay, Mom, have a good time." *Thank god, they're leaving the house all day.*

"See you later—love you," Mrs. Parker said through the door.

"Love you too. See you when you get back." *I hope!* Gisabella thought, knowing if they couldn't make Jennifer better, the Parkers may never see their daughter alive again.

When Gisabella heard the bedroom door shut and footsteps retreating down the steps, she relaxed her shoulders. Within ten minutes' time, she watched as Jennifer's parents pulled out of the driveway. With a wave of her hand, Gisabella placed an energy protection alarm around the house and yard before she transported back to her granddaughter's bedside.

"Everything is all set," Gisabella greeted the moment she returned. "I placed an energy alarm to sound the moment their car pulls into the driveway. They should be back by dinnertime, but I have a feeling it could be earlier."

"That gives us at least another ten hours earth time, so ten more days' time here in your dimension," Josh calculated.

"If you don't mind, I'd like to at least paint my granddaughter's nails and brush her hair. I think she could use a little pampering." Gisabella headed into the master bathroom and returned with a bottle of pink polish, hand lotion and Jennifer's hairbrush, then went to work while Josh headed downstairs to find food for Talos.

"It's been six days and two batches of tonic—why isn't Jennifer responding?" Josh blurted out in frustration.

"I pray this final injection will help her," Gisabella said.

~Gisabella, why don't we go talk somewhere private?~ Merlin messaged, blocking it so as not to alert Josh.

"Merlin and I are going to go make some tea. Can we get you something?" Gisabella offered.

"No thanks," Josh replied, his eyes never leaving his soulmate.

Gisabella followed Merlin out of the room and into the kitchen. Summoning a protection spell, she surrounded the area with enough of a barrier that Josh wouldn't hear them.

"What is it?" Gisabella asked.

"Jennifer should've improved by now. I'm afraid the poison may have done too much damage to her system. If this is the case, there's a greater risk this dosage will put her into a permanent coma." Merlin's eyes closed, and his face scrunched—the only visible signs of how badly the wizard was struggling to fight back his rising emotions.

"There must be something else we can do. What if we were to create another tonic—stronger in strength?"

"Any stronger and it could instantly kill her. My love, we must be realistic. If our granddaughter were to go into a coma here in your dimension, or any other dimension besides earth, we could be found out by the Council and disintegrated for treason."

"But what other choice do we have...," Gisabella's voice faded. "You're suggesting we give up and send Jennifer back to earth?!"

"If we send her back now, when Jennifer dies, Josh can transport her soul to heaven. It'd give us a chance to make things right. You and I could figure out a way to rebirth her soul into another life path. Providing she hasn't suffered any lingering side effects, we can continue with her high priestess training."

"What about Josh?"

"He could remain her protector."

"Merlin, you know I can't do that to him or Jennifer. Suppose she doesn't remember him? We must consider all our options. What about our plan to produce the next heir to the throne? We need them together to accomplish that part!"

"Alright, I'll administer the final injection, but that's it! If it doesn't help Jennifer, then we must let the cards fall where they may."

"I don't approve, but I guess I have no choice but to agree. Now the question is, what are we going to tell Josh?" The color drained from Gisabella's face.

"Let me handle it. He'll take the news better if it comes from me." Merlin pulled Gisabella close for a comforting hug. "Maybe Jennifer will respond, and we won't need to act upon our decision."

Josh felt Gisabella and Merlin return, but he didn't turn around. *Why does their energy feel so different?* He tried reading their minds, but each was blocked, giving nothing away.

"We have the final tonic shot with us. Like before, hold Jennifer in case she has a reaction," Merlin said, holding up the syringe.

"Don't worry, baby, this is the last one. This is going to help you get well so we can spend the rest of eternity together," he whispered close to his wife's ear. "Go ahead, I'm holding her." Josh shut out all the what ifs threatening their happily ever after from creeping into his thoughts. *Please let this one work.*

Merlin squirted the air out of the shot before he inserted the needle into Jennifer's vein, once again slowly injecting the fluid while watching for any signs of reaction.

"*Stop!*" Josh shouted, gripping Jennifer's shoulders tighter. "She's convulsing."

Merlin removed the needle and pressed his finger on Jennifer's vein to stop any chance of bleeding while Gisabella helped to quiet her.

"Her breathing's erratic." Josh watched helplessly as his wife gasped for each precious breath. "Do something! For the love of God, please do something to help her," he cried out.

Gisabella pulled out a tiny blue bottle from her pocket. Opening it as fast as she could, she filled the dropper with the liquid. "This will calm her." She squeezed the bluish liquid into Jennifer's mouth, and within a few seconds, Jennifer went limp.

"Josh," Gisabella said with tear-filled eyes. "We've done all we can do."

"No—there must be something else we can do to save her. This is heaven, isn't it? There must be a cure here—find a cure," Josh begged, breaking down.

"We must return her to earth," Merlin said, his eyes visibly clouding over from the emotional tide surely building within his heart. "Jennifer has slipped deeper—she's in a coma, and as her protector, it's your duty to transport her back to earth."

"Are you asking me to give up hope?" Josh asked before the truth sank in. "You want me to bring Jennifer down to earth to die?"

"As her protector, you're the only one who can transition Jennifer's soul to heaven," Merlin explained, maintaining a dry-eyed gaze.

"I promise to keep you on as Jennifer's protector in her new lifetime," Gisabella sniffled, wiping away the stream of tears.

"But you can't promise she'll remember who I am, or if she'd be able to see me like she could in this lifetime. We were supposed to be together for all eternity, and now you're telling me I need to let her go?"

"I'm sorry, Josh, but our hands are tied. Now her life and destiny are in the hands of a greater power—God. If you bring her to earth, there's always a chance for a miracle to happen. Unlike here, miracles have been known to occur on earth," Gisabella offered, giving Josh something to cling to while doing the hardest thing she'd ever asked of him.

"A miracle? Days ago on earth, Jennifer and I were celebrating Christmas—laughing and decorating her parents' house, and now I'm bringing her back there to die. How can I ever live with myself knowing I'm the one responsible for her—" He couldn't bring himself to say the words.

"Do you want me to help you transport Jennifer?" Merlin offered.

"I'd rather be alone with my wife." Josh stood and gathered Jennifer into his arms, letting his tears fall freely as Gisabella said her goodbyes to her granddaughter, followed by Merlin. With one last blurry glance at the high priestess and wizard, Josh transported Jennifer back to earth for the last time.

CHAPTER THREE

*J*osh arrived back at the lake house on earth solid in form with Jennifer cradled in his arms. He placed her in their bed, then sat down on the edge close to her.

"Are you warm enough?" He waited for Jennifer to reply. "What am I doing? Hoping by some miracle, you'll answer me. Baby, please give me a sign you can hear me. I'd give anything to lose myself in your *cioccolato*-colored eyes—please open them for me." He waited expectantly, but once again nothing happened.

-Sir, if I may, I'd like to come up on the bed with Jennifer—to provide comfort.-

"What the hell are you doing here?" Josh snapped at Talos, who now looked like an average domestic black cat.

-I tagged along.-

"Well, then tag on back!"

-Please let me stay. I feel horrible about what happened. If only she'd eaten the rabbit I caught instead of running off on her own.- Talos lowered his head in shame.

"I guess we all played a part. Fine, you can come up—just stay out of my way." *All I wanted was a few precious moments alone with my wife, just in case these are the final seconds we share together.* He didn't have the heart to make the crestfallen panther leave. Ignoring Talos, he covered Jennifer with their favorite comforter and knelt next to the bed. Clasping her chilled hand in his, Josh began to pray to a far greater entity than every soul alive on earth or in spirit form combined.

"God, I haven't always been the nicest man, but please don't take my shortcomings out on Jennifer. If you could find it in your heart to let her live, I promise I'll serve you well. She's my everything, but I guess you already know that. You probably also know how we lost each other once before, maybe even more than once in previous lifetimes, but I have no memory thanks to—never mind, that's not important." Though Josh couldn't remember his last lifetime on earth as Demetri, he was sure they'd loved each other then as well.

"God, the only thing that matters is my wife. Of course, I'm assuming you're the only other one who knows we're married, other than Gisabella and now Merlin. You must also know I'd do anything for this woman—just name it, and it's yours! I've honestly never loved anyone the way I do Jennifer. My entire world revolves around her; she's the sun and the moon—and every breath I take, I do so only because of *her*. If Jennifer dies, then I have failed her, not only as her protector but also as her husband. She's my best friend, and I hold her above all others. If only I'd told her about Sarnia sooner, and I hadn't pushed her so hard to study, my wife might be here with me smiling as she lay in my arms instead of barely holding on to life.

"Please, God, you're our only hope. I know if Jennifer were able to speak, she'd ask you to give our forever marriage another chance to be. If you take her home now, I fear I'll lose her forever." When Josh was done speaking, he blessed himself while still gazing at Jennifer's closed eyes. Then, using his thumb, he made the sign of the cross on Jennifer's forehead and said a blessing in preparation for the inevitable. Her breathing had grown shallow, and he swore he heard traces of a rattle as she struggled to breathe—all signs death was coming for her.

When the time comes, I must take Jennifer quickly so she doesn't suffer. He choked back a sob at the thought of transporting the love of his life to heaven. "We haven't had enough time together! Baby, please, don't ask me to let you go."

~You must transport Jennifer to heaven *now*!~ Gisabella's message broke into Josh's thoughts.

No! "Please, God—don't take Jennifer from me! All she needs to do is finish her life-path so we can be together in heaven forever. I can't bear to lose the woman I love again!" He poured the very depth of his undying love for his wife into his final prayer to the Lord.

All hope was lost when his desperate plea went unheeded, and soon another message broke into his pained thoughts: ~If you wait any longer, Jennifer's soul will be lost forever. You *must* transport her soul to heaven now!~

Josh clasped his hands over his ears, hoping to block out Gisabella's words, but it was useless. He knew she was right, and if he waited much longer, his wife's soul would cease to exist, removing all hope for Jennifer and his soul to ever meet again.

"Jennifer, my love, please wake up. I'm begging you to give me a sign that you can hear me. Baby, please just open your eyes before I'm forced to end your life and our forever marriage," he whispered softly before bringing his lips to hers for one last kiss.

One by one, each of Josh's tears trickled a path down his cheek to land on her face before sliding off onto the pillow. One very special tear that was larger than all the others somehow forged a different path, seeping its way through the crease in the corner of her lips and into Jennifer's mouth.

"I promise never to forsake you, my love. There could never be room in my heart for anyone but you, Mrs. Smith." Josh brought Jennifer's limp hand to his lips before he broke down. *I need to be strong for the woman I love so her soul will find peace—but how do I say goodbye or keep my soul intact on the off chance our souls might connect once again? That—I cannot fathom.*

"Please don't cry, Josh," Jennifer whispered softly.

"Jennifer!" Josh gazed down in disbelief. "Was that you?"

"Where am I?" Jennifer's eyelids fluttered open to gaze up at the man she loved.

"Are you really back? Please say something else," Josh begged anxiously.

"When did you grow a beard?" Jennifer raised her hand and caressed her husband's overgrowth. "I've never seen you look so tired."

"My love, you have no idea how much hearing your voice means to me—and those luscious, espresso eyes of yours—they're all I need to stay by your side forever."

"I heard you praying and ordering me not to let go," Jennifer said, trying to sit up.

"No, baby, you need to save your energy. You've been unconscious and haven't had anything solid to eat during those six days in Gisabella's dimension, to be exact."

"Days? What happened?"

"I'll explain everything once I transport you back to our honeymoon house so you can get the care you need." Josh lifted Jennifer into his arms. "My darling, I can't wait to see the look on your grandma and Merlin's faces when they see you're alive!"

~Hey, Talos, prepare to transport.~

Before Josh initiated transport, he sent a quick message to the only one who could've saved Jennifer's life. ~Thank you, God—I meant it: just say the *word*, and I'll do whatever you ask of me. I give you my promise that I will cherish Jennifer for all eternity and give thanks in your name each and every day Jennifer and I are together.~ Once done professing his eternal gratitude, Josh transported Jennifer, Talos, and himself back to their honeymoon house.

"My poor child," Gisabella blubbered, rushing over to Josh and Jennifer. "I hope you made it in time to save Jennifer's soul."

"I think I timed it right," Josh said, trying to tamp down his joy.

Gisabella took hold of Jennifer's hand. "She still feels warm, so we should be okay."

"I don't suppose you can feed me before you take my soul?" Jennifer asked dryly.

"What? How? When did this happen?" Gisabella sputtered, joined by Merlin, who immediately grabbed hold of Jennifer's wrist to check her pulse.

"Her pulse is a little low, but that's to be expected after being in a coma."

"You were right when you told me the only place miracles happen is on earth—with God's help, of course!" Josh carried Jennifer toward the bed.

"Oh no you don't! If you insist on carrying me anywhere, you'd better head toward the kitchen. I'm starved!" Jennifer wrapped her arms around Josh's neck, holding on as he carried her downstairs to deposit her into a chair at the kitchen table.

"What are you hungry for, my love? We have chicken or beef broth?" Josh's grin widened.

"You've got to be kidding me! I'm starved, and all you have to offer is colored liquid!"

Josh turned his eyes toward Gisabella for help.

"It's okay—here in my dimension, Jennifer should be able to eat whatever she wants." Gisabella glanced Merlin's way and shrugged her shoulders.

"I'd kill for one of your omelets! Better add a slice or two of toast and a glass of orange juice with a cup of tea."

"Coming right up," Josh said with a quick kiss before hurrying to the fridge where he pulled out several ingredients and poured orange juice into a tall glass.

"Did you paint my nails? Hey, where are my rings?" Jennifer held up her naked hand.

"No worries, I have them tucked away in a safe place," Josh said vaguely. *I sure hope Jennifer's too hungry to ask for more details!*

"I painted your nails hoping it'd make you feel better. I hope you can forgive me for the terrible things you over heard," Gisabella pleaded.

"What things?" The puzzled look on Jennifer's face matched her confusion.

"Don't you remember overhearing Josh and me fighting?"

"I have no idea what you're talking about, Grandmamma. The last time I remember seeing you was when you greeted Josh and me at your house. I believe I was arriving for my psychometry lesson." Jennifer's eyes sought Josh's, looking for some sort of sign about what Gisabella meant, but his poker face revealed nothing.

"You don't remember walking in on Gisabella and me before you transported yourself?"

"Maybe it's best you make the poor girl something to eat and worry about all this stuff later." Gisabella flashed Josh a warning glare.

"Let me guess—the two of you were fighting. That was it, wasn't it? Not that the two of you don't go at it all the time."

"You know us so well, Jennifer. Josh, shouldn't you be cooking?" Gisabella attempted to change the subject.

Not so fast, Grandmamma. "What was this fight about?" Jennifer probed.

"You know how Gisabella and I are always bantering. Honestly, baby, it wasn't a big deal. I'll tell you all about it tomorrow, but for the time being, you need to concentrate on regaining your strength."

"Josh is right; there'll be plenty of time to talk tomorrow," Gisabella added before sending a private message to Merlin: ~Did you have anything to do with Jennifer's recovery? If so, what are the possible side effects of whatever potion you used?~

~Me? I thought you found some magical spell,~ Merlin admitted.

~Wait a minute, you don't think some rogue spirit took over Jennifer's body, do you?~ As Gisabella messaged the words, her eyes widened, turning once again to study Jennifer. ~You know how some of them like to sneak in just before the person's heart stops, so they can experience what it's like to be alive.~

~Anything's possible. After all, Josh would've been too distraught to notice another spirit entering the room. Although, if that were the case, I find it hard to believe he wouldn't have noticed when it got close enough to enter Jennifer's body,~ Merlin debated.

~Maybe that stray cat you sold Josh had something to do with this? It's possible Talos could have distracted Josh to allow some spirit from the dimension where he and Jennifer were stranded.~ In unison, they glanced at Talos, who was busy cleaning his paw.

~Nonsense, I personally vetted Talos.~ Merlin turned to the panther seated across the room. ~Talos, what do you know about Jennifer's improvement?~

~Josh was speaking to God one moment, and the next, he was telling

Jennifer how he must transition her soul. Oh—and he kissed her on the lips! *Yuck*! I could've done without *seeing* that!~

~Are you sure that's all?~ Gisabella's eyes narrowed.

~Yes, Your Excellency, come to think of it, Josh seemed just as surprised by her recovery as you and Merlin. He also muttered something like, "Miracles do happen here."~

Gisabella looked on as Josh placed a large plate containing a vegetable omelet, toast and sliced strawberries, along with juice and tea in front of Jennifer. Then she watched in amazement as Jennifer dug into her meal with gusto.

~Jennifer sure is hungry,~ Gisabella messaged to Merlin.

~Maybe we'd better observe her. I'm not sure what Josh meant by a miracle, or if God played a part in her sudden recovery. Either way, I wouldn't share any information or classified teachings with the lass until we're sure Jennifer's the same girl.~

~Should we say anything to Josh about keeping his eyes open for anything strange about her?~

~I think it's best if we keep this to ourselves. If Josh were to catch wind of our suspicions, he may accidently alert Jennifer.~

~Good thinking. Maybe if you volunteer to check Jennifer's vital signs, you may find something.~

"Jennifer, when you're done eating, I'd like to do a quick check of your vital signs, you know, blood pressure, heart rate, and temperature," Merlin said.

"But I feel great." Jennifer popped another piece of buttered toast into her mouth.

"I can see that, but after what you've been through, I think we'd all feel better if I did so. It'll only take a few minutes."

"If you must." Jennifer put down her fork to gaze at the unknown bearded man. "May I ask if you're some sort of doctor?"

"Jennifer, I'd like you to meet the man you once told me didn't exist —Merlin!" Josh's grin doubled in size at the sight of Jennifer's expression as it changed to one of disbelief.

"Nice to meet you," Jennifer mumbled.

"Aren't you a polite lass?" Merlin let out a chuckle. "Don't let her fool you, Josh. She was a little hellcat as a child! So much so that her grandmother had a hard time controlling her antics."

"Gisabella, I'd have liked to see that!"

"Jennifer got into so much stuff that watching over her was a fulltime job!"

"Hey, I happen to be right here," Jennifer admonished.

"See what I mean, boy?" This time Merlin laughed so hard he sent Talos scurrying under the kitchen table with his tail between his legs. "Ye better be careful, Jennifer, before Josh takes to calling you 'hellcat' as well. The things you used to get into! Honestly, lass, you wore the title well."

"Nothing like picking on a helpless girl." Jennifer fluttered her lashes.

"I'm so thankful you're still with us, Jennifer," Merlin gushed. "I don't wish to tax your memory, but I don't suppose you have any idea who I am to you?" When Jennifer stared back with a puzzled expression, he added, "I'm your grandfather."

"What the fuck?!" Josh gasped.

"Jennifer, remember how I once explained how I was your soul's grandmother; well, Merlin is your soul's grandfather," Gisabella quickly clarified, ignoring Josh's shocked expression.

"Um—okay," Jennifer answered tentatively.

"I guess I should've waited a while before I dropped that wee bit of news," Merlin offered sheepishly. "But I couldn't help it."

"I sure hope I didn't inherit your profound sense of timing." Jennifer jumped when her comment caused a roar-like laugh from Merlin.

"That'd be just like you to say such a thing to your elder! See what I mean, boy? Jennifer's hellcat nickname was well earned!"

"Wait a minute!" Josh said, scratching his chin. "I thought Gisabella was married to her life-path husband?" Josh glanced between his boss and Merlin, both of whom shrugged as if they hadn't dropped a bomb in the middle of the room. When he noticed Jennifer's anxious expression, he quickly changed the subject.

"Hellcat or not, I don't have to tell you how thankful I am to have my wife back." Josh leaned in closer and pressed his lips to Jennifer's. "Promise me you won't ever scare me like that again, baby." He smiled when he saw how much color his kiss brought to her cheeks.

"I'll try my best," Jennifer vowed as she gazed into her husband's warm but tired eyes.

"You better try your best, my little hellcat; otherwise, there'll be hell to pay." Josh whispered the warning so no one else but Jennifer could hear.

"Mmm, I like the sound of your sexy threat," Jennifer sighed half to herself while the two pink spots of color on her cheeks grew in size. *Why does my man's dark side sound so sexy?*

"Oh no you don't, Mrs. Smith—for god's sake, woman, you were in a coma less than two hours ago. Get this through your head: I'm not touching you until you're fully recovered and we've had a chance to talk," Josh scolded after reading Jennifer's private thoughts.

"Hey, Merlin—I think you'd better check Jennifer's vital signs before Josh heats her blood! Any hotter and she'll be burning up!" Gisabella laughed when both lovers turned toward her with mouths agape.

A little while later, once Merlin was satisfied Jennifer was in good health, he and Gisabella took their leave. Within moments, they were standing in his home scanning his vast book collection for anything that could provide them with answers. Merlin stood and stretched before he went back to the bookcase in search of more tomes with potentially useful information.

"I hope that book is more helpful than this one," Gisabella sighed. "Do you honestly believe we have a chance of finding information on the berries Jennifer consumed in a book?"

"I sure hope so because we need to figure out if she'll suffer any lingering side effects. Our plan may need to be altered depending on what obstacles might get in our way. Once we find Josh and Jennifer's unborn child's soul and the berries Jennifer ate, we'll have a better idea what we're dealing with." Merlin placed two more books on the table and took a seat across from Gisabella, where they continued flipping through pages for the next few hours in silence.

"These look similar in size, but they're red." Gisabella turned the book around so Merlin could see.

The wizard studied the photo then read the description. "These could be related to the berries I found, but I can't be sure. Why don't we keep these in mind while we look further?" He reached for the latest book he'd brought to the table and began flipping through the pages.

"I think I found them!" Merlin pointed to the blueberry lookalike. "It says here they only exist in several uninhabited dimensions." He continued to skim the text until he found what he was looking for. "Sure glad we found this when we did."

Merlin's grave tone alerted Gisabella. "How bad is it?"

"The lasting effects are known to shorten the survivor's life by many years."

"There must be something we can do to extend Jennifer's life. She has so much to learn before taking over my position. And what about our plan for the baby and her life-path? Our granddaughter must complete her destiny for Josh and her to be together. In case you're forgetting, we need him by Jennifer's side to help her reign. Without proper training and Josh's help, she's sure to falter!"

"Calm down, love," Merlin coaxed. "What if we were to accelerate Jennifer's destiny?"

"How long do you think she has?"

"Ten years tops, but she'll become ill much sooner. To be on the safe side, I'd say Jennifer could have as few as six years left."

"Six years?! That's right around the corner—how in the world are we going to hide this from Josh? You know he'll flip if he finds out what we're up to." With each word spoken, Gisabella's voice rose an octave.

"Six years is better than none," Merlin reminded her how close they'd come to losing Jennifer and having zero options.

"We'll need to move Jennifer's required marriage to soon after she finishes college. I've been thinking of a way to get them into the same dimension, you know, for the sake of having a baby. I suppose I can offer Josh some sort of trip with Jennifer where he'll be solid in exchange for his help with her lessons. Now, all we need is to find their baby's soul."

"So you plan on tricking him as you did me?! Aye, lass, even though I should still be furious for the way you deceived me, I'm more thankful to have had Olivia with you and my lovely granddaughter. I must say it's a dicey hoodwink of a plan, but if it works, it'll be worth the risk! I doubt Josh will suspect a thing, and later when he finds out he's a father, I hope he'll be too happy to care that we tricked him." Merlin's forehead creased. "Please tell me you don't plan on placing Josh in Jennifer's dimension the entire time they're on this supposed trip?"

When Gisabella blanched, Merlin cringed.

"I know it's a huge risk, and no one other than the two of us can ever know what we've done. I just hope we can pull it off! I mean, technically Josh will still be considered a spirit, and it's not like he'll have a new life-path or destiny assigned to him during that time."

"Aye, lass, I swear you could reason your way out of a starving lion's mouth. Don't think all your jibber-jabbering has convinced me your plan is foolproof! But if that's the best we can come up with to make this all happen, then so be it." Merlin sighed. "I guess I should ask if Jennifer's life-path holds any other requirements I should know about?"

"Only a few minor things that can be easily changed."

"Maybe I could teach Jennifer some basic wizardry techniques," Merlin offered.

"I bet that'll go over well with Josh! I wonder how he'll react when she learns all his magic tricks?"

"Kind of makes me feel sorry for the lad! I mean, he sure has his hands full—not unlike myself with you!" Merlin chuckled when his comment earned him a dirty look.

"While we're together, why don't we use the time to search for their unborn child's soul? With any luck, he or she hasn't lived many lifetimes or won't currently be alive on earth. I hate to have to take the child's soul away from a loving family."

"Let me make some room on the table." Merlin set to work removing the stacks of books. "To think their child will not only be the first between a spirit protector and his appointed charge, but it's also the second interdimensional baby born on earth. Not to mention Jennifer herself being born to the first interdimensional child—our daughter, Olivia."

"I don't know about you, but I'm getting giddy just thinking about it! Either way, we'd better keep our heads about us."

"Aye, lass!"

"I think we'd be better off starting in the Hall Of Records," Gisabella suggested.

"Maybe only one of us should go as not to attract attention."

"Good point," she agreed.

"Why don't I go and see what I can find while you check on the kids?" Merlin offered.

"I'll have you know that one of those so-called kids is almost as old as I am," Gisabella retorted before bidding Merlin goodbye.

Once alone, Merlin donned his magical cloak and transported to the Universal Hall Of Records, where he easily walked past the guards unseen. He headed to the section that held all the ancient life paths. The collection was sparse, the only records remaining after a band of rebels vandalized the building over a thousand years ago. They'd had some stupid notion that if they could muck up millions of souls from completing each of their necessary lifetimes, those souls wouldn't be able to reside in heaven, and some would be unable to become spirit guides to others alive on earth.

Let me think—what year did Josh die in the Colosseum? I believe Gisabella said 180 A.D. Upon reaching that section, Merlin scanned the folders until his intuition blared loudly in his mind. A quick check of the folder proved it to be Demetri, Josh's name during that previous lifetime. After that, it was easy to find Jennifer's former soul, Astraea. Then Merlin helped himself to the seven possible folders that could be their unborn child. Since there were only a few, he was able to easily to locate each of their current life-path folders before anyone discovered what he was doing.

Merlin tucked the folders under his cloak and skedaddled out of the building before he transported himself home.

Merlin immediately ruled out all the babies who'd survived months into the pregnancy since Astraea had been no more than a day or two pregnant when Demetri was murdered and she killed herself. A couple other souls had gone through the birthing process in 180 A.D., narrowing the search down to two possible souls. Upon closer examination, one had lived many long, untroubled lifetimes. The other soul, however, had never made it past a few hours after being born each lifetime. If this were the child they were looking for, its soul had remained pure and untouched since the day it'd been conceived by Josh and Jennifer's former selves.

This has to be their child! A new soul full of unconditional love, who's never known anger or hate means no bad karma could hold it back! I must find this child's soul! Merlin rose with the life-path in hopes he'd picked the right soul.

~Gisabella, come quick, my love,~ Merlin messaged, eager to get started. He didn't have to wait long for Gisabella to appear.

"Did you find the baby?" she asked eagerly.

"I believe I have—take a look." He handed Gisabella the life-path folder.

After flipping through the pages, she looked up with a huge smile. "If this is the one, it's a miracle this soul has remained untouched. Why, it's almost brand new! Think of how pure all this soul's intentions will be, never having experienced anger, hate, greed, deceit, or any other emotions that leave behind everlasting scars. Think of all the possibilities!" Gisabella's eyes danced as she took another quick look.

"My thoughts exactly!"

"Where's the soul now?" Gisabella asked.

"It's being returned to heaven after being aborted."

"Aborted? Oh dear, that's sure to leave a scar on the soul. Then again, it's a scar that will help the soul develop a deeper sense of compassion and love. When Astraea unknowingly killed their baby after taking her own life, that too gave the soul a lesson in compassion and love. Surely, even though it had only been conceived hours earlier, the soul would have felt Astraea's insurmountable grief of watching her lover being murdered in the arena."

"As this is their child, we better intervene and claim it as ours," Merlin warned. "Once we do so, you and I can work out a timeline for our plan."

"Speaking of timing, Jennifer must return home in less than nine days of our time in case her parents come home earlier than expected."

"How soon before we can move forward with the baby?"

"We can hold the baby's soul in limbo until Jennifer's last year of college. Hopefully we can speed up her life-path before the aftereffects of the poison take hold. Either way, we must keep this between you and me," Gisabella warned. "If Josh finds out, he might try to stop us or refuse to let go of Jennifer and his baby. I pray we can pull this off without anyone finding out about our plans. I guess all I can do now is push Jennifer harder so she'll be fit to take over my position. Things have sure become a lot harder now that our granddaughter's cut her original life-path, which was designed to be thirty-plus years."

"It's the only shot we have, love. As soon as you leave, I'll see about collecting the baby's soul. The last thing we need is your name to be linked in any way with taking this particular soul. Off you go; the sooner I get going, the less chance I have of getting caught. You know how those crowds of friendly spirits show up every time a soul comes home to heaven. I'll let you know when everything's secure. Until later, my love." Merlin sealed his words with a kiss then watched as Gisabella transported back.

Now I must find Josh and Jennifer's child's soul before anyone else does! Merlin declared before placing Jennifer, Josh, and their baby's life-path folders into the fireplace.

CHAPTER FOUR

"Behave yourself, Jennifer," Josh warned, taking a couple steps backward.

"What's wrong; don't you trust me?" Jennifer took a few steps closer, reaching out her hand toward Josh, but before she made contact with his newly grown beard, his hand shot out with lightning speed, encircling her wrist firmly.

"I think we should take things slow until you're feeling more like yourself." Despite his attempt at a blank façade, he failed to stop the increased need to blink. "If you're starving, I can make you something else. What're you in the mood for?"

"I thought I was making it clear—I'm in the mood for *you*!" This time Jennifer employed her most seductive voice.

"But, Mrs. Smith, you've been unconscious in this dimension for almost a full week. I think it's best if we wait until you're feeling more like yourself."

"I don't know what you're talking about; I feel great, and I'm hungry for you." Jennifer almost added a foot stomp, but that would have been a little over the top.

"You were in an undiscovered dimension and may have picked up something we don't know about. So, for now, we should abstain." Josh studied her intently, accentuating the creases in his forehead he'd acquired since she'd run out on him. "Perhaps you'd like some apple pie. I think there's one from the bakery around here. Gisabella didn't make it, so it should be safe."

"What kind of something would I have picked up?" Jennifer asked, trying to free her wrist.

"Oh, you know, something lying about."

"Not you too! Did you see the way Gisabella and Merlin were studying me? Geez! I bet if they had a magnifying glass, they would've used it! They were giving me all sorts of sideways glances mixed with intermittent raised eyebrows the entire time I said or did anything. Call me paranoid, but I swear they were messaging each other back and forth. Talk about making me feel like I am some freakazoid from another planet! Honestly, what's wrong with all of you?"

"Try to understand, baby—up until a few hours ago, you were unconscious and barely alive after eating some berries from the uninhabited planet you landed on. When you worsened, I was sent to Earth with you to transition your soul. I only had a few moments left to take you to heaven and was saying my goodbyes when you snapped out of your unconscious state. And now, you're acting as if nothing happened, devouring two plates of food—then eyeing me like I'm next on the menu. What else am I supposed to think?"

"I almost died from eating berries? Well, I feel great now. I mean—I only wanted to taste you. I promise I'd have only taken a pint or two of your blood." Jennifer did her best to keep a straight face, but when Josh sank his teeth into his bottom lip with a worried expression, she burst out laughing. "Look at you! I almost had you ready to run out of the house!"

"Not even close! I just wanted you to think I was alarmed."

"Then how do you explain your vise grip on my wrist?" She eyed his long fingers that easily encased her slender wrist. *Make love to me, damn it!*

"Oh—right." Josh hesitated before loosening his hold. "Are you really hungry or just playing around?"

"Only for you," she toyed, staring intensely once again at the pulsing artery keeping time with Josh's heartbeat.

"Alright, Jennifer—you had your fun! How about I run a nice hot bath for you?"

"As hungry as I am for my man, I guess your offer sounds better than a few pints of your blood!" she razzed with an impish grin.

"Be thankful I need to treat you with kid gloves for the next few days." Josh raked his eyes over his wife and added, "But after that, I plan on taking matters into my own hands." Josh held up his palm with a devilish look and watched Jennifer squirm.

"You wouldn't dare!" *Geez, his offer sounds so hot, I'm almost tempted to take him up on it—providing he follows it up with a few rounds of sex and a couple of orgasms!*

"I think you know the answer to that, my little hellcat. Now let's get you upstairs and into the tub. If you behave yourself, I'll wash and dry your hair too."

"Then will you tell me what happened and give me my rings?"

"Maybe—I'll see how tired you are." *The last thing I want to do is risk losing Jennifer all over again when I tell her about Sarnia. What if it causes her to remember all the other things Gisabella and I said that night?*

When he finished drying Jennifer's hair, Josh carried his wife to bed, pulled the blanket over her and gave her a quick kiss. "Sleep, baby, we'll talk later."

"Your beard tickles," Jennifer mumbled sleepily before drifting off into a deep slumber.

Once Josh was sure Jennifer was asleep, he wasted no time sending a message, ~Gisabella, why were you and Merlin scrutinizing Jennifer so closely? Whatever you two were doing made her uncomfortable.~

~Don't blame me; I was only following Merlin's suggestion. Other than Jennifer's bountiful appetite and energy, I saw nothing unusual.~

~Either way, she picked up on your behavior and the way you were secretively messaging each other. Keep it up and you'll alienate your granddaughter more than you already have. It's only a matter of time before she recalls us arguing and all the stuff you and I said to each other.

I, for one, plan on coming clean tomorrow so she doesn't find out about Sarnia from anyone else but me.~

~Jennifer may seem like herself, but I'd like you to keep an eye on her. None of us know what other effects those berries had on her, or whom she may have come in contact with. If you notice anything odd, you must tell me.~

~Fine,~ Josh shot back.

~I, for one, want to believe Jennifer's well enough to resume her high priestess training.~

~Are you fucking kidding me? You'll be lucky if Jennifer agrees to visit you on holidays! And if she remembers the bogus life-path marriage you've locked her into in eight years' time—scratch that, seven years now, you can say goodbye to Jennifer forever.~

~Do I need to remind you of your responsibilities as your wife's protector?~ Gisabella chastised. *Thankfully it doesn't appear Josh has picked up on the revised timeline for Jennifer's life-path.*

~You can keep playing that losing card because, as far as I'm concerned, other than playing some protection games with Jennifer, she has no need to learn all the stuff you expect of her.~

How dare he defy me, Gisabella cursed. *Too bad he's the only protector strong and talented enough to teach Jennifer, but he'll never fall for threats like my other protectors. I got it!*

~I can see you have me at a disadvantage.~ Gisabella began setting her impromptu plan into action. ~What if I were to reinstate you as my number one protector in exchange for your help in convincing Jennifer to fulfill her title?~

Sounds like she's desperate enough to eat crow? Josh smiled at the thought of his boss being at such a disadvantage. ~Nah, I don't care about titles. Jennifer's not the most eager visionary; in fact, she's quite a handful, as I suspect you already know. Didn't you and Merlin used to call her a "hellcat?"~

~Fine, why don't we just cut to the chase? Tell me what you want in exchange for Jennifer's training and to help convince her to accept her destiny?~

~Erase the part in Jennifer's life-path that says she must marry another man.~ Josh cringed, knowing his request would earn him an earful.

~You're lucky I don't replace you as Jennifer's protector for asking such a thing! However, seeing as though I'm feeling extra generous toward you for bringing my granddaughter back to me alive, I'm prepared to give you and Jennifer a second honeymoon in Italy—say, five days alone together.~

~What good is that? Me being a spirit in another dimension following my wife around while a bunch of horny Italian men hit on her? Not on your life!~

~What if I can make it possible for you to enjoy Italy—solid the entire time, without any of the normal restrictions? That way you can fend off all the guys yourself!~

~So, let me get this straight. Unlike the limited times I get to be solid on earth, during that time Jennifer and I would be in Italy, I'll be allowed to interact freely with everyone? Even strangers?!~

~Yep, as if you were alive on earth! Don't worry, I have my ways of getting around the time limits and interaction stipulations.~

~You mean your illegal methods?~

~Do we have ourselves a deal or not, Josh? If so, I'll honor my part after Jennifer's been trained—but no sooner than her last year in college. Being such a good friend, I'll even reinstate you as my top protector, explaining how it was all a misunderstanding.~

~Make it seven days in Italy, and I'll even make sure Jennifer knows how to properly transport and manipulate dimensional time zones.~

~Excellent! You can start while she's here recovering.~ *That was easy! Looks like Josh hasn't gotten any better at negotiating deals. Poor guy, doesn't he know I was prepared to offer a whole lot more than a week's vacation in the same dimension?*

~First, I'll need to tell Jennifer about Sarnia before you cause her to dump me again.~

~Again? I hadn't realized you'd patched things up. As far as I could see, my granddaughter's left hand still looks naked.~

~Her wedding rings wouldn't have left her hand if it weren't for you!~ Josh snapped back, reminding her how big of a mess she made between himself and Jennifer.

-You sound a little grumpy; maybe you should take a nap.- Gisabella cackled loud enough for Josh to hear.

Ignoring Gisabella's irritating message, Josh headed to the bathroom. Once he'd shaved his beard off, he undressed and slipped into bed next to Jennifer. Wrapping his limbs around his wife, he nuzzled her neck through her silky hair, reassuring himself that she was alive and well.

An hour later, Josh woke with a start, throwing all his senses into high alert. Glancing at Jennifer showed her to be peacefully sleeping, but to his dismay, he found Talos stretched out by their feet. *That cat must have weaseled his way onto the bed!* Scanning the house for any sign of unwelcomed energy revealed all was well and eased his adrenaline rush.

-Seriously, cat—what are you doing on our bed?- Josh messaged.

-Helping you protect Jennifer,- Talos replied before lazily standing and arching his back. After stretching, he lay back down and curled back into a ball of midnight black fur, nose to tail, and closed his eyes.

-Hey—you mangy cat!- Josh glared at his Christmas gift to Jennifer. -Don't get used to sleeping in our bed because after tonight you'll be on the other side of the door.-

-If you don't mind, I'd like to go back to sleep,- Talos messaged with a low growl.

-Fine, but you'd better watch your step before you find yourself sleeping outside.-

Talos lifted his head. -If that'd been the case tonight, seeing as though you were sleeping, who else but me would've been alert enough to protect Jennifer?- Once again the panther rested his head on his paws and closed his eyes.

I need to speak to Merlin about that beast! I should've given Jennifer a watch for Christmas! Josh turned his attention to something more palatable than the ornery black panther—his sleeping wife—and concentrated on not dozing off again.

A new day rose with rays of sunlight streaming through the chandeliers, casting rainbow-colored sparkles around the room.

"Good morning, baby," Josh greeted the moment Jennifer's eyes fluttered open.

"Huh? Oh, good morning," she grumbled.

"How are you feeling?"

"Um, good—why?"

"Just asking. So, no bad dreams or ill effects from the berries you ate?"

"Not unless you count the odd way you're staring at me." Jennifer bit her bottom lip. "Perhaps a kiss would've been a better greeting."

"You're so right." Josh lowered his mouth to her puckered lips for a tender kiss before raising his head. "Why don't we go downstairs and have breakfast? You can keep me company while I cook."

"But your lips taste so good, and I love how smooth your face feels minus the beard." She ran a pink-polished fingernail along Josh's jawline. "Couldn't we just stay in bed a few more hours?"

"As tempting as your suggestion is, you need to eat, and I need to talk to you about what happened before I agree to make love to you."

"This is the second time you've mentioned needing to *talk*. What's wrong? And, for that matter, I'd like to wear my wedding rings. You're not breaking up with me, are you?"

"You think I'm breaking up with you? You've got that all wrong. I have your rings in a safe place, and I promise to get them once we've eaten breakfast." He lifted Jennifer's left hand to his lips. "You gave us all a scare. Honestly, I never saw Gisabella so worried. Please try not to be too hard on her, though I admit she sometimes has an odd way of showing her love."

"I hope she stops staring at me like I have three heads! Honestly, what does she think I picked up?"

"Don't mind her—she's just overly protective."

"Great! Having one protector is more than enough!" *Yes, that comment was directed at you, Josh.*

"I see we'll need to work on your blocking skills," Josh said sardonically.

"I think we better go make breakfast before I fade away. No need to concentrate on blocking skills, not with such a busy day ahead of us: cooking, kissing, eating, talking, having sex, and more sexy stuff." She lost all attempts to squelch her rising fit of giggles.

"Are you laughing at me?" Josh asked. Much to his dismay, she only laughed harder. The way she was laughing, complete with tears running down her face, transformed his expression. "Go ahead and laugh all you want. I swear it's the most musical sound I've ever heard. To think I could've lost you over—" He caught himself before he said too much.

I wish he'd just spit it out already. "Since you won't tell me or give back my rings until after we've eaten, then we need to go downstairs." Jennifer pulled on her robe, cinching it tightly, and stomped out the door, leaving Josh and Talos in her wake.

CHAPTER FIVE

"You make the best blueberry pancakes," Jennifer sighed, putting down her fork. "It's great having a chef in the family."

"Don't you mean as your husband?" Josh's tone held no humor.

"Of course—although, you refuse to give back my wedding rings until you speak to me. About what, I don't know, but my imagination is coming up with all sorts of unsavory scenarios."

"You have it all wrong; I'm the one worried you'll leave me." Josh reached over and took hold of her hand while he continued, "You're so pure and loving that I'm the one who feels undeserving of you."

"Nothing could be further from the truth. Don't you realize what an amazing man you are?" she expressed, but her words seemed to fall on deaf ears.

"Promise you'll hear me out and give me a chance to explain before you leave again," Josh said, giving her hand a gentle squeeze.

Leave him—again?! Oh no, it must be bad. "Of course I'll listen."

With his other hand, Josh reached into his pocket and pulled out her diamond engagement ring and wedding band, then placed them on the table, trying to keep his frayed nerves in check. If he couldn't convince her that Sarnia had never been anything to him—*that he could remember*—he might lose Jennifer forever.

"The night you left, you were asleep, and I'd gone downstairs to speak to Gisabella, but our conversation didn't go so well. In fact, it became very heated, and before long we were shouting at each other. We were so busy yelling, neither of us noticed you coming down the steps. It wasn't until the rings you threw hit my cheek that I saw you standing there. You were so angry, and you wouldn't let me explain..." his words trailed off.

"What did I hear?" Jennifer croaked out.

"Before we were married, I'd transported to my apartment to get dressed. When I arrived, I ran into a neighbor who was drunk out of his mind—so much so, he let a woman into my apartment whom I wanted nothing to do with."

Jennifer paled and shut her eyes momentarily before she spoke, "Did you ask her to leave?"

"Absolutely. In fact, I told Sarnia I wanted nothing to do with her, and when she didn't leave, I threatened to have her fired."

"Good!"

"That was after I found her waiting for me in my bed—naked," Josh confessed, knocking the air out of Jennifer's lungs. "I swear I never touched her—I could never do that to you. For centuries, I've been telling Sarnia I wasn't interested in her, but somehow, she'd gotten some crazy idea we were lovers. No idea where she got that from! I don't even like the girl. If you don't believe me, ask Gisabella."

"So, this Sarnia woman was naked in your bed a few hours before our wedding, and you didn't think this was important enough to tell me?"

"I immediately threw her out of my apartment and told her if she ever came back, I'd have her fired. Once she was gone, I concentrated on your wedding gift, then showered, shaved and got dressed. Please try and understand—I've not been in a relationship for centuries, maybe even thousands of years. Honestly, I have no memories of anyone other than you, and even then I believe you're the woman in my dreams who used to haunt me. It's the only explanation of why the dreams stopped the day I caught you flying off your horse."

"Were you and Sarnia ever intimate?" *I must focus on the questions and not on our first encounter, or rather, the first time I saw him solid. At the* moment, it's too painful to remember the many butterflies my conversation with him caused in my tummy.*

"No—at least not that I can remember. My accident has taken many fragments of my memory away, but I honestly don't believe I ever touched her."

"Have you seen Sarnia since our wedding night?" *Josh is an old soul; surely he's had other lovers before me—even if he can't remember them. What if Sarnia was one of them? He claims she means nothing to him now, right?* Jennifer's thoughts did little to dispel the dull ache in her heart. *What if he suddenly recalls how much Sarnia meant to him? Will he pick her over me?*

"I only saw Sarnia once—at the protector meeting just before Christmas. Up until that night, I'd forgotten about what happened. In fact, it wasn't until I ran into Richard, who began running his big mouth, commenting about Sarnia and saying he wished she'd come knocking on his door, that I recalled that night. Things escalated from there and neither of us noticed how everyone stopped talking to listen to us. That was about the time I cursed Richard out for breaking into my apartment to let Sarnia inside, then blamed him for her being naked in my bed."

"What happened next?" Jennifer asked, forcing her voice to portray calmness even though she felt anything but serene.

"Gisabella's booming voice caught my attention; I've never seen her so infuriated! She pitched a royal fit, telling me how I should've mentioned the incident with Sarnia when it happened. Claimed I made her look like an idiot in front of her army of elite protectors. I heard later on how Gisabella threatened to disintegrate Sarnia if she didn't leave immediately. She also dismissed her as a protector forever and demoted Richard to a basic protector."

"What did Gisabella do to you? I'm sure you didn't escape her wrath." Jennifer clenched her jaw.

"Well, for one, Gisabella threatened to castrate me, but thankfully, with you being her granddaughter and my wife, she decided against that option." Josh released an audible sigh. "She decided instead that I had to tell you how Sarnia showed up before our wedding. Oh, and she demoted me to the second highest protector, but has since reversed that decision."

"So, the *only* reason you decided to tell me there was a naked woman in your bed a few hours before our wedding is because my high priestess grandmother forced you?" Jennifer yanked her hand away and pushed back her chair.

"Jennifer, please don't run—I'd give anything to do things differently. I was stupid not to tell you when it happened, but the only thing I was thinking about that day was being with you. Afterwards—well, you know, I forgot all about it," Josh stammered.

"What day is it on earth?" she demanded with her arms folded.

"Um, it's December 27th," he gulped.

"You realize our first wedding anniversary is in eighteen days. How am I supposed to react to this admission, knowing you were forced into telling me something as important as a naked woman in your bed?" Jennifer asked, unable to stop her lips from quivering. "My grandma was right: you should've told me sooner than a year later!"

"Please don't leave," Josh cried out as he stood, ready to grab hold of Jennifer if she tried to transport herself like last time. "I can't take losing you again. The last time, I vowed if I lost you forever, I'd cease to exist."

"What do you mean you'd cease to exist?" Jennifer blanched.

"Without the possibility of you in my life, there'd be no reason for my soul to live on. Baby, when you ran out, and I couldn't find you, my world collapsed. I thought I'd lost you forever, but then I found you, only to come so close to transporting your soul to heaven. If that happened and you were reborn, there'd be no guarantee you'd be able to see or hear me, let alone remember us." He raked his fingers through his hair. "Who am I kidding? Even without any hope of a forever marriage like we have now, I'd never be able to leave your side."

"Why would our forever marriage have been annulled if I'd died on earth?"

"Because you would've died prior to finishing your required life-path lessons. Until you do so, you'd be reborn and sent back to earth to finish the ones you hadn't completed in this lifetime."

"But I thought Gisabella said once I died, I'd have to take over her position."

"Yes, but only after you've completed the mandatory items."

"But you can't tell me what those lessons are?" she huffed, balling her fists in frustration.

"Even if I knew what your future held, I'm not at liberty to discuss it," Josh explained calmly so as not to upset Jennifer any further.

"Then I'd best head back down to earth and get them over with so you and I can be together, because without you, I'd cease to exist too! You mentioned how memories of me from a previous lifetime haunted you—I know for certain my memories of you would've done the same. I wish you'd told me about Sarnia earlier, way before Gisabella forced you to, but I believe nothing happened between you and her. Is there anything else about the night I left that you failed to tell me?"

Other than your life-path requirement to marry another man? "I guess I should warn you how you told Gisabella off, refusing to study or become the next high priestess—before you disowned her. After that, you said you were divorcing me, and then you illegally transported yourself and Talos before we could stop you. Thank God you took Talos with you because he was able to show Merlin the poisonous berries you'd eaten."

As Josh's words sank in, the color drained from Jennifer's face. "I said all those things? My grandma must be furious with me. And, you—how could I have said such a terrible thing to you?" As realization dawned, her eyes darted to his. "Is that why you haven't given me my wedding rings back?"

"I have them right here, but only if you vow to never utter the word 'divorce' again. If you can promise this one thing, I'd love to place these back on your finger where they belong for the remainder of eternity. *Even when some other man places a ring on your finger, our wedding vows and rings will prevail.* Josh blocked the thoughts that threatened to tear his soul apart. The knowledge of how once Jennifer fulfilled this nonnegotiable part of her life-path, and how she would once again be his when she transitioned to heaven would need to be enough to carry him until then.

"I give you my word, Mr. Smith." She wiggled her ring finger with a shy smile.

He kneeled before Jennifer and slid both rings on her finger, then raised her hand to his lips and sealed them with a kiss. "You're all mine once again." Josh beamed as he got to his feet.

"Yes, completely yours." Taking his hand in hers, Jennifer began leading the way up the steps. "I think it's time for a second honeymoon." She didn't get the response she hoped to receive when Josh became an immobile object. "Why are you stopping?"

"I'm not sure you're ready for that level of excitement," Josh warned.

"Oh no you don't—according to you, I've been lying around here for days doing nothing, and I want you to make love to me!"

"Demanding little wench, aren't you? I guess I've no option other than to obey my wife. By the way, if Gisabella ever asks, that's my excuse," he claimed before scooping his wife up and carrying her to their bedroom to stand next to the bed.

"I think we should start by getting you naked." He slid the soft material of his wife's nightgown up over her head and gazed upon her mostly naked body wearing a huge smile. "I'll never tire of looking at you." His voice was thick with carnal appreciation. "Promise you'll let me know if this becomes too much for you."

"Okay." Her voice came out breathy, and she visibly shivered with anticipation as Josh lowered himself to kneel in front of her and began sliding her panties down her legs. Holding on to his shoulder for balance, she lifted one foot at a time while he removed them. She ran her hands through his thick hair, then twisted her fingers and gently tugged when she felt his hands on her backside and his mouth on her sex. Delicious waves of pleasure built rapidly as her husband kissed and sucked her sweet spot and his fingers kneaded her fleshy backside, all the while increasing her pleasure through firm flicks of his tongue.

Oh my—this is too fast. "So close," Jennifer cried out before her release took over her senses. Coming down from her orgasm, she found herself lying face up in bed.

"You taste exquisite, baby. Far better than anything else in the entire universe," Josh proclaimed.

"I love the way you taste, too. You know how much I love it when you use strawberry flavoring." Jennifer's eyes sparkled.

"Oh no you don't, I want to lose myself inside you." Josh quickly unbuttoned his shirt and removed it and his pants, followed by his black briefs.

"That's a sight I'll never get tired of—you naked. Mmm, why, Mr.

Smith, have I ever told you how much you resemble *David*? That is, with one very large exception," she snickered, eyeing Josh's erection. "He didn't have your—um—physical attribute." *Why am I feeling so shy?*

"I don't believe I've ever heard my dick called a 'physical attribute' before."

"Really? Well, I think it's a magnificent attribute to have inside me." Jennifer opened her arms invitingly. She was lost the moment Josh looked into her eyes and slowly slid his well-endowed attribute deep inside her, stretching and expanding her sex with his thickness. Every millimeter of his snail-paced strokes in—then out, then in and out again and again, increased her need.

"What's wrong, Jennifer? Not giving you what you want?"

"Feels—agh—you're driving me—crazy," she gasped, digging her fingernails into his muscular biceps.

"I want to make sure you'll remember this moment forever."

"Do you think you can help me remember it a little faster?!" Jennifer's words rushed out.

"Are you saying you want me to speed up the pace?" Josh chuckled.

"Stop teasing me!" She wrapped her legs around him and began swatting his butt with her feet. "Giddy up before I fetch a riding crop!"

"Go ahead, but don't be surprised when you find yourself receiving the same." His eyes glimmered excitedly.

"Mmm, is that a fantasy of yours?" Her blood began racing through her veins at the thought of being at his mercy, causing an involuntary moan to escape.

"Sounds like it may be one of yours too." Josh lowered his mouth to her earlobe, capturing it between his teeth and giving it a gentle squeeze before releasing it. "Just say the word, and I'll make that happen."

"Oh god!" Jennifer called out before all her senses shattered as she came over and over, vaguely aware of Josh calling out her name as he found his own release. Afterward, they lay joined together while catching their breath.

"Jennifer, I don't think there are enough mortal words to express how much I love you." His emotionally charged voice added many dimensions to their meaning.

"My heart and soul are yours forever, as is all my love," she spoke the words in her heart. When she winced, Josh looked at her with alarm. "It's nothing—just a little twinge," she promised.

"Relax while I slowly pull out of you and fetch a damp washcloth."

When he returned, he used the washcloth to clean her, then insisted she take a nap before lunch, not letting any amount of protesting change his mind.

Chapter Six

With each passing day, Jennifer grew stronger and so did her demand for more freedom.

"Seriously, Josh, I feel great. Why can't I go riding?"

"For the tenth time, the answer's no!" Josh loomed large with his arms crossed, effectively barricading the back door. "I'll let you know when you're well enough to ride D'Artagnan. Until then, you should read one of the many books I brought you."

"You mean the books you cluttered our bedroom with? Maybe you should've asked me what I like to read before you crammed the bookcases full of boring high priestess books!"

When her husband didn't waiver, Jennifer huffed and turned on her heel, departing the room with a final comment, "Have it your way—I'll be in the dance room."

"That's not allowed either!" *Why does she have to be so stubborn?!* He'd spent the last two days monitoring her activity level while making sure she ate enough to regain some of the weight she lost. *How does Jennifer intend to explain the weight she's lost in less than twenty-four hours on earth?* Taking large strides, he entered the dance room long before Jennifer began her warm-up stretches.

"Oh no you don't," he called out, covering the distance between them before his wife could react. "Either you pick a different activity, or I swear, I'll put you back to bed and force you to stay there until it's time to bring you back home!"

"Tyrant!"

"Bed it is then." He hoisted Jennifer over one shoulder, ignoring her pounding fists against his back as he carried her out of the dance room.

"Put me down, you big lug!" Jennifer demanded, continuing her assault on Josh's back while trying to wiggle out of his grasp. "I'll tell Gisabella you've been keeping me up all night, begging me for sex." Unfortunately, her outright lie earned her several swats on the butt. "Cut that out!"

"Keep it up, and I promise you'll find yourself draped over my lap."

"As fun as that sounds, I'd prefer you put me down—in an upright position," she added to be on the safe side.

"Under one condition: you find something to do that doesn't burn a lot of calories." Josh couldn't help grinning knowing she was bound to figure out he left her no other option besides reading. *That's one way to get her to study!*

"Fine, but for the record, sex burns tons of calories!"

"Looks like *you're* out of luck, then." He slowly slid his wife down the length of his body, making sure to give her a good indication of his arousal.

"Umm—maybe we can compromise." Jennifer tried her best to keep the neediness out of her voice, but seeing the change in Josh's irises, now darkened to emerald green, she hadn't succeeded.

"What're you offering?"

"I dunno—maybe if I were to spend a few hours painting and agree to eat a little more, we can visit the horses. Then, afterwards, you can make me dinner, and I'll let you make love to me."

"How kind of you, Mrs. Smith—such a generous wife to let *me* make you dinner and make love to you—in the same day, no less! Maybe I've been a little too harsh in my demands. I'll tell you what, after you've finished painting, we can make dinner together, then afterwards, depending how much energy you have left, I may let you make love to me. But only if you're a 'good girl' and eat all your food." Josh stood poised waiting for a blowout.

"Dream on, Mr. Smith!" She skirted around Josh and headed toward her art studio, all the while hearing his laughter in her head. *He's so annoying!*

~I heard that!~ Josh messaged as a reminder she'd forgotten to block her thoughts.

"Good—you were meant to!" Jennifer shouted back before she imagined a large, brick wall in her mind to prevent Josh from reading her thoughts and block any further messages from him.

A few deep breaths later, she selected various colors of paint and deposited a smear from each onto her wooden palette. Like most artists, Jennifer had her favorite hues: the reddish brown tones of burnt sienna, the earthy pigment found in burnt umber, yellow ochre, titanium white and ultramarine were amongst her choices. Before sitting, she lifted the cloth to reveal the painting she'd begun before Christmas and laid out the brushes she'd need with a small cup containing turpentine. After selecting Journey's "Evolution" album with her favorite singer, Steve Perry, she immersed herself in the task at hand.

Talos slinked into the room to sit by her chair, and soon she lost track of time until Josh came up behind her and began rubbing her shoulders. "I think it's one of your best pieces."

"Hey—you weren't supposed to see this until it was done."

"Sorry, I'll hide my eyes."

"It's okay, you can look—it's almost finished," Jennifer said, tugging on Josh's arm until he uncovered his eyes. "I was going to wait until our anniversary, but after all you've been through, I want you to have it now. Happy anniversary, darling!"

Josh studied the canvas painting of Jennifer riding D'Artagnan by the fence with her hair sailing behind her in the breeze as she soared by him at breakneck speed. But it was the lead rope she added into the painting that she'd used to lead him into the barn after reading his mind for the first time that caused Josh to look up with a huge smile.

"I see your brush with death didn't cause you to forget that day. For the record, that was one of my all time favorite fantasies. Thank you, Mrs. Smith, for such a thoughtful gift." He lowered his lips to hers for a much-needed kiss. "Happy early anniversary, baby."

"Maybe we should continue this early celebration with strawberries and champagne, naked by the fire," Jennifer suggested, running her fingertips up her husband's jean-clad inseam.

"Sounds perfect, except your grandma invited herself over for dinner." He didn't bother to hide his disappointment. "If we weren't on Gisabella's radar, I'd reschedule, but she's been good enough to wait a couple of days before pushing her title around."

"Do you think she's angry with me? I honestly don't remember anything the night I supposedly transported myself."

"Everything will be fine. Just promise to hear her out and hold your comments until after you've thought about them for a day or two. Whatever you do, don't start yelling about what a horrible leader you think she is or dismiss her as your grandma." Josh stopped speaking when he noticed most of the pigment in Jennifer's face had faded.

"It's official—you need to cancel dinner. Tell her I'm not feeling well."

"Seriously, Jennifer? All she'd do is glance into her crystal ball, and she'd know you were lying."

"Ugh! Why do I have to be related to the high priestess? It's hard enough that I'm married to my protector, but with both of you lurking around all the time, I have no privacy. I'm fed up with you and Gisabella trying to read my thoughts and watching whatever I'm doing through your crystal balls, or whatever other magical device you come up with."

"If you want privacy, all you have to do is study. Everything you need to know to beat us at our own game can be found in the books Gisabella wants you to read. Best of all, if she thinks you're studying to take over her position, she'll leave you alone."

She studied Josh for signs of trickery, but his poker face gave nothing away. *Looks like I'll never get them off my back unless I can match their level.* The thought did nothing to improve her mood. "Fine, I'll *pretend* to study."

"Good girl! Dinner's sure to go a lot easier this way." Josh silently patted himself on the back. "I've prepared most of tonight's dinner, so all we need to make is dessert. How would you like to learn how to make biscotti?" *Making Italian cookies is perfect way to celebrate our Italy vacation!* Josh hid his celebratory thoughts so as not to cause any suspicion.

"Okay." *Baking with Josh is so much better than reading a bunch of silly old books.*

After Jennifer cleaned up her workspace, they headed toward the kitchen with Talos at their heels, where she noticed Josh had all the ingredients laid out.

"I took the liberty of setting up two workstations, so we can work side by side while I show you each step."

"Cool." Jennifer went over to the sink and washed her hands, preparing to get to work.

"First step is to combine some of the dry ingredients: flour, baking powder, salt," Josh instructed, verbally giving each of the measurements.

"Now cream the butter and sugar together in the mixer until smooth, and add the vanilla." He demonstrated so she could follow along with her mixer. "Now slowly mix in the dry ingredients, in small batches."

"Wait! You're going too fast," Jennifer protested, still measuring out the vanilla, but the roar of his mixer overpowered her voice. She reached into the flour and gathered a small handful, then, with a devious look in her eye, she tossed it in his direction, pleased by the immediate stoppage of his mixer.

"So, you'd rather play?" Using both hands, Josh gathered enough flour to coat them completely before turning to his wife and grabbing both of her breasts.

"Agh!" A glance down at her navy t-shirt showed two large handprints as if they'd been printed there on purpose. She quickly coated her hands with flour, but before she could retaliate, she felt his hands on her ass. In a bold move, she scooped a half-cup's worth of flour and tossed it directly at his chest, sending up a huge dust cloud. When it dissipated, she had handprints all over her body, and she was sputtering with laughter.

"I'd say we're even!"

"Animal!"

"Behave! Or next you'll be on the floor naked, covered in butter," he taunted.

"As tempting as that sounds, I think I'll pass." Jennifer continued working on her dough until she'd caught up with him. They finished by adding chopped hazelnuts for flavor.

"Now we roll out the dough." Once he finished, he demonstrated by reaching around Jennifer and placing his hands over hers.

Geez, the way he keeps rubbing my hands and using them to form the dough feels so sensual. I'd like to continue this naked, please. "You heard that, didn't you?"

"Maybe after we get these in the oven and return from visiting the horses, we can take a shower together."

"Actually, the floor is looking good!" Her needy words went ignored, and before long, her baking pan held similar-looking cookies as her husband's.

"Now we place them in the oven and go outside for some fresh air." He grabbed two apples off the counter and slipped them into his shirt pocket before reaching for Jennifer's hand. He turned expectantly toward Talos. "Want to go for a walk with us?"

~Thanks,~ Talos messaged, though he hesitated a moment to make sure he'd heard Josh correctly before he hurried out the door Josh held open.

"I'd like to go see D'Artagnan; I owe him and Misty a thank you," Josh said before they set off in that direction.

"Okay." Jennifer glanced his way but decided not to ask why. "I hope we don't run into grandma looking like this."

"It's not like she doesn't know my hands are always all over you."

The three continued down the path until they reached the horses, who, though they eyed Talos with suspicion, soon cantered over to them.

"Hey, boy," Josh greeted, rubbing the black Friesian stallion behind his ear. "I owe you a huge thank you for all your prayers. You too, Misty." He produced two apples and fed one to each horse.

"I've missed you so much, D'Artagnan." Jennifer rested her forehead against his lowered head. They stayed like that for a while until she lifted her head and looked into his soulful eyes. "Thank you for your prayers and for giving Josh your support." She repeated the same with Misty, and before long it was time to head back to the house.

When they returned, the timer was almost ready to chime. Soon, they pulled the pans out of the oven and stood back admiring their finished cookies. "These look great," Josh declared.

He's got to be kidding, Jennifer thought, looking at the two trays. Normally, everything she attempted to cook under Josh's tutorial turned out perfect—except for *her* biscotti. Looking at the two, it was easy to tell which one of them had made the flat, "pancake" version. Being the gentleman he was, Josh insisted her flopped cookies would be presented as proudly as everything else.

"Have I told you I like working with you way more than with your grandma? I enjoy the perks and rewards you offer, too!" Josh teased, planting a kiss on her lips.

"I have plenty of other perks for you, in addition to my kisses." She reached for one of her flattened cookies and held it out. By the look on his face, he'd expected something other than her failed baking attempt. She tried her best to keep a straight face as he gallantly attempted to bite into it. After nearly breaking a tooth, he gave up.

"Damn, woman! What recipe were you following?"

"You were my teacher. You tell me what I did wrong." She was laughing so hard, she barely got the words out between breaths.

"I haven't a clue. Are you sure you used flour and not cement?" He too was gasping for air.

"If I did, then you must have given me the cement. Obviously, you were so worried my superior baking skills would outshine your biscotti. Bad enough you covered me in handprints, but you felt the need sabotage my efforts too!"

Her laughter finally held at bay, she continued razzing, "Were you not the person who taught my grandma to bake? Oh, I see, Mr. Smith, maybe underneath it all, Gisabella's a better cook than us both!" She paused a moment and contemplated the absurdity of her comment. "Maybe not!" she admitted, reaching for a cookie from Josh's tray.

"We'd better go get ready before Gisabella arrives," Josh warned. Although his wife's first biscotti attempt didn't go so well, he'd be sure to point out how advanced her skills were, unlike Gisabella's.

Once showered and dressed, Jennifer scanned a few books in the bedroom. Selecting an armful of required reading material, she carried them downstairs and positioned the books in various places so they'd be easily spotted. Then she arranged her crystal orb and several gemstones on the coffee table with some sage that promised to ward off evil spirits and bad energy, or at least that was what the description read on the back cover of one of the books.

Josh was busy in the kitchen when the doorbell rang, forcing her to welcome their guest. *Show time!* Jennifer held an opened book in her hand, appearing to be preoccupied with the content.

"Hi, Jennifer," Gisabella greeted, glancing at the book Jennifer held. "You're looking exceptionally well."

"Come in, Grandmamma; Josh is in the kitchen," Jennifer greeted blandly, carrying on her pretense while making sure to block her thoughts.

"Good book?" Gisabella asked.

"Huh? Oh—sorry, I didn't mean to be rude. Why don't we have a seat in front of the fire?" Jennifer led the way to the seating area she'd staged. She didn't have to wait long for Gisabella's gaze to drift over the items she arranged or for the older woman's expression to break into a gleeful smile.

"I see you've been working with your crystal ball. Maybe we can play a game after dinner," Gisabella exclaimed in delight.

"A game?" *Oh dear!*

"Don't look so worried; I'm sure you'll do great. Besides, it's a fun way of practicing working with your crystal orb." Gisabella attempted to test Jennifer by prying into the girl's thoughts, pleased when her granddaughter thwarted each of her tries.

~Cut it out, Gisabella! Otherwise you'll have to deal with me!~ Josh messaged with a fake smile as he joined them.

"Hello, Joshua," Gisabella feigned like nothing unusual had been said.

"Glad you could make it," Josh spoke on their behalf, reaching for Jennifer's hand. The unexpected sight of his wife's montage of gemstones, books, and other items laid out in front of them caused the briefest kink in his poker face. *Leave it to Jennifer to push the envelope with Gisabella. Oh, baby, it's never a good idea to play with fire.*

"I see you've been working with Jennifer," Gisabella gushed. "It gives me such hope for the future." Turning to her granddaughter, she added, "I suppose Josh has told you never to smudge him with sage because you could harm his aura."

You'll have to do better than that, Grandma. "I read quite the opposite in this book." Jennifer picked up one of the books and flipped it open to the page she'd creased earlier. "Sure enough, here it is, 'spirit guides are immune to sage unless they've been stripped of their power and have fallen into a lower dimension.'" She leveled her eyes, challenging her elder to try and trick her again.

"So it appears you're right—my mistake," Gisabella fluffed it off and turned to Josh. "We've decided how much fun it'd be to play our favorite orb game."

"Not tonight! Jennifer's stamina is not up to par, so I'm afraid we'll have to wait until another time." Josh slammed the door shut on the so-called game, no doubt designed to expose Jennifer's lack of training. "Speaking of tired, we'd better head into the dining room before my wife's eyes begin drooping."

"Yes, of course, we should forgo playing tonight," Gisabella said coyly. "Jennifer, you're very fortunate to have such a thoughtful husband. Perhaps I can come back tomorrow night, and we can play then." She followed it up with a searing message to Josh. ~You're gonna have to take the kid gloves off sooner or later and make Jennifer fend for herself.~

~I'll be the one to decide when! In the meantime, it'd serve you well to back off until she's better prepared.~

~Tsk-tsk, you're such an overprotective protector. I promise to mind my manners for now, if you agree to a short orb game before Jennifer heads back to earth.~

~Fine, but so help me if you try and play up to your normal *cutthroat* standards, I'll call the game off and send you packing!~

"If the two of you would like some privacy, I can leave the room," Jennifer spoke up, putting an end to their obvious message conversation.

"That won't be necessary—Gisabella and I are good. Come, let's eat." Josh offered Jennifer his arm and escorted her into the dining room.

After enjoying a large Italian feast, they retired to the family room for tea and dessert. Jennifer's plan of hiding her failed biscotti cookies didn't work as well as she'd hoped when, much to her dismay, it didn't stop Josh from describing them in detail.

Once she finished her tea, Gisabella rose. "Jennifer, you look tired. I'm afraid I've overstayed my welcome. Why don't you head to bed while Josh and I clean up the mess?"

"I am kind of sleepy." Jennifer blinked, looking as if she could no longer keep her eyes open.

"Don't worry—I'll clean up later. I'd better get Jennifer to bed." Josh looked toward Jennifer with concern.

"Good night, then." Gisabella hugged them both before she headed home.

"I'm glad that's over," Jennifer sighed, appearing to be wide awake the moment the door closes.

"You little sneak!" Josh roared with laughter. "You better hope Gisabella never finds out you played her! Damn, I don't think I've ever felt so proud as I do at this moment!"

"Wait until Grandma discovers I've no clue how to use my crystal ball," she admitted.

"How did you manage to mark the exact page you'd need in that book?

"Simple—I knew my grandma would mention one of the objects on the table, so I read the book blurbs and a few lines in several chapters of each book. I never expected her try something underhanded to trick me! Thank goodness I was particularly interested in what items would bother you," Jennifer revealed with a straight face.

"Maybe I should've said yes to her orb game!" He flashed her a wolfish smile.

"Thank you for saving me," she cooed, wrapping her arms around his waist. "I don't suppose you'd be willing to teach me how to use my orb?" she sugarcoated her words while gazing adoringly up at him.

"After the way you played Gisabella, I'm starting to wonder how many times you've managed to do the same to me?"

"Never—you're too smart to be tricked, Josh." Jennifer stroked her husband's ego.

"Now I know I'm being played!"

"But you'll still teach me, right? Please, Josh, I've never pulled such a pretense with you! Gisabella just gets on my nerves with all her high priestess talk."

"Alright, but you'll need to listen to me and be a good student," Josh said while inwardly celebrating. "For now, I need to get you to bed." He lifted Jennifer, instructing her to wrap her legs around him before he headed to their bedroom, leaving Talos asleep by the fire.

CHAPTER SEVEN

"Good morning, baby." Josh placed their breakfast tray on the table closest to the bookcases stacked with Jennifer's required reading material.

"How obvious can you be?!" Jennifer kicked the comforter off and begrudgingly clambered over to where Josh was waiting.

"I have no idea what you're talking about," he played innocent, pushing Jennifer's chair in before he took his seat and draped a napkin across his lap.

"If you expect me to believe that—I must be the Queen of England!"

"Baby, you're destined to rule the entire universe and every dimension in existence, not just *one* measly little country."

"Correction—according to you, I already quit! Now I'm free to do whatever I want, whenever I choose." Jennifer's jaw tensed, and her lips tightened into an uncompromising line.

"That's a pretty selfish thing to say. Have you no regards for how much this means to all of us? If you refuse your role as high priestess, you can kiss heaven and earth as we know them goodbye." Josh tossed his napkin onto the table and stood.

"Please don't leave! I—I don't know what to say. Can't you try and put yourself in my place? Until I met you, I was a normal teenager, but then we fell in love and I married you—a spirit who turned out to be my protector. It was the best day of my life, and I felt secure in what we had, in our marriage and our future—until my grandma, who happens to be your boss, told me I must take over her reign after I die. Heck, I never even heard of a high priestess before I met you!"

Jennifer paused to gather her thoughts before she continued, "Now, both of you tell me that my future's set in stone. Worst of all, you keep laying on the guilt whenever I contemplate not accepting my destiny or want to do something fun instead of reading one of these boring books!" She waved her hand toward the wall filled with bookcases. "All of this is just too much for me to handle!" Jennifer covered her face with her hands to hide her tears.

"No, baby, please don't cry," Josh soothed, squatting down to blot her tears. "Don't you realize you have a chance to do something for every soul in existence? Now isn't the time to think only of yourself—not when you can reach out and make a difference in all people's lives and every soul in existence."

"I'm not thinking of just myself!" She pushed Josh away with both hands and studied him through blurry eyes." Using a softer tone, she tried a different approach. "If I take on the high priestess role, all my time will be spent working, and everyone will expect me to be available round the clock—there'll be no us." Her lips quivered.

"Baby, that's not true. Gisabella and Merlin are together, and if they've managed, so will we."

"Explain to me why we haven't seen or heard of Merlin until now. It's simple—Gisabella had to choose her title over the man she loved. I don't want to give you up, but I don't know how to keep you and run all the universes and dimensions at the same time!"

"Didn't you hear Gisabella? I'll be by your side always, meaning you don't have to rule alone—I'll be there to help guide you. All I'm asking is for you to read about stuff that's important to me. Once you do, you'll be better equipped to hold your own against Gisabella and me. Then, when the time comes, you can step into your role as high priestess, and if you're miserable, maybe Gisabella could find a solution. If not, and you absolutely hate it, there is a way you can relinquish your title and step down.

But that's the worst-case scenario and only if the two of us together can't make it work."

"You make it sound so easy," Jennifer sighed.

"And you're making it sound much harder than it needs to be. No one's asking you to become Gisabella. I'm certain she could've made a better life with Merlin if she wanted to, but she's the one who decided to devote every minute to her job."

"Like a workaholic?"

"Yeah, I believe that's what Gisabella would be called on earth."

"If I do as you say and accept my title, you must promise to tell me if I'm becoming a workaholic, or if I become too controlling like my grandma."

"Do you honestly think I'd let either of those things happen? Although, the stunt you played on Gisabella reminded me of something she'd have done. Consider yourself lucky she didn't make you play the crystal ball game last night! That reminds me, when you're finished eating, we'd better start working on your scrying skills in case Gisabella insists on playing sooner than expected."

"Do you think she'd do that?" Jennifer gulped.

"I wouldn't put it past her, especially if she suspects you were fibbing."

"You'd better hurry up and finish your breakfast," Jennifer said, putting down her fork.

"You only ate two mouthfuls! We'll begin only after you've cleaned your plate." Josh eyed the amount of Jennifer's untouched food and rejoined her at the table.

"What's up with your obsession with food lately? Not that you haven't always been a pain about my eating habits!"

"You only have approximately four and a half days left in Gisabella's dimension to gain back most of the weight you lost; otherwise, if I brought you home to earth, everyone would wonder how you'd managed to lose so much weight in less than nineteen hours!"

When Jennifer's eyes reflected doubt, he challenged her. "If you don't believe me, go look in the mirror." He watched as Jennifer headed into the bathroom only to return wearing a worried look.

"I guess I can finish the toast." Jennifer slathered on a thick layer of butter and topped it off with jam.

"Good girl," he rewarded, holding back from patting Jennifer on the head. To do so would have landed him in hot water.

Once they finished eating, they cleared the table for Jennifer's lesson.

"Wait here while I dim the lights. It's easier to relax and see stuff that way. While I'm at it, some soft music would be nice too," Josh said, selecting a classical album. With the volume adjusted to low, he returned to the table where her crystal sphere sat on a black velvet cloth.

"It helps if you begin by bringing yourself into a meditative state," he instructed, only to receive a protesting groan. "Your choice, but I'm letting you know when you're first learning scrying, meditation's essential."

"Are you sure this isn't one of your tricks designed to get me to meditate more often?"

"If that were the case, I'd have taught you to read your orb sooner," he taunted. "Once you're relaxed, simply gaze at your crystal ball without focusing your eyes."

"Don't focus on the orb? How will I see anything that way?"

"Trust me, baby, that's how it's done."

Jennifer did as she was told and gazed into the round orb for the next two hours before she gave up. She looked at him, rubbing her eyes for the tenth-plus time to exclaim, "This thing's broken! We've been at this for hours, and I still haven't seen anything!"

"You can't expect to see something right away; it takes lots of meditation and practice. Unlike some of your other gifts that came so naturally, this is the first thing you've actually had to work at learning. It doesn't mean you won't eventually be good at scrying."

"But what will Grandma think?"

"Gisabella doesn't expect you to be great or even good at orb visions yet. She only wants to know you're putting forth the effort. When she sees the way you look into the orb, she'll know you're ready for the images inside to relinquish their knowledge."

"So you're saying Gisabella will be okay even if I fail miserably?"

"For now, but she'll expect much improvement as you continue to practice. Trust me—I'm a much better teacher than she is. Scrying didn't come easily to me at first either, but her way of motivation was setting unrealistic time limits on how quickly she expected information."

"Oh! Thank goodness my grandma isn't teaching me!" Jennifer stretched and rolled her head from side to side. "I don't suppose my teacher can find it in his heart to let me ride my horse?" She clasped her hands together as if praying.

"Sure—I can use a break too!" Josh stood, holding out his hand.

"I'm that bad at scrying?"

"Have I mentioned how much I love you?" Josh added, changing the subject and following it up with a long kiss.

With plans to practice later after a ride to the oasis for a picnic lunch, they headed to the barn where D'Artagnan and Misty were grazing in the field.

The next day after eating lunch with Gisabella, Josh and Jennifer cleared off the table and pulled out their crystal balls in order to play the game Gisabella swore was her favorite.

"Well, should we get started?" Gisabella asked.

From what Jennifer had been told, the object of the orb game was to match wits against each other. There were no dice, game pieces, or cards used—only their crystal balls. Each player used their scrying skills to see something about each of the other players that had to do either with the past or the future. It was up to the other players to determine if they'd spoken the truth or were only bluffing.

Once she'd heard how the game was played, Jennifer's excitement fell flat on the floor. *This feels more like a test than a game!* Even though she'd practiced for hours, she hadn't had much success, so what were the chance she'd see anything?

"You first, Jennifer," Josh encouraged, even though his wife was playing with a significant disadvantage against Gisabella and himself. Never mind how ruthlessly Gisabella and he normally played, where even the most experienced player would be intimidated.

Jennifer concentrated as she gazed into her crystal orb. *Please work this time,* she willed her sphere. *Preferably with something that doesn't sound like I'm hallucinating!* Like in practice, she unfocused her eyes and continued to stare, only this time the fog dissipated, making it so her mind could travel inside to the center where makeshift mountains of varying colors gave way to clarity. *I had a vision!* She had no idea what it meant, but she didn't care—it felt like a win.

"Grandmamma, I see you sitting in a chair holding a baby wrapped in a pink blanket." Jennifer continued to stare into her crystal ball to see if she could give any more details. "The baby has green eyes like Josh!" Jennifer exclaimed as if she'd struck gold. *I did it!*

"Excellent, Jennifer." Gisabella thought it best to agree so she didn't discourage the girl—until another thought occurred. "I must have been feeding my daughter—your mother—the one who birthed your original soul!" Gisabella put extra blocking on her thoughts so neither would discover that Jennifer may have been catching a glimpse of her and Josh's future child!

"She had green eyes?" Josh narrowed his eyes while studying the high priestess, but Gisabella gave nothing away.

"When Olivia was a baby, she did, but once she turned two, her eyes darkened, becoming more brown than green," Gisabella lied.

Gaining confidence, Jennifer concentrated on her orb, once again traveling deep into the center, only this time she saw a pair of dark eyes staring back at her. The sight took her breath away, but it was the voice she heard that caused her to let out a high-pitched scream.

"Jennifer!" Josh leapt out of his seat and snatched the orb away from her. "Look at me," he commanded, shaking her by the shoulder. When he caught sight of her glazed-over eyes, he slapped Jennifer out of the trance she'd been pulled into.

"It was horrible!" Jennifer cried out, gripping Josh tightly.

"Tell us what happened!" Gisabella demanded. This was no time to coddle the girl if someone had formed a link to her.

"I saw dark eyes, and then—a voice said, 'I know who you are.'" Jennifer visibly shivered.

"Could you tell if it was a man or a woman?" Gisabella asked.

"I only saw their eyes, but the voice sounded much deeper than a woman's." Jennifer hesitated before adding, "I guess I could take another look."

Her suggestion was instantly turned down with a unanimous "Absolutely not!"

"You're not to touch this crystal ball again until I get you another," Gisabella warned, wrapping her granddaughter's orb in the black velvet cloth. "I'll give this one to Merlin to see if he can figure out what happened."

"So we're done playing?" Jennifer's face fell. "Figures! We stop when I was ahead!"

"You're not missing much," Gisabella played off how intense their games usually became.

"Not missing much!" Josh accused. "What Gisabella doesn't want you to know is how most of our games end in a no-holds-barred energy battle!"

"Seriously? You mean to tell me you fire bolts of energy at each other until someone gives up?" Jennifer could tell by their expressions the energy they used wasn't the pleasurable, orgasmic kind her husband used with her. "Thanks for telling me this—after the fact!" *Will they ever learn to play nicely together? Probably not.* She blocked her thoughts and climbed into Josh's lap, where she felt safe from strange black eyes and dark voices.

Josh took advantage of Jennifer's closed eyes to message Gisabella. -What do you think she saw?-

-I'm not sure? You know yourself when someone's new to scrying, their ego could produce some bizarre visions.-

-If there'd been some powerful energy connection, I'd have felt it when I grabbed the orb away from Jennifer.-

-After you leave, I'll bring the orb to Merlin so we can study it for any signs of black magic or tampering. With any luck, Merlin can tell us if it's clean or find enough evidence to figure out who said those words to Jennifer.-

-In that case, I'd better get Jennifer home. I'll be surrounding the house with extra protection, so you may wish to knock before transporting yourself inside.- Josh cracked a smile, in spite of the possible seriousness of the conversation.

-Who do you think taught you how to disarm energy alarms? Now you and Jennifer shoo so I can bring her crystal ball to Merlin.-

-Well, be forewarned I've improved my skills since you taught me!- Josh stood with Jennifer cradled in his arms and transported back to their honeymoon house, where he promptly took all necessary precautions to keep Jennifer safe.

Once Josh and Jennifer left, Gisabella transported to Merlin's house so they could talk privately.

"Gisabella, what is it, love?" Merlin asked, his eyes etched with apprehension.

"I need you to take a look at this." Gisabella unfolded the cloth to reveal Jennifer's crystal ball. "Something unusual happened during our orb game."

"Bring it over here and place it on the table," Merlin instructed as he sat down. "Has anyone other than Jennifer touched it?"

"Josh grabbed it out of Jennifer's hand, but it couldn't have been more than a minute before I wrapped it in this cloth." Gisabella placed the velvet and orb on the table and looked on as Merlin did a thorough inspection of the crystal ball.

"Tell me what happened," Merlin mumbled while peering at the orb through a jeweler's eye loupe with his right eye.

She relayed what happened, making sure not to leave out any details. Then she watched as Merlin ran his wand over and around the ball while his face remained expressionless.

"You say neither you or Josh saw or felt anything?" he asked while tying a bunch of dried leaves and herbs together.

"Nothing, it came as a complete surprise." Gisabella wrung her hands.

"What happened before Jennifer had this vision?"

"She saw an image of me holding a baby wrapped in a pink blanket." Gisabella worried the corner of her lip with her teeth. "I told her it was Olivia."

"You don't suppose she saw into the future?" Merlin's eyes lit up.

"I didn't think her ability would be developed enough, but then Jennifer saw the baby's eyes were green!"

"Green! Like Josh's?" His eyes widened in disbelief.

"That's what Jennifer said!" As Gisabella spoke, her eyes twinkled.

"Well, I'll be a rat's uncle!" Merlin slapped his thigh. "Wow, Josh and Jennifer will have a baby girl—doesn't that beat all?"

"Before you break out the champagne, you'd better listen to what happened next."

"Go on, love," Merlin said, leaning forward to give Gisabella his full attention as if he was unable to quell his excitement.

"Listen carefully because we need to keep our stories straight. I told them Olivia had been born with green eyes, but they'd darkened to mostly brown."

"Good thinking. Did Josh grow suspicious?"

"I'm not sure if he believed my answer, but Jennifer began her next turn before he could ask any further questions."

"Did Jennifer see more of their child?"

"No—she described a pair of dark eyes looking back at her from inside the orb. She was fine one moment, and then the next she let out an ear-piercing scream. That's when Josh slapped her out of the trance and grabbed the orb away." Gisabella continued to explain about the voice and words Jennifer had heard.

"Poor little lass, I bet that frightened her." Merlin leaned back with a sigh.

"Yeah, Jennifer was pretty shaken up; even so, she was willing to have another look to see if she could tell us more. Other than that, Josh and I never saw or felt anything unusual."

"This trick should tell us if anyone or anything attached themselves to the orb." Merlin struck a long, wooden match across the stone fireplace and used it to catch fire to the dried buddle he'd tied. Then he blew on the embers until smoke billowed freely in curls before placing it into a copper bowl and covering it with a mesh grate. Merlin carefully placed the crystal ball on the grate as Gisabella looked on.

The two studied Jennifer's orb for any signs of activity as the smoke wound its way around the ball, engulfing it completely in a thick cloud until no trace of the orb could be seen.

"What are we looking for?" Gisabella asked, no longer able to hide her curiosity as the smoke turned various colors.

"You'll know if and when it happens." As if on cue, the smoke dissipated, revealing a pair of eyes etched in the otherwise smooth surface of the crystal ball. "This is what Jennifer saw." Merlin gestured to the obvious.

"Is that it? A pair of eyes with no distinguishing features? What about the voice Jennifer heard—or what kind of magic locked her into a trance?" Gisabella shouted as she smacked the table with her hand.

"Calm down, the smoke would've revealed any lasting tie to Jennifer if it existed, and as for the voice, well, that's a different spell." Merlin shrugged as he picked up his wand. "Listen carefully because this will only work once."

With a few waves of his wand, a deep monotone voice was heard saying, "I know who you are."

"Well? Do you recognize it?" Merlin asked, awaiting a reply.

"It was too muffled. Do you think whoever it was used something to disguise their voice?"

"Probably, unless you were set up by the person you obtained the crystal ball from."

"I purchased it so many years ago from the same shop where I've gotten all my orbs and potions, and I've not had any issues before." Gisabella's brows furrowed. "My first thought was of the foretold prophecy of the person who'll try to destroy all dimensions but one."

"Of course we need to consider that as well, but I don't think he'd bother to play a cat and mouse game. This feels more like a prankster than anything else. For all we know, it could have been hidden away inside this crystal ball for centuries by some teenage wizard playing a harmless prank."

"That's highly unlikely since they only sell new merchandise. If what you said is true, then how do you explain Jennifer's trance?"

"Simple, our granddaughter's gifts are too powerful for such a young student to be subjected to one of your orb games. Honestly, lass, I thought you had more sense than to goad Jennifer into playing that game until she'd gotten used to scrying?"

"It was a harmless game!" Gisabella's features hardened.

"What you mean is it was harmless to you and Josh. As for an untrained young visionary who's doing her best to keep up with her high priestess grandmother, Jennifer must have felt extremely pressured to meet your expectations."

"You mean both Josh's and my expectations."

"No—I meant only yours. Jennifer knows Josh will love her whether or not she's gifted." Merlin watched as the meaning of his words clouded Gisabella's features. "Don't worry, my love, she'll get there; just give the poor lass time."

"Thanks to me, time's something we don't have." Gisabella turned her eyes to the fire, momentarily watching the flames dance until she was able to rein in her emotions. "I've been giving Jennifer's life-path a lot of thought, and I think we should take action sooner rather than later. I'm afraid if we wait until the aftereffects from the poison take hold, we'll run out of time," she said, turning her eyes away from Merlin.

"One little prank and you decide to rush this decision?" Merlin's nostrils flared.

"We can't afford to take any chances," she replied before turning around to face Merlin. "I love Josh as if he were my own flesh and blood, but we can't risk losing Jennifer's soul or the opportunity to create a child from them."

"I hope you know what you're doing."

"Perhaps I need to remind you of my title," Gisabella lashed out from behind her frostbitten blue eyes.

"Forgive me, Your Excellency; I await your instructions," Merlin acquiesced, bowing his head in respect.

"Do whatever you can to speed up Jennifer's life-path! I guess you should have gotten Jennifer's current life-path from the Hall of Records when I sent you for her former life-path as Astraea. Anyway, the one there was altered in order to hide her destiny, but it has the real name of her future earth husband. If for some reason there's absolutely no way to speed up his life-path in time to marry our granddaughter within a few months after she graduates college, then do whatever you can to find a replacement. We must act now to insure our plan works! When the time comes, I'll get Josh to take the trip to Italy I promised. Hopefully he won't suspect anything or realize how alive he's feeling is the real deal."

"I should hope not! Last thing we need is for Josh to have an inkling what we're up to. If I must manipulate another man's life-path to marry

Jennifer, what do you suggest I do with Jennifer's original life-path husband?"

"If that turns out to be the case, then get rid of him. Do whatever it takes! If we don't finish Jennifer's life-path journey, we could lose her soul forever—or worse, we could all be banished when the Council finds out what we've done." Gisabella paused long enough to lower her head and release a sigh before she met Merlin's worried gaze. "I'm sorry for dragging you into this mess—I mean, the mess I created. This is all my fault. If I hadn't agreed to give Josh a life with his former lover or changed Jennifer's soul over to our lineage, you wouldn't be in danger." She covered her mouth to stop a wrangled sob from escaping, but there was no way to hide the tears she was unable to hold back.

"I choose to be here with you. I wouldn't change having you back in my life for anything, not even if this all gets me banished. You and I, along with Josh and Jennifer, will pull through this, and so will their child. We haven't come this far to lose everything, and if it's any consolation, Josh would feel the same way. I'll begin a new timeline for Jennifer's life-path straightaway. Once I have everything in order, you may wish to talk with Josh. I hate to deceive him."

"Absolutely not! You said so yourself: Josh can't find out what we're up to. We both know if he gets the slightest inkling he's due to lose Jennifer sooner than expected, he may try to stop us."

"Gisabella, that was before we decided to make so many changes in her life-path." When her expression darkened, Merlin corrected his words accordingly. "Have it your way, but eventually you'll need to face him. After all, Josh will remain Jennifer's protector, so you should keep him in the loop."

"I'll decide when the time is right to tell Josh and not a moment sooner."

"Of course, Your Excellency." Merlin's eyes softened.

"Please don't be that way, my love. I feel terrible enough dividing Jennifer and Josh when they're so in love. If we can't pull this off, I may lose them both for good. Don't you think I realize they may never speak to me again?!"

"Surely when they are together in heaven for the remainder of eternity, neither will have anything but respect and love for you."

"I only hope you're right," she said as she stepped into Merlin's welcoming embrace.

Once alone, Merlin hurried unseen through the Hall of Records until he reached the proper life-path section. It took him a while to locate Jennifer's fraudulent life-path Gisabella had spoken of and a few more minutes to flip through its contents to find the name of her future husband. Slipping it under his cloak, Merlin backtracked to the section containing all the A's.

There you are. Merlin pulled Jennifer's future husband's life-path and placed it under his cloak with Jennifer's. Then he transported himself back to his cabin in his private domain where he removed his cloak and laid both envelopes on the table. *Now, let's have a look at both your futures and see if we can move things along.*

CHAPTER EIGHT

*I*t was just after midnight when Josh received an incoming message from Gisabella.

-Merlin did some tests on the crystal ball and found nothing unusual. He concluded it must have been the random work of a prankster. Even so, I'd like you to concentrate on teaching Jennifer more forms of protection and energy cleansing techniques.-

-Tell me you don't really believe Merlin's theory?- Josh asked, doing his best not to sound off with a tangent of unfit words.

-Why wouldn't I? I watched him do several magical tests, and I agree with him.-

You would!

-What was that?- Gisabella automatically called Josh out, expecting him to say something under his breath.

-If you believe him, then I do too.- This time Josh made sure to block his thoughts.

-Don't you think we would've picked up on any energy force if it entered the room?- Gisabella reasoned. -In the meantime, I think it'd be wise to place some extra protection around Jennifer.-

-So you're *not* a hundred percent sold!-

~I never said that! Shouldn't you be in bed with your wife?~

~She's next to me, sound asleep.~ He smirked knowing his boss had enough of their conversation and was hoping he'd drop this line of questioning. ~What tests did Merlin do?~

~Do me a favor and take a nap! Maybe it'll help your attitude.~

~There's nothing wrong with my attitude.~

~Good night, Josh!~

Josh folded his hands behind his head and reclined against the headboard with a huge grin. *Good to know I can still get Gisabella's goat.* He spent the remainder of the night going over all the possible angles of what had happened earlier and how scared Jennifer had become. By morning he'd reached no conclusions other than it wasn't a random act.

By morning, Josh's restless mind wouldn't calm, and he couldn't be happier to see his wife's eyes open.

"Good morning, baby. I've been thinking we should practice your protection lessons today, maybe even add a few other kinds of methods so you have other options to fall back on." Josh's words sped out like race cars zooming around and around the racetrack. *I think I'd better skip the coffee this morning!*

"Good morning." Jennifer rubbed the sleep from her eyes. "As wonderful as that sounds, I was thinking we could ride the horses to the oasis. Maybe even bring a picnic lunch," she suggested.

"Alright, why don't we plan on leaving in five hours. Until then, I think we should spend some time going over some of the stuff you'll need to know." He couldn't miss the way Jennifer's nose crinkled at the first hint of studying for her future position. "You know, in order to fool Gisabella into believing you're studying," Josh managed to add with a straight face.

"Are you sure this isn't your way of deceiving me into studying that high priestess stuff?" Her brows creased. "Now, if you told me I could read a dozen books about the stuff I'm interested in learning, I'd happily agree."

"I thought we decided you'd accept the position? At least give it try before you go running to Gisabella and beg her to find a solution out of your destiny. Who knows, you may actually enjoy the position," Josh added before his wife could balk.

"Fine—but it better be something fun without scary voices or eyes!"

"What about learning to clear negative and stagnant energy by smudging? Doing so will add another layer of protection that will help keep away anything scary." Josh employed his best sales approach in hope of making it sound more exciting than it was.

"Please tell me I don't have to read one of those boring books!" She waved her hand in the direction of the bookcases. "I'd much rather learn by way of hands-on demonstrations."

"I promise, no books—and when we're done, my hands will be all over you." A wicked grin accompanied his promise.

"Okay, but just so we're clear, you promised me a lunchtime picnic!"

"I wouldn't dream of missing our picnic. How about we go eat breakfast and feed Talos before we smudge the house?"

How does he do that? Go from hot sex god to innocent-looking boy next door? Yikes, either way Josh is hot enough to melt my defenses and make me beg! Oh no, I did block my thoughts, right?!

Once they'd finished breakfast and cleared the dishes, Jennifer and Josh headed into the family room.

"Wait here while I go get my smudging kit," Josh instructed, hurrying out of the room.

He has a kit? Seriously? What kind of geek have I married? Soon her snicker morphed into laughter just as Josh returned with a candle, a bowl, a feather, and something that looked like a rolled-up bunch of dried leaves tied with string. *He did say this was going to be fun, right?*

"Are you ready?" Josh asked, ignoring his student's blaring thoughts she'd blasted so loudly, he couldn't help but hear them. *Geek, eh? If that's what my wife wants—that's what she'll get!*

"Go ahead—smudge away, but if anything bad happens today, I'm out of here!"

"Oops—I almost forgot my first aid kit—you know, in case we have any issues." Josh rushed back out of the room, and when he returned, he was carrying a first aid kit, fire extinguisher, safety glasses, rubber dishwashing gloves, and some elastics.

"What's all that for?" Jennifer suspiciously eyed all the stuff he was carrying.

"Prevention management. Here, use these elastics to pull your hair back and put these on." Josh handed her a pair of gloves and safety glasses. "Maybe you'd better put these on too." He passed her a hat and air filtering mask.

When she was all set, he looked her over and nodded his approval. Then he lit the candle and held the tied bundle of white sage over it until it caught fire before placing it in the bowl. He blew the flames until they dissipated and smoke curls drifted upward.

"Shouldn't you be putting on your safety gear?" Jennifer asked, failing to notice the way Talos had curled his lips at Josh.

"Nah, as a spirit guide, I'm safe from fire and burning sage." Josh turned away, trying to reinstate his poker face and not laugh at her ridiculous outfit. *Talk about looking like a geek!*

"When you're on earth, you should make it a habit to sage your house a few times a year to clear away any unwanted energy and to create a barrier of only positive energy. It's actually something everyone on earth should be doing to prevent the buildup of negative and stagnant energy. I'll show you how it's done and let you do the rest of the house."

She watched as Josh turned around and raised the bowl, letting the smoke rise before he waved the feather, guiding the smoke into the corner and around the front door.

"The next part is very critical, so listen carefully." He waited until he had her full attention before he continued. With his face turned away to hide his expression, Josh issued a series of made-up commands: "Be gone! I tell you—be gone bad energy and take your sorry ass friends with you!"

Once finished, he hopped on one foot three times, then spun around twice counterclockwise. Finally, he followed up his act by bowing toward the cleansed corner, where he remained facing away from Jennifer until he'd erased all signs of humor from his face. "Now this area is completely free of bad energy. Do you want to give it a try?"

"I think I got it," Jennifer said, holding out her hands to take the bowl and feather. "Where should I head next?"

"You could finish the entry. Start by doing this wall first." Maybe he should have felt guilty by his student's eagerness, but he couldn't back down now. Instead, he stood back and watched Jennifer smudging the wall, following his instructions to the letter. She'd made it as far as the dining room when the doorbell sounded.

"That must be Grandma. Can you let her in?"

"Sure." Josh cringed as he waved his boss inside. "Hello, Gisabella, I wasn't expecting you."

"Where's Jennifer?" Gisabella asked, but when she heard her granddaughter saying, "Be gone, I tell you, be gone," she walked into the dining room to watch the show.

Once Jennifer bowed to the wall, she turned to face Gisabella. "Hi Grandmamma, Josh taught me how to smudge. I never realized it was such an involved process."

"Neither did I." Gisabella turned and scowled at Josh. "It's nice to know I've personally entrusted you to teach my *granddaughter*. I must see to it that you're *rewarded* for your exemplary teaching methods."

"How kind of you, Your Excellency," Josh said with an exaggerated bow, following it with a private message. ~If your granddaughter wasn't such a disrespectful student, I would've shown her the easier way to smudge.~

~I see. Well, then, carry on,~ Gisabella messaged before speaking out loud. "I'm sorry, I didn't realize you were in the middle of smudging. I must leave so as not to change the energy pattern. Great to see you learning helpful clearing *techniques*. Perhaps tonight you should read the book on smudging so your clearing efforts will last longer. If you don't, you may have to smudge the entire house again tomorrow. Goodbye." Gisabella hurried out, closing the door behind her before laughing. *Boy is Josh going to get it when Jennifer finds out what he's done!*

Jennifer continued her tedious task of smudging every room in the house. It was well over an hour later when she pulled off her protective safety gear, removed the elastic from her hair and collapsed on the couch next to Josh, holding a book.

"You finished already? Are you sure you did every corner?" Josh asked, eyeing the book in her hands.

"Yes, every corner, wall, doorway, and room in the entire house."

"I have our picnic basket all set. Why don't we leave now? You must be starving."

"But I need to read this book so all the work I've done stays around longer than a day."

"There'll be plenty of time for reading later tonight." *I don't want to be anywhere in the area when she reads that book!* Suddenly his joke didn't seem so funny.

"I'm too tired to go riding. Why don't we have a picnic here in front of the fireplace? I'm sure Talos would enjoy it too. Won't you, boy?" When Talos came over to sit in front of her, Jennifer reached down to pet the panther.

~I disagree, Josh! I think Jennifer's right; she should read that book now. Then I'll be the one curled up in bed with her, while you'll be sleeping on the floor,~ Talos messaged, glaring at Josh with his copper eyes.

~I'd be quiet if I were you, cat; otherwise, you'll find yourself living outside! I'm sure once I explain everything, Jennifer will find it funny.~

~Fat chance, old man!~

"Hey! What are you two up to?" Jennifer glared at their guilty faces.

"Nothing—I'll grab the picnic basket and a steak for my friend Talos," Josh offered before finishing his thought in a message meant only for Talos' ears. ~Who'd better keep his trap shut!~

~It'll take the prime rib and some catnip to keep me from talking,~ Talos messaged, following Josh into the kitchen while licking his chops.

It took a few minutes for Josh to gather the last minute things for their picnic and find a suitable snack for the panther. "Here you go, cat," he said, feigning a happy tone as he handed the panther a slab of frozen meat. ~Try not to choke on it!~

Josh carried the picnic basket of food and a large bottle of wine with two glasses out of the kitchen, only to arrive in the family room to find Jennifer curled up, fast asleep.

"We'll have our picnic when you wake up," Josh whispered and covered his wife with a blanket. What had seemed like a great way to teach Jennifer a lesson about respecting her protector and his teachings may not have been as brilliant of a plan as he once thought. In his defense, his student did call him a geek. *Maybe I'd better be prepared with roses and an apology for when she wakes up! Better yet, I have an idea that Jennifer will love so much that she won't care how I tricked her when she discovers the* real *way to smudge.*

~Talos, stay here and keep an eye on Jennifer. Alert me if she wakes up or if anything seems amiss. I'll be back in a little while.~

Josh rushed around the house gathering items before transporting them to the oasis. Once he had everything in place, he transported to the stables where he bridled both D'Artagnan and Misty and headed back to the oasis. Once everything was all set, he transported back to the house.

Jennifer opened her eyes to find Josh gazing down at her. It didn't take long for her to notice the dozen red roses in his hand.

"How long have I been sleeping?"

"A while. Come with me; I have a surprise for you." Josh held out his free hand.

"The roses are beautiful. Where are we going?" she asked sleepily.

"If I were to tell you, it'd ruin the surprise." When Jennifer stood, he lowered his lips to hers and began transporting them to the oasis, where he pulled away, releasing her mouth.

It took a moment for her eyes to focus and for the transformation of the oasis to sink in. "When did you do all this?" Jennifer said the only words that came to mind as she took in the twinkling lights hanging from the trees, floating candles in the water, welcoming mats with pillows and blankets, and his promised picnic for two set up on a small table. Most of all, her eyes lit up when she saw her beloved D'Artagnan grazing next to Misty a few yards away.

"I figured we can ride back," Josh answered her unspoken question.

"Under the moonlight?"

"Absolutely."

"As long as I make it back to the house in time to read the smudging book. I don't want to do that again anytime soon!"

"Umm, about that. Gisabella was pulling your leg," Josh confessed.

"Why would she do that?"

"Probably as a way of getting back at me. Let's eat," he added, hoping to change the subject.

"What did you do now? I swear the two of you are always irritating each other."

"I—eh—didn't do anything to *her*."

"Well, you must have done something," Jennifer accused.

"Maybe we should eat first."

"What are you hiding?" She narrowed her eyes at Josh's reprehensible expression.

"I did something as a joke that didn't turn out to be very funny—*to you*."

"What kind of joke? Tell me!"

"Many of those smudging precautions, sayings, and some of the rules I had you follow aren't exactly…required."

"Seriously?" Jennifer's mouth dropped open. "You mean...," her voice trailed off. "Why would you do such a thing?"

"Well, it all started when you broadcast your thoughts, saying I was a geek." His reasoning didn't sound as valid as earlier in the day when he'd decided to deceive her.

"You're right; I was wrong. You're not a geek—you're a jerk! If I were you, I wouldn't bother coming to bed tonight. Not unless you're in the mood to be kicked to the curb. You—you made me wear all that junk!" As mad as she was, she couldn't stop her lips from forming a small smirk over the trouble he'd gone through to make it up to her. "I suppose jumping around on one foot like a fool was fake—wasn't it?" *I must ignore how adorable he looks—all sheepish and embarrassed. Maybe I could use this to my advantage?*

"Yeah, it was pretty much all fake. On the other hand, you looked so cute."

"How did you keep a straight face?"

"That was really hard, and honestly, I was going to tell you sooner, but when Gisabella arrived, it was too late."

"Too late for what?" A renewed need to pay Josh back surged from within.

"Honey, I'm sorry. How can I make it up to you?"

"You can start by smudging the entire house tomorrow morning following the same rules you gave me!"

"If that's what it'll take for you to let me back in bed, consider it done!"

"Can you please pass the chicken?" Jennifer asked with a big *smile. I'm gonna have so much fun paying him back!*

CHAPTER NINE

The next day, Jennifer enjoyed watching Josh put on the so-called protective smudging gear.

"Don't forget these," she taunted, holding out the rubber gloves and hat. "I think you need this too." She handed Josh a hair net. "Unlike my hair, yours isn't long enough to tie back, and heaven forbid you lose any of it—after all, a man of your age needs all the hair he can get." She ignored Josh's scowl, knowing full well his selected age was one that would keep his hair, features and body intact indefinitely.

"Are you sure that's it?" Josh asked with a foolish smile.

"Almost." As if on cue, the doorbell rang. "Oh good, our guests are here."

"Guests? As in more than one?" *Shit! It wasn't my fault Gisabella saw her dressed in this getup!*

"Come on in," Jennifer greeted Gisabella and Merlin. "You're right on time to learn the proper way to smudge your home."

"By the looks of it, I've been doing it *all* wrong!" Gisabella said, laughing.

"Wow, Josh! I'd sure like to know what you did to deserve this getup."

"You mean Grandmamma didn't tell you?" Jennifer snickered.

"Honey, I think you should show us all how it's done. Hop to it; we haven't got all day." *Wait until they start taking photos! Yikes! I'm so going to pay for inviting witnesses!*

They spent the next hour following Josh around laughing and snapping photos.

"Why the hell are you taking my picture?!" Josh glowered at Gisabella.

"Oh, you know, for posterity," she replied, snapping another shot.

"I think you mean for blackmail purposes!" Looking at Jennifer with a crooked smile, Josh took a step toward her. "I think I've more than earned my way into your panties."

"Joshua!" Jennifer flamed red from her roots to her toes while everyone fell into a fit of laughter.

"So that's why you agreed to make such a fool out of yourself," Merlin roasted.

"Can you blame me?" Josh shot back.

"Not in the least! If I did something that stupid, I'm sure I'd also agree to anything to make peace and get laid."

"Good lord, Merlin, you're as crass as Josh!" Gisabella reprimanded, swatting the wizard's arm and making everyone laugh harder.

"What are you talking about, Gisabella? You're just as bad, if not worse than Merlin and me!" Josh chimed in while ripping off his ridiculous fake smudging outfit. "I want my prize now!" He sauntered toward Jennifer with a lascivious grin.

"Don't you dare look at me that way. You haven't finished… Agh!" she yelped as Josh grabbed her around the waist and lifted her into his arms. "Put me down—we have company!"

"It's not like they haven't seen us kiss before. Besides, I'm sure when I carry you upstairs, they'll get the hint."

"If you don't release me this instant, you'll be sleeping on the couch for months!" Her threat worked, and soon she was lowered and released.

"Jennifer, you could've avoided all this if you'd read the smudging book instead of relying on Josh's bizarre teaching methods," Gisabella reminded her.

"Gisabella makes a good point, lass," Merlin spoke up. "I can tell you from personal experience, Josh is one of the nicer teachers. I could go on for days about the crueler stunts other protectors have used to teach their visionaries valuable lessons. Unlike the others, you have a valuable bargaining chip—sex! Just remember not to overplay your cards because there'll come a time you won't like the results. If that happens, don't come running to Gisabella or me, because we'll side with your protector. A word of warning, little hellcat, your lessons are far too valuable to all of us than your pride."

"How about we call a truce, baby? I don't wish to spend our last night here fighting." Josh followed it up with a gentle kiss on the top of her head.

"Truce." She turned into his embrace, snaking her arms around her husband's waist while looking up expectantly. "Please kiss me for real."

"Love—isn't it grand?" Merlin planted a swift kiss on Gisabella's lips.

"Mmm, it sure is," Gisabella agreed.

"Josh, why don't you bring Jennifer to my house in two weeks so I can help her get caught up with her lessons?" Merlin suggested. "When I get done teaching you, Josh and Gisabella will never be able to gang up on you again." Merlin's eyes twinkled with mischief.

"Count me in!" Jennifer piped up.

"I'm not sure I like the sound of that. What exactly are you planning on teaching my wife?"

"Never you mind, boy. Just make sure you bring my granddaughter to my domain in two weeks. Once you drop her off, you can make yourself scarce."

"I don't know what you're up to, old wizard, but you better watch your step." Much to his dismay, his warning only made Merlin chuckle.

"What'd I tell you, lass—the sooner you learn how to wield your power, the easier it'll be to keep your husband and Gisabella in line."

"Looks like we got ourselves a deal. I'll see you in two weeks, and I promise to be a perfect student. After all, with such an incentive, how could I go wrong?"

~Great job, Merlin!~ Gisabella cheered. ~You'll have Jennifer caught up on her lessons in no time at all.~

~Thank you, my love. With how lovesick Josh is for Jennifer, it's no wonder she gets away with murder. I seem to remember a certain young girl doing the same to me many centuries ago.~ Merlin messaged with a wink, enjoying Gisabella's rosy cheeks.

Josh gazed down at his wife. "I love you more than I ever imagined possible." His eyes glistened as memories of how close he came to losing her forever drifted uninvited into his thoughts.

"I love you too." Jennifer rose on her tippy toes to kiss him once more.

With one arm wrapped around Jennifer, Josh turned to their guests. "Seeing as though Jennifer has to leave tomorrow, would you like to join us for dinner?"

"Yes, of course," Merlin accepted on behalf of himself and Gisabella.

"How about I get started on dinner while Jennifer gets your drink orders?" Josh suggested before heading into the kitchen with Talos slinking after him, salivating in hopes of being rewarded with scraps.

The next day, Josh and Jennifer rode up to the barn on their last horseback outing in Gisabella's dimension before returning to earth. Once her steed came to a stop, Jennifer slid off D'Artagnan to land in a patch of mud. "Agh! Why do we have mud?" She looked down in dismay at her boots and jeans. "I've never seen it rain here."

"What are you talking about? If it didn't rain, nothing would grow."

"So it rains in heaven?"

"Of course it rains in heaven but does so while you're sleeping. Never longer than an hour, and there's no thunder or lightning, just rain. Guess it poured harder than usual," Josh commented, looking at her muddy boots. A glance at his watch made him grimace. "Holy shit! We only have ten minutes to get you home!"

"Ten minutes? That's not enough time to change my clothes!"

"Grab my hand," Josh commanded. The moment her hand locked hold with his, Josh transported them back up to their honeymoon house, where they picked up Talos. Then he transported the three of them into Jennifer's bedroom on earth, arriving just in time to hear her mom.

"Jennifer, are you home?" Mrs. Parker yelled up the steps leading to her daughter's bedroom.

"Coming." Jennifer turned to Josh, unsure what to do.

~Quick, throw this on.~ Josh handed her a robe. ~Better slip off your boots too.~

After she complied with his orders, Jennifer opened the door and raced down the steps. Though she and Josh had been in Gisabella's dimension for a little over eighteen days, with the difference in the movement of time, she'd only been gone for eighteen hours.

"Hi, Mom!" She wrapped her arms around her mother, catching her off guard.

"Hello to you too." Mrs. Parker patted her on the back. "We'd have been home sooner, but we hit a so much traffic. You know how it is, a couple of snowflakes reduces everyone to a crawl." Her eyes drifted up and down her daughter's figure. "Please tell me you weren't locked in the house all day drawing? You're looking awfully pale. Make sure you get some fresh air, and for goodness sake, eat something before you fade away!"

"Did you and Dad have a good time in Vermont?"

"Yes, it was very nice. Millie and Bill's two sons came home in time to join us for coffee. I wish I'd known they were home from college because I'd have brought you with us. The twins have grown up into fine-looking young men. Who's that?" Mrs. Parker's eyes grew large as she looked past Jennifer.

Jennifer whipped around, expecting to see someone other than the black domestic cat, who was innocently licking his paw. She reached down and gathered Talos to cradle him in her arms. "You haven't noticed him hanging around outside the past few weeks? It was so cold last night and this morning, he was at my window meowing to come in. I didn't have the heart to turn him way. I'd like to keep him, if that's okay."

"How did he get up that high?" asked Mrs. Parker as she fixed the collar on her shirt, thinking. "I guess he could have jumped from the tree over to the ledge."

Jennifer held her breath as she waited for her mother to work out the details of the impossible feat she claimed the now normal-looking house cat was capable of doing.

"If you're sure he doesn't have any family, and he doesn't destroy the house, I guess he can stay." Mrs. Parker pursed her lips and studied the ordinary-looking cat for a moment. "Does he have a name?"

"Talos."

"He looks a little scruffy and thin. There's some leftover chicken and fish in the fridge you can feed him." With a glance at her watch, Mrs. Parker hurried back down the hall. "I think I'll join your father for that second cup of coffee and some of those delicious Christmas cookies you baked."

Jennifer watched her mom hurry down the hall toward the main part of the house, then turned toward Josh. Since it was no longer Christmas, a full moon, an emergency, or one of the few other days or extenuating circumstances Josh could be solid on earth, his appearance was translucent. She was able to see him and feel his energy, but unless he densified his energy, her hand or other parts of her would pass right through him.

~Whew, that was close,~ Josh messaged, looking down at the bottoms of her muddy jeans. ~Let's get you cleaned up and fed. Your mother's right. You need to eat more; you're still too thin.~ An expression of remorse flickered across his face, but Josh squashed it before Jennifer noticed. ~I suppose Talos is hungry too. Well, you'll have to wait until Jennifer's had a hot shower.~

Josh turned and led the way back up the steps and into their bathroom, turning expectantly toward Jennifer. ~Time to get you undressed.~ Josh eyed his wife with his ever-changing smoky green eyes, now darkening on their own to a color that reflected Josh's lusty thoughts.

"If you put it that way," Jennifer whispered, sliding off her bathrobe. Once she removed all her clothing, she joined her now-translucent husband under the hot water spray and grabbed the shampoo.

~I'm surprised your mother didn't say you smelled like horses!~

~*What?* Do you think she noticed?~

~Nah, she was too consumed with their Vermont outing to notice anything other than you looking pale and underweight.~

~It seems hard to believe it's only a little after six p.m. on December twenty-eighth.~

~Be thankful your parents decided to leave town for the day.~

~That's for sure. I don't know how I'd have explained where I was for all those hours?~

Once she dried her hair, Jennifer put on leggings and an oversized sweatshirt with thick socks. ~It's a lot colder here than Grandma's dimension.~

~Is it?~ Suddenly, as if recalling something painful, Josh's expression darkened, and every muscle in his face tightened. ~I swear to God, Jennifer, if you ever do something so stupid as transporting yourself to another dimension or eating poisonous berries again, I'll spank your bottom so hard, you'll won't be able to sit for days!~

Josh can't be serious, can he?!

~Oh, I'm serious alright—so don't push your luck. Got it?~ Josh glowered.

~Then you'd better not mess around with any other women!~ Jennifer scrambled toward their bedroom door only to come face to face with Josh, who'd transported across the room. ~If you hadn't given me a reason to leave you, I'd have *never* run away or transported without you!~

~Dammit, Jennifer! The last time we were here, I was on my knees praying for a miracle!~

~I'm sorry, that was a terrible thing to say to you. The thought of never seeing you again is far worse than if you'd cheated on me.~

~Baby, get it through your head: I didn't, nor will I ever cheat on you. When I found Sarnia in my bed, I couldn't get rid of her fast enough. She could never be half the woman you are.~

~I still don't get why I disowned my grandma—I mean, Gisabella.~

~Umm,~ Josh stalled, searching for *believable* words other than the truth. *I can't say how she overheard Gisabella talking about her life-path marriage to another man. My wife would never understand that—or my promise to let her go.*

~It's that bad?~

~No, I'm just trying to remember what it was you overheard that caused you to turn against her. I guess I was too busy trying to explain about Sarnia to notice what else was being said.~

~Maybe I should ask Grandma what she said?~

~I think that'd be best. You and Gisabella should work things out on your own. I'd hate to get in the middle of my wife and my boss.~ He sighed in relief.

~Whatever happened to dinner?~ Jennifer changed the subject to a more palatable one. ~Talos and I are hungry, aren't we?~

"*Meow*," Talos did his best earthly cat impression. ~What's a cat got to do to get some food around here?~

~Fine, I get the point,~ Josh groaned. ~I'm sure we can scrounge up something to eat for you and the cat. Come on, you two,~ Josh said, leading the way toward the kitchen, glad he had successfully changed the subject away from Gisabella and Jennifer's life-path.

CHAPTER TEN

JANUARY 10, 1980

*T*wo weeks had passed since they'd returned from their honeymoon house, and it was the final Friday before college classes resumed. With Jennifer's parents on their way to work, Josh and she had the kitchen to themselves.

Once all the ingredients were gathered, Josh busied himself dicing onions and peppers while Jennifer sliced the mushrooms. When done, he glanced Jennifer's way to find her painstakingly working on the task at hand.

-Would you like some help with those?- He nodded in the direction of her cutting board.

-I get it—I'm nowhere near as fast as you are,- Jennifer messaged, looking down at her finished work with a frown. -Apparently I'm incapable of slicing them as paper-thin too.-

-Since you asked—I've been saving this lesson until you were ready, and today's as good a time as any.- Josh walked up behind Jennifer, getting close enough for their energies to mingle. -I'll need you to relax and place all your trust in me. Remember, you're safe as long as you don't think too much—better yet, don't think *at all!* Now, empty your thoughts, and when you have successfully done so, I'll show you how us chefs do it.-

When Jennifer did as she was told, he moved forward until his energy successfully coexisted with hers while he co-inhabited her consciousness. When she stayed relaxed, he used his energy to guide Jennifer's left hand to pick up the two-inch blade knife and move her right hand to position the mushroom in place. At first, he began slicing the mushroom slowly until he was sure she wouldn't panic. Once she gave no sign of resistance, he moved the knife faster, while he curled her fingers holding the mushroom to prevent accidentally slicing her fingertips. Once again, he increased his speed, leaving paper-thin slices of mushrooms in the blade's wake.

Jennifer stared down at her hand gripping the knife tightly with the tip resting on the board, moving rapidly while barely leaving the mushroom's surface. Like magic, it looked as though the blade hadn't moved at all. *Yikes, I sure hope he knows what he's doing!* Her thoughts took over, kicking Josh out and leaving her once again in control of the knife. The result was an unusually thick slice.

~Now look what you've done,~ Josh remarked, pointing at the cutting board. ~See what happens when you think?!~

~But—it didn't look like the knife was slicing into the mushroom.~ Jennifer used her fingers to fan through the pile of uniform slices. ~How did you get them so paper thin?~ Each slice was the same until she came across the one where her thoughts had taken back her reflexes. *Oops!* ~I can tell which one was my handiwork. So you took over my mind and my body?~ A chill ran through her over how easily Josh was able to take control of her.

~As you saw, I'm able to do so in a way that makes it easy for you to kick me out, ensuring you're never in any danger. As for being able to slice mushrooms so thin, I have to admit, with you being left-handed, unlike someone who's right-handed, you're at a disadvantage because, depending on the size blade you're using, you can't necessarily see what you're doing. Whereas, a right-handed person's line of vision sees each slice as it happens, regardless of the knife selected.~

Jennifer cocked an eyebrow and picked up the knife with her right hand, then she carefully cut into the next mushroom. ~I see what you mean—this way is so much easier!~

~Which reminds me, you should be using a special left-handed knife that's been honed differently than the knives you've been using. Do you think you'd be comfortable enough try again?~

~Sure, just try not to tire out my hand!~ This time, she kept her thoughts at bay until the next mushroom was sliced.

~Now that you know how it feels, if I ever had to take over driving your car for you for some other reason in order to keep you safe, you won't panic—*right*?~ Josh hoped his comment would go over well, but his wife's stubborn look made him elaborate a little more. ~It'd feel very similar to cutting mushrooms with you, only I'd be using your hands and feet to control the car, but you'd still have the ability to use your free will.~

~We should stick with slicing mushrooms for now,~ Jennifer messaged while shifting uncomfortably. *Josh presiding over my entire body? Geez, talk about being way too close for comfort!*

~Mushrooms it is, then!~ *For now.* ~Remember to keep your thoughts blank.~ When she did as he asked, he once again picked up the knife with Jennifer's left hand and made quick work of the remaining three mushrooms.

~Whew, that was fast!~ Jennifer exclaimed, taking back control of her body while rubbing her arm after her husband's impromptu slice and dice workout routine.

~What are some of the things Merlin has taught you?~ Jennifer asked, now seated at the table while taking a bite of her mushroom omelet.

~Oh, you know—the usual stuff like turning people into frogs, shrinking their heads and making them howl at the moon.~

~Be serious—I really want to know.~

~Merlin is great with potions and magic, in addition to things like being able to walk on water or transforming himself into various forms of wildlife.~ Encouraged by Jennifer's full attention, Josh continued, ~He used to drive me nuts showing up as different characters, each of his transformations crazier than the one before. As far as healers go, Merlin and Gisabella are equally matched, and they're one of the main reasons you're still alive. However, it was a far greater being—the overseer of all, including the high priestess—God himself—who saved you.~

~What did you mean when you said Merlin showed up as different characters?~

~Oh, he has an entire repertoire of them! One time he showed up as a woman with horns sprouting from her head and a slithering tongue. I found it especially hard to concentrate on what Merlin was saying while his forked tongue darted in and out.~

~Eww, if Merlin shows up to teach me looking like that, I swear I'll run the other way!~

~No use in doing that—Merlin would only turn himself into an owl and fly after you.~

~He wouldn't dare do that, would he?~ She worried her lip and glanced around as if they were being watched. ~Don't laugh at me!~

~Relax, baby, I guarantee Merlin isn't here spying on us, and you can be damn sure he'll be treating you with kid gloves. If not, he'll not only have to answer to Gisabella, but to me as well. He knows better than to mess with one of my visionaries, especially the one who holds my heart captive.~

~Is that right, Mr. Smith?~ Jennifer put down her fork and stood while holding out her hand. ~Come, I want to go back to bed—all your body invasion and talk of the things Merlin may have taught you is turning me on,~ she messaged with a wink, and soon Josh's energized hand was holding her solid one.

~Talos, feel free to clean off the breakfast dishes,~ Jennifer messaged as she led Josh out of the kitchen with a huge smile.

A few hours later, Jennifer was standing in Merlin's domain with Josh and Talos, looking around expectantly.

"There you are," a raspy voice called out as the man who belonged to it shuffled forward as fast as his long robe would allow without tripping. With eyes a shade darker than a bluebird, his lips widened as he moved closer.

"Good to see you, Merlin," Josh greeted, holding out his hand.

"You too, Josh." The wizard grasped the protector's hand firmly. With a large owl perched on his shoulders, the older man glanced at a very nervous Jennifer, and his smile grew twice in size. "Poor lass, you look as if you've seen a ghost!" Merlin doubled over laughing, sending his feathered friend flying off to the nearest tree.

"I'm not scared, if that's what you're thinking," Jennifer balked, squaring her shoulders. *Maybe just a little, but neither of them need to know that.*

"Still my little hellcat!" Merlin said, making Jennifer blush.

"I am not a hellcat—or whatever else that means!" She stomped her foot, but her rebuttal only made Merlin let out a laugh so loud that a flock of birds took flight. *Great, bad enough Josh and Gisabella tease me, but now I have Merlin making jokes at my expense too.*

The moment both sets of eyes narrowed in her direction, it became crystal clear she'd forgotten to block her thoughts. *For once I wish the playing field between them and me was equal!* "What? It's not like I said anything in my thoughts that wasn't true!" Jennifer lashed out.

"She does have a point, Merlin." Josh's eyes twinkled with amusement.

"Yeah, I'd hate to be in her shoes."

"If you both would like to continue talking about me like I'm not standing here, I can try transporting myself back home to earth." *Yikes!* Jennifer's stomach felt as if a herd of angry buffalo had taken up residence. *Wow! I don't believe I've ever seen Josh's face turn so red before! At least not since my run in with Mr. Burk!*

"Umm, I think I'd better take my granddaughter up to the house now and begin her lessons," Merlin spoke up, taking Jennifer's hand in his. "Don't worry, she'll be safe here with me. Why don't you run along and take a little time out to go enjoy yourself?"

Josh walked forward and brushed his lips to Jennifer's before whispering in her ear, "I'm not about to forget your transporting remark." When she tensed, he flashed her a secretive smile. "Have fun while you're safely tucked away in Merlin's domain, Mrs. Smith."

Then he turned toward Merlin. "I'll come back in a few hours. I'll leave Talos here—maybe he can help thin out your bird population." Talos looked to be the only happy one as he purred in response to Josh's offer.

The moment Josh transported, Jennifer exhaled with an audible whooshing sound.

"No need to fret, lass." Merlin squeezed Jennifer's hand. "Not to worry, he's sure to cool down by the time he comes back to pick you up. But I'd caution you to never threaten to transport on your own—ever again! Not after the hell you put him, Gisabella and myself through. I've known Josh for centuries, and I've never seen him look as devastated as the day he was ordered to transport you back to earth to die."

"I hope you're right; otherwise, I may opt to hang out here for a few days."

"Sorry, but even as your grandfather, I have *no* say over how your spirit protector decides to reprimand you. And you can be sure as hell Gisabella isn't going to step in and save you from Josh's wrath either."

"That does it; if he shows up looking mad, Josh can go cool off some more." Her intention only made Merlin laugh harder, causing the buffalo inhabiting her tummy to stampede.

"Come, lass, we have lots to do." Merlin led the way toward his home. Once inside, he motioned in the direction of the two chairs in front of the crackling fire. As Jennifer settled herself into one of the overstuffed chairs, he went into the kitchen and returned a moment later with two steaming mugs. "Go ahead and drink this; it will take the chill out of you."

"Thank you." She gratefully accepted the ornate pewter mug and tentatively sipped the amber liquid. "Mmm, this is delicious."

"I used to make this when you were a wee lass."

"Sorry I don't remember," Jennifer voiced with a trace of sadness.

"None of that—looking back never gets us moving forward." Merlin lifted his mug to his lips and took a sip before he spoke. "You know who I am now; that's all that matters—right?"

"Yes—of course it is." She smiled kindly at her grandfather from many lifetimes ago.

Merlin cleared his throat before speaking. "I've come up with a list of lessons for you to choose from: moving objects in and out of dimensions, how to read blocked minds, or a lesson on basic potions. There's another choice that most of my students prefer, which is how to make yourself invisible." When his student's eyes brightened, he smiled knowing which she'd choose. "Well, which lesson should we concentrate on today?"

"If I learn how to make myself invisible, would anyone be able to see me?"

"If you're speaking about Josh—you must first practice hard and manage to perfect your technique—only then will the lad have a hard time finding you. But mind you, I'll not be held responsible for his actions when he locates you!" Merlin guffawed. "You haven't changed a bit, little hellcat. It's a wonder Josh hasn't taken you over his knee—or *has* he?"

"He wouldn't dare," she said unconvincingly, causing Merlin's grin to broaden.

"No, of course he hasn't," Merlin said, nodding his head in a way that indicated he thought otherwise. "It's settled then: invisible lesson it is!"

When she nodded, Merlin began, "There are a few rules you must adhere to; otherwise, you'll become visible, possibly putting yourself in danger."

"I understand," she said, hoping to hurry Merlin along in case Josh decided to return earlier than expected.

"First you must clear your mind of all thoughts but the one needed to become invisible to others."

"Got it! Will I be invisible to Talos and other animals, too?"

"Of course, but don't be surprised if Talos smells you and walks your way. This has been known to happen after eating meat or spicy foods."

"Okay, no meat or spicy foods. What else?" She leaned forward.

"Once you clear your thoughts, you'll need to find a place to stand where you can blend in with your surroundings, preferably a colored wall or one that has been wallpapered. Those are the two easiest places to start since you have something to camouflage with. Once you have camouflaging down pat, you can work up to other backgrounds and eventually to being unseen while you're in an empty space."

"That's amazing! Will I still be able to message or be heard out loud?"

"It will take lots of practice before you'll be able to message without breaking your concentration. If you did that, you'd become visible to everyone within sight. As for speaking out loud—that'd be counterproductive—wouldn't it? I mean, what'd be the point of being invisible if you're going to talk out loud?" Merlin slapped his thigh while he laughed at his own joke.

"Good point," she snickered. "Can we start now?" There was nothing she could do to hide the eagerness in her voice.

"You can begin whenever you're ready. The easiest place to start is with your hands. For first timers, I recommend facing your background and holding up a hand a few inches from it, so you can see your progress for yourself."

She headed over to the brown wall Merlin pointed to and held up her hand as instructed. At first nothing happened, but when she unfocused her eyes, like Josh had instructed her to do when reading her crystal ball, one by one her fingers seemed to disappear, and Merlin cheered. In a short time, she was able to make hands and feet invisible, each blending into the brown wall. Within an hour, she was able to make all but her ears and hair unseen.

"Great job! You almost did it! Try concentrating on wearing an invisible helmet that covers your ears and hair."

Helmet! Okay—I'm wearing a helmet that no one can see, not even Josh. Just think of the jokes I could play on him. I must concentrate! A helmet— covering my ears and my long hair.

"Keep doing whatever it is you're doing, because it's working! Well done—I can't see you!" Merlin looked down at his watch, and when five minutes passed and his student remained unseen, he clapped his hands together in a round of applause. "Amazing job, Jennifer! That's enough for now."

When she failed to appear, his eyebrows knitted together. "This is not the time to play jokes, lass. I command you to make yourself visible now!"

"What are you talking about? I am visible," Jennifer insisted.

"But I can't see you!" The wizard stared earnestly at the brown wall, hoping to catch an outline of Jennifer, but no matter how hard he stared, he saw nothing. "Oh no, Josh is gonna kill me," he muttered under his breath.

"But I'm completely visible!" Jennifer stifled a giggle at the poor wizard who appeared to be panicking.

"No, you're not, and I'm afraid no one will be able to see you," he cried out in despair.

"Turn around, and you'll be able to see me for yourself."

Merlin whipped around to spot Jennifer standing in front of the shelves full of books and his mouth dropped open. "How—when?" he stammered. "You better not have transported yourself across the room, or Josh won't be the only one who'll want to tan your hide!"

"I walked here," Jennifer rushed out her response before she was added to yet another *in big trouble* list. "I thought you were being kind—you know, pretending you couldn't see me when I moved."

"You walked right past me? Either I'm slipping, or you're more gifted than we all thought! Lass, I've trained thousands of the most gifted people in all the universes, including Gisabella, but it took them longer than you to make themselves disappear. Most of them spent months to a year practicing before they were able to walk around a room unseen." Merlin chuckled. "Boy is Josh going to have his hands full now!"

"Surely he'll be able to see me or at least sense where I am!"

"If you're playing a game with him, Josh may be able to pick up on your sexual energy. Other than that, *no*, I don't believe he'll be able to pick up on your energy or know you're in the room. More importantly, neither will anyone else. Jennifer, you may never be strong enough to defend yourself in an *energy* battle against a rogue or evil spirit, but with enough practice, you'll be able to effectively hide from all of them."

"So, maybe you can tell Josh to stop being so overprotective?"

Merlin took Jennifer's hands in his. "The sooner you accept your destiny and the fact you require a strong protector to watch over you, the easier your life will become."

"Why can't I just have a normal life and a husband who's only my spouse?"

"You sound just like your grandmother! Gisabella hated being guarded. Although, back then, there wasn't the level of protection you have now. She used to balk and refuse to heed her guards' advice. Never mind the attitude she gave me when I showed up to begin her high priestess lessons." Merlin snorted before once again becoming serious. "As time went on, though, we fell in love and both of us were glad we had the excuse of her lessons to fall back on, providing us with a cover for all the time we spent together."

"Then Gisabella should understand how I feel." Jennifer's shoulders slumped.

"She has a job to do, and although Gisabella loves you, there are too many lives at stake not to make sure you're prepared to assume your title and her position. This isn't about you, Jennifer; it's seeing that every soul in every dimension is given a chance to live in harmony, so that each is capable of fulfilling the purpose for which they were created. I'm sorry you think you've been dealt a bad hand with a future you never wanted, but there's nothing any of us can do about it other than offer our love and support and teach you all the skills you'll need to succeed."

"I guess Josh was right when he said I sounded selfish. I don't mean to make things so difficult or act like I don't care, but, Grandfather—I'm scared. What if I fail and ruin everything? Suppose I cause everyone's soul to be disintegrated or the dimensions all to collide with one another or merge together into one big mess?" Jennifer's eyes blurred, and she found herself instantly whisked into her grandfather's embrace.

"There now, child, please don't fret. We'll all be there to make sure nothing like that happens. We have faith in you and believe, one day, you'll be a great high priestess. All we ask is that you listen to Josh; he knows what he's doing and has a good head on his shoulders. I may tease the boy, but there's none better to protect and care for you than Joshua. He's like a son to me. How wonderful that my granddaughter has married such a great protector—forever, no less! Good choice, lass." Merlin hugged Jennifer tighter before releasing her just in time to watch Josh appear looking much happier than when he'd left.

"Wow, you must have done a great job, baby," Josh said, eyeing the older wizard. "Merlin never hugged me after my lessons."

"Had I known you needed to be coddled, boy, I'd have kicked you to the curb!" Merlin bashed.

Ignoring the wizard's dig, Josh swooped Jennifer into a full body embrace. "I missed you." He nuzzled until his wife clung to him tightly. "How did you do, baby?"

"Umm, good I think," she said flatly, not to give any indication of her newfound invisible abilities.

"She did fairly well for a new student. You know, she's not the worst visionary I ever taught. With some practice, Jennifer will get better," Merlin played along, enjoying their private joke.

Josh noticed the glimmer in the wizard's eyes, giving him a clue there was more to what they were saying. *Talk about two of the worst liars.* Now all he had to do is figure out what they were hiding. "Don't worry, I'll help you practice so next time you can whoop Merlin's ass." He followed up his comeback with a crooked grin.

"Remember you must practice what you learned today with Josh, and do so often—okay?"

"If you insist. I'll try to be more dedicated to my high priestess lessons. I'm so glad I have a husband like Josh who inspires me to practice so much," she said using her best poker face.

"Now run along home to earth with Josh and behave yourself, little hellcat, because I have a feeling he won't have any problem controlling you better than your grandmother and I ever could." Merlin was positive once Jennifer played her invisible trick on Josh, she was sure to pay a price for making her protector look like a fool.

When she received a playful swat on the butt from her husband, she blushed from head to toe. "Agh! I don't care how highly evolved you both are—you men are all the same!"

"That we are, baby, and you love us more because of it! That being said, I'd better take Talos and my wife home before I get myself into any more hot water. Thanks for your help with Jennifer's lessons. I'll bring her back in a couple of weeks for her next lesson."

"See you then, kids," Merlin called out as the two faded away. *I'd give anything to see the expression on his face when Jennifer becomes invisible.* A vision of Josh's reaction to Jennifer's disappearing act flashed into his mind. The look on the younger protector's face was one of utter shock, causing Merlin to fill the room with boisterous laughter. *Oh that poor boy!*

CHAPTER ELEVEN

The moment they reappeared in the lake house bedroom, Talos began winding in and out of their legs, rubbing against them just like an ordinary domesticated cat.

~Your parents won't be home for another four hours,~ Josh messaged with a wink.

~Mmm, are you suggesting what I think you are?~ she replied, eyeing his translucent physique with unguarded hunger. ~I'd love nothing more than to lie underneath you while you give me energized orgasms—a dozen of them would be great!~

~As wonderful as that sounds, I thought we could practice what you learned earlier; you know, since we have the house to ourselves.~ *Ouch, guess that wasn't on my wife's wish list!*

~As appealing as your idea is, Merlin said I should rest. You know how it is—being an earthling and all, I'm afraid I don't have the stamina you have.~

She unbuttoned her blouse and let it fall to the floor with her jeans, bra and panties. Though her husband's expression remained relaxed, the deepening emerald shade of his irises and the way his jaw tightened was all the proof she needed that her plan was working. If that wasn't enough, the bulge pressing against the zipper of his jeans left no doubt she was about to get her own way. With the grace of a dancer, she sashayed her hips invitingly as she walked over to their bed in hopes Josh would follow.

By the time she laid her head on the pillow with her limbs stretched out in a way to provide him with the best view of her glistening arousal, her man was standing at the foot of the bed buck naked. *He's so sexy!*

Jennifer skimmed her fingertips over her breasts, leisurely stroking her peaked nipples before traveling south…leaving a trail of goosebumps all the way down her torso. Slipping her hand between her thighs, she could feel the wetness of her burning desire as she closed her eyes. It wasn't long before she gave into the rising moan of pleasure begging to escape her lips and was rewarded by her husband's sharp intake of breath.

When she reopened her eyes, she found Josh's gaze pinning her in place as if his hands were holding her hostage. It was then she noticed his hand wrapped around his erection, stroking up and down while looking at her.

-What do you want, Mrs. Smith?- he taunted.

If Josh didn't take her soon, he'd possibly lose his mind, or worse, come too soon before he was inside her.

-You! I want only you. Please, Josh, I need you.- Her pleas sounded so pitiful to her own ears, but she didn't care.

-I hate how weak you make me, woman! Do you know how much I need to be inside you? Hell, if I don't claim you this minute, I swear I'll lose my mind!- Josh transported himself until he was suspended in midair above her with his now energy-dense erection poised at the brink of her beckoning sex. He gave Jennifer a moment before he took her with one thrust, a move that caused ripples of her pleasure to caress his length and forced him to once again fight off the urge to give in to his orgasm.

-God, woman—all I can think about is making love to you. Tell me you feel the same, like you can't live without me.-

"Without you, there'd be nothingness," she called out, no longer able to form messages in her mind. "I love you, heart and soul." Salty, emotional tears streamed down her cheeks only to be kissed away by Josh.

-That's right, baby—let go—do it for me,- he coaxed. He was rewarded when Jennifer tightened around his throbbing erection before he gave in to his desire. Lying joined together in a pool of ecstasy, their love further intertwined them for all of eternity. They remained until his manhood ebbed and his energy subsided, making him once again impossible to touch without passing through him.

~Are you sure you're feeling strong enough to go back to school on Monday? You can always miss a few days,~ Josh reasoned, hoping to avoid taxing her newly regained strength.

Jennifer bristled until she noticed the look on Josh's face. ~Honestly, Josh, you've kept me under house arrest for eighteen days in our honeymoon house since Christmas, then made me hang around here for two weeks! The last thing I need is more rest.~

~Don't you mean since I almost lost you forever?!~ His eyes darkened, and his forehead creased.

~It was you who caused me to run away!~ Jennifer retorted. *Great, nothing like making his blood pressure skyrocket! Good thing spirits can't give themselves a stroke!*

~Run away!~ Josh shouted. ~Running away doesn't begin to describe what you did! Fuck it! Jennifer, don't you understand how serious of a law you broke when you transported on your own? I hate to think what would've happened if we didn't find you when we did!~ Josh's chest heaved with each angry breath he took.

~Fine—I get it—I shouldn't have transported on my own. Must you constantly rub my nose in it? You need to let it go before you drive a wedge between us,~ Jennifer tried to reason.

~As your protector, it's my *fucking job* to keep you safe!~ Josh sat up and turned away, running a hand through his hair in an attempt to calm his energy. But when he turned back around, his wife was nowhere in sight! *What the?*

~Jennifer, where are you?~ He spun around, but she was nowhere to be seen. ~This isn't funny! So help me, if you transported yourself again, you're gonna be in for one hell of a rude awakening!~

When his threat didn't make her step forward, he turned toward Talos, who was seated across the room with his back toward him, absorbed in licking his fur coat clean.

~Well, did you see where Jennifer went, cat?~

~I have a name, you know,~ Talos scratched back.

~Yeah, but unlike you, I have access to the freezer!~ When Talos favored cleaning his paw over acknowledging him, Josh sighed. ~Talos, did you happen to see where Jennifer went?~ he acquiesced.

~Just because you cannot see something, doesn't mean it isn't there,~ Talos purred.

~What the hell does that mean?~ Josh scratched his chin until a name popped into his thoughts—*Merlin!*

~So you want to play, little wife? I see you've learned a new trick.~ He closed his eyes momentarily and inhaled. ~Mmm, there's no way you can hide your delicious scent from me.~ A quick scan of the room helped him picked up on her energy. ~Oh baby, the last thing you should attempt is an invisibility trick so soon after sex.~

He walked toward the other side of the room, purposefully stalking her. ~I will find you, and when I do, I plan on punishing you, and there's not a damn thing you can do about it!~

I get the feeling he isn't as happy about my prank as I am. Maybe I can manage to remain invisible while I run out of the room—like a bat out of hell?! She cringed when her protector chuckled.

~Tsk-tsk, Jennifer! Not blocking your thoughts is such a rookie mistake. Here I thought you had *that* lesson down pat. Now I have another lesson to teach you.~

Jennifer closed her eyes and cringed again. *Another lesson?* She inwardly groaned as she watched Josh head toward the desk, and when he opened the top drawer, her insides quaked. *Surely he's only trying to intimidate me?* Her thoughts did nothing to calm her nerves when she watched him densify his hands enough to take out a wooden ruler and swat his energized palm.

~Why don't you come out now and make things easier on yourself?~ Josh continued to circle the room as if delaying the inevitable: Jennifer draped over his lap.

As Josh headed in a different direction than where she stood, Jennifer made her escape, somehow managing to remain invisible all the way to the bedroom door. None of it mattered, though, when Josh became solid and she lost her concentration. Doing so, Jennifer became completely visible and at Josh's mercy before she could get away.

Josh becoming solid is a bad sign! The fact he was able to do so gave her a clue how much trouble she was in with her protector. Within a few seconds, she found herself flung over his shoulder like a ragdoll before she'd gotten the chance to escape.

"I think it's time I finally make good on all those warnings I've given you," Josh said, grinning while he carried her over to the loveseat.

Ugh, how does he make that sound so hot? Talk about embarrassing! She made sure to block her wayward thoughts. Too bad she couldn't block her body's reaction.

When Josh lowered her off his shoulder, he did so slowly and in a way that made her pubic bone rub the length of his erection. *Oh...he's excited too!* She didn't have much time to digest this information before she found herself lying across his lap, naked and at his mercy.

"Let's see, arguing with your protector and husband. Using an unauthorized invisibility trick to hide from me while making me think you'd transported out of the room. Plus forgetting to block your thoughts. I'd say that adds up to a well-deserved spanking, wouldn't you?"

Surely he doesn't expect me to answer him?! The feeling of Josh's hand caressing her butt made her moan. So sensual was the feeling that soon she relaxed and gave in to the sensations. *Mmm, this is more like a reward for being on my best behavior than a—Ouch!* She was snapped out of her dreamy thoughts by a somewhat painful, but not too hard swat from the ruler. Her natural reaction was to rise up, but all attempts to do so were thwarted by Josh holding her in place with his other hand resting on her back.

When his hand once again caressed her behind, she embraced the blissful sensations. "Mmm, that feels so good," she moaned, but instead of being rewarded with more caresses, the ruler landed a little harder than the previous smack.

"Aren't you going to tell me how great that felt too?" Josh taunted, once again caressing her butt.

"Bad enough you're spanking me, but do you have to make such a big deal out of it? Ow!" she exclaimed before once again finding herself giving in to Josh's soothing caresses. *Oh, this is too much.* The mixture of bliss, lying across his solid lap, and the ruler smacks was making her crave more of each. As if Josh read her thoughts, he continued his creative punishment until she was panting with need.

"After this final swat, I'm going to carry you back to bed and take you from behind!"

"Yes, please." She was unable to keep her neediness out of her voice. Soon she was rewarded when Josh slid a finger inside her wanton sex. "Oh please," she cried out, only to receive the final promised ruler smack.

"Agh! Please, I can't take any more—I—need you!" she begged, past all caring about her mixed reactions to his punishment. She was rewarded when Josh carried her back to the bed where he proceeded to live up to his endless energy.

Two hours hour later, Jennifer sighed with contentment and snuggled closer to Josh while resting her face on his shoulder.

"Tell me, Jennifer, when were you planning on letting me know you learned how to become invisible?"

"Um, I—wanted to wait until I was—uh—more proficient before boasting," she stumbled through her explanation.

"I see, so you planned on playing your little joke on me from the get go."

"Either way, the results were extremely satisfying." She looked up to see Josh's eyebrows rise.

"Yes, the outcome was certainly pleasurable—*this time!* Be forewarned: next time you decide to become invisible without my permission, I won't be so understanding." He flashed her a dark, smoldering look before he planted a kiss on top of her head.

"Okay—I need to forewarn you before disappearing from your sight! Got it!" she said, beaming up at Josh. *Yikes, he looks like he's ready to spank me again!*

"I'd give anything to have seen Merlin's face when you disappeared! I bet he was shocked, you disappearing on your first lesson. That's incredible! Way to go, baby!"

"At first I thought he was pretending he couldn't find me. It wasn't until his eyes grew wide, and he started mumbling to himself about how you and Gisabella were going to kill him that I realized Merlin was in full panic mode. Oh Josh, I wish you could've seen his face! His worried expression was hysterical!" She swiped at the tears of laughter trickling down her cheeks and was close to stopping until Josh's booming laugh started her up again.

"Merlin must have been blown away by your ability! Let's face it, you're a direct descendent of two of the most gifted souls: Gisabella and Merlin. You can't get any better than that."

"Yeah, but being their descendent is the part that forces me to learn all this stuff and become a high priestess." All traces of humor faded from Jennifer's face, and she found herself being pulled into her husband's loving embrace. *Mmm, there's no place I'd rather be.*

CHAPTER TWELVE

TWO YEARS LATER—JANUARY 7, 1982

"I have no idea where the years have gone, Merlin." Gisabella brought the froth-filled mug to her lips while keeping her focus on her lover, who was adding more logs to the fire. "Why, it seems like just yesterday Josh and Jennifer were standing before me, pledging their hearts and souls to each other, and now, next week is their third wedding anniversary! What do you suppose is a proper gift for three years?"

"That'd depend on the couple." Merlin ran his hands down his robe to brush off any debris. "That should warm the place up."

"You weren't listening to a thing I said, were you?" Gisabella chastised. "Fine, I'll give them something from us both, and if they don't like it, I'll tell them you picked it out!" She waited for a response, but none came from the relaxed wizard, who was staring into the fire like it held the answer to some great mystery of life.

"I don't get why you insist on chopping logs and building a fire from scratch? It must be a man thing—or is it some sort of survival skill test you give yourself? With all your magical skills, surely it'd be nothing for you to instantly poof some smokeless flames to warm your cabin, without all the work."

"My dear woman, I find doing some menial tasks rewarding. For all we know, there may come a day that our magical powers will cease to exist." When he saw Gisabella's loss of color, he immediately regretted his words. "Nothing will happen, my love; I just like to maintain my basic earthly skills. You really should try some of them."

"Well, I do love to cook and bake new creations, so I guess I do, as you say, practice menial survival skills."

Merlin bit back the retort resting on the tip of his tongue while trying to come up with something a little more flattering. "And a lot of *practice* you do, my love." He sat down opposite Gisabella before he continued where they'd left off prior to fetching the logs. "Getting back to Jennifer. There are still things I feel she needs to learn before she'll be able to fill your shoes."

"I agree! I have many things to teach her, and I'm sure Josh still has a list of things, too. Do you think if we doubled our efforts, she'll be ready before her arranged marriage? Honestly, once she marries her life-path husband, we can forget Jennifer's lessons. As it is, she's been falling way behind with them. Not to mention all the extra credit projects she insists on doing for college. Too bad Jennifer doesn't put the same effort into her high priestess lessons."

"Yes indeed, the poor thing already has her hands full between school and everything we expect her to learn. Why, it's been over two months since Jennifer has shown up for her lessons with me, and the time before was over four months. Let's face it, Jennifer's not you, and I get the feeling no matter how much time we spend teaching her, we're going to run out of time. What we really need is another ten lifetimes before she's required to take over as high priestess!"

"Thanks to Josh taking it upon himself to marry the girl forever, that option no longer exists!"

"There's one way, but I'm not sure how legal it'd be to carry it out."

"I think the hole we've dug for ourselves is already too deep to care about adding another infraction—I mean, what's the difference now?" Gisabella asked with a shrug of her shoulders.

"What if, when the time comes for Jennifer to join us in heaven, we keep her existence a secret?"

"For how long?" Gisabella perked up.

"We could say indefinitely, Your Excellency." Merlin bowed his head in respect.

Gisabella took another sip from her mug while considering Merlin's suggestion. "Then, when Jennifer's skills are up to speed, we can produce her to the Council. Afterwards, we'll be free to do as we please." Gisabella's rose-colored lips widened.

"Exactly! By then, I'm sure Josh and Jennifer won't mind taking over, given all the time they'd have to themselves as a family beforehand."

"You're right! Josh would jump at the chance not to be tied to the throne until necessary."

"Then it's settled: we'll continue training Jennifer at this pace, and then, when her life on earth is over, we'll secretly transition her to your private domain," Merlin reiterated.

"Brilliant, my love! No one will be the wiser, and they already have a house there, so I see no issues with our plan. Unless, of course, someone were to find out about their marriage, or how Jennifer's my—I mean, our granddaughter."

"Would you like more?" Merlin nodded toward the cup Gisabella held in two hands.

"No, thank you—I'm good."

"In that case, do you want to stay the night?" Merlin suggested.

"Sure." Gisabella placed her mug on the book table next to the chair and stood.

"I think we should hit the sack now, don't you?" With a come-hither smile, Merlin took hold of her hand and led Gisabella toward his bedroom.

Unaware of the plans being made in another realm, Jennifer concentrated on the canvas in front of her until her art teacher's voice broke into her thoughts.

"Miss Parker, if you have a moment, I'd like to speak to you after class."

"Of course, Mrs. Tisdale." *I wonder what she wants?* Jennifer shrugged and turned her concentration back to the task at hand.

Before class was about to end, she cleaned her brushes and straightened up her workspace. Most of the other students had exited the room when she finished sliding her final palette knife into its proper place amongst her art supplies. After closing the lid and snapping the latches in place, she picked up the wooden art case and headed over to where Mrs. Tisdale looked to be grading papers.

"Ah, Jennifer, your work was top notch today," Mrs. Tisdale complimented, lowering her thick, wire-rimmed spectacles.

"Thank you, Mrs. Tisdale. I love Michelangelo, and I consider it a treat to be replicating a small part of *The Last Judgement*. I never realized how much expression Adam and God's hands contained until you had us concentrate on painting them."

"It's your appreciation of each detail that led me to recommend you to my friend Oscar. He owns one of the largest galleries in New York, and he's currently in need of a part-time employee who's able to work weekends. Should you accept the position, you'll be greeting visitors, answering phones and helping various artists with their gallery openings, including organizing the refreshments and press releases. I can't stress enough what a great opportunity this will be for your career. No matter whatever direction you choose, there's no better teacher than Oscar and his staff." Mrs. Tisdale finished the sentence with the annoying clicking sound she often made by her tongue hitting the roof of her mouth.

"I—um—thank you for your recommendation, Mrs. Tisdale. Does Oscar know I'm not set to graduate until next year?"

"Yes, and he's already agreed to let you work part-time until you graduate, upon which, I'm sure he'll offer you a full-time position. Why don't you think about it tonight and let me know what you decide tomorrow? Just don't wait too long because he's desperate to fill the position as soon as possible."

"It sounds perfect! I just want to run it by my—um, parents before I accept," Jennifer said with flushed cheeks.

"Very good. If you stop by my office tomorrow with your answer, I'll set up a meeting between you and Oscar. I know you'll love working for him."

"Thank you, I'll see you tomorrow."

Art being her last class, Jennifer scurried toward the exit, beaming ear to ear. She was on cloud nine when her sports car came into view. *So much for hoping Josh will extend his usual warm welcome,* she thought, taking in the sight of her man standing with his arms crossed and his usually handsome face marred by a frown. *Great, there's no way I'm having a conversation about my new employment here in plain sight.*

A quick glance around at the somewhat empty parking lot showed a few students lingering close by. *He better not dare broach the subject until we get home! The last thing I need is someone to notice me arguing with my invisible husband.*

~Hello, Jennifer,~ Josh greeted smoothly. ~I take it you had a good day at school.~ Other than the storm brewing in his eyes, he almost looked the picture of tranquility.

~Good to see you too, Mr. Smith,~ Jennifer messaged, risking a small smile and hoping the group of students nearby wouldn't notice. Once seated inside her vehicle, it didn't take long for the atmosphere to change from cordial to heated.

~So, did anything happen today I should know about?~ Josh inquired.

~You do that all the time! Why do you always start bugging me the second I turn the key? To top it off, after you distract me, you complain about my driving! Well, not this time, mister! If you've got something to say, you'll have to wait till we're home.~ Jennifer finished messaging as she rolled to a stop for the red light. A quick glance in Josh's direction gave her a false sense of security. *I stunned him into silence! Good!*

With each mile, the electricity in the car sizzled, and it was all Jennifer could do to concentrate on where she was going. *One more turn and I'll be home. Now all I have to do is hold it together and get out of the car fast!* The moment she turned off the car and set the brake, she bolted toward the front door. Once inside, she leaned against the door with her heart thumping.

~If I didn't know any better, I'd think you're trying to avoid me.~ Josh leaned forward and placed his hands above her head, looming closer until no gap existed between their bodies, only their combined coiled tension.

~Do you mind? I have to get changed and—~ Jennifer stopped mid-message as waves of pleasurable energy took over her senses.

~No, I think it's best if we talk now. Unless, of course, there's something you don't wish to share?~

"Since you obviously listened in on my private conversation with my teacher, you know about the position at the art gallery that I've decided to accept. Whether you like it or not, the opportunity is too fantastic to pass up. End of discussion!" Jennifer said out loud, if for no other reason than to hear her own words over her husband's messages.

~On the contrary, I believe we have a whole lot to discuss before I agree to let you accept the position.~

"This isn't up to you!" Jennifer tried to push her husband out of the way, but in his translucent state, her hands went right through him, causing chills to rush up and down her spine. "Ugh! I can't even have the satisfaction of shoving you out of my way! Don't you dare laugh at me." Jennifer huffed and closed her eyes before she rushed forward through Josh's translucent figure, re-opening them in time to run up the steps before Josh had a chance to recover from her surprise move.

~I dare you to try that tomorrow when there's a full moon!~

Drats! I forgot he'll be solid! Stupid full moon! To make matters worse, her parents weren't due home until Sunday night. Jennifer reached the bedroom where Talos was curled in a ball, soaking up the last remaining rays of sunlight. *Why is he always so unreasonable? I bet if Josh didn't have to guard me, he'd be a whole lot more fun!*

~Jennifer, we need to talk.~ Josh calmed his energy as he carefully approached her, trying not to escalate their much-needed conversation into a bigger fight.

~There isn't much to discuss. I've decided to accept the position unless you and my grandma can come up with several valid reasons why I must turn it down. Even then, I refuse to do so!~

~But what about your high priestess lessons?~

~If I work at the gallery on weekends and change our trips to our honeymoon house to two nights during the week, I'd have plenty of time to do both. Please try to understand that this job will jumpstart my career and provide enough money for a place of our own after I graduate.~ When Josh's worried look didn't soften, she added, ~You need to let me finish growing up and let me make my own decisions.~

~Alright, but if your mandatory lessons suffer, Gisabella and Merlin will back me up when I pull the plug on you working!~

~Does this mean you agree with me?~

~Only if I you can prove you're able to handle the extra work.~

~With a few extra visits to our honeymoon house, it'll be a piece of cake!~ Jennifer squashed the desire to break out in a happy dance after winning the small battle. When Josh remained tight-lipped, she attempted to lighten the mood. ~Think of all the benefits you'll be receiving during those extra trips back to our honeymoon house.~

~I'll be the judge of that.~ Josh pulled off his sweatshirt then unbuttoned and unzipped his jeans before lowering them to the ground with his briefs.

~I love makeup sex.~ Jennifer messaged, eyeing Josh as he stepped out of his clothes.

~Me too, Mrs. Smith.~ Josh raised his eyes before he turned and headed in the other direction, toward the bathroom.

Where's he going? ~Didn't you just say you loved makeup sex?~

~I sure did.~ Josh chuckled, letting the water from the shower run over and through his body. ~Too bad there's no such thing as makeup sex if we didn't have a fight.~

Jennifer entered the bathroom and closed the door behind her. ~Sure, you're only claiming it wasn't a fight because I won! Maybe I should start another fight with you?~ She stripped and joined Josh in the shower. ~Or maybe not fighting would be better.~

Jennifer eyed his erection and swallowed hard as her primal need for him grew, and desire gathered and pooled from deep within. As if Josh sensed she was ready, he now stood before her, dense enough to touch.

~Please touch me,~ Josh implored, then groaned when her hand wrapped around his erection. It felt good, really great, but he needed more. The only thing that'd satisfy his raging lust was to fuck her with everything he had in him. Without any warning, he turned her around, and, grabbing each of her wrists, he stretched out her arms and guided her hands toward the tiled wall while steam engulfed them. Grabbing her hips, he pulled Jennifer toward his stiffened manhood and took her with one thrust. He established a steady rhythm, but it still wasn't enough. He needed to claim every bit of her; it was as if his very existence depended on it.

Without any warning, Jennifer felt the ground disappearing from underneath her feet, and the shower wall she'd been so desperately clinging to vanished from beneath her fingertips. Without knowing what was happening, it felt like time stopped for hours. Panic rose, and her blood pounded in her ears before she could reason everything must be okay since Josh hadn't withdrawn from her. Then she was hit with an intense feeling of pain as her womanhood began to stretch to accommodate something huge. A scream cut into the silence, but she had no knowledge it'd come from her.

"I'm here, baby. I didn't mean to frighten you. I just thought it'd be nice if I transported us to our honeymoon house. You know, so we'd have lots of extra time to make love," Josh soothed. "Are you okay?"

She glanced at her husband's hands to discover they'd become solid, as had the rest of his body. "Get off of me!" She reached down and shoved his hands away, only to cry out in pain when he tried to pull out of her. "Stop!"

"Try to relax, and whatever you do, don't panic."

"What have you done?" Her eyes watered.

"I—I'm not sure. I mean, it probably has something to do with transporting us while I was inside you."

"No shit!"

"I wonder if we try standing under a shower of cold water?"

"And how do you suppose we walk there? So help me, if you say transport, you better not plan on ever having sex again." She swiped a few stray tears of pain away. "We'd better message Gisabella."

"Don't even think about calling her!" Josh paled. "Maybe if I were to transport only myself, when I turn into pure energy, I'll slide right out of you. You won't feel a thing."

"So help me, if you don't call my grandma, I will!"

"Gisabella will have my head if she finds out what I've done."

"And I'll gladly hand it over to her on a silver platter!" Jennifer grimaced. "What makes a man impotent?"

"Why? You can't be so furious you're prepared to do *that* to me!"

"You said cold water, but what other things would cause your erection to shrink?"

"I dunno, I guess a warm shower would too."

"Seriously? What is it with you? You get a hard on, and it reduces the size of your brain!"

"You yelling at me isn't helping our situation."

"Fine, I'll stop yelling when you're no longer inside of me."

"Believe me, I'd rather be anywhere else about now."

"Well, as soon as you're finally out of me, you can go anywhere you'd like—without me!" Jennifer's eyes opened wider. *It's working!*

"If that's what you want, it can be arranged!"

"Then I suggest you withdraw yourself and go take a hike." She crossed her fingers, hoping her words would do the trick.

"Fine!"

Jennifer breathed a sigh of relief when she felt how easily Josh slid out of her. The moment she was freed, she headed to the bathroom and began running a bath, but she wasn't alone for long.

"Do you mind if I join you?"

"I thought you wanted to get away from me."

"Not *you*, just your yelling." He raked his hand through his hair and gave Jennifer a crooked grin. "I guess I should've checked the transporting manual before I attempted that move."

She pursed her lips as she studied his face for any trace of ill-timed humor. "Fine, if you promise to behave yourself, you can wash my back."

"Scouts honor!"

"I don't suppose you messaged Talos so he knows where we are?" She looked his way expectantly.

"I let him know we'll be gone for a couple of hours. I think we could use the time alone, even if I can't touch you."

Jennifer lowered herself into the oversized tub piled high with mounds of bubbles. To her surprise, Josh held two glasses of wine.

"Here's to making it up to you," Josh toasted once he'd joined Jennifer in the tub, sealing his promise with a kiss.

CHAPTER THIRTEEN

~This must be our stop,~ Jennifer messaged with a fleeting, nervous glance at her translucent husband as their train pulled into Grand Central Station.

~Remember, keep your pocketbook close and stay next to me,~ Josh warned.

I'm nervous enough; the last thing I need to deal with is his over-the-top protector persona!

~Do you know how many muggings, murders and other crimes are committed in the city each day?~

~I can't say that question ever came up during a game of *Trivial Pursuit*,~ Jennifer replied automatically while gazing up at all the tall buildings.

~In 1980, there were 710,153 reported crimes!~

~You've got to be kidding me! How many is that a day?~

~1,945.62!~

The huge number caused her to stop walking, forcing people to swerve to avoid her, several muttering curses under their breath.

~Walk, Jennifer!~ Josh commanded, taking hold of her arm to guide her through the busy intersection. ~The gallery's up there on the left.~

~Please tell me you won't interfere with my interview.~ A glance in his direction did little to appease her apprehension, even though Josh's expression revealed nothing but an innocent façade. *What's he up to?* She blocked her thoughts while acting as if she didn't suspect him of anything, having learned it was easier to catch her husband up to no good when hiding her suspicions.

~Relax, I'm not planning on interfering. As a matter of fact, after doing a quick check, I concluded this is the perfect place for you to cut your teeth in the art world.~

~Here we are.~ Jennifer paused in front of the massive glass doors with cylindrical brass handles.

~I'll wait out here until you're done.~ Josh flashed her a disarming smile.

~You promise you're not going to try anything funny, right?~

~Why, Mrs. Smith, I'm appalled by your lack of trust. Don't look now, baby, but you're causing a scene.~

Me? A quick look around proved Josh's point. *Oh no. This was not how I pictured my first job interview starting off.* Three college-aged employees were poised on the other side of the door, staring back at her with perplexed expressions. *Sure wish Josh didn't put a moratorium on my becoming invisible in public! Not that he approves of me doing so any other time either! Geez, he can be such a control freak!* Jennifer was snapped out of her reverie by the sound of Josh's voice invading her thoughts.

~Just tell them this is your first trip to the city, and everything will be fine. No worries—you've got this, baby!~

With a deep, cleansing breath and a little white light protection, she walked forward with a fabricated air of confidence, even though she didn't feel the least bit at ease. A man who looked to be in his early forties hurried toward her with a warm smile and outstretched hand.

"*Ciao, bella*, you must be Jennifer. It's a pleasure to meet such a prized student of Delores's, I mean, Mrs. Tisdale."

"Thank you. You must be Mr. Balarini." Jennifer extended her hand to the middle-aged man with the most infectious toothy smile.

"Please call me Oscar, like everyone else."

"Thank you, Oscar. I brought my resume, although I'm afraid it's rather empty other than a few art awards and recommendations from my teachers."

"Based on Mrs. Tisdale's referral, there's no need for resumes and interviews. Instead, why don't I show you around and introduce you to some of your coworkers? Then we can go over your hours and salary."

Jennifer took notes as Oscar guided her through several rooms and various floors. As they walked through the gallery, she noticed each featured artist had been arranged by their style and types of medium used. Along the way she met all her future coworkers, many of whom were art students like herself, but most of them attended dedicated art schools. Afterward, she followed Oscar into his office, where she received a slip of paper with a generous starting salary printed on it and another with her starting hours. *Surely this isn't the norm for a college student with no experience!* A few additional forms completed her hiring packet.

"Do you need a ticket for the ride home?" Oscar asked.

"I have a round-trip pass."

There was a knock on the door, and a tall gentleman dressed in a well-tailored suit entered the room as if he lived there. The diamond stud in the man's ear sent sparkles around the room. That and the man's indigo pocket square made him appear better dressed than anyone she'd ever seen, other than Josh on their wedding day.

"Lover, what a wonderful surprise!" Oscar exclaimed, embracing the younger man. "When did you get back?"

"My plane got in an hour ago. I'd have been here sooner, but the traffic was atrocious." As if the gentleman remembered they weren't alone, he turned to address her in a British accent. "My apologies, miss, I didn't mean to spoil your conversation."

"That's okay, I was just leaving," Jennifer said, standing up. "I need to catch the train." *I should've blocked their energy before the full force of their love for each other filled the room.* She tried to squelch the color in her cheeks, hoping neither man noticed or got the wrong impression. *If two people were ever meant to be together, it's them!*

"I'm sorry, Jennifer, I'm afraid we've made you feel uncomfortable. It's just that Derek has been away on business for a month and...."

"No need to explain." She held up her hand with a huge smile. "Clearly the two of you are deeply in love. I don't know what I'd do if I couldn't see...," she stopped short of blurting out *my husband*, leaving her new boss and his lover waiting for her to finish.

~Someone I love,~ Josh jumped in before either man suspected anything was out of place.

"If I couldn't see someone I loved," Jennifer tried her best not to sound like a babbling idiot. *Ugh, they must think I'm daft!*

"As you heard, my name is Derek. It was so nice to meet you—um—"

"Forgive me, lover, this is the newest member of our gallery family, Miss Jennifer Parker," Oscar made the quick introduction while Jennifer accepted Derek's outstretched hand.

After exchanging a few more pleasantries, she made her escape from Oscar's office and left the gallery, where she found Josh waiting in translucent form. ~Talk about receiving my dream job!~ she messaged while risking a brief smile his way.

~Congratulations, baby!~

~Thank you! I take it you're pleased my new boss is in a relationship! Makes sense why you thought this gallery was the *perfect* place for me to work.~

~No need to roll your eyes at me. I guarantee if situations were reversed, and you were the one no one could see or know about, you'd feel the same way.~

~What way is that, Mr. Smith? Overprotective? Jealous? Or perhaps both?~

~We better hurry before you miss your train.~ *All of the above! Just once it'd be nice if the shoe was on the other foot. I bet that'd put a stop to her insolent tone.*

With a hint of a smirk occupying his features, Josh placed an energized hand on Jennifer's arm as he effectively guided her down the crowded sidewalk toward the train station. Once they boarded the train, he located two empty seats and surrounded them with protective energy, making sure no one would sit next to them.

~Baby, why don't you take the window seat so you can enjoy the view?~ *And, I can protect you more easily.* As Jennifer gazed out the window at the boarding passengers, Josh scanned each of the new passenger's energy, making sure his visionary wife would remain safe.

It had been two months since Jennifer started working at the gallery, and she was seated with her friends in the college cafeteria while her sentry stood with his arms crossed, surveying the area from no less than ten feet away. It was one of the rare breaks she was able to enjoy without anyone wanting something from her. *Study, write papers, make dinner, read these five hundred high priestess books, practice your energy protection, you can't miss another one of Merlin's lessons, help package a painting for shipment* were only some of the reasons her time was no longer her own.

Ugh! That reminds me, I so need to call Sarah. I wonder how my little niece is doing? Lilly is so much fun now that she's almost two years old and talking! I wonder if the doll I sent is still Lilly's favorite toy? Maybe I can call Sarah later tonight? Jennifer quickly subdued the pang of desire to have a little girl of her own. *It's not like you didn't know you wouldn't have a child with your spirit husband!* Jennifer quickly chastised her thoughts before Josh picked up on them.

"Jennifer, you're so lucky! I'd be in my glory working so closely with so many struggling artists. Especially the bohemian-looking male ones," Mary exaggerated while fanning herself, pretending to swoon. "Have you met anyone famous yet? You know, like Michelangelo or Picasso?"

"What are you talking about, Mary?" Colleen jumped in, looking up from her study notes long enough to stare at Mary as if she'd completely lost her marbles.

"I said, *like* one of them!" Mary admonished before turning her attention back to the matter at hand—Jennifer's dating life. "Surely there must be a few men wandering about the gallery who've caught your eye. For once, tell us something more interesting than the latest painting you loved or that same bronze statue of Hercules you keep talking about! Geez, I bet if the real Hercules walked into the gallery, you wouldn't even notice him!"

When you're married to a spirit who looks like a Greek god, why look at anyone else? Jennifer answered silently.

"Mary, what do you mean, you'd be in your glory working with so many men? Didn't Fred just propose, and you said yes?" Elizabeth interrogated.

"Why yes, he did," Mary cooed, holding up her left hand to admire her engagement ring. "I didn't say I wanted to date one of them; I just like being around men." She pouted her glossy watermelon-tinted lips.

"Have you set a wedding date?" Jennifer interjected. *Come on Mary, take the bait.*

"I was going to wait to tell you all until the save the date announcements arrived. Wait until you see them—I think there's a picture in this bridal magazine." Mary reached into her canvas tote, pulled out a magazine and began flipping through it, evoking a conspiratorial wink from Elizabeth.

Josh scowled at the memory of how the latest artist at the gallery kept glancing in Jennifer's direction. Worst of all, the jerk had requested her to oversee his opening night reception. *If that ass thinks he's getting anywhere near my wife next Saturday night, he's in for a rude awakening!*

A glimmer of self-doubt crept into Josh's soul. *What the fuck?! This can't be him? It's too soon, right?* The thought of another man stepping in to marry his wife tugged at his emotions. *There's no way I can let Jennifer go. There must be some way of changing her destiny?* The thought did nothing to appease his mind or offer the slightest glimmer of hope. Jennifer's life-path was set in stone, and their marriage agreement included giving her up in eight years' time. Three years had already passed, and the thought that it could be anyone punched him in the gut.

~Josh, are you alright? You look like you're about to vomit!~ Jennifer messaged to her scowling husband who'd moved and was now leaning against the wall with his arms crossed and his foot propped up.

~Nothing—just thinking about that so-called artist you'll be babysitting next Saturday. How someone could think a single red or blue square in the middle of a blank canvas is art is beyond my comprehension! How does he get away with charging people thousands of dollars to take if off his hands?~

~Please tell me you're not jealous of Dalton? Do you think just because he's a successful artist, I'm going to go flying into his arms? Dalton must be at least thirty-six years old, or older!~ Jennifer wrinkled her nose.

~Are you ready to get out of here?~ *I wonder what Jennifer would think if she found out how old I really am? As in ancient—many times over!*
~I promised Merlin I'd deliver you for your lesson on time. He wasn't

pleased with how late we arrived last time or about the four lessons you cancelled.~

~If you remember correctly, one of those cancelled lessons was your fault!~ When her retort deepened his visible annoyance, Jennifer pushed back her chair and stood up.

"Yikes, I just noticed the time! See you all Monday; I've gotta run," Jennifer blurted, grabbing her books and hurrying out the door with her invisible husband in tow.

~We'd better hurry and get you home so you can change first. If you hadn't begged off so many of your previous lessons, we could have enjoyed our afternoon alone,~ Josh messaged with a frown as they got into Jennifer's car.

~I get it! Please stop reminding me how many lessons I've missed or how I'm letting everyone down if I don't study every moment of the day. For once I'd love to have a conversation that didn't ultimately make me feel guilty for not being perfect.~

Josh sighed. ~I'm sorry, baby. How about after your lesson with Merlin, we stop by our honeymoon house? With any luck we'll be able to have a peaceful night to ourselves before you need to return home to earth.~

~On one condition.~ Jennifer pulled to a stop at the red light and glanced at her husband. ~If we can have one night of you not bringing up anything to do with high priestess lessons, boring books, responsibilities or anything else to do with my afterlife destiny! All I want to do is curl up with you and feel loved for who I am—no matter how badly I might stumble through this lifetime.~

~For the record, I do love you for who you are, every single moment of each day. I'm sorry if there have been times I haven't been as understanding as I should have been. How about tonight and all next week, I promise to give you a vacation away from all your mandatory priestess studies? That is, as long as you let me show you how much I love you every chance I get.~

~I'm holding you to your promise, Mr. Smith!~ Jennifer glanced at her translucent husband and flushed before pressing the gas pedal. ~Especially if your plan includes a lot of sexy interludes!~

~Absolutely, baby!~

CHAPTER FOURTEEN

*H*ours later, Jennifer was seated across from Merlin, trying to choose what lesson she wished to learn. Merlin had already taught some basic potions and herb remedies. And between him and Josh, Jennifer had more uses for gemstones than she cared to know.

"Here's something you're sure to love, lass!" Merlin jumped up from his chair to fetch a tome from the stack of books balanced on what looked to be a tiny, wobbly table that was ready to collapse from the excess weight.

"If it's more potions, forget it!" Jennifer groaned.

"Nope, you made it quite clear how you felt about those during your last lesson. You should be thankful I didn't tell your protector how badly you behaved. Rest assured, if you insist on balking, I'll see to it Josh takes care of your attitude!"

"You wouldn't dare!" Jennifer retorted, unable to disguise the way her voice trembled when saying the words.

"I'll be happy to summon Josh this minute and watch to make sure he properly punishes you. A couple of energy shots or perhaps something a little more old-fashioned would curtail your behavior." Merlin pointed his unwavering gaze directly at Jennifer's throat chakra, a method often used to encourage a student not to talk back.

"Please don't call him." Jennifer blanched.

"Given you're my granddaughter, I fear I've been too lenient with you."

"I promise if you select something other than potions, I won't give you a hard time." Jennifer sighed in defeat.

"There is a lesson I was saving, but it might be something we can both enjoy working on. I haven't taught it to anyone else, not even Josh, so maybe you and I can reach a truce."

"What kind of a truce?"

"You need to agree to show up for each lesson, willing and ready to learn the moment you arrive in my realm."

"You said you never taught this lesson to Josh?" Jennifer leaned forward, ready to hear more.

"That's right! Best of all, he'll have no clue how to prevent you from using your newfound gift."

"I don't suppose you'll tell me what this unusual gift is before I agree to your terms?"

"Nope! But I *will* tell you it'll be far better than the alternative—Josh showing up madder than hell," Merlin taunted with a boisterous laugh.

"Come to think of it, this supposed unauthorized lesson is sounding more intriguing by the moment."

"Good choice, lass!" Merlin cheered and quickly retrieved a pocket-size leather bound book from its secret location. "Here it is, my pride and joy. Otherwise known as my 'little black book.'" Merlin guffawed at his own humor.

"If you say so."

"Please tell me you didn't just roll your eyes at me."

"What is this secret lesson?" Jennifer quickly leaned forward, eager to learn.

After fanning through the book, Merlin laid it out flat on the table in front of them. "Once you learn this forbidden spell, you'll be able to transform any animal's appearance or species to another," Merlin said in hushed tones.

"Really?!" Her eyes opened wide. "You mean I'd be able to change Talos into, say, a bird or dog, or some other animal?"

"That's exactly what I'm saying, lass."

"That's pretty cool. Josh has told me stories of how you used to transform yourself into different images and animals!"

"Flipped him out, I did—and often! I'd do the same to the other protectors I was teaching, but they weren't as entertaining to mess with as Mr. Cool, as I used to call Josh. His eyes would almost bug out of his skull, and he'd break out into a sweat." Merlin let loose a belly laugh. "It was great while it lasted—until Josh caught on to my ulterior motives and was no longer fazed by anything I turned into."

"Will you teach me how to transform myself too?

"Aye, but you are a wee bit of a troublemaker, little hellcat. A chip off the old block, I'd say." Merlin winked. "Maybe someday, when your gifts have matured, and you've proven you're able to harness your power, I will teach you the magic that only I, myself am privy to—no one else!"

"Now you're talking! Although, I'm not sure what purpose transforming animals into other creatures would serve, other than playing a couple of jokes on Josh."

"Aye, but you're failing to think like a high priestess. Imagine if you and Talos were surrounded by a group of rebels, or even a rogue spirit, who were after your soul. Since Talos is nothing but a small cat on earth, you'd be able to transform him into something deadly that would help you fight."

"But I already have a protector in Josh."

"In your position, it's always best to know how to defend yourself or have a backup plan in place. Sure, Josh is always around, but suppose you're attacked, and Josh comes to your rescue, but more attackers show up before Josh is available to help you? Jennifer, you should always be aware of possible danger and have the ability to defend yourself. Not that we have the level of turmoil like when my daughter—your soul's mom, Olivia—was murdered, but as the leader of every soul in existence, you must always be prepared in case you run into trouble when Josh isn't able to swoop in to save you."

Jennifer's shoulders sagged. "Oh," she said in a dull voice.

"No need to fret, lass. We'd better get started before we run out of time." Merlin reached inside the pocket of his azure-colored wizard robe and pulled out a long, thin wooden box. "I was saving this for your birthday, but I think this spell calls for a little extra something. Go ahead, open the box."

Jennifer placed the box on the table and flipped open both latches before lifting the lid. "Oh my goodness, it's a wand! Looks similar to the one you have." Her eyes lit with excitement as she gingerly lifted the matching thin, lightweight English oak wand.

"Carved from the same branch as mine, that one is. I had it made special for your mom, but I never got the chance to give it to her. If I had, she might still be with us."

Jennifer leaped up and wrapped her arms around the older wizard. "I know I can never be Olivia, but I promise to do my best to make you proud. Please don't worry; I'm a lot stronger than I look, and with Josh by my side, and you and Gisabella around, I'm not going anywhere. Especially once you teach me how to use this thing." Jennifer waved the wand through the air, causing several books and a vase to crash to the floor.

"Uh oh!" Jennifer clamped her hand over her mouth as she looked toward the mess she'd created with an unusually large amount of the whites of her eyes visible.

Merlin roared with laughter. "Well, well—it looks like this wand was meant to be yours! Just try not to wave it around until you learn how to properly harness its power."

"I'll keep that in mind." She slowly placed the wand back in its original resting place in the box.

"I think it'd be best for now if you practice on a stuffed animal until you get the feel of your wand," Merlin said while fetching four stuffed bears from a wooden chest next to the fireplace.

"Sure you trust me with those?"

"You shouldn't have too much of an issue with these. Either way, I have a fire extinguisher, you know—in case you cause them to explode!" Merlin roared.

"Ha ha!" Jennifer sassed back.

An hour and three incinerated teddy bears later, Jennifer slumped in the chair. "It's no use. No matter how many innocent stuffed animals I kill, I'm never going to get the hang of it." She eyed the remaining innocent stuffed bear. "You better save yourself now!" Jennifer warned it.

"Maybe I should show you again. You may pick up on something I do that I failed to mention." When Jennifer nodded, Merlin set the toy on a wooden stool and stood back four feet. Once he was sure his student's attention was fixed on him, he raised his wand and voiced the normally silent commands out loud for her benefit while swirling the tip of the wand in a small clockwise motion. He continued the rotations until the stuffed animal levitated a couple of inches before it transformed from a bear into a horse.

"I think I know what I was doing wrong!"

"What don't you try changing it back into a bear?"

Jennifer stood up and took Merlin's place. After she took a deep breath, she repeated the steps like she'd done earlier; only this time, she used very tiny circles with her wand. Within a couple of moments, a bear was sitting on the stool where the horse once was.

"I did it! Look, he's not even singed!" she called out, doing a happy dance around the room.

Over the course of the following month, Jennifer returned weekly to Merlin's domain, where she learned how to transform living creatures such as insects, mice, and even a bird into various living things. Each practice transformation, Jennifer selected a wide variety of bugs, frogs, or other small animals before changing each back to their original state. Once Merlin explained that none of the animals experienced any pain or suffered when being transformed, Jennifer began to relax.

When it was time for her next lesson, Josh transported her and Talos to Merlin's realm.

"Baby, I don't know what Merlin did to inspire you to learn, but it's sure nice not having the same quarrel about why you need to study this stuff!" Josh accompanied his words with a wide smile while he casually leaned against the wizard's house with his arms folded.

"Oh no you don't, I've been fooled way too many times by your laid-back stance and your disarming smile. Nope—not going to happen! I know you too well not to realize underneath your Mr. Cool persona, you're getting ready to pounce!" Jennifer quickly pulled back the knocker on the wizard's door and rapped three times before Josh could react to her words.

"I don't suppose you'd like to tell me what you're working on with Merlin?"

"Not particularly," she responded flatly. *Hurry up, Merlin!* Her thoughts were answered when the door swung open. "Okay then, honey, I'll see you in a few hours."

But before she was able to disappear through the door, Josh grabbed hold of her sleeve.

"What—no kiss goodbye?" He loomed closer with a salacious grin, only to be met with Jennifer's heavenward gaze. Ignoring it, Josh clasped her face and lowered his mouth to hers for a slow, lengthy kiss before he released her and transported out of there with a wave goodbye.

~Don't think I won't be paying you back for ruining my concentration!~ Jennifer messaged before turning to greet Merlin.

Once she and Talos were guided into the cabin and given a hot, soothing beverage, Merlin began what he referred to as her advanced transformation lesson.

"I think it's time for your final exam!" Merlin declared.

"Final?" Jennifer gulped.

"That's right, lass. It's time for you to transform an animal you care for greatly. It's the only way you'll move forward enough to be able to use this spell under pressure. Best you practice now while I'm close at hand in case something goes wrong." Merlin readied his wand.

Jennifer glanced at Talos. "You don't expect me to transform *him, do you?*" She pointed her eyes at the panther slinking in the direction of the door.

"Get back here, you mangy scaredy-cat!" Merlin commanded.

~Oh no—don't look at me!~ Talos shook his head back and forth.

"Nonsense—get a grip, cat! I'll be here the entire time, and Jennifer is more than ready—honest!"

~She better not blow me up!~ Talos glowered at Merlin before padding back to the center of the room where he sat down facing Jennifer.

"Go ahead, Jennifer," Merlin reassured.

What?! Jennifer slammed her eyes shut momentarily, but found Talos and Merlin waiting expectantly when she reopened them. "I don't suppose you have any preferences, Talos?"

~Something alive would be nice!~ Talos curled his lip, exposing just enough of his fangs to let Jennifer know he was being serious.

Great! Everyone's a critic! I can't help it if I haven't always been the best trainee. Maybe they should look for another high priestess if they think I'm so horrible at this stuff! Jennifer picked up her wand while selecting the first thing that came to mind before she waved it at her wide-eyed panther.

"Umm, what is Talos supposed to be?" Merlin chuckled at the half-dog, half-horse standing in the middle of the room where the panther once sat.

"Oh!" Jennifer exclaimed when she saw what she'd done. Hooves, dog face, curly pink hair with blue polka dots and bright yellow long whiskers similar to a walrus's looked back at her with a foul expression. "Oh dear! I guess I couldn't make up my mind what you should become. Maybe next time you'll do a better job helping other than just saying 'alive!'"

"No harm done, Jennifer. Now concentrate on turning Talos back into his normal self."

Jennifer did as she was told, and soon, Talos was his normal-looking, majestic self.

"Great job, lass! Congratulations—you've officially graduated and are allowed to use this spell whenever you'd like. That is, of course, if no one sees you using it! Whatever you do, never tell Gisabella I taught it to you; for that matter, you better not tell Josh either, unless he catches you using it!"

"So I can actually use this one! Nice to finally have permission to use something I've learned besides the approved visionary stuff like gemstones and my crystal globe, in addition to the endless protection methods you all insist I do every day."

~Not on me, you're not!~ Talos messaged with a snarl.

They were interrupted by a knock on the door, and Josh strolled in earlier than expected to find them all laughing at his failed attempt to figure out what Jennifer had learned.

CHAPTER FIFTEEN

It was an especially hot Saturday in June, making the ride into the city seem longer than normal as she and Josh messaged each other amongst the weekend travelers.

~I can't wait to see who the next new artist is! All I know so far is he's supposedly known for using several different methods and multiple kinds of media to achieve uniqueness. Apparently, the larger pieces in his collection are touted to be worth millions! I heard he has a huge following, so the gallery is sure to be busier than usual. The only thing I don't know about him is his name! I can think of several artists it could be, but I don't want to jinx it by guessing,~ Jennifer blurted without taking a breath.

~Oh, he's a piece of work alright.~ Josh didn't bother to hide his sarcasm.

~Not again! Honestly, Josh, you don't like any of the artists in the gallery.~

~That's where you're wrong—I like you—and you're an artist in the gallery.~ When his remark made Jennifer snicker, his smile brightened.

The moment the train pulled to a stop, she exited as if she'd been doing so all her life. Even Josh was more at ease now that they'd come up with a routine that worked well for them both. Each week, they took two trips to their honeymoon house, Monday and Thursday nights, leaving Friday night free in case Jennifer had to work or wanted to do something with her friends, and she worked every Saturday and Sunday at the gallery.

Jennifer all but skipped alongside Josh, excited at the prospect of seeing the rumored famous artist's collection.

-Do I look okay?- she asked nervously before opening the door.

-You look beautiful.-

-Thanks, see you at lunchtime, which looks to be in a half hour.- Jennifer rolled her eyes at the absurdity of being scheduled so close to lunch.

-I'm looking forward to it.- He blew an exaggerated kiss her way before she disappeared inside, then he continued watching over her from above.

Once inside, she found Oscar rushing about, waving his arms and giving directions to the staff where each painting was to go. Hanging a new collection always seemed like utter chaos with staff members dashing about unwrapping crates and paintings while a few were on ladders positioning prized pieces. Under Oscar's guidance, everything always came together in time for the unveiling.

"I'd like that one over there, next to the window," the new artist instructed while pointing.

It was the artist's French accent that caught Jennifer's attention first, but when he turned his eyes and their gazes met, her heartbeat quickened. His hair was much lighter than Josh's, without one hint of a wave or curl. The artist's face was free of stubble, and even from a distance it appeared to be baby soft, giving him almost an angelic appearance. Dressed in a short-sleeved navy denim shirt, it was easy to see how muscular his arms were. *He must lift a lot of paintings!* Then she noticed his white jeans. *Who in the world would wear white while setting up a display? Say goodbye to those clean pants!* Jennifer tried to stifle her sudden need to giggle and was about to fail when he called out to her.

"Hey there, miss. Yes, I mean you with the lovely dark hair. I don't suppose you could find me some tags? I seemed to have forgotten mine."

Jennifer nodded and went to fetch some. When she returned, everything was quiet. *Where is everyone?* A glance at her watch verified it was lunchtime and the gallery was now closed for one hour. With a frustrated breath, she headed over to the only person left standing in the expansive room.

"I wasn't sure how many you needed, so I brought the whole box," Jennifer said demurely, holding out the blank tags.

"I'm the one who should be asking for your forgiveness for delaying your lunch. I don't believe we've been properly introduced. Please allow me to rectify the situation. I'm Alexander B. Cavadoir." He offered his outstretched hand.

Jennifer's eyes widened as recognition hit. "Oh—I've heard of your work. I mean, our class studied your pieces," she said, unable to hide her excitement.

"Don't you mean dissected them?" Alexander chuckled. "Don't look so horrified—it was a joke, though rather a bad one."

"You weren't very far off. As a matter of fact, we *did* take each one of your famed pieces apart and put them back together again—for over a month. My name's Jennifer Parker." She took hold of the hand Alexander offered, causing an immediate rush of adrenaline, then she snatched it away in horror. To his credit, Alexander pretended like nothing was unusual about the way she reacted.

"I don't get to the city very often, and I'm afraid I don't know my way around town. Since everyone seems to have left without us, I don't suppose you'd consider joining me for a bite to eat? I'm not a fan of dining alone, and I'll try not to talk your ear off, but I can't promise I won't bore you to death. While we're eating, you can fill me in on how badly my paintings faired in your class," Alexander offered with a disarming smile.

"Why not? I have no other plans for lunch," Jennifer replied in a daze.

What's my wife talking about? We always eat lunch together, and even though I sit beside her unseen, we talk the entire time! Josh's stomach clenched when he watched Alexander place a hand on Jennifer's arm to guide her out of the building. *He better not try anything funny!*

Josh drifted above until they'd entered a restaurant, then made himself invisible even to Jennifer. He stood off to the side, close enough to prevent anything from happening to his wife.

At first Alexander made small talk about silly things like the weather, but by the end of their meal, he'd upped his game, increasing the furrow in Josh's forehead.

"Why did you decide to incorporate manmade things like wire, Styrofoam and, for lack of a better word, trash in your masterpieces?" Jennifer focused her complete attention on Alexander as if her life depended on his answer. Or at least that was how Josh saw it. *She used to look at me that way. True, we've had our ups and downs, but that's what marriage is all about, isn't it? Maybe I haven't always been as understanding as I should, but damn it—Jennifer knows I have a job to do, even if it means keeping her in line.*

"Several years ago my work hit a dead end. I was bored of painting landscapes and the kinds of paintings people expected of me. I tried a few nudes, but I tired of that quickly." Alexander paused to take another bite of his steak while keeping his eyes focused on Jennifer's pinkened cheeks. "Painting the female body wasn't nearly as simulating or beautiful as admiring a woman's curves while making love."

What the fuck was that about? Josh shouted in his head. *Try that again, mister, and you can say goodbye to your career and my wife!*

When Jennifer's cheeks glowed pink, Josh's heart sank. *Who am I kidding? Jennifer's acting like I'm not even here.* Realization slammed his heart. *This must be him!* But *her life-path husband isn't due for another five years!*

Josh paled. *Damn it, Gisabella!* He groaned at the realization his boss had only indicated Jennifer would marry her life-path husband in eight years' time. *How convenient of Gisabella to omit how soon Jennifer and Alexander would meet!*

Jennifer took another sip of wine and sighed. "That all sounds so interesting. I envy you for being able to travel the world painting." She folded her napkin and pushed back her chair. "I really must get back to work. Thank you for lunch."

"If you give me a moment, I'll walk back with you. I hate to see a pretty girl like you walking alone in the big city," Alexander said with a mollifying smile. After he paid the bill, he stood to pull out Jennifer's chair.

"Why, Alexander, you're like old-fashioned gentleman." Jennifer brushed a stray hair from her face.

"Not really—I just want to spend more time with you."

What do I say to that? she mused, too flustered to think straight.

Josh perked up when he read Jennifer's thoughts. ~Tell Alexander you're seeing someone, and it's serious.~

Once she repeated Josh's words, the artist looked so crestfallen, she had to stifle a snicker.

"Doesn't your man worry about you wandering around the city all by your lonesome? I know if you were my girl, I wouldn't be able to relax until I knew you were home safely."

"I think worry is a bit of an understatement," Jennifer replied with a smirk as they exited the restaurant. "Sometimes, I could swear he's hired a bodyguard to watch over me. My poor, sweet man will worry himself into the grave if he's not careful."

~I'm glad you think your lunch date with another man is so funny!~ Josh scorned.

"Now I know you're making fun of me." Alexander's smile widened. "But he does worry about you—*right?*"

"Yes."

"Well then, I have an idea that will work out well for both of us, especially since you're such an innocent." Alexander took hold of Jennifer's hand as they approached a busy intersection.

"An innocent?" She wrinkled her nose at his choice of words.

"Jennifer, you're very sweet, if not a little naive. I find it very endearing, which is probably why I'm so attracted to you," Alexander admitted half to himself.

"You only think you are because I'm not available."

"Trust me, I know the difference between real attraction and possession, and this is real. So much so, that if there comes a time your boyfriend is no longer in the picture, I'll be the first in line to ask you to marry."

Marry? He must be insane! Jennifer thought, trying to wiggle her hand free.

He wants to marry my wife already? This can't be happening! I agree with Jennifer. Alexander must be crazy with a capital K!

"Please, *cherie*, don't let my declaration scare you off." Alexander released her hand and stuffed it into the pocket of his jeans. "Consider this: I'm in the process of moving here for my work, and since you work at the gallery, we'll be seeing a lot of each other. So, what harm would it do if I take you out to lunch, and on nights you and I work late, maybe we could have dinner? As far as gallery openings, if it's okay with your boyfriend, I'd appreciate it if you'd pretend to be my escort. It would keep the wolves that are sure to be lurking around you at bay."

"But I don't even know you. How do I know you're not a wolf who's pretending to be a sheep?"

"I promise to be a perfect gentleman the entire time we're together. Plus, I can help your boyfriend out by offering you my protection. Don't give me that look—I mean strictly as a friend with no fringe benefits. Unless, of course, there comes a time you decide you want more from me." Alexander played off the last sentence as if his suggestion was purely innocent.

~Jennifer, ask him to clarify what he means by *his* protection. His thoughts are all over the place, making it hard to decipher what he's implying.~ Josh begrudgingly sent off the message that would either help him protect Jennifer or send her flying into the other man's arms. If Alexander was his wife's destiny, there was no escape for either of them, and if he tried to change it, Josh could lose her forever and risk damaging Jennifer's soul in the process.

"For starters, I'd feel terrible if I didn't escort you to and from the train station, or at the very least, have my driver give you a lift. As a matter of convenience, I can arrange to have my driver at your disposal, that way you can come and go as you please without me. It really can be a dangerous area, especially if you're walking alone. I shudder to think what could happen to you, Jennifer."

"What do you get out of this deal?" She narrowed her eyes at the handsome artist.

"Honestly—I'll be able to concentrate on my work without a bunch of bimbos hounding me. I can't tell you how many people come out of the woodwork the moment your name appears in the media, or worse— the tabloids! Spending time with a pretty girl, with whom I share a love of art, and who doesn't seem to have any problem calling me out on the carpet, would be a refreshing change," Alexander said, capturing Jennifer's hand once again.

Will he promise not to try and make you fall in love with him? Josh held back from asking that question in lieu of another. ~Does he promise not to kiss you?~

~Are you out of your gourd? Get this through your head, Josh—the last thing I want is another man's lips on mine! I can't believe you're actually considering his offer! Have you lost your senses?~

~Just ask him, Jennifer.~

~Fine!~ she messaged her retort before addressing Alexander. "I'm not sure why I'm considering your suggestion. Before I agree to be friends with you, I want to make sure you won't attempt to kiss me or try to steal my heart away from my significant other."

"I promise I won't make any advances, nor will I try to kiss you, but you can't hold me responsible for secretly hoping my charms will win you over."

"I wouldn't hope too much." *I'm too deeply in love with my husband to fall for anyone else—even you, Mr. Alexander B. Cavadoir.*

"Maybe I can hold on to a trace of hope. What do you say, Miss Parker—friends with no benefits, then?"

~As much as I hate to say this, Alexander's right, he can keep the wolves at bay and do wonders for advancing your career.~ Josh's heart ached as he messaged the words that would lose his wife earlier than he'd expected. *All I can do now is hope Alexander has a weak heart and dies young, ending my wife's commitment as soon as possible. Once that happens, she'll be forever mine!*

"Sure, why not?" Jennifer shrugged. If Alexander noticed her lack of enthusiasm, he gave no indication.

"Then it's settled—we're officially platonic friends!" Alexander declared with a broad smile and a brief kiss on Jennifer's cheek, totally oblivious to the death stare he was receiving from her spirit husband.

"Since Oscar's pretty protective of his staff, you can be the one to explain *us* to him."

"Consider it done, honey."

~*What the fuck?!* Tell your *friend*—no pet names are allowed!~ Josh shouted.

~Why don't you tell him yourself, Mr. Smith? After all, *you're* the one who suggested I accept his offer!~

Why does doing the right thing always suck? Josh thought as he followed Jennifer and Alexander into the gallery. *I need to find out if this smooth talker is definitely Jennifer's destiny. If not, I'll kick his artist ass to the curb!*

CHAPTER SIXTEEN

Once Alexander's attention was finally focused back on his work and not on Jennifer, Josh concentrated on the best way to approach Gisabella. The minute he was satisfied his idea would work, he put his plan into action.

~Gisabella, your granddaughter and I will be arriving tonight and would like to meet with you.~ *So what if I lied a little?* He didn't have to wait long to receive a panicked message back.

~Is everything okay?~

Gotcha! ~Kind of—I'll explain when we see you tonight.~ He kept his message vague.

~Okay.~

Maybe I need to give Gisabella something to keep her busy until our meeting. ~I don't suppose you can go to the bakery and pick up some cookies or a cake for Jennifer and me?~ Josh counted down as he waited for her response, ten, nine, eight, seven...*bingo!*

~Better yet—I have a new recipe I've been dying to try.~

She can never miss an opportunity to make me ill! ~Thanks, we'll see you later.~ With his boss busy baking and the first part of his plan in place, he spent the remainder of Jennifer's workday observing Alexander eyeing his wife. *Enjoy it now, dirtbag, because after I meet with Gisabella, you'll be out the door!* Josh's thoughts did little to soothe his mood, knowing it'd be a hard sell.

The closer it came to the end of Jennifer's schedule, the more doubtful he grew. And Josh had seen enough smiles between his wife and Alexander to haunt him for a lifetime, even his everlasting one.

"Good night, Alexander," Jennifer called up.

"Sorry I can't take you to the train station myself! I'm gonna be a few more hours, but my driver's out front waiting," Alexander said from his perch on top of the ladder.

"You needn't have bothered. I'll be fine."

"Jennifer, it's no trouble. As a matter of fact, if you refuse my driver's escort, I'll be forced to walk you there myself," Alexander relayed with a smile so wide, it crinkled the corners of his eyes. "Honey, it looks like we're expecting a storm. Please accept my offer."

"Alright already, stop with the pleading; I accept your offer," Jennifer cried out, laughing.

"Thank you, I feel so much better now." Alexander pulled out a level and pencil from his tool belt. "Are you working tomorrow?"

"I'll be here early—ten a.m."

"My driver will be at the station waiting for you." Alexander frowned when he saw Jennifer's look of dismay. "It's supposed to rain all day tomorrow, and I wouldn't want you to catch a cold."

"I gotta go. Thanks again for lunch." She gave a quick wave goodbye before she scurried out into the night just in time to see a jagged flash streak across the sky, followed by a loud boom. *Yikes! Alexander was right!* Seeking cover, she ran to the waiting limo.

"Good evening, Miss," Alexander's driver greeted with an open door and a smile. Once he'd taken his place behind the wheel, he turned around to address Jennifer sitting in the back seat. "There are some beverages in the fridge; please help yourself. My name is Claude, and here's my card with a number where you can reach me. Mr. Cavadoir left instructions that you're to be driven to and from the gallery and anywhere else you'd like."

"Thank you, Claude. Please call me Jennifer. I usually like to walk, but tonight I'm very thankful for the ride." She sighed, leaned back in the plush leather seat and closed her eyes, knowing Josh was probably following the limo from above. *I'll have to face him sooner or later! How will I explain so easily breaking our lunch date? Better yet, how will he justify accepting Alexander's deal?*

When the limo pulled up to the train station, Claude jumped out and opened her door, holding an umbrella to shield her from the deluge of rain. "Thank you, Claude."

"My pleasure, Jennifer. I'll be waiting in this area tomorrow morning at 9:45. Until then, have a safe trip home." Claude tipped his hat and offered his umbrella, but she declined.

The moment she walked through the sliding doors, her husband appeared in his usual translucent state, only tonight Josh was holding a dozen red roses accompanied by a worried expression.

~I come bearing roses,~ Josh messaged uncomfortably. *She doesn't look as pleased to see me as I'd hoped.*

~Thank you.~ Jennifer kept her expression blank while she weaved her way through the bustling station. ~I was planning on apologizing for breaking our standing lunch date before I began demanding answers about accepting Alexander's stupid deal.~ She bit back the threatening emotions that begged to be unleashed.

When he didn't say anything, her mood plummeted further. *What's going on with him?* ~Why aren't you saying anything?!~

~I already told you I thought his offer would benefit your career. Plus, he seems like a nice guy, and I welcome another pair of eyes to help keep you safe.~ Josh feigned nonchalance, adding, ~I have a few things I'd like to run by Gisabella, so we'll be visiting our honeymoon house tonight.~

~Like what?~

~Just some new protocol rules she's put in place.~ He snaked his arm around Jennifer's waist and slipped his energized hand into the back pocket of her jeans. ~What do you say, baby? Want to spend a few days together in heaven?~ He accompanied his question with a gentle squeeze of her butt that brought color to her cheeks.

At the stroke of midnight when her parents were fast asleep, Jennifer closed her eyes and welcomed Josh's kiss as he transported them and Talos to their honeymoon house.

"Mmm, more kisses," she sighed, pulling Josh's solid mouth back on hers.

"I love kissing you, baby," Josh agreed. "Before we get carried away, I need to speak to Gisabella. Do you think you can find something to do for an hour?"

"Don't worry about me; I could use some time to myself. Tell my grandma I said hello."

"I'll see you later, baby." He planted another kiss on her lips before he headed out the door. A few minutes later, he was staring at Gisabella's front door, waiting for it to open.

"Come in," Gisabella welcomed, motioning Josh inside. "Where's Jennifer? I thought she wanted to meet with me, too?" she questioned before she realized Josh may have set her up. "My granddaughter *is here* with you?"

"Of course she's here!" He hoped she wouldn't call him out on his ruse. "I needed to speak to you about something that's come up."

"As you're the only one here, I need you to taste something." She ignored Josh's grimace and led the way toward the kitchen.

Upon entering, Josh waved his hands back and forth in an attempt to clear the smoke-filled room. "What the hell were you trying to do—burn the house down?"

"What are you talking about? Relax, it's just a little smoke." Gisabella placed seven unidentifiable blackened lumps on a plate. "I did as you asked and baked! You must try these—I swear they taste amazing!"

Josh stared down at the plate. *I'll be amazed if they're edible!* Ignoring Gisabella's expectant gaze and the lumps of coal she called cookies, he cut to the chase. "When did you plan on telling me my wife's earthly husband would arrive far earlier than agreed upon?"

"They're mincemeat cookies with chocolate chips and…" Gisabella attempted to dodge the question.

"I don't give a crap what's in those things! As Jennifer's protector, I should've been notified well in advance of Alexander's arrival!" he shouted, playing the only kind of cards Gisabella understood. "Well?!"

He took satisfaction in the way his command caused his boss to jump. *That's rare!*

But she regained her composure as quickly as she'd lost it. "If you were only Jennifer's protector, things would've been handled differently. However, since you took it upon yourself to marry my granddaughter, that information needed to be withheld until after Alexander arrived."

"So it is *him*! I knew it!" He shoved the plate, scattering the cookies across the table. "How long?!"

"I'm not sure."

"What the fuck does that mean? This must have been your plan all along. Of course you knew how long it would be before my wife weds another man. Cut the bullshit, Gisabella! How long do we have left?!"

"Try to understand, after Jennifer came so close to dying, Merlin and I grew concerned you'd interfere with her life-path destiny."

"You and *Merlin* were concerned? So what? You took it upon yourselves to speed up Jennifer's marriage to another man and thought it best to keep me in the dark?" His eyes narrowed as he poured all the contempt he could into his gaze. "That makes no sense. Where's my wife's fabricated life-path? As her protector I demand you hand it over this minute!" His fist landed on the table, causing the cookies to jump.

"Merlin's the only one who has access to her information." Gisabella retorted. "Before you think of running off to demand answers from Merlin, don't bother; he won't tell you anything."

"Of all the lowest tricks you could've pulled, this takes the fucking cake!" He lowered his energy, knowing if he lost control of his emotions, there was no telling what he'd be capable of doing. "What about our forever marriage? It can't be changed—*right*?" He searched Gisabella's icy glare for some sort of sign.

"Rest assured, Merlin and I want you to remain Jennifer's eternal husband. That will never change." She picked up the cookies one at a time and returned them to the plate.

"What possessed you to match my wife up with some famous guy? It only increases her public exposure, never mind attracting every crooked person within a five-mile radius!" Josh knew his case was weak at best, especially since he hadn't read Jennifer's life-path file years ago when he had the chance. But now that Jennifer's destiny had been altered, he had to do something before he lost her sooner than expected. *I bet anything the earlier date has already been imprinted on her very soul, along with Alexander's name.* He didn't let the hopelessness of the situation stop him from laying his cards on the table.

"If he presents such a high risk to my granddaughter, then it's a good thing I assigned you to protect her."

"Is that why you picked such a dirtbag who has swarms of bimbos hanging all over him? How could you do that to a granddaughter you claim to love so much?" Josh played the guilt card, but his boss didn't look amused.

"At the time, I found Alexander to be the best choice for the lessons Jennifer needed to learn during this lifetime. As you know, her destiny has been engraved in her soul since birth, so nothing you say or do will change the outcome. Maybe I need to repeat myself so a man of your ancient years can understand: Jennifer will be returned to you upon the end of her lifetime," she spoke the words loudly. "Look, the best thing you could do for your wife and the rest of us is to start backing away so Jennifer lives the life she was destined to complete. Then, once her life and destiny are finished, she'll be free of all her earthly obligations."

"You want me to start backing away from Jennifer *now?*" Josh fell back in his chair and raked his fingers through his hair.

"Not this very moment, but soon. Remember, the closer Jennifer becomes to Alexander, the greater your risk of scarring her soul if you try and pull her back toward you." Gisabella hardened her expression to let Josh know she meant business.

"Suppose after all this, Jennifer changes her mind about wanting to be with me at the end of her life? I can't imagine spending eternity without her." He picked up a cookie and studied it until his emotions were under control. "You didn't see how easily she fell in line with Alexander, all googly-eyed, accepting his lunch date without giving me a second thought."

"If you're asking for suggestions, all I can tell you is to use the time you have remaining to make every moment so special, it'll withstand the test of time."

"I can do that. My wife loves to go horseback riding and jogging. Maybe if I learn to enjoy running, it'll mean a lot to her."

"Those are both good examples of what you *should* already be doing with your wife." Gisabella sighed. With her cheeks coloring, she elaborated, "Women want to be cherished and loved in a way that's creative. You and Jennifer have a wonderful relationship, and by the looks of the way you two act, there's not much lacking in the—um—bedroom area."

"You mean I should sex my wife more? If I do that, I may kill the girl!"

"Heavens, don't do that!" Gisabella exclaimed. "I don't mean more times, I mean more special. You know, something unique." Gisabella squirmed uncomfortably. *Why is this so difficult? We've been friends for centuries; surely I can say this in a way that will sink into his thick skull.* "I'm talking more along the line of playfulness. You know, maybe once a week, do something out of the ordinary. I can recommend a few books on the subject. I don't suppose you've read the *Kama Sutra*? If not, that'd be a good place to start."

"You want me to read a book about sex? I think that's the one area in which I excel." Josh folded his arms.

"You may excel at sex, but do you excel at the art of seduction or erotica, or playful bondage? Trust me, most men could learn a few things in that department. If you want Jennifer to remember you long after you have to let her go, then you have nothing to lose by reading the book."

Josh pretended to closely examine the cookie he held. "I don't suppose you have a copy handy?" He took a bite, hoping it'd help cover up how awkward their conversation had become.

"As a matter of fact, I do." Gisabella quickly walked out of the room and returned with a book. "Here you go." She handed him her tattered copy. "Don't just look at the pictures! There's lots to be gained in addition to sexual gratification if you take the time to read."

"So you're saying, even though my wife is destined to marry this Alexander guy, if I mixed things up in the bedroom, she'll remember *us* on several levels?"

"Exactly. She'll never forget who you were to her once her life on earth ends, but if you go a little out of your way to spice things up, you'll be engraved in her psyche forever. You'll possibly even deepen your spiritual connection to each other. Just remember to keep doing all the important little things like jogging and spending quality time together!"

"I don't suppose there's any way you'll consider changing Jennifer's timeline back to its original?" he asked, even though it was a lost cause.

"I'm afraid not. If it's any consolation, Merlin and I will see to it that Jennifer's life-path ends sooner than expected."

"As of yet, she hasn't shown any recollection of overhearing about her predestined marriage. But I can't promise she'll continue to remain oblivious to the plans that lie ahead," Josh said, pressing his fingertips to his temple. After a moment, his eyes met Gisabella's. "What do you mean—her life-path will end sooner than expected?"

"You brought up a valid point about Jennifer not remembering the details before she transported herself."

"Try again—the truth this time."

"Fine, we may have come up with a way of bringing her home earlier. You know, so the two of you can be together." Gisabella withered under her top protector's steel-green eyes.

"If that's the case, I need to push her to study harder."

"That won't be necessary. The slower pace she's been learning at will suffice until Jennifer comes home." Gisabella busied herself clearing the cookies. "Now that we've covered everything, you'd better head back to your wife. She must be lonely without you."

Looking down at his wedding band, Josh's eyes clouded. "I have no clue how I'll survive losing Jennifer for even a day, never mind the remainder of her lifetime."

"I'm sorry, Josh, I know this will be the hardest thing you've ever had to do, and if you ever need a break, Merlin and I can step in and help."

"If it's okay with you, I'm gonna head home." He brushed off the offer. "Maybe I'll glance through this book along the way." Josh headed toward the door, and as he turned the handle, he looked back. "How did Merlin get through your separation?"

"You'll need to ask him."

"Right."

On the walk home, Josh flipped through the used book. At one point he turned it sideways, stopped and stared at the tangled couple on page twenty-eight. *How in the world did they get into that position? Thank goodness Jennifer's limber! Although, I'm not sure if I can contort my body into a pretzel! Maybe there are some easier positions. No to this one! What the hell are they trying to do?!*

A few more photo examples later, Josh closed the book. *Maybe I should try something a little more basic to start, like super romantic, or maybe something with a touch of spice, or a little darker? She seems to enjoy it when I'm dominant while we're making love. Come to think of it—I enjoyed spanking her, and it sure seemed to excite her! There must be something sensual or different enough to make her remember me.* By the time he arrived back at their honeymoon house, he'd come up with a plan.

Tucking the book into the waistband of his jeans so it was hidden from sight, he opened the door. A quick energy search helped him pinpoint Jennifer's location: the bedroom. *That's a good place to start!*

"Hey, baby, I'm home!" Josh called out while walking up the stairs. When he walked into the bedroom, Talos was the first to greet him with a low growl. Brushing the panther's ornery attitude aside, he headed to where Jennifer sat at the table near the bookcases with her head resting on an open book and her eyes closed.

"Hey, baby," Josh whispered, trying not frighten her.

"Oh, I must have dozed off." Jennifer stretched with a yawn.

"I see you're hard at work—good girl!" Josh glanced at the book she was reading, *Wizardry for Fledglings,* and his lips quirked. "Interesting choice."

"Um—it was on the shelf with the others," she stammered, looking as if she'd gotten caught with her hand in the cookie jar.

"Just remember what happened the last time you played a wizard trick on me." Satisfaction bloomed when Jennifer visibly squirmed in her seat. "Looks like you have fond memories of the event." *That's the deepest shade of blush I've ever seen my wife wear.*

"Yes, I seem to recall your god-awful, boorish behavior," Jennifer retorted, doing her best to appear stern.

"Well, I, for one, can't wait for you to mess up so I have an excuse to spank you again." Josh winked. "Remember, little hellcat, next time I'm using this." He held up his hand with a salacious grin.

Jennifer gazed up at his strong, long-fingered hand, and her eyes widened in size as she gulped. *How does he make that sound so delicious? Oh no, please tell me I blocked my thoughts.*

The glimmer of humor playing in Josh's excited eyes gave her the dreaded answer—*she hadn't!*

"What would you like to do first?" Josh smiled down at Jennifer as if he hadn't heard her. "We can ride the horses over to the oasis and spend time reading and swimming."

"You mean, study more of these books?" She indicated the three books she'd selected to read before she'd found the one she settled on.

"Nope, you can pick any book you want or bring your sketchpad; whatever you want to do is fine with me." Josh thought for a moment before adding, "If you don't want to do either of those things, we can lie back, gaze up at the sky and pick out cloud formations like we used to."

"When was the last time you saw a cloud in this dimension?" she smirked.

"Okay, scratch the clouds. Surely there must be something you'd like to do together."

"Mmm, let me think about this—you and me together in the same dimension." *Me totally turned on by the sight of your raised hand.* "I can think of a few things I'd like to do."

"Why, Mrs. Smith, I like your style."

"Good, then you won't mind teaching me how to do the tango." When Josh's face fell, she tugged on his shirt until he lowered his lips close enough to trace them with her fingernail. "I guess we can always start with a kiss and see where it leads us."

"Now you're talking." Josh pulled her upright to rest her against his length and lowered his lips to her moistened ones.

"Bed," Jennifer said the first chance her lips were free. That one word did the trick, and soon she found herself being carried off.

CHAPTER SEVENTEEN

While Jennifer was horseback riding, Josh went to work on preparing their date for the following night. Gisabella was kind enough to help him with some of the more feminine touches, offering to provide Jennifer with a special dress and shoes to wear, so all he needed to worry about was the romantic ambiance.

The next night, Josh was putting on the finishing touches in anticipation of their special date. While he was lighting the candles, Josh messaged Gisabella. -Hi, boss! Is my bride ready?-

-Jennifer's dressed and anxiously awaiting your arrival. I swear my granddaughter's more nervous tonight than she was on your wedding day!-

-That makes two of us—I want everything to be perfect tonight.-

-I'm sure it will be. Just remember to loosen up and have fun.-

-I'll be there in ten minutes. Do you think you can watch Talos, so my bride and I can be alone without that cat watching us?-

-Sure, bring that beast over here, but he goes back to your place before sunrise.-

-If I wasn't so worried about tonight, I'm sure I'd have a great comeback. But for the life of me, all I want to do is see my wife.-

-Then come and get her, Prince Charming!-

~Prince Charming, huh? Okay, I can do that for Jennifer.~

Eleven minutes later, Josh rode up on his Andalusian mount with roses braided into her tail and mane. He donned his ceremonial protector uniform that Gisabella used to insist upon for special occasions until it became impossible to keep track of who needed what uniform. Either way, it was befitting of something Prince Charming would wear.

"Jennifer, please use some restraint, dear. You should make Josh work harder to please you instead of running out to greet him before he even arrives." Gisabella hadn't finished the sentence before Jennifer exited the house in a blur of red silk. She grabbed the camera and dashed outside in time to see Josh's arrival.

"Grandmamma, is that really Josh?" Jennifer whispered, barely able to breathe as a dashing figure of a man on a horse cantered up the lane toward them.

"That's him, alright." *Talk about making an impressive entrance! Heck, even I feel like swooning.*

The moment Jennifer waved, Josh urged Misty into a gallop, skidding to a halt and jumping off when he reached his wife. "You look amazing." The awe in his voice was palpable.

"You look like you jumped out of a fairytale." She swallowed, trying to calm her racing heart long enough to breathe. "You're in a uniform," was all she managed to say.

"If I knew how much you'd like my attire, I'd have worn it for our wedding day."

"I had a hard enough time breathing that day!"

"So did I, baby." Josh lifted her hand to his lips. "Now, let me admire you." He took a step back to get a better look at the vision she made in the clingy red dress that showed off her slender curves. "You look breathtaking. Are you really *all* mine?" A pang of doubt crept into Josh's heart knowing how close he was coming to losing her, but he chased away the disturbing thought, not wanting anything to ruin their evening.

"Always, Mr. Smith." Jennifer encircled her arms around his waist as if she was unable to contain her need to be closer. Unbeknownst to them, Gisabella snapped several photos before escorting Talos inside and waving goodbye.

"This is for you, my love." He handed her a red rose before lifting her up to sit sideways in front of him on Misty as they rode back to their honeymoon house. When they arrived, he jumped off the horse then lifted her off, placing Jennifer's feet on the ground in one fell swoop. Once he removed Misty's bridle and saddle, Misty galloped back toward the barn to join D'Artagnon.

With her hand in his, Josh opened the door to reveal a fantasy presentation.

"When? I mean, how did you do all this?" Jennifer asked while taking in the many candelabras and vases full of red roses in their family room and the table for two positioned in front of the fireplace.

"I have my ways," Josh teased. "I hope you're hungry." He escorted her to the intimate table and pulled out her chair.

"Come to think of it, I'm starving. Did you tell Gisabella not to feed me?"

"No, but if I had, you'd be thanking me. Especially if she tried to force those god awful charred mincemeat cookies on you."

"Ew, enough talking about her cooking before I lose my appetite."

"I agree." Josh retrieved the bottle of champagne from the ice bucket and popped the cork, pouring them each a glassful before sitting down across from her.

"To the only woman I have ever loved—thank you for being my wife." After clinking glasses, they each took a sip.

"I don't know what I've done to deserve such an amazing husband. I thank God every single day for giving you to me," Jennifer toasted while dabbing an emotional tear, which earned her a sweet kiss.

During the half hour, Josh served a light meal of several small plates featuring various delectable delights.

"That was delicious," Jennifer declared, sitting back in her chair. "Have you ever wished you could have pursued a career as a chef?"

"There were times I thought about going back to live another lifetime on earth, but once I was assigned to you, the thought has never entered my mind."

"I'm very happy to hear that." Jennifer blushed and started to fiddle with her fork, suddenly appearing shy.

"Jennifer, I love what I do, and once you became my wife, I've never wanted to leave your side."

"I feel the same way." Her eyes pooled as she gazed lovingly into Josh's.

"Good to know," Josh purred. "I have something planned for us that I thought you'd enjoy. Come." He stood up and held out his hand.

"Like what?" She accepted his proffered gesture and stood.

"Oh no you don't—it's a surprise!" He began leading the way toward the dance room. Jennifer balanced on red heels in heady anticipation, wondering what he had in store for her. Before Josh turned the door handle, he flashed her a dazzling smile.

"Are we going to dance?"

"Maybe." Josh grinned when his noncommittal answer earned him a sweet pout.

When he opened the double doors, Jennifer noticed how busy her husband had been. She walked alongside him to the middle of the dance room, then watched as he walked around the room with a lighter, making each of the many candles come to life. Her gaze drifted over vases of white calla lilies positioned around the room and the way the mirrored wall had been draped with billowing white curtains, only allowing a few glimpses of reflections to be seen.

Caught up in the moment, she didn't notice Josh walking toward her with a red rose between his teeth until he was only a couple steps away. Her eyes widened when she caught the look of excitement in his eyes, and her gaze remained fixated on him as he made a production of removing the rose from his mouth and tucking it behind her ear. It was then she noticed the music playing, surmising he must have clicked on the stereo.

"My love," Josh said to her huskily, stirring all her senses into a primal dance of their own. The music was a tango! *Yikes!* She'd never danced the tango before, and apprehension bloomed in her belly knowing what an accomplished dancer Josh had turned out to be.

"Relax, baby, I got this!" Josh reassured, taking her in his arms until her body was pressed against his, with one of her legs in between his and the other the outside until she was effectively straddling his right leg. There was no denying how well their bodies fit together or how it was like they'd been made to fit together since the beginning of time.

"I—I don't know how to tango."

"Consider this your first lesson then. No worries—I've watched you dance often, and I know how your body moves. I guarantee you'll do great! Give me your right hand," he instructed, holding his left hand up. Once their hands were clasped together, he stretched out his arm until hers was straightened.

"I'm going to send you images of the dance moves as we go along. If it gets too confusing, let me know, and I'll switch to the old-fashioned way of talking you through the steps. The tango is a seductive dance of love, so it's best if we let our bodies do all the talking."

When Jennifer nodded, Josh turned his head to the side until he was looking toward the end of the room, and she followed his lead, doing the same. At first, Josh took his time, slowly walking her through the steps, leg movements, and spins. Once she'd learned the basics, he sped up the pace. The feel of his body rubbing against hers and his dark, intense expression made her want to dance closer, but if Josh were to hold her any tighter, they may have combusted into flames.

"Faster?" Josh challenged.

"Yes!" Jennifer said, enjoying the feeling of her hair swaying to and fro across her exposed skin, courtesy of her backless dress. Soon, their moves became a synchronized rhythmic dance of seduction as he guided her around the room until she was completely breathless.

"Enough," Jennifer gasped before breaking into a fit of laughter.

"You did amazing!" He clasped her face with his hands and kissed her solidly on the lips.

"Thanks to your lead! We should dance like this more often."

"I'll be happy to dance with you—anytime you want."

There was something in the way Josh said the words that made Jennifer give him a second look. *Did I imagine his hesitation? Maybe he was partly out of breath?* But looking at the steady rise and fall of his chest debunked her theory.

"What do you say to some dessert?"

"Are you on the menu?" she flirted, failing to feign even the slightest hint of innocence.

"Oh no you don't. Tonight is for romance, and I intend to make this a special night you'll remember for many years to come."

"Okay, romance it is. Please tell me you didn't bring home any of my grandma's baking horrors?"

"Bite your tongue, woman!" Josh excused himself before he walked around blowing out the candles. Once done, they headed back to the family room where he motioned toward the couch closest to the fireplace while he opened a new bottle of chilled champagne.

"May I ask you something?" Jennifer hesitated, knowing her question could lead to an argument.

"You can ask me anything."

"Why did you have me accept Alexander's offer?" *There it is again! That look!*

"Because—he can help me protect you." Josh was careful not to raise his eyes until he was sure his blank expression was in place.

"By taking me out for lunch and dinner? Or having his limo driver cart me around town?" Jennifer ignored Josh's flinch and continued. "What's changed?"

"Nothing's changed. Look, Jennifer, Alexander's able to help us out by acting as a sort of first line of defense. He was right, you know—about it not being safe for you to walk around the city looking as if you're on your own." *Please drop this line of questioning!* Josh silently begged.

"What is it about Alexander that's making you push me toward him? Don't try and tell me it's my imagination because I'm feeling you doing so!" She wrapped her arms around herself, suddenly feeling chilled. "It's as if you're hiding something, but I don't know what it is, and it scares me. Tell me! I know it's something big, but the way you look tonight and danced the tango is distracting—to the point of being unable to think."

"Jennifer, please drop it."

His soft-spoken warning sucked the breath from deep within her lungs. "You expect me to drop it? I'm your *wife*. If anyone deserves an answer—it's me!"

"Don't ruin our night." Josh sighed.

"I can see the pain in your eyes."

"It's nothing. There's nothing going on," Josh raised his voice.

"If there's nothing going on, then why do I feel as if I'm losing bits and pieces of you, like tiny fragments of who we were?" Her eyes brimmed with tears. "This has to do with Alexander; I just know it does. Are you hoping to make things easier on yourself?"

"What are you talking about? Easier? Do you think standing by watching you eating lunch with another man is easy?" He ran his fingers through his hair, but it failed to calm his energy.

"Then why?"

"Jennifer, you know I can't discuss my job with you."

"And I'm your *job*." Jennifer slugged back the remainder of her champagne to gain strength. "Damn it—get this through your head: I'm your wife, not a fucking job! How would you feel if I were to tell you how attracted I am to Alexander? He's really quite the catch, you know. On paper, we fit together perfectly, and he seems to be sweet and kind."

When her brazen comments failed to break her husband's façade, she pushed a little harder. "Josh, please open up to me. Don't you understand how scared I am? I'm sitting here begging you to throw me a lifeline, but instead I feel as if you're kicking me out of the boat."

"You have to live your life!" Josh said through his clenched teeth.

"I don't care how great Alexander adds up on paper, I only want you! Talk to me, damn it! I—I need answers." She choked back a sob.

"Baby, no, please don't cry. I love you and only you—but—I cannot discuss this." Josh wrapped her in his embrace and began to kiss away her tears. "I love you; I love you; I love you...," he cried over and over as he stroked her hair.

"God, how I love you, Joshua. Promise me you won't disappear. I'm so worried that you're going to leave me because you have some preconceived notion that Alexander is a better fit for me, just because he's alive in my dimension."

"Baby, I could never leave you. Besides, we married each other forever, and I take my wedding vows very seriously."

"I never want to be parted from you." Though Jennifer could see the sadness in his eyes, her husband's mouth remained closed. *He looks so lost.* She risked trying to read his thoughts, but they were sealed up like a Wells Fargo bank safe. She had no choice but to postpone her line of questioning until a later date. Instead, she was forced to resign herself to enjoying the rest of their evening.

"Hope you have a little bit of room for dessert. I promise it'll be well worth it!" Josh voiced, trying to get their night back on track.

"Judging by the way your irises have become the color of the Mediterranean, I'm ready for dessert!" Jennifer's heart fluttered of its own accord, but her smile was forced.

"Not so fast—I want to make tonight last forever." *If only I could.* Josh tried his best to brush away all thoughts of Alexander and losing his wife.

"I think from the moment you caught me in midair, that's all I've ever wanted—a chance to be with you forever," Jennifer declared, missing the undertone of sadness in Josh's eyes before he brought his lips to hers.

"Are you ready for something a little more indecent?" Josh reached behind the pillow to hold up a long, two-inch wide length of black silk. Jennifer licked her lips, sending a bolt of anticipation through his body. *Don't rush—this needs to be memorable enough to last a lifetime.*

"Close your eyes," he commanded, his voice husky with desire. When she complied, he covered her eyes with the blindfold and tied the silk in a bow. "Can you see anything?" he asked, making funny faces so when Jennifer's answer came out so soft even a mouse would struggle to hear, it didn't matter. "I'll be back in less than a minute—stay here." He brushed her lips with his thumb before he exited the room to return with a tray of assorted desserts. Once he refilled their champagne glasses, he sat back down.

"Because you were such a *good girl* for not moving, I have a special treat." Josh selected a chocolate-dipped strawberry and slowly began to rub it on Jennifer's bottom lip.

She captured the sweet treat between her top teeth and bottom lip. "Mmm, I love the way you serve dessert." Her lower region clenched in anticipation of what was to come, as thoughts of her husband pushing her toward another man faded into the background.

Without answering, he lifted the flute of champagne and rested it on her bottom lip until she parted them enough to tilt the glass, giving her a sip of the chilled bubbly. Next Josh selected a bite-sized éclair he'd made last night while she was asleep.

Jennifer opened her mouth, allowing Josh full access, biting down on the creamy, chocolate-covered treat. Being blindfolded heightened her senses, making each nibble fill her entire body with pleasure. "Was that an éclair? When did you find time to make those?"

Once again she felt the chilled glass against her bottom lip to receive another sip of sweet wine. His mouthwatering seduction continued with bite-sized pieces of chocolate-covered fruit and other tasty treats he'd baked, giving her sips of champagne between each offering while remaining silent.

Josh bit into a juicy strawberry and brought his mouth to hers, sharing the sweet fruit as they kissed. When her fingers tangled in his hair to try and take control, he caught her hands and brought them to rest in her lap, then captured her bottom lip with his teeth and gave a tug, eliciting a protesting groan from his wife.

"Please, take me to bed," she pleaded, only to receive another kiss. This time Josh shared a mouthful of champagne while he held her wrists hostage, so she was helpless to do anything but accept his far-too-gentle kisses.

"I can't take much more..." Jennifer moaned, only to have Josh's mouth cover hers again as he continued with his game. She eagerly sucked some of the whipped cream from his mouth and swallowed. Breathless and wanton beyond anything she thought she was capable of withstanding, Jennifer was forced to wait, accepting another sip of liquid she'd come to expect. A few kisses later, to her relief, Josh patted her lips with a napkin.

"What would you like to do now, Mrs. Smith? Perhaps watch a movie or read a book?"

"I *want* to make love!" Jennifer managed to say through her shattered senses.

"I love how desperate you sound for me," Josh answered, causing Jennifer to moan in frustration. When she'd reached her limit, he stood and lifted her in his arms then carried her upstairs.

"I want to make love to you—blindfolded," Josh whispered when they reached the bedroom.

"Okay." Jennifer's voice came out shaky, reflecting how overwhelming she found his intentions.

"If this becomes too much for you, tell me to stop and I will. Baby, nod if you understood what I said." When she nodded, he lowered the straps of her dress off her shoulders, leaving a trail of kisses in their wake. While he was doing so, her hands slid from his shoulders to his chest, where she felt her way around until she found and undid the buttons on his uniform. "I love how eager you are, baby."

"So eager," Jennifer cried out, working quickly to remove his jacket.

"Relax, my love, we have all night to enjoy each other."

She pushed his jacket off and felt for the buttons on his shirt that stood in the way of his naked chest, fumbling until she'd successfully gotten them all undone. She ran her hands up his bare chest, enjoying the feeling of his manly, taut, muscular body.

"Turn around so I can unzip you," Josh ordered as a way of slowing the pace. When she did as told, he lowered her zipper very slowly, doubling her breathing. Without a bra, it was easy to remove her panties with the dress in one swift move, then he positioned himself so he was facing her.

"I bet you're wet for me." Josh lowered himself to his knees and held Jennifer in place with his hands on her hips. Inhaling her musky scent was enough to nearly undo him. *I think I'd better hurry up before I drive myself crazy!* With a huge smile his wife couldn't see, he brought his mouth to her quivering sex and began nibbling and sucking, pushing her over the edge of ecstasy within a few moments.

"Josh!" Jennifer screamed as she gave in to her body's powerful orgasm. She was left standing on shaky legs, and the only thing keeping her upright was the man she'd always love.

"I think we'd better lie down," Josh said half to himself as he carried his wife to bed then laid her down and removed the blindfold. "Let me finish undressing—then I'm going to make love to you all night long."

"Yes, please!" With their earlier conversation forgotten, she rolled on her side to get a better view.

"See anything you like?" Josh asked, wearing a huge grin and nothing else.

"No," Jennifer paused before adding, "I love everything about you."

"Good—because I'm all yours." He lay down on the bed and pulled Jennifer on top of him, positioning her so she was straddling his erection. "I can't think of a better view than you riding me as hard as you do your horse."

Hours later, after making love several more times, Josh lay on his side watching Jennifer sleep. Everything about their date was perfect until his wife had brought up Alexander's name. Now, in the dead of night, the reality of what he'd be facing in the not-too-distant future threatened to collapse his world and crush his heart.

I can't bear to lose her. If only there was a way I could answer her questions and express how I'm feeling—without breaking my vow of secrecy. As he gazed down at Jennifer, he could no longer bear to hide the facts from the woman he'd promised never to lie to or withhold the truth from ever again.

"Baby, I need to tell you something, but I made a promise to your grandma, and as your protector, I vowed to keep your life-path a secret. Even if I hadn't promised, I couldn't tell you. It would be like placing an albatross around your soul if you ever found out what your future held for both of us," Josh spoke his confession softly. "Soon, I must begin to pull away—not because I no longer want you, but because I love you too much to make you choose between Alexander and myself. Please try to understand, if I'm by your side as your lover and husband when your feelings for Alexander become stronger—"

Josh paused to rein in his emotions. "It'd be selfish of me to hold you back from the destiny given to you at birth. I love you too much to tear your soul apart. Alexander has been etched into your very soul since the day you were born—that, combined with Gisabella's magic—is too powerful for you to fight off. When the time comes, I must willing let you go, even though it will kill me to do so."

Jennifer snuggled closer and rested her head on his arm, making him smile. "I love watching you sleep, especially the way you're always snuggling closer. Sometimes I swear you're on a mission to take over the entire bed!" Josh took a painful, deep breath in an effort to steady his emotions.

"Regardless of what happens, know that I love you with all my heart and that I'll always be there for you even if there comes a time you can no longer see me. I give you my word: I'll never leave your side, and I vow to *always* protect you. I hope someday when I transition your soul home, you'll remember tonight and all the wonderful memories we've created during our time together, and you'll choose to stay by my side as my wife forevermore. Even if you make a different choice, my heart and soul will always be yours."

Josh lay down, though heavy-hearted. He enjoyed the feeling of Jennifer's nakedness against his skin and dozed off, holding her as if his life depended on it.

CHAPTER EIGHTEEN

Jennifer awakened to the smell of bacon, roses, and the heady afterglow of last night. A glance next to her and around the room held no sign of Josh. Donning her robe over her nakedness, she found a notecard addressed to her.

Jennifer,

Thank you for a lovely evening I'll always hold deeply in my heart. I apologize for not being there to wish you good morning, but I had some business to attend to. Talos has agreed to keep watch over you until I return.

Love, Josh

While the note sounded sweet enough, something about his words fell flat, and Jennifer couldn't tell if she was imagining Josh distancing himself from the level of intimacy they shared last night. *Does this have anything to do with my questions about Alexander?* A knot tied itself in her stomach, but she shook off the encroaching feeling that something was wrong.

Once she alleviated her bladder, Jennifer headed over to the sink and washed her hands, catching sight of her reflection. The woman looking back at her had tangled hair and swollen lips, both signs of their torrid lovemaking. *How could he call last night "a lovely evening"? Seriously? It was passionate, all-consuming and epic—"lovely" in no way does it justice!*

She wandered over to the table that now held breakfast for one, the sight of which turned her stomach and doused all hints of her euphoric afterglow like a bucket of ice water had been dumped over her. The single red rose placed next to her breakfast cheered her up a little as did the side of chocolate-covered strawberries, but they didn't help to shake off the feeling in the pit of her stomach that something had changed.

After picking at the lukewarm blueberry pancakes, she pushed them aside in favor of heading to the barn. If anything, she needed to remove the roses from Misty's mane. *Maybe I'm overreacting, and Josh just had to attend a meeting or something! So what if my forever husband missed one breakfast? For goodness sake—get a grip, Jennifer!*

She shrugged off her thoughts, dressed and headed downstairs where she followed another note she found taped to the refrigerator door, this one instructing her to give Talos the whole chicken. *Josh sure was into writing notes this morning. It'd have been nice if he woke me to say goodbye.*

"I'm going to the barn," she said to Talos, who was too busy gnawing on chicken bones to say much, other than to message, ~okay.~ *Ugh, talk about disgusting!* She made her escape out the back door before she lost what little she'd eaten.

She kept herself busy at the barn most of the day, grooming both horses, cleaning tack, and sweeping out the barn until she noticed the sun was setting. That's when she saw Talos walking toward her with a scowl, licking his chops.

"Fine, I get the hint. I'm sure there must be something for you to eat in the fridge. I don't suppose you heard from Josh?" Jennifer couldn't tell if the dirty look from Talos was meant for her, or Josh.

~No, my lady. The last I saw of him was when he left at three in the morning.~

"Three a.m.?" *Where did he have to go at that hour?*

-That's right,- Talos messaged, padding alongside Jennifer, who instantly sped up her pace until he needed to lope to keep up.

After a quick check in the fridge, she handed the panther a steak. "I hope this wasn't anything Josh was planning on serving. Talos, you'd better stay here in case Josh returns while I run over to Grandma's house."

Jennifer hurried through the house and out the front door, then ran the entire way to Gisabella's and pressed the doorbell in rapid succession.

"Hold your horses, I'm coming," Gisabella mumbled under her breath before opening the door. "Jennifer! Are you alone?"

"You sound surprised." Jennifer wrapped her arms around herself in an effort to ease her growing concern.

"Of course I'm surprised. Usually Josh sends me a heads-up when you're coming over."

Nothing like monitoring my every move! When she realized her grandma was staring at her, Jennifer confided, "As you know, Josh and I had a special date last night. It was perfect! He was so romantic and attentive, but when I woke this morning, he was gone, and all I found was breakfast and a note. I thought it was odd at the time when he referred to our night as lovely, but other than that, everything seemed fine."

"Did he tell Talos where he was going?"

"No, Grandmamma, but Talos just informed me that Josh left the house at three in the morning. I'm worried there might be something wrong."

"I'll be right back." Gisabella headed into another room where she consulted her mystical pond. "Where are you, Josh?" Swirls of mist circled round and round, eventually clearing to reveal the protector's location. "That does it! They're in so much trouble!" Gisabella said mostly to herself before she hurried back to where she'd left Jennifer standing on the front stoop.

"I don't know how it slipped my mind, dear, that I'd asked Josh to help Merlin go through some new protector candidates. I guess the time must have gotten away from them. Anyway, Talos will be here momentarily to escort you back to the house, where he's to keep an eye on you."

"But I want to go with you." *Dammit!* Jennifer added silently.

"Jennifer, between Merlin and Josh's antics, I've enough to deal with without you tagging along."

"But, Josh is my husband, and I deserve to know what's going on!" Jennifer tried not to cringe at the change in Gisabella's expression. *No wonder everyone's afraid of Grandmamma!*

"Josh knows his job comes first—as should you," Gisabella warned. "Talos has arrived, so do as you're told, and I promise to bring Josh home in time to transport you back to earth in the morning." Gisabella bustled inside and closed the door, leaving Jennifer with Talos.

"Wait a minute!" Jennifer huffed. *Why does everyone insist on treating me like a child? Fine, so I'm not as old as they are, but I'm not a fragile doll they have to protect, either!*

"Talos, I suggest we get going before Gisabella changes her mind and banishes us to the outer limits." When Jennifer noticed the terrified look on the panther's face, she quickly added, "I was kidding—I doubt Grandma would never do that to *me*."

-If it's all the same to you, I'd like to keep my fur coat,- Talos messaged as he began trotting off in the direction of the honeymoon house.

"Hey—wait for me." She hurried to catch up.

Josh chugged most of the golden liquid in his glass, letting it blaze a trail down his throat and into his stomach. He'd lost all sense of time after the third hour of talking to Merlin and the two bottles of booze that now sat empty on the table. He was surprised when the wizard proved to be a bottomless drinker who was far better at holding his liquor than he was.

"As I was saying..." Josh finished what little there was left in his glass. "Where was I? Oh right, so—um—so you had issues too?" he slurred while trying to put Merlin's fuzzy expression into focus.

"Absolutely, boy! Who wouldn't have issues with letting the woman they love run off with another man?"

"Damn straight! How dare my wife ditch me for some rich asshole artist! So what if he can lay the world at her feet? I have benefits too, you know—" Josh's head slumped, jerking him awake. "Lots of them. She loves the way I fuck, you know. That's got to be equal to the millions of dollars Alex—an—der can give her. Shhhh, don't tell no one—I transported her to Gisabella's do—main—we have a house! She loves that damn horse, too! I can't compare to that four-legged demon. Four legs is better than the three I've got. Should count my cock as three legs? Or one leg with two balls? D'Artagnan—aw, fuck his stupid name. Anyway, my three legs and two balls are better than all five of his! Legs—I don't think he has any balls? Have you seen the size of that fucking horse's fifth leg—damn, no wonder Jenn—ifer likes him!"

Merlin squelched his mirth at Josh's drunken blabbering. He remembered what it was like when he was in his shoes, and even if Josh were sober, there was nothing he could say that would make what the younger protector must face any easier.

"Hey, boy, don't you think you should see how Jennifer's doing?"

"Talos—that worthless cat you sold me—is with her. Jennifer loves me more than him," Josh expressed proudly, momentarily sitting upright before leaning forward onto his propped elbows to keep from face-planting onto the table.

"Glad to hear you beat out the cat." Merlin tried not to laugh but failed miserably.

"Hey—you! You—you—wizard—said you'd help save my wife. Save my wife, Jennifer. You know her—she is your grandfather—no, or are you her granddaughter?"

"Leave it all up to me. But either way, win or lose Jennifer, you need to be strong. You'll get her back."

"Love her way too much. That's the problem—I fell in love. You know I love my wife, right?"

"I think you've said that fifty times since you arrived over sixteen hours ago." Merlin sighed. "How about I transport you home to Jennifer—remember her? She's the woman you love, who amazingly manages to put up with you," Merlin roasted.

"You think she loves me more than her horse?"

"You can cook, can't you? I'd say that fact alone makes it a done deal." Merlin shook his head over the fact Josh hadn't passed out hours ago. "Like I told you this morning, I've been in your shoes and know how you're feeling, but the only thing you can do is be there for Jennifer, so when her life ends, she'll be yours forever. That's a much better deal than I ever got with Gisabella, and we ended up together."

"I can cook, you know," Josh said, jerking his head upright at the sight of his boss.

"What do you think you two are doing?!" Gisabella shouted, earning both of their attentions.

"Hey, Your Excellency! About time you got here." Josh raised his glass and finished the contents, then refilled it, spilling more than a few drops. He couldn't care less that he was pushing Gisabella into a corner with his lack of respect. He no longer cared what happened to him. The liquor was doing his thinking now, and he'd come up with all sorts of ways to solve his problems. One solution was to tick off the high priestess until she banished him forever. Then, his soon-to-be ex-wife would be able to find happiness in another man's arms—one who was alive on earth!

"Aren't you going to offer me a glass of whatever poison you're drinking?" Gisabella said to the inebriated protector before her, who just last night had ridden in on a gray horse looking like Prince Charming. She eyed his disheveled appearance and his red puffy eyes.

Josh tipped the bottle and poured the remaining liquid into his glass before he looked up and said, "No can do—the bottle's empty!" He held the bottle upside down to prove it.

Gisabella walked over to the table, picked up his glass, and drank the remaining contents before slamming it down so loudly that Josh and Merlin both jumped.

"Hey! That was mine!" Josh spat in anger as he glared through his bloodshot eyes in the direction of the dancing Gisabella twins before him.

"And you!" Gisabella turned toward Merlin. "What do you have to say for yourself?"

"Not my fault the boy came knocking on my door. Good thing I was here to let him in. By the sound of him, Josh had started his drinking binge long before he transported here." Merlin squirmed uncomfortably under Gisabella's gaze. "Have I mentioned lately how much I love you?"

"Buttering me up will do you *no* good. Apparently our grandson-in-law left Jennifer alone when he left their house in my realm around three this morning without telling her where he was going."

"I wrote a note." Josh held up his index finger before he sagged in his seat. His thoughts drifted in and out through the fogginess in his brain. *I need another drink.* He doubted Gisabella would be willing to oblige him by fetching another bottle out of the liquor cabinet.

Josh's cloudy look and blank expression didn't fool Gisabella, who was able to read the protector's thoughts. If she weren't so livid, she'd have called him out on his request for another bottle of booze.

"Joshua!" Gisabella snapped, redirecting Josh's focus on her and away from the bottles of gin in Merlin's cabinet. "We need to get you sober so we can get home to Jennifer. She's been worried sick about you. What in the world happened last night? I told you to use your time left with Jennifer to create special memories; I never said to disappear afterwards!"

"Do you think Jennifer still loves me?" Josh muttered, running both his hands through his mussed waves of dark hair.

"I don't suppose he told you why he ran out on his wife in the middle of the night?" Gisabella asked Merlin, who looked a lot better off than Josh.

"From what I gathered, the night was beyond anything he had experienced before. Afterwards, he apparently confessed everything to Jennifer while she was asleep. Sounded to me like he spoke from his soul. Told her how he'd need to back away from her so she could fall in love with and marry Alexander."

Gisabella cringed over the huge rule breakage her top protector had committed, but now wasn't the time to throw the book at him.

"I can't let Jennifer marry *him*!" Josh moaned.

One look in Josh's eyes, and it was obvious how desperately in love he was. So much so, he was willing to do anything for the girl, even if it meant getting himself banished in the process. The two loved each other and truly belonged together forever, but Gisabella had made it clear that unless Jennifer completed her life-path, he'd lose her anyway.

"Josh, I know for a fact that Jennifer loves you. I also know you are, and will always be, the only man she'll ever love. Her life-path husband will only be an obligation, and Jennifer's heart will always belong to you. All Merlin and I ask is that you protect our granddaughter and love her for all of eternity."

"How do you expect me to watch some other man kiss her? Wasn't putting Merlin through hell enough for you?" Josh spat.

"That's enough, boy," Merlin warned. "You're a strong man and an honorable protector who *will* do the right thing in the end. Don't make the same mistake I did when I pulled away long before I needed to. It's taken us thousands of years to work things out. If only I'd been strong enough for the woman I loved, we'd have had so much more time together."

"I'll hurt Jennifer's soul. Tear it to pieces if I pull too hard."

"That's only partly true. You'll need to pull away from her, but you don't have to leave her completely. Jennifer will always need your friendship and protector abilities, and once she marries, she'll be given the freedom to make her own choices. Seeing as though you will remain her husband in every sense of the word, Jennifer may encourage you to spend time with her."

"You mean like an affair with my own fucking wife?!"

"It wouldn't be an affair since you're already married! Look, all I'm saying is that you'll have chances to be together. Nothing says Jennifer must sleep with her husband after the honeymoon!" Gisabella explained.

"I fucked up last night by leaving, didn't I?" Josh groaned.

"Jennifer seemed more worried about you than angry. From what she told me about last night, it was pretty darn special. How about I get some coffee into you?" Gisabella handed him a quart-size espresso that was sure to give him the jitters for days. She hid her grin from the faltering warrior, who was in no position to tolerate any amusement.

"Where the hell did you learn to make espresso? From my mother-in-law?" Josh complained, forcing another gulp down.

"I believe this is the first time I've ever seen you completely shit-faced." Gisabella had her friend at a disadvantage, not thinking clearly. "I bet if I hadn't drunk the last of the gin, you'd be lying on the floor now passed out, wouldn't you?" she toasted, making up for ruining her night and getting Merlin too soused to be of any use to her.

"I was perfectly capable of finishing that last glassful. In fact—you owe me more gin!" he declared, bringing his fist down on the table.

"I think you've had enough to drink. I only hope you don't throw up all over our granddaughter!" Gisabella said, knowing there was a good chance he'd do so.

"If I do, it'll be all your fault." Josh took a couple gulps of espresso. "Better not vomit on my wife."

"I'd better help you transport him," Merlin offered. "Maybe afterwards, you'll let me spend the night."

"That depends on whether or not you drank too much to function," Gisabella said, bringing a touch of color to her cheeks.

Merlin stuck his hand in his pocket and magically pulled out two dozen red roses. "Here you go, boy; these roses are sure to make our ladies forgive our drunken binge."

"Maybe I should put my uniform back on. Jennifer liked that a lot!"

"Come on, boys," Gisabella said, preparing to transport them back to her house as a group.

CHAPTER NINETEEN

Gisabella and Merlin reappeared at Jennifer's front door, each doing their best to keep Josh from sinking to the ground.

"Wake up, boy—you're home," Merlin declared, grabbing a handful of Josh's hair to lift the younger protector's head until his eyes were facing the door.

"I'd better use the doorbell. Once Jennifer answers, we can drag him into the house and make our escape!" Gisabella planned, using her free hand to press the bell.

"He's all hers now!" Merlin seconded.

"If you remember correctly, you were partly responsible for his condition. If not for the amount of liquor you provided him, Josh wouldn't need both of us to hold him upright."

"This doesn't look like a tavern!" Josh slurred, leaning closer to the door, squinting. "It doesn't have a name. Every bar has a name—unless—it's a club! Jennifer better not be in there! She's dancing for other men—gonna marry one."

"Shit! He better not open his big mouth to Jennifer!"

"Open mouth? Ohhhhh—Jennifer's a—dentist!" Josh claimed before opening his mouth. "Ahhhhhhh," he sounded, sticking out his tongue just as the door flung open. Startled, Josh's eyes shot open before he doubled over and vomited mere inches from Jennifer's feet.

"Nice, Josh!" Merlin exclaimed, patting the protector on the back.

"Josh! Are you alright? What happened?!" Jennifer turned to Gisabella for answers.

"Better out here than in the house," Gisabella said matter-of-factly. "Don't worry, for the most part, he's fine, but I'd suggest you make a huge pot of coffee."

"Where have you been?"

"Jennifer! I love you—wife. When did you become a dancer—oops, dentist. Mrs. Smith, you're gonna leave me—aren't you?"

"What is he talking about?" Jennifer asked before her entire demeanor changed when realization hit. "You're *drunk*!"

"Bravo!" Merlin verified before he hoisted Josh over his shoulder and carried him into the house. "Where do you want him?"

"You mean all the time I've been worried sick, you were getting drunk at some—bar!"

"He wasn't at a bar; he was with me," Merlin admitted.

"You got my husband drunk?"

"He was the one who came knocking on my door liquored up in the middle of the night."

"Merlin, put him down on the couch, and let's get out of here before you get yourself and Josh in deeper hot water," Gisabella ordered. "Sorry, Jennifer, but try to understand that Josh was doing what guys do, making a total ass out of himself. I suggest you lock him out of the bedroom for a week! Oh, and you might want to give him a garbage pail in case he gets sick again. Other than that, whatever you do with him is up to you."

Gisabella tugged on Merlin's cloak and very quickly led the way out the door.

"What am *I* supposed to do with you?" Jennifer demanded with her hands on her hips.

"Not so loud," Josh moaned. "Someone may hear us!" He fumbled with the button on his jeans. "Can you undo this?" He pointed to his waistband. "Got strawberry, here—you like straw—berries." He tried tugging at the button again, but he was all thumbs. "Only want you," Josh slurred before his eyes rolled back and he became silent.

"Josh!" Jennifer cried out, falling to her knees. "Wake up!"

~Best to let him sleep it off, princess,~ Talos said with a catty grin. ~Sure is a lot quieter without him jabbering nonsense.~

"I can't leave him here by himself! What if he gets sick again or does something stupid and hurts himself?"

~Stupider than leaving you in the middle of the night to go off drinking with Merlin? I think Josh has already cornered the stupidity market. Besides, you need sleep more than he does.~

"You're right! He was the one who disappeared while I've been worried sick!"

~I think Gisabella had the right idea—we should kick him out of bed for a month or two.~

"We?" Jennifer glowered at the panther.

~Without your protector close by, I need to stay by your side. If Josh were awake, he'd insist I do so.~ Talos purred, only it came out more like a growl, earning him another angry glare.

"Talos is right, Josh! You can sleep it off down here, but tomorrow morning, I expect some serious groveling and an explanation why you snuck out last night. How could you have gone drinking after we shared the most amazing night together?" She choked back a sob as she ran from the room with Talos on her heels.

Once they were in the master bedroom, she closed and locked the doors before she curled up in bed, sobbing.

~There now, princess, I promise everything will be alright. Talos is here to keep you safe.~ Talos gently stroked Jennifer's heaving back with his paw.

"Suppose he leaves me again? I—I couldn't bear to go on without Josh."

Talos rolled his eyes. ~Seems to me he was more concerned with you leaving him.~

"Do you think I was too hasty in leaving him alone? He was really drunk—suppose he needs my help?"

~Do I need to remind you that he left you in the middle of the night to go drinking with Merlin?! If you go down there now, he'll only do it again. Best to ignore him until tomorrow. Meanwhile, I'll stay here and keep you warm while you sleep.~

"You're such a good friend, Talos." Jennifer sat up and hugged the midnight-colored panther before she lay back down, pulling the comforter over them both.

Four hours later, Jennifer awakened with a start. "What's all that noise?" She shook the warm body lying next to her.

Talos raised his head and perked his ears. ~Sounds like Josh is trying to crawl upstairs.~ Talos tucked his face under his paw once again.

Jennifer bolted upright, straining her ears. "Are you sure he's alright?" A loud clatter followed by a cry of pain had her jumping out of bed and running to the door. When she yanked the door open, she found Josh on his knees, covered in food, holding a tray in one hand and a cup in the other.

"I made you breakfast," he said sheepishly while trying hard to keep a straight face.

Jennifer picked a piece of jam-covered toast off his shoulder and took a bite. "I don't suppose that cup of tea is for me?"

"It is!" Josh lifted it toward her.

"Thank you." She lifted the tea to her lips and took a sip. "I guess I should be happy you showed up for breakfast today instead of going out drinking again."

"Jennifer—I'm sorry."

"Why would you leave our bed to go get drunk with Merlin? I tossed and turned all night trying to figure it out, but nothing makes sense." Her voice came out louder than she meant, making Josh shut his eyes as if in terrible pain. "Hangover?"

"The worst!"

"Really? Spirits get hangovers?"

"I think Gisabella had something to do with it."

"Well, you certainly deserve a killer of a headache! She and I are furious with you."

"I know." Josh lowered his head to examine the mess he made.

"Look, Josh, the sun hasn't even come up, and I haven't slept much.

So, unless you find a way of explaining how tired I look to my parents, I need to go back to sleep."

"I'd like to join you in bed," Josh said with sad puppy dog eyes.

"I'm not having sex with you or sucking your dick—got that?"

"My head hurts too much to do anything other than shut my eyes and pray it doesn't explode. Thanks, you laughing at my pain isn't helping." Josh crawled closer and wrapped his arms around her legs. "I think you should join me—down here." He lifted her up and gently set her on the floor in front of him.

"Agh!" She reached under her butt and retrieved a glob of runny egg yolk with a little purple jam mixed in. "I think this was your egg, sir." She smeared the mixture all over his face.

Josh licked the corner of his mouth. "Actually, Mrs. Smith, I believe that was yours. This egg was mine." Josh scooped up the egg he was wearing and attempted to return the favor.

"Oh no you don't!" Jennifer tried to wiggle out of his grasp, only to find herself lying down with Josh over her. "Let me go!"

"Not without a kiss." He brought his mouth closer.

"Ugh!" She pinched her nose and turned her face. "Not without mouthwash!"

Josh cupped his hand over his mouth and did a quick breath check. "I've smelled worse."

"Where? In an ancient mummy's mouth? Because I'm sure your breath is worse." Despite trying not to, she began to giggle.

"Laughing at me, are you? I'll take that over shouting!"

"I'm still mad at you and have a lot of questions you need to answer."

Josh held up a hand. "I know—but do you think it could wait until morning? You need some sleep, and I have a huge mess to clean up."

"Fine." Jennifer turned to see Talos watching them closely. "I have an idea. Talos, help yourself to breakfast while Josh and I get cleaned up. We'll see you in the morning." Jennifer got to her feet and offered Josh a hand up.

~So much for keeping Josh out of your bed for a month or two.~ Talos' retort fell on deaf ears, made clear when the door closed in his face. Lowering his head, the panther quickly cleaned the carpet and curled up with his eyes closed.

In the morning, Jennifer woke up to Josh carrying a fully intact breakfast tray and apologetic flowers.

"Good morning, beautiful," he said with a dazzling smile.

"Morning," Jennifer acknowledged stiffly.

"Do you want to eat breakfast in bed or sit at the table?"

"Table—it's neutral territory."

"Okay then." He headed toward the table and began setting up breakfast for two. *I sure hope her favorite vegetable frittata gets me out of the doghouse.* "Allow me," he offered, pulling out Jennifer's chair.

"Thank you." She immediately noted breakfast included many of her favorite foods. *What time did he get up?* Either way, the thought was endearing.

"Since we have until noon before we need to head back, would you like to go riding?" Josh offered.

"That'd be fine. It'd give us a chance to talk about last night. Or maybe we should talk beforehand."

"I'd hoped cooking you breakfast would show you how sorry I am."

"Josh, I know you're sorry, but sometimes showing me how sorry you are isn't enough," Jennifer said, shielding her heart from his hurt expression.

"What do I need to say to make things right?"

"You can start by explaining why you left our bed in the middle of the night to go drinking with Merlin without saying anything to me?"

"I needed to talk to him. I didn't plan on staying, but he was in a talkative mood, and once he opened a bottle of gin, one glass led to another. I guess time got away from me."

"What did you talk about?"

"Protector stuff," Josh said vaguely. "We talked about his relationship with Gisabella and all they'd gone through to be together."

"Did you talk about us?" Jennifer dug deeper.

"Kind of." He studied the food in front of him.

"Tell me!" she demanded when Josh avoided making eye contact.

"I told him how much I love you and how I'd do anything to make you happy. Baby, I want you to know, no matter what the future holds,

I'll never leave you. Other than that, there's nothing more to tell you." Josh donned a perfect poker face, despite his guilty conscience.

"I take it this was all spawned by our conversation about Alexander?"

"Please eat your breakfast before it gets cold." It was clear by the look on his wife's face, she wasn't pleased by his attempt to change the subject. "Look, I'm sorry I went out last drinking last night without at least giving you a heads up, but as much as I'd like to tell you more, my hands are tied. Just know our marriage is forever, and there's no way I'll ever leave your side."

"Okay." *Maybe I can broach the subject at a later date.* "I still can't believe how drunk you got."

"I was somewhat coherent until Gisabella showed up! Not funny, Jennifer," Josh shot back when she started laughing at his expense.

"Hey, she's your friend!"

"What do you say we finish this conversation in bed so I can show you how sorry I really am?" He stood and held out his hand.

"Not fair, Mr. Smith—you know I love sex with you too much to resist your sexy temptations. To top it off, you're only solid for a few more hours."

"Please, baby, it's the only way I'll know for sure that you've forgiven me."

"Okay, but just so you know, you're currently only eighty-seven percent forgiven." She bit down on her lip, trying to squelch her rising smile. "You can work off the other thirteen percent in bed!"

She placed her napkin on the table and accepted his hand, but Josh held up a finger, silencing her from saying another word. *Now what?* she cringed.

"Sorry, Jennifer, that was Gisabella. Your grandma demanded I go to her house if I want any hope of remaining your protector."

"What? She can't do that!" Jennifer's eyes darkened, and her pupils dilated as she hopelessly watched her husband's expression change, catching just enough scent of anxiousness to elevate her apprehension.

"I'm afraid she could. Can I take a raincheck on that thirteen percent I owe you?" Josh asked, tossing his napkin on the table.

"I really wanted that thirteen percent and *more*," Jennifer groaned in frustration.

"For the record, I planned on giving you a hundred percent of pure pleasure. Sorry, baby, but I'd better get out of here before she transports me." He planted a kiss on Jennifer's lips and transported himself to Gisabella's before his boss did it for him.

When Josh reappeared, he did so in front of Gisabella and Merlin, who were seated at a boardroom-style table. The first thing he noticed was there were no extra chairs, forcing him to remain standing. That was a sign of trouble to come.

"I summoned you here this morning with the intention of stripping you of all your protector abilities," Gisabella spoke in a grave tone, letting Josh know the severity of the situation. "You can thank Merlin for saving your ass, your job, and for allowing your marriage to Jennifer to remain intact."

Josh's Adam's apple bobbed rapidly several times before he was able to regain control of his nerves. A glance in Merlin's direction made it clear the older wizard hadn't faired too well last night, either. In fact, Merlin looked paler than the face looking back at Josh this morning in the mirror.

"What in the universe possessed you to tell Jennifer about her life-path marriage?! Not only have you put me in an awkward position, but I'm no longer sure I can trust you with my granddaughter's life, never mind her training." Gisabella folded her hands on the table and straightened her spine. "If not for the undying love you have for her and the knowledge you carry of who Jennifer is to become, I'd kick you to the curb!"

Josh tried to steady his heartbeat while doing his best to remain calm as he emptied all comeback thoughts from his mind. It didn't take a brain surgeon to figure out how one wrong word at this moment would result in serious ramifications.

"I can't believe what an uncompromising position you've forced me into. Even though we've been the closest of friends for centuries, you've given me no choice. If Jennifer were to recall your words in the future, we could all be held accountable. If not for you getting yourself so inebriated, this would've never happened!" Gisabella picked up the gavel in front of her and twirled it between her thumb and four fingers, letting the seriousness of the situation sink in. "I cannot let your actions go unpunished. What kind of a high priestess would I be if I didn't enforce some kind of consequence for breaking protocol?"

Typical—Gisabella wants her pound of flesh, Josh internalized. "I agree, Your Excellency." *Satisfied? Go ahead and tell me I must give up drinking, or whatever other stupid penance you believe will make me regret confessing to Jennifer.*

"Joshua! Are you listening to me?!" Gisabella shouted.

"Yes, Your Excellency." *Geez, someone didn't get laid last night.* A glimmer in Merlin's eye let him know the wizard had tapped into his snarky thoughts. Flitting his eyes back to Gisabella, Josh was glad to see she hadn't read his comment.

"For Jennifer's sake, it pains me to take back the offer of the trip to Italy and the chance for the two of you to experience a week in the same dimension—"

Josh's change in stance upon the one thing he wanted most of all being taken away proved her number one protector had been successfully chastised.

"With Jennifer's life-path husband in the picture, you must start slowly backing away from her. Above all, you must consult the protector manual and begin following all procedures to start guiding your visionary charge toward her future husband. Trust me, it'll make it easier on Jennifer if you start easing your affections away now, instead of all at once. It'll be less of a shock for her." She briefly closed her eyes, blocking out the devastated look in Josh's eyes. "Do you have any questions?"

"Not at this time," Josh responded. *Please let me leave before I do something stupid like drop to my knees and beg Gisabella to reduce my penance. Not that it'd make any difference in the outcome; in fact, I'd probably incur more penalties, or worse, lose Jennifer much sooner than anticipated.*

"Jennifer's due back home soon, so you'd better get going. I suggest you work on your poker face before she sees you looking like that!" Gisabella berated while rising to her feet holding out her ring-adorned hand.

Great, she wants more flesh! Josh blocked his thoughts as he walked forward, bowing and kissing her ring before transporting himself back to their honeymoon house.

"I knew you were going to call Josh out, but did you have to throw the entire book at him?" Merlin asked with disgust in his tone.

"You're lucky I didn't do the same to you!" Gisabella chastised, unable to hide the pain in her eyes. "If I let him get away with what he did, when the time comes, it will only be harder for him to give Jennifer up."

"What about Italy? I thought they needed to go to Italy in the same dimension before Jennifer marries someone else?"

"We'll just have to come up with another plan." Gisabella flashed her lover a frosty glare.

"Is that before or after she falls in love with her future fiancé?" Merlin rose. "I'm heading home."

"Merlin, wait! I could've thrown the entire book at him, but I didn't." She watched Merlin fade away, leaving her alone with her self-loathing thoughts. *Merlin knows it's my job to keep everyone in line no matter how much it hurts.*

Merlin appeared in his cottage and threw a ball of fire into the fireplace, partly out of anger and partly for warmth. His nerves were rattled, and the bottle of unopened gin was looking a whole lot better than it had last night after Gisabella showed up.

I thought I knew the woman I loved, but after the way she cut Josh to the core like some cold, heartless ruler, it's only a matter of time before she might try and do the same to me. All in the name of power! That's the thing about power—it's a drug that addicts even the nicest of people, pushing and driving them harder, just so they can stay at the top. Outsmarting everyone is the name of the game, and Gisabella sure outsmarted me. Would her feelings for me remain the same if I were no longer of use to her?

Merlin headed to the liquor cabinet and pulled out the gin. *How could she have taken so much away from Josh? All he did was confess his feel-*

ings of love and voice what he was being forced to comply with per Gisabella: to push Jennifer into another man's arms.

Merlin elevated himself to the highest shelf and reached behind a row of leather bound tomes to pull out Jennifer and Alexander's folders. *I think it's time I had another look at Jennifer's future husband. If I remember correctly, he's a little too perfect for her to suit my taste. After all, Josh and I need to stick together if we have any hope of surviving these high priestess women.*

Once seated at the table with a glass of gin, Merlin took a few gulps before he began reexamining the folders in front of him. He only made it a few pages into Jennifer's future husband before he slammed the file shut. *I'll be damned if I put Josh through the same pain I had to endure!* Tipping back his glass, he finished the contents and threw the glass into the fireplace, shattering the empty room's silence.

I love you, but not so deeply to sit back and watch you destroy Josh and Jennifer's future! What can Gisabella do to me afterwards that could be worse than being her lovesick puppet? As Josh would say—fuck that!

Merlin transported to the Hall of Records, where he spent the next three hours searching through countless life-paths until he found a willing pawn to right the wrong he'd been delivered thousands of centuries ago. Once Merlin found what he was looking for, he returned to his cottage.

An hour later, once satisfied with the changes he'd made, Merlin closed all three life-path folders and put his head in his hands.

"God, please forgive me for what I'm about to do," he prayed out loud. "When you spared Jennifer's life, we all thought it was because of Josh's prayers—only now I believe you had a far greater purpose in mind than the plans Gisabella and I made for Jennifer's future. I hope you understand why I cannot let destiny risk Jennifer and Josh's happily ever after. They must stay united! It's the only way to make sure Jennifer will lead Josh to the one weapon powerful enough to prevent the destruction of every dimension but one.

"I know in my heart you sent Josh to us because he's the only warrior strong enough to stop what you do not wish to happen—the demise of all other souls in existence except those living in the only foretold dimension that will remain standing. With Jennifer by his side, Josh will do your bidding and be victorious! Together they will birth the greatest and most compassionate leader any of us have ever seen. Their child will be the one who'll carry on your wish, succeeding where all others have failed you, and uniting every soul for the greater good of all."

Merlin looked down at the folders on the table and glanced skyward. "I only hope by changing these two men's life-paths, you'll find it in your heart to watch over Josh and Jennifer once I'm gone."

Grabbing the bottle of gin, Merlin sagged into the chair closest to the fire. *Here's to Josh and Jennifer, may you avoid the mistakes Gisabella and I have made, and choose your love for each other first!*

CHAPTER TWENTY

"I hope Josh comes back soon." Jennifer glanced out the front window expectantly.

~I hope he comes back, period!~ Talos swished his tail back and forth. ~There's no way I'm transporting with you again!~

"Talos! Shame on you! I thought you were my friend."

~Friend or no friend, you almost killed us both!~ Talos rubbed his head against Jennifer. ~I'm sure glad you didn't.~

"Oh, Talos, I'm glad too. It'd have been different if I would've joined Josh in heaven, but I shudder to think how I could've lost him forever. And you too—of course," she quickly added when she saw the hurt in his eyes.

They were both peering out the window when a voice from behind caused them each to jump.

"What are you two looking at?" Josh asked, doing his best to cover up his anger with Gisabella. The last thing he wanted was for Jennifer to notice anything was wrong.

"We were worried you wouldn't be back in time." Jennifer ran over and was pulled into a hug.

~I was telling Jennifer how I refused to transport alone with her ever again,~ Talos spoke up.

"You better put all thoughts of doing such a thing out of your head! Got that, Jennifer?!" Josh growled.

"Thanks a lot, Talos," she admonished before turning back to Josh. "For the record, I had no intention of leaving here without you."

"Good, because I promise you wouldn't like my reaction!" Josh released his hold and walked away. "We need to leave soon. I have a couple of things to take care of before we head back." Without saying another word, Josh stomped off in the direction of his study.

What was that all about? Jennifer glared before she ran upstairs to pack a few things to bring home. Once she grabbed her riding boots and a few personal belongings, Jennifer eyed the bookcases in the corner. *I wonder if Josh received another lecture about my training—rather, my lack of abilities?* With that thought in mind she pulled out the overnight bag she'd found on the shelf in her closet and hurried over to the high priestess books. Once she selected a bunch that didn't look too dull, she stuck them in the bag. Eyeing the High Priestess manual, Jennifer opened the cover and read the instructions on how to reduce it in size.

She ignored the warning not to remove the manual from Gisabella's realm that zip-lined through her mind so fast, it hardly made an impression. Using her most authoritarian voice, Jennifer said the words, tapped the cover three times and stood back, fingers crossed. *It worked!* She picked up the manual, now the size of a quarter, and slipped it into the pocket of her jeans before zipping the bag packed with books.

Once downstairs, she left her bags and went in search of Josh, only to discover the door to the study was closed. She knocked timidly—she'd never had to deal with the door being shut until today.

"What is it?" Josh called, slamming the desk drawer closed.

"May I come in?" *Why do I sound so meek?*

"Sure." Josh steepled his hands and tried his best to calm his aura, but he was too far gone. It didn't help his mood when Jennifer slowly opened the door as if she were afraid of him.

"I'm ready to go whenever you are."

"Fine. Why don't you make sure that cat of yours is all set." *Please give me a few more minutes to compose myself.* Josh swallowed. He would've been better off unblocking his thoughts because, instead of leaving,

Jennifer walked over and climbed into his lap, where she curled up with her lips pressed against the base of his neck.

"I take it your meeting didn't go so well." She reached up and brushed back his hair, running her fingers through the thick waves.

"Yeah." It was all Josh could choke out before he claimed Jennifer's mouth as if it would be the last time she was his. Her freshly showered scent was intoxicating, and before he could stop himself, his hands found their way under her shirt to all but tear off her bra. A moan escaped his lips when his fingertips found her nipples, twisting and squeezing them as Jennifer writhed on his lap, driving him to the brink of desperation. He undid her jeans with his other hand, yanked the zipper down, and with her help, she was out of them in no time.

"Please," Jennifer begged, using her hands to undo Josh's jeans and free his manhood. Once freed, she grasped his stiffened length and began moving her hand up and down, over and over until her man cried out for her to stop.

"Not like this! I need to feel all of you," Josh growled, then he stood, taking Jennifer with him, and laid her out on the desk. "If you don't want this, you better say so now because once I enter you, I'm not stopping. Got that, princess?!" His words came out harsher than he intended, but the flames of his desire were reflected in Jennifer's eyes.

"Don't you dare call me princess, not if you want to fuck me as hard as I need to be fucked."

"Damn—you're hotter than any woman I've ever known." Josh spread her creamy thighs wide and stroked her wetness before he slammed inside of her. He couldn't help but quirk his lips at how Jennifer cried out from his sudden move. Trying not to be a complete asshole, he stilled for moment before he began his harsh rhythm. To his wife's credit, she managed to keep up with him, at times digging her nails into his arms while encouraging him to go deeper, harder and faster. She was all over him like a rash, and he was loving every minute.

Fuck Gisabella's rules, Josh thought just before he gave in to his orgasm and came with a vengeance as Jennifer joined him. It was when he looked into her eyes that he felt ill. *What have I done?! How will I ever be able to pull away if I can't even keep from fucking her for only one hour?*

The look in Jennifer's eyes reflected Josh's confusion, seeming to question what just happened.

"We'd better get going before someone misses you," Josh said, handing her a wad of tissues while he used a couple on himself. "You have everything you need?" He took her nod as a yes and finished straightening his clothes before helping her stand and do the same. He ignored Jennifer's swollen lips and did his best to smooth her disheveled hair while she held on to his arms for support. He couldn't help but notice how shaky she was, and if not for the time constraint, he may have given her a lavender bath, or at the very least, used Reiki to calm her surely sore muscles and legs.

"My stuff is packed." Jennifer dashed away her tears before Josh noticed. *Why is he acting so cold or like he's disgusted with me? What happened to Prince Charming?*

"Come, we'd better get going," Josh said, grabbing hold of Jennifer's hand just when the doorbell sounded. "What the fuck now?!"

The moment Gisabella saw the condition of Jennifer's lips and hair, she shot Josh a bolt of energy that nearly toppled him to his knees.

"I came to say goodbye to Jennifer," Gisabella said warmly.

"Goodbye, Grandmamma." Jennifer hugged Gisabella.

~You better make sure Jennifer takes a shower before anyone else hugs her,~ Gisabella messaged. ~She reeks of sex! To think I came over here because I felt badly for the way I treated you.~

~It won't happen again,~ Josh messaged.

~Wanna bet?~ Gisabella challenged.

"We must be going," Josh said, failing to hide the frostiness in his voice. ~Message me the terms and stakes, and I'll let you know.~

Jennifer looked between the two, who, at the moment, looked more like arch enemies than friends. The atmosphere was filled with such a mixture of energies, Jennifer was finding it hard to breathe.

"Thanks, Grandmamma, see you soon." Jennifer pointed to her heavy bag, forcing Josh to step away before things escalated between Gisabella and him worse than they already seemed to be.

Without a word, Josh grabbed the bag, and once Talos leaned against him, he lowered his mouth and thrust his tongue into Jennifer's mouth in an act of defiance as his boss looked on.

The moment they arrived in their bedroom at the lake house, Jennifer stepped out of his energy field. "What the hell was that all about?"

-First of all, you'd better use messaging so we don't end up in deeper trouble. Secondly, that was for Gisabella's benefit.-

-What's gotten into you? First you give me an amazing romantic evening followed by epic lovemaking, only to disappear the next morning. Then you come home drunk out of your gourd and throw up, only to plead for my mercy before you run to Gisabella's side the minute she commands! That's it, isn't it? What did Gisabella do to you at the meeting?-

-Nothing.- Josh managed to hold on to one of the best poker faces of his life.

-I don't believe you.-

-Well, it's the truth.- He stood firm.

-How you can stand there lying to my face is beyond me. Something changed the night you went to see Merlin, and I demand to know the truth.-

-Truth is, you and I had an amazing evening, and I couldn't handle it.- Josh turned away to glance out the window until he was able to continue. -My love for you is beyond anything I've ever experienced. So much so, I'm afraid if I don't get my feelings for you under control, I'll miss something stupid and fail to protect you. Damn it, Jennifer! Don't you know what you've done to me?-

-Done to you? Look what you've done to me. You loved me when I felt like a silly schoolgirl. Taught me everything I know about heaven, gemstones, spirit protectors and energy battles. Most of all, you've been by my side every step of the way, encouraging me to succeed, and you've given me the most intoxicating pleasure I shall ever know.- She reached out to touch Josh, but his translucent state made it impossible. He'd remain that way until the next full moon unless she asked him to densify his energy. She kept silent.

-You have to go to work in a few hours, so why don't you take advantage of this time to catch up on the sleep you missed?-

-You're not going to tell me what happened at Gisabella's, are you?-

-Even if I were able to tell you, I wouldn't.-

~I see.~ *It must be bad! Now what? Do I tell him off and walk away, or try to work it out in bed?*

~I have to do a search of the perimeter to make sure no one followed us. If you want to lie down for a while, I'll wake you when it's time to get ready.~

He transported before Jennifer could respond, leaving her alone with Talos, unsure where she stood. *I wish I could ask Elizabeth what to do, or Sarah. My sister has had a wealth of dating and marriage experience; surely she'd be able to give me some advice.* The realization she had no one to talk to about being married or even dating hit home. As far as everyone knew, she hadn't dated other than the one time Josh had showed up at Sarah and Dave's wedding.

She reached down and unzipped the tote bag full of books. *Maybe I was correct, and Josh got chewed out because of how far behind I am with my reading? They both have made it clear on numerous occasions how I must study. If that's the case, I can easily remedy the situation. Either way, it can't hurt.* After placing the quarter-sized High Priestess manual in a safe place, she selected a book and curled up in bed, trying not to give in and message Josh.

CHAPTER TWENTY-ONE

*J*osh returned to find Jennifer asleep with an open book resting on her chest. Upon closer examination, it proved to be one of the books on her required reading list. *That must be why her travel bag weighed so much!*

He glanced down at the book to discover she was in the middle of a chapter on how to read auras. *Of all times for her to develop that gift! Trying to maintain a happy aura while keeping my facial expressions in check—God help me!* He glanced at the other books and shook his head. *You mean all I had to do was tell her* not *to study?!*

A glance at his multidimensional watch showed it was time to awaken his wife. His usual wakeup call method would have been to stir her energetically, but after being such a jerk lately, he opted to kiss her forehead instead.

~It's time to wake up, baby.~ The last word caught in his heart. *I've been such an asshole! It's not Jennifer's fault—she has no clue she's going to betray me. Like Merlin said, I need to man up. Boy does that hit home. I need to tell Gisabella the bet's off!*

~What time is it?~ Jennifer squinted through swollen eyes.

~You only have enough time for a quick shower. Come on, sleepyhead, rise and shine.- Josh tried to play the part of Mr. Cool, but it came across like Mr. Scared-of-Losing-You Jackass.

-Alright.- Jennifer folded the page she was reading and closed the book, all the while avoiding Josh's expression.

Once dressed, she led the way to the car, and together with Josh, they began their excruciatingly silent ride to the train station. Their silence continued until they'd reached the art gallery.

-Jennifer, I...,- Josh began, but he was shut down.

-Please don't do this now. You had the entire ride here to say something, and you choose now? I have to go.- Jennifer opened the door and slipped inside.

I must be in hell! Fucking Gisabella has really messed things up for us! Josh stared through the glass door until Alexander greeted Jennifer with a kiss on her cheek. *Now I know for sure I'm in purgatory! I must get Gisabella to reconsider my penance!*

"What's wrong, Jennifer?" Alexander greeted with an affectionate kiss on the cheek. "You look so sad, *ma cherie*."

"I'm fine; it was just some nightmare I had last night." *Not that my morning or the entire ride here was any better.*

"Please tell me you like pizza because someone mentioned there's a place people swear transports them to Italy."

"Name me one college student who doesn't like pizza?" Jennifer grinned. *Why can't someone else be in as happy of a mood as Alexander?*

"Then it's all set—a pizza date with my beautiful friend."

"I better get to work," Jennifer said to Alexander before she headed off in a different direction. *It's not a date—Alexander is just being friendly. I'm not cheating on my husband, who seems to be doing his best to sabotage our marriage. This is so messed up!*

Great—Alexander thinks he has a date *with my wife. Who am I kidding? My first date with Jennifer was pizza while we set up the Christmas tree. I'd give anything to relive that moment with her.* It took effort, but Josh managed to restrain the urge to message Jennifer. After all, he owed her an apology, and, until doing so, he didn't think she'd care how much he wanted to curl up and watch television, run alongside her, or make love. *How am I ever going to make love to her knowing soon she'll belong to Alexander?*

Gisabella mentioned Jennifer could choose me as her lover. Could I ever be happy as my wife's spirit lover? The question is, would Jennifer even consider that option? Now that he had time to calm down, he realized being a part of Jennifer's life, no matter how small, was better than nothing at all.

-Gisabella, it doesn't matter what the wager, all bets are off.- *Step one completed,* Josh thought with satisfaction.

-What a shame, Josh, here I was prepared to offer you the trip to Italy in exchange.-

Exchange for what? No sex? My help in pushing my wife into another man's embrace? Talk about typical Gisabella nonsense! After a little while of not answering his boss, Josh received another message.

-Did you not get my message? A trip to Italy with Jennifer—both of you solid the entire time. Come now, even you can give up sex for a few months.-

I'm sure there's some sort of catch tied to her offer. -I'll agree not to hold Jennifer back from her destiny with Alexander, but there was nothing in the protector manual about abstaining from having sex with *my wife.*-

-How are the two love birds doing?- Gisabella taunted.

-Gisabella, you must have better things to do than ruin what little is left of our friendship. I'm sure you can find some other poor soul to talk to besides me. For the record, you've already done enough damage when you caused Jennifer to transport on her own. If not for your words, she'd have never left me.-

-But you're so much more fun to taunt.-

-Goodbye, Gisabella.-

-Okay, but—promise you'll try to keep it in your pants as much as you can. The less intimate you are with Jennifer, the easier it'll be on her soul and heart.-

-Fine—I promise to try and ease away for Jennifer's sake. Is that what Merlin did for you? Made it easier by disappearing from you and your baby's life?- He didn't have to wait but a heartbeat for a response.

-Merlin did the *right* thing in the end, and while it was rough on me, it was for the best. Now we're—um—Merlin and I are working things out.~

The pauses in Gisabella's message spoke volumes about how she and Merlin were really doing. ~Jennifer's leaving the building for lunch, so we'll have to continue this conversation another time.~ *If you and Merlin are doing so well, why don't you bug him for a change?* Josh kept his retort in his thoughts, hoping to avoid another fight.

An hour later, after watching his wife seated next to Alexander in a booth, laughing and smiling, Josh had all he could stand. *I need to make up with Jennifer before she runs off with Alexander sooner than her destiny calls for!*

With plans to talk to her later that night, Josh spent the remainder of the afternoon watching Alexander flirting with his wife. When it was time to walk Jennifer through the train station, Josh calmed his energy, hoping to enjoy their ride home together.

Jennifer exited the limo to find Josh waiting for her at the curb. *Why does seeing Josh still give me butterflies, even when I'm mad at him?*

~Did you have a good day, baby?~ *Of course she did—with Alexander!* Squelching his unwanted thoughts, Josh reached for Jennifer's hand and fell into step.

~Work and lunch were very nice, thank you,~ Jennifer messaged back, unable to hide the smile that formed when she glanced at Josh's energized hand holding hers.

~Sounds like your parents are attending a party tonight. What do you say to a night out? We could go to the movies if you'd like.~

~Don't get me wrong, I appreciate your offer, but I have school tomorrow, and if you recall, I didn't get much sleep while we were away.~

~Do you want to get a bite to eat on the drive home?~

~It'll be after nine by then. If it's all the same to you, I'd like to just go to bed.~ *To sleep!* She made sure to void her thoughts of all things romantic.

~Okay. There's a seat halfway down on the right.~ Josh pointed, but when Jennifer breezed by it to select a middle seat between an older lady and a much younger man closer to her own age than himself, Josh knew he'd been thrown into the doghouse. *Well played, Jennifer! Well played indeed!*

The moment Jennifer arrived home, she unlocked the door and let herself in before she turned to Josh. ~I'm not sure where you're sleeping tonight, but after how chilly you were to me, I'd rather be alone.~ She steeled herself against his look of hurt.

~Jennifer, please, we need to talk.~

~We can talk tomorrow after school. Hopefully by then, I'll have a clear head and won't feel so emotional.~

~Can I stay on the couch, or are you kicking me outside?~

I'd kind of planned on crying myself to sleep, and you being in the room doesn't fit the plan. Jennifer changed her mind upon seeing Josh's eyes, now a muddied, olive color she'd never seen before. ~Fine, you can sleep on the couch in our bedroom, but Talos will be sleeping next to me.~

Nothing like rubbing fur in my face! ~Thank you, I'd feel better sticking close to your side—you know, in case you need me.~

Jennifer led the way upstairs and carried her nightgown with her into the bathroom. A moment later, she climbed into bed and called for Talos to join her.

~I told you someday I'd be in Jennifer's bed, and you'd be sleeping on the couch. I must be psychic, eh, Josh?~ Talos purred, rubbing in his elevated status over the well-known protector.

~If I were you, cat, I'd watch out! If not for Jennifer, you'd be outside hunting mice for your dinner.~

~You have that all wrong—I'd be leading the life of luxury while you...~

"If the two of you don't stop—I'll throw you both outside, then you can hunt mice together!"

Jennifer was able to read my blocked messages? That's new! Josh surmised it must have been due to the energy behind his messages that enabled Jennifer to pick up on his conversation with Talos. As tempted as he was to toss a pillow at the domestic-looking cat, he tucked it behind his head and propped his knees up to better fit on the couch. *Stupid cat better watch his step!*

The moment the sun came up, Josh greeted Jennifer with breakfast that he managed to cook before her parents had gotten out of bed.

~Thank you. Aren't you having anything?~ Jennifer ran her fingertips over Josh's five o'clock shadow. ~I like this.~

~I love your touch.~ Josh caressed Jennifer's hand, then brought it to his lips. ~I've been such a jerk lately. Eat your breakfast, baby—we'll talk later after your classes.~

~Please join me; I don't want to eat alone.~ Jennifer patted the mattress next to her, causing Talos to scurry off the bed. When Josh took his place, she held up a piece of toast and watched as Josh took its duplicate into his dimension. ~It's funny how breakfast for one serves both of our dimensions.~

~That it is.~ Josh took a bite of toast and made his energy dense enough so Jennifer could feel him next to her.

CHAPTER TWENTY-TWO

After meditating with the intention of creating a backup plan, Gisabella summoned Lawrence. He was the first step needed to insure some sort of safety net, just in case things were to blow up in her face. Most of all, she needed a way to keep Josh in line and a way to ensure Jennifer would go through with her life-path marriage. *I think a little motivation is in order.* The threat of Lawrence had worked to her benefit once before, so why not use him again?

She quickly made some tea and readied a few scones from the bakery to serve her guest before she transported Lawrence to her private domain. Unlike her business meetings with Josh, she didn't relish sitting down with Lawrence. He was too stiff and way too formal for her taste, and the quicker it was over and he was out of her house, the better. With that thought, she transported the protector to stand before her.

"Hello, Lawrence," Gisabella greeted with an indulgent smile. "Please join me for some tea and scones while we talk."

"Thank you for your kind gesture, Your Excellency," Lawrence replied, looking surprised by the elder's informality. He quickly recovered his facial expression and bowed to kiss the high priestess's ring.

Gisabella studied the strong protector before her. At first glance,

SHATTERED DESTINIES

Lawrence seemed older and wiser than the last time she'd seen him. He still looked young for his afterlife and selected age, and Gisabella surmised it was his blond hair and loose, tousled curls that made him youthful-looking. He was tall, lean, and muscular, with the most disarming Mediterranean-blue eyes she'd ever seen. She could only imagine that his eyes plus his blond and boyish good looks had helped to charm many a woman into his bed. That, and the fact he looked like the Greek god Apollo—a name Josh had taken to calling Lawrence, who seemed to get under her top protector's skin.

If ever looks were deceiving, it'd be in this case. Lawrence had been known to use his angelic looks to disarm his opponents into believing he was too pretty to own any serious fighting skills. Often his opponents believed the protector had little more than his playful magic to rely on until the Apollo lookalike wielded his powerful, sword-toting arm and left their heads on the ground, looking up at him.

Gisabella turned her attention back toward her guest, who looked to be waiting for permission to sit. One thing the man had was impeccable manners. Now she hoped, when the time came, Lawrence would be capable of handling everything she'd ask of him in the future, though that would come much later. Today's meeting was only a precautionary measure.

"Please sit down and join me." Gisabella poured them each a cup of tea and passed the sugar his way. He declined the cream. "Why don't you try one of my favorite baked scones with some honey butter?"

"Thank you, Your Excellency," Lawrence's deceivingly tender voice responded with well-mannered, proper etiquette.

If we are going to get anywhere, I need to do something about Lawrence's excessive manners before I go out of my mind! Maybe this was the reason she didn't have the best feeling about him. Then Gisabella recalled the time the lower level protector had taken it upon himself to teach one of his charges how to transport, breaking one of the most basic rules. She wasn't thrilled when protectors transported their charges—but even then, it was usually done for a valid reason. In Lawrence's case, he'd taught his charge to transport on his own! He was lucky she hadn't banished him on the spot! Then again, Jennifer had read and transported herself, and look how badly that almost ended. *Lucky for Josh, he hadn't been the one to teach my granddaughter to transport!* Either way, Lawrence proved he wasn't afraid of breaking a rule or two, which could work in her favor if the need to do so arrived.

"Lawrence, if we're going to work together, it'd be best if you relax. When you're in my home, there's no need to stand on ceremony." She hoped her frankness helped get her point across.

"I understand. Thank you, Your Excellency."

Gisabella inwardly grimaced at Lawrence's unchanged formality. "Lawrence, I'd prefer you call me Gisabella during our meetings."

"Yes, ma'am, I'm sorry—I mean—yes, Gisabella," he stammered.

"Good. I'm sure you're aware of Sarnia's departure from my elite protector army. You may or may not have heard the reasoning behind my decision, but rest assured, even though it was a personal matter, I had no other choice than to take action."

"Yes, Gisabella." Lawrence's bland expression didn't give anything away.

"In light of Sarnia's position remaining open for too long, I've decided it's time to bring in someone who possesses fighting skills worthy of Josh's level. Seeing as though there is no one in my entire elite squad who comes close to his abilities, I'm considering you for the position."

She sat back and sipped her tea, playing close attention to Lawrence's actions. She was glad when he didn't jump at the chance to win her over by boasting about all his successes or selling his endless skills; instead, he leaned back and crossed his leg so his ankle rested on his other knee. Even better—his thoughts were like an impenetrable fortress. *I think Lawrence could give Josh a run for his money!*

"I see, Gisabella," the Apollo lookalike replied, taking another sip before continuing, "I'm honored to be under consideration. Surely, you have a vast amount of candidates who are well suited and remain in better standing with the Council than me."

"If chosen, your standing will, of course, be elevated greatly, second only to Joshua, and you'd be starting off with a clean slate. I'd see to it that your infraction from the past is erased, and you'll have a chance to prove yourself worthy of being the best."

"Are you implying a promotion to your top protector position is a possibility?"

"I guess you can say anything's possible, but I wouldn't count on it for centuries to come." *If Lawrence turns out to be as good as I hope, it could happen the day Jennifer's life on earth is finished.*

"Of course not, Your Excellency."

"As my second highest protector, I'd expect your complete devotion and loyalty to me, not necessarily to my position. I say this so you understand if anything were to happen to either overthrow or replace me, I'd expect your allegiance."

"Yes, Your Excellency, I'd vow to stand by your side until the end of time." Lawrence bowed his head in respect.

"If you'd be so kind to wait here, I'll fetch your uniform. Since you're currently in between assignments, I expect you to attend the next elite protector meeting, where I will make the announcement welcoming you as my second highest protector." When Gisabella rose, Lawrence stood out of respect. *Maybe he can teach my grandson-in-law some manners!*

Gisabella returned with a garment bag containing an identical uniform to the one Josh had worn on his date with Jennifer. "I believe this will fit you well. I'll message you with the meeting details. Be prepared for a backlash when your appointment is announced. I fear there'll be many who had their eye on Sarnia's position, but I think your skills will speak for themselves as time goes on."

She was pleased by Lawrence's impeccable thoughts and the strong blocking he'd put in place the moment he'd arrived. In addition, he had not let his guard down, which was something she admired in her protectors. It was something her number one protector had become a little lackadaisical in doing.

"Thank you, Gisabella. I've been hoping for an opportunity to make up for my past indiscretion and a chance to prove my worthiness to you and the Council. I solemnly swear my allegiance to you directly, and if there comes a time where I must choose between the Council and you, on my word of honor, I will protect you until my last breath."

Though she found him a bit dramatic, Gisabella smiled warmly. "I'm grateful to have you on board, Lawrence," she replied with a slight bow of her head—meanwhile, on the inside, she was jumping up and down, doing a happy dance while cheering loudly in her head. She knew Lawrence was the only protector other than Josh who'd be capable of handling Jennifer's protection if needed. *I think it could be time to begin considering protection for my number one protector.* Gisabella bit back a secretive smile, matching her newest, second highest protector in giving nothing away.

After bidding farewell, she transported Lawrence back to his apartment before she began to dance around her kitchen, pulling out baking pans and ingredients for a creation. *Now who can I get to try it when I'm done?*

By Jennifer's last class, she found herself only partially listening to Professor Martin's lecture on Pavlov's dog and how, in theory, the same principles could be used in marketing. Mostly, she kept checking the clock, wondering if it was broken. Half-tempted to retrieve the messaging pen Josh had given her the Christmas before they were married, she reconsidered, not wanting to start up a conversation with him in the middle of class.

When it came time to drive home, the ride was disturbingly quiet and way too calm, giving Jennifer an indication of the storm that was sure to follow. She tried to obey every traffic law in existence, not wishing to make things between them worse than they already felt. Jennifer turned the sports car into the driveway and shut off the engine before she turned to Josh and yelped. "Nothing like scaring me to death!" Her heart rate and breathing accelerated now that he'd become solid. "Tonight's a full moon?" *How did I lose track of such important information?!*

"Explains why you jumped in surprise!" Josh failed to hide his amusement. "Full moons do have certain advantages." He reached for Jennifer's hand and studied her palm, tracing her lifeline with his thumb. *What the hell happened to Jennifer's lifeline? Maybe it reflects the lesser number of years left on earth Gisabella mentioned?* He blocked his thoughts, vowing to study it more closely that night when she was asleep.

"What's wrong?" Jennifer spied his perplexed expression.

"You have a new wrinkle, but it's so small it hardly seems worth mentioning." *Talk about a lame cover-up!*

"What are you talking about? I don't have any wrinkles on my hands, or anywhere else." She flashed him a dirty look, then snatched her hand away and exited her sports car, which seemed too small for the conversation they needed to have. "We should have our talk outside." *That's one way to refrain from jumping his bones. Ugh! Of all days for Josh to be solid. Great—now he's grinning like a fool.* "How dare you read my thoughts!"

"Don't blame me! As my visionary charge, every single one of your thoughts is fair game." Josh took a seat in the grass and invited Jennifer to do the same.

"You're not in a position to be funny." Jennifer knelt down.

"You're right, baby—I owe you so many apologies after the way I've behaved. Go ahead and call me an idiot for taking my frustrations with Gisabella out on you. It's not your fault your grandma's a controlling woman with a bug up her skirt!"

"Josh!"

"Sorry." He squirmed.

"Look, I forgave you for getting drunk and almost throwing up on me. Though I'm not happy with the way you disappeared in the middle of the night, none of that matters as much as your coolness toward me after your meeting with my grandma." Jennifer picked a blade of grass and pretended to study it closely.

"Please tell me this has nothing to do with—um—fucking me on your desk?" She tossed the blade of grass aside before glancing up to see Josh's apprehensive expression. "You know, if I were keeping score, I'd have to rate desk sex—*freakin hot!* Not for nothing, but I never thought anything could be so rough and incredible at the same time. Not that I want that all the time—maybe once a month. I just don't understand why you shut me out afterwards?"

"For the record, I thought that was hot too, but the fact I used sex to calm my foul mood was wrong." A movement out of the corner of his eye caused Josh to whip his head around to find Talos sauntering toward the front door and lying down in a small patch of sun. He turned his eyes back to Jennifer and exhaled. "Sorry, that oversized cat interrupted me."

"Doesn't matter, but you do owe Gisabella an apology for the way you behaved. Just to be clear, slamming your tongue down my throat because you're angry is unacceptable!"

"I deeply regret doing that to you—and Gisabella. I don't know what came over me." *Other than your grandma taking away our trip to Italy! Oh yeah, and losing you to Alexander years sooner than agreed upon.*

"You're not off the hook yet. I need you to explain why I get the feeling something's changed after our date night. Did I do something wrong?"

"Baby, no, you didn't do anything wrong." Josh caressed Jennifer's face with his fingertips, then, no longer able to hold back, he brushed his lips against hers. "Look, when I almost lost you—I mean, the thought of letting you go..." his voice trailed off, unable to handle the painful memories. He absentmindedly tucked Jennifer's hair behind her ear while trying to corral his emotions. "That was the worst day of my life."

"That was a few years ago, and you didn't lose me; I'm right here." Jennifer placed her hand over Josh's heart. "Our hearts still beat as one and always will, no matter what the future holds. Josh, I have no interest in Alexander, or any other man, only you. However, I get the feeling you're holding back something, and that night when you told me how you couldn't talk about it because your job came first, do you have any idea how that makes me feel?"

"I know he's just a friend. As for my job coming first, I wish I could change that, but I can't. I—I want you to know I trust you. Jennifer, it was never about doubting you or your love for me. Just know, no matter what the future holds for us, I'll never leave your side, and I promise I *will* be the one who'll transition you to heaven! The most important thing is that we'll be spending all of eternity together."

"I guess I have to accept your word and hope the remainder of my time on earth includes you by my side. As for my time in heaven, you had better be next to me, or I *will* come find you and drag you back. After all, you need to help me keep all the universes and souls in place. Lord knows what a mess I'll make of things without your help." Though the ache in her chest was heavy, Jennifer did her best to remain stoic. *I must be strong—he's hurting too.*

"You'll drag *me* back, eh? Now that I'd like to see." He fisted Jennifer's hair and gently tugged her mouth closer to his. "I can play rough too." His mouth was on hers before his wife could reply with one of her usual sarcastic retorts. His hands followed suit, and soon he and Jennifer were lost in their lusty need for each other, pushing back against how quickly the little time they had left together was slipping away.

CHAPTER TWENTY-THREE

*J*osh did up the brass buttons on his uniform for the second time in many years. On this occasion, he was obeying the order Gisabella had sent him the night prior, moments before his uniform appeared in Jennifer and his shared closet on earth.

-As I was saying, I'll be back as soon as my meeting is over and I talk with Gisabella,- Josh messaged, glancing up at Jennifer, who was sitting cross-legged on the bed eyeing him with interest.

-No problem, I should be home by then.- Jennifer smiled sweetly until she saw how stormy Josh's expression had become. -I'm kidding! Stop stressing; Talos and I will be right here waiting for you to come home.- Upon hearing his name, Talos jumped on the bed and began kneading the blanket.

-Not funny, Jennifer! Look, if you wish to go out, you need to give me an advanced warning—say at least four hours, so I can place enough protection around you and scout out where you're going.-

Once Josh answered Jennifer's sour expression, he turned his attention to Talos. -Cat—you'd better keep an eye on her.-

-I'll be by her side all night long.- Talos abandoned his latest hobby of fluffing blankets in lieu of rubbing his head on Jennifer, leaving enough of his scent to irritate her protector.

~I wouldn't get too comfortable, cat! The minute I come back, you're on the couch!~

~How long do you think you'll be?~ Jennifer turned and scooped up Talos, then kissed him on the head.

~No idea, although, I can't imagine why your grandma decided to hold an impromptu meeting. If I know Gisabella, she's got something up her sleeve! Too bad she'll probably drag out the meeting for ten or more hours of other realm time.~ Josh did his best to ignore the way Talos had begun kneading Jennifer's sweater. *Damn cat!*

In an effort to change the topic to something more palatable than her grandma, Jennifer unfolded her legs and placed Talos on the bed. Then she stood and took a few steps until she was wrapped in Josh's energized embraced, his energy now dense enough to lean on without falling through him.

~Mmm, you smell good.~ Josh inhaled deeply while tightening his hold.

~Promise you'll wake me up when you get back. I want to be the one to take this off you.~ Jennifer smoothed her hands over Josh's uniformed chest before her gaze fell upon Josh's breath-robbing smile. ~You still give me butterflies, Mr. Smith,~ she whispered while clasping Josh's biceps, savoring the way his hands traveled down her body where they came to rest on her hips.

Her lips parted to receive his inviting kiss: sweet and slow with just the right about of deliberation to skyrocket all her senses until she was unaware of anything but him. Her tongue sought refuge inside his mouth, where it entangled in a provocative dance that spoke of what awaited him upon his return. Teasing morphed into hardened need that had her grinding against his thickened, energized body until Josh broke the kiss and pulled back.

~Whoa, I'd do anything to stay here and finish this, but I can't be late —this time.~ Josh traced the V-neck of her t-shirt and dipped his finger inside. ~This is mine,~ he said, circling her nipple with his finger several times until it peaked.

~Yes, yours.~

~I need to leave while I still have my wits about me.~ He rested his forehead against Jennifer's. ~God, woman—I can't believe what you do to me.~

~What you do to me, too.~ She sighed when Josh lifted his forehead and stepped back before he completely faded from the room. *There'll never be anyone for me but you, Mr. Smith.*

Josh arrived at Gisabella's with a reluctant smile on his face. "Your Excellency." He bowed and kissed her ring before rising to make eye contact with his old friend.

"Joshua," she coolly nodded her acknowledgement. "I believe the last time I saw you, your tongue was shoved down my granddaughter's throat."

"I'd say that's an accurate description." He paused as Jennifer's words came back to him. *"You owe Gisabella an apology." Damn!* "Look, when I did that, I was angry, but it was inappropriate, and I'm sorry."

"Jennifer's a good influence on you."

"Yeah, she wasn't too happy with me."

"Well, it's water under the bridge now. Would you like a drink before we go?" Gisabella walked over to her bar cart and selected a bottle of gin with two glasses. "Gin okay with you?"

"I'll pass." Josh paled and held up a hand. "Just hearing the word gin makes my head hurt."

"Maybe a glass of wine, or perhaps I should pour you a glass of milk."

"I think we'd better get going. I don't wish to leave your granddaughter on her own any longer than necessary."

"I take it you used several layers of energy protection shields, and Talos is watching over her." Gisabella pulled her priestess robe over her shift dress and tied the braided silk cord in place.

Josh faked a smile. "All that plus a few extra precautions." *As if I do anything less!*

"Of course you placed extra protection—how silly of me to ask." She bit her lip, trying not to laugh at her friend's irritation as she slipped her feet into her gold-colored shoes and picked up one of her favorite crowns.

"Let's go," Gisabella said, placing her hand on Josh's proffered arm.

"Okay, Talos, now that Josh is gone, let's do some reading," Jennifer spoke to the domestic-looking cat, who was more interested in licking his paw than anything else. She clambered out of bed and retrieved the High Priestess Manual from its hiding place before rejoining Talos on the bed.

Saying the words she'd memorized, Jennifer watched the quarter-size book grow to its full size. "We probably only have fifteen or twenty minutes our time before Josh returns! I sure wish there was a way I could read it on the sly without Josh finding out. Not that you'd understand how frustrating it is to be watched over all the time. I'm sure he'd love to gloat how he got me to study and read this manual, but I'd much rather surprise Josh by using a spell or playing a trick on him."

~That can be done easily. I believe the instructions for hiding the manual's appearance can be found on—um, let me think a moment.~ Talos grew silent, appearing deep in thought. ~I believe it's on page 2,567. Yes, I'm certain that's where you can find it.~

"Thanks, Talos!" She flipped to the page number and read the heading: *How to hide your manual from prying eyes.* Jennifer skimmed the section and cheered. After a few attempts, she was able to make the book invisible from Talos and hoped that meant that no one else, not even her powerful husband, would be able to see it. "This is awesome!"

Never did it occur to Jennifer to ask how Talos knew this information.

When Gisabella and Josh arrived at the protector meeting, the first thing Josh noticed was the casual attire everyone else was wearing.

"I see you're up to your usual tricks," Josh commented out of the corner of his mouth. With a forced smile in place, he nodded to his fellow elite protectors while they made their way toward the stage.

"But you look so handsome," Gisabella teased under her breath while smiling at the 733 strongest protectors in the universe, knowing the newest inductee would be joining them momentarily.

"Flattery will get you nowhere. I know you're up to something, old woman, but for the life of me, I can't figure it out."

"I do believe you've become overly paranoid in your ancient years."

"Gee, I wonder why? I'm sure it has nothing to do with your antics." They'd reached the top step, putting an end to their banter. Once he walked Gisabella to the podium, Josh took his position as the only protector allowed to stand to the high priestess' left.

"Welcome, my most valued protectors in the entire universe and all dimensions. Thank you all for being here on such short notice. As you know, Sarnia is no longer with us, leaving her position as my second-highest protector vacant. With so many highly trained men and women, my decision became harder than ever. There was one candidate, though, whose skills could no longer be denied. I've watched him for centuries, and as the years flew by, his maturity and success rate have soared. This by no means overshadows my top protectors standing on the stage with me." Gisabella turned to her left first. "My number one protector, Joshua." Once the applause died down, she turned to her right. "Third highest, Cornelius, and fourth, Lancelot."

The deafening applause rang out for several minutes until Gisabella raised her hands, motioning for the crowd to quiet down. "At this time, I'd like to call forward my choice for second highest protector, who, if for any reason Josh is unable to fulfill his duties, will step forward to take his place until I decide otherwise."

Josh shifted his stance. *What the fuck does she mean—take my place? Sounds an awful lot like I'm being set up!*

"Without further ado, please join me in welcoming our latest member to the elite protectors, and our newest, second-highest protector, Lawrence."

Holy fucking cow! Has Gisabella gone mad? She knows how I feel about that Apollo look-a-like fucker! Josh gritted his teeth before he said something that would give Gisabella a reason to promote Lawrence and replace him on the spot.

He eyed the stage along with everyone in the room, watching as Lawrence appeared. *For fuck's sake, did she have to dress him in the same uniform?!* Josh's scowl deepened as the younger blond male greeted Gisabella, bowing and kissing her ring before he knelt in front of her. Josh was too angry at that point to listen to Gisabella reciting the oath that bestowed upon the Apollo clone membership in the elite group but also promoted him to the second-ranked amongst so many others who were just as worthy of the title. If she'd at least promoted Cornelius and Lancelot, and brought Lawrence into the group as fourth-highest protector, he could've understood, but this was surely Gisabella's way of warning him that he'd better stay in line.

While the applause was courteous at best, Josh joined the others on the stage in congratulating their newest top protector.

"Congratulations, Lawrence. I'm sure Gisabella had her reasons for promoting you to such a prestigious position. I wish you all the best." Josh forced himself to recite the sentiments with a touch of sincerity.

"Thank you, sir! It's a pleasure to finally meet you," Lawrence said warmly while vigorously pumping Josh's arm. "If there's anything I can ever do for you, Josh, let me know."

"That's okay; I think I got it." *That'd be the day I ever let you anywhere near my wife!* If the younger protector noticed his coolness, he hadn't shown any sign.

Six hours later, after lots of lengthily drawn out talking points in Gisabella's lecture, she transported herself and Josh back to her house.

"I'm glad that's over," Gisabella said, kicking off her shoes. "I've been dying to take those off."

"I should get back to Jennifer," Josh said, hoping to leave before she mentioned Lawrence.

"Let the poor girl enjoy some time alone. Talos is watching over her, and it's not like you've been gone for hours on earth. Why, I'm sure your wife has barely noticed you're gone." Gisabella headed toward the kitchen, refusing to take no for an answer.

Great! Just what I want to do, spend my night sipping tea when I could be enjoying my wife. Maybe there's a way I can be excused quickly. Josh rapidly developed a strategy and waited for Gisabella to return with tea and whatever god-awful creation she was sure to serve.

"Let me carry that for you." Josh rushed forward to take the laden tray. Once he placed it on the coffee table, he took the seat across from her, trying to hold back from laughing at the flat, speckled object on the tray. *What did she do—run out of baking powder?*

"I think you'll love this; it's pepper cake," Gisabella gushed. After using two hands and much effort, she finally managed to cut a slice and place it on a plate.

"Thanks." *How much pepper did she add—an entire cupful?! I hope she doesn't seriously expect me to eat this!* He put the plate down before he began sneezing and opted for a sip of tea. "So this Apollo guy—Lawrence. I suppose the Council was surprised by your selection." He enjoyed the briefest withering expression before Gisabella regained her composure.

"Whom I select for my personal army is my choice."

"So that's how you managed to select someone, who, up until tonight, had been on the blackball list? After all, a boy with infractions against his character is the perfect choice for your second-in-command. What did Merlin say when you told him of your choice?" *Uh oh, looks like I scored another hit.*

"Merlin's been away at some retreat, so he doesn't know about Lawrence. In case you're forgetting, as the high priestess, I can select anyone I want, and I chose Lawrence."

"Instead of promoting someone who's proven their loyalty for thousands of years? That's rich! How do you expect Cornelius and Lancelot to respect your future decisions after you've stepped over them? Look, if your selection had anything to do with getting back at me for breaking a rule or two..."

"I'm sorry if you think Lawrence isn't up to your standards or that I picked him as a way of getting back at you for some silly drunken night, or for confessing to your sleeping wife she must marry another, but you're way off-base. Lawrence was the *most* qualified candidate to hold that position. You may not realize it now, but eventually when Jennifer transitions home to heaven, your responsibilities will completely change. Have you not given any thought to how different your life will be? You'll be removed as a protector in my army the moment Jennifer's life on earth is over, possibly even weeks earlier, depending how much she needs you by her side." She watched the protector's expression alter as her words registered. "Don't tell me you haven't given any thought to what will happen?"

"I—um, I guess I figured I'd remain Jennifer's protector when she joins me in heaven. I mean, she'll need a protector then as well."

"Of course she does, and you'll remain by her side, but surely you realize when Jennifer takes her position, you'll be expected to stand by her side as her husband, and she'll be assigned a new protector."

"Jennifer and I *will* have a say who's assigned to protect her, right?" A few tiny beads of perspiration appeared on Josh's forehead.

"Correction, Jennifer will have a say, and at that time she may consult your opinion."

"If you promoted that Apollo fucker to become my wife's personal bodyguard, then you'd better think again!" Josh's eyes turned the color of coal.

"I happen to think he'd make a great protector, but who Jennifer selects is not up to either of us."

"Why do I get the feeling my time with Jennifer is coming to an end far sooner than expected?"

"Speaking of which, by the middle of September I expect you to refrain from bedding your wife. It'll will only confuse Jennifer if you continue to hold on to her. I ask this as your high priestess, not as her soul's grandmother."

"I understand." There was no poker face in all the dimensions that could have hidden his shock.

"I knew you'd understand. Merlin and I believe it best for our granddaughter's sake if you let her go sooner than needed, but we understand how great your love for Jennifer is, so we've granted you more leeway."

"Speaking of Merlin, where has he been?" Josh asked, not missing the flicker of doubt in her eyes. Either way, his boss didn't look pleased.

"I told you, he's off at some retreat."

"Really? He didn't mention one coming up to me."

"I'm sure he'll be back soon." Gisabella wrung her hands.

"Why don't you send your newly appointed Apollo man to go look for Merlin? If he's as good as you say he is, Lawrence will have no problem locating the wizard." The corners of Josh's mouth twisted wryly.

"Would you look at the time? You'd better run along before Jennifer falls asleep. I'm sure she's anxious for you to come home, seeing as though you look so handsome in your uniform. I'll even wrap up your piece of cake so you can eat it later."

"Fine," Josh acquiesced, accepting the sample of cake. "Make sure Merlin gets in touch with me so I can arrange Jennifer's next lesson. Good night, Gisabella." Josh gave her a peck on the cheek before transporting home to Jennifer.

~My lady, you may find page 3,089 of interest.~ Talos messaged, leaning closer to get a better view.

"I think I've done enough reading for the night." Jennifer closed the book and stretched her arms. "I'd better put this away before Josh finds out I brought it home. I get the feeling my butt won't be safe if he finds it here." She quickly used the words needed to shrink the book before tucking it back in its hiding place, then climbed into bed just in time to see Josh reappearing.

~You're back!~ She bounded out of bed to run her hands along his translucent arms while trying not to go through him.

~Did you miss me?~

~Of course I did.~ Jennifer's smile faded. ~What's wrong?~

~Nothing you need to worry about.~

~If you expect to groom me for my position as high priestess, then you need to take off the kid gloves. Josh, I'm your wife—if you can't trust me with your problems, who else can you trust?~ *Please don't say my grandma's name!*

~Forget it, baby. I have more important things on my mind—and all of them involve you.~

"Oh!" Jennifer yelped before her senses gave in to her body's release, dissolving into Josh's energized embrace. "Not fair! Now all I can think about is making love. Afterwards, you better tell me what happened, but for now I need you to kiss me."

One kiss led to another and another, and soon she was lost in Josh's tangled web of desire.

CHAPTER TWENTY-FOUR

SEPTEMBER 15TH, 1982

*S*ummer had come and gone, and before long, Jennifer was beginning the second week of her final year of college. Lately, time had passed by so quickly, she found herself constantly rushing about. Today was no different as she hurried out of class and down the hall into the cafeteria. A quick glance at her watch verified she was a few minutes late for lunch with her friends.

"It's about time you showed up!" Mary chastised, waving the latest copy of their favorite tabloid. "When were you planning on telling us?"

"Telling you what?" Jennifer glanced around the table for a clue.

"Don't act so innocent. I have proof right here on the front of this magazine." Mary held it up.

Oh no! Jennifer cringed.

"I have to agree with Mary," Elizabeth said with a uncharacteristic edge in her voice. "It says you attended a party with this famous artist—Alexander Something-or-Other."

"He sure is cute," Colleen added, grabbing the magazine to take a closer look.

"I told you guys about him. Alexander's just a friend who begged me to be his date for some gala." *His fake date!*

"You never told us how *hot* he is!" Mary rolled her eyes.

"Is he? I hadn't noticed." *Please don't get Josh started. Not when things are going so well between us, or at least they had been going great until a few weeks ago. How many times must I tell my husband that Alexander's just a friend?*

"Hey! Earth to Jennifer!" Elizabeth waved her hand in front of Jennifer's blank expression. "Looks to me like Alexander is a whole lot more than a some ordinary date!" she teased. "What is that?" Elizabeth pointed to the watch on her friend's wrist. "Don't tell me—Alexander bribed you to attend the party with him."

"Um, not exactly. I mean—Alexander gave me the watch, but he did so only because he didn't wish me to miss the train." *Geez, that sounded lame.*

"Did you hear that? Alexander gave her a gold watch so she wouldn't miss the train," Colleen mimicked.

"Isn't that a Rolex?!" Mary jumped up from her chair and grabbed Jennifer's wrist to take a closer look.

"Alexander has a friend who sells them," Jennifer clarified. *Great, they seem almost as shocked as Josh had sounded. Maybe I should've tried harder to reject it, but Alexander looked so dejected when I told him it was too expensive.*

"Sure wish I had a friend who sold Rolex watches," Mary laughed. "Seriously, Jennifer, this Alexander guy sounds like a keeper."

"Make that a drop-dead gorgeous keeper!" Colleen gushed, focusing her attention on the photo. "This is a great photo of the two of you. I hope you bought extra copies for yourself."

"Your mom must be in seventh heaven at the thought of you dating. To top it off, he's a celebrity!" Elizabeth added, knowing how often Mrs. Parker bugged Jennifer to find a man.

"Is she ever! Mom keeps pestering me to introduce Alexander to her and Dad," Jennifer said with an exaggerated skyward gaze.

"Oh, I'd love to be a fly on the wall when that happens!" Elizabeth chuckled.

Josh scowled. *I can't believe how quickly Alexander has worked his way into Jennifer's life. Soon he'll be the one seated at Christmas dinner, and I'll be left out in the cold! Not that I wasn't already.*

"So, when do *we* get to meet Alexander?" Mary leaned forward, waiting for an answer.

"Not you guys, too?" Jennifer rolled her eyes.

"I think you should invite him to dinner with us. Think of it as your chance not to be the odd woman out."

"Mary!" Elizabeth chastised.

"Don't worry, I'm used to Mary's comments," Jennifer answered with a sigh.

"I'm sitting right here," Mary took offense.

"Fine, I'll ask Alexander if he'd like to join us," Jennifer caved. The way her girlfriends laughed caused her stomach to tighten. *Not good! I hope Josh doesn't get the impression I'm dating Alexander!*

Jennifer glanced around the room with a sinking feeling when she saw no sign of her husband. He'd been doing that a lot lately, disappearing or turning himself completely invisible. At first Josh claimed it was to give her space or time alone, but he'd begun doing so more frequently, leaving Jennifer to wonder if Josh thought he was doing her a favor by removing himself from the picture. The realization that Josh might think Alexander would be better for her because he was able to interact with her family and friends hit home. *He better not think he's doing the right thing by being a martyr!*

"I can t wait to meet your boyfriend!" Colleen said, shaking a French fry in Jennifer's direction. "If Alexander's as hunky as he looks in this photo, I plan on staring at him all night long!"

"So, it's okay for *you* to stare at a boy when you've got a significant other, but it's not okay for me to do the same?" Mary huffed.

"Two words—engagement ring!" Colleen wiggled her vacant finger.

Why did I have to become friends with someone so famous? I never asked for a new watch or a limo driver to cart me around the city. Sure, Alexander's a sweet man who's fun to hang out with, but I'm married. We can be nothing more than friends no matter how great everyone thinks he is! Deep inside, something nagged at Jennifer's subconscious—*what if Alexander is meant to be more than a friend?*

"Jennifer!" Mary snapped. "You can't fool me; I know that far off look. I bet by Christmas you'll be wearing a ring!"

"What?!" Jennifer hyperventilated. *Has Mary lost her mind?*

"Jeez, Jennifer, you lost all your color," Elizabeth said, poised to perform CPR.

"Relax, Elizabeth, Nurse Colleen is here to save her if she passes out. Seriously, Jennifer, someday you're going to get married—so why not pick a famous, handsome, rich guy, who loves the same stuff as you? Imagine the cute kids you and Alexander will have! I can just see it, a house full of little artist clones." Mary sighed dreamily, as if caught up in the image she'd described.

"I have no plans to marry Alexander," Jennifer protested again. "Would you look at the time?" She barely glanced at her watch. "Sorry, I promised my mom I'd run errands."

"Ask Alexander!" Mary called out as Jennifer made a mad dash toward the exit.

Jennifer didn't slow down until she was seated in her car. *Why can't they mind their own business?* Things had become awkward enough between Josh and her since Alexander's arrival, never mind how the last couple of months, she'd begun to accompany Alexander to art openings and a couple of charity galas. Things had become complicated enough between them without her friends stirring up rumors.

Isn't there a song about being torn between two lovers? What am I saying? Alexander's a nice guy, but he certainly isn't Josh!

Then again, Josh and she hadn't been to their honeymoon house in over a month. *The only reason I agreed to accompany Alexander in the first place was because Josh said it'd be great for my career!* Proof that Josh had been right was in the bonus she'd received and the full-time position she'd secured before she began her final year of college. Still, his reasoning for her spending so much time with another man seemed odd. *I wish we were a normal couple, then I could spill my guts to Elizabeth. I bet she'd help me find some insight into Josh's actions.*

When Jennifer backed out of her parking space, Josh followed her from above while thinking of ways he could try to spend time with his wife. *If we curled up and watched television until Jennifer dozes off, I won't break*

Gisabella's latest rule of no making love to my wife. Who am I kidding?! We used to make love all the time, and then afterwards, we'd stay awake for hours, talking.

He grimaced when Jennifer didn't see the light change, but his quick action of slowing her vehicle avoided possible accident number thirty-six! *Where was I—oh right; it pains me to see the look in Jennifer's eyes each time I kiss her goodnight and don't want to make love. Or the times I pretend I must stay vigilant from up above the house. Who knew months ago I'd be in fucking hell and have a serious case of blue balls to boot? I sure wish Alexander was a spirit, then the playing field between us would be equal. If that were the case, I'd bet my soul that my wife would choose me over that wealthy creampuff artist!*

~How was school?~ Josh messaged with a dazzling *welcome home* smile.

~It was good—I had lunch with my friends,~ Jennifer stated, adding, ~I didn't see or feel you around?~

~I thought you'd enjoy having some space,~ he messaged, checking to make sure his emotions didn't give anything away.

~Is that your new motto—to give me *lots* of space? Because it sure feels like that's what you're doing.~

~For years you've wanted more freedom, and now that you've learned how to protect yourself enough to keep someone at bay until I take over, it's time I took a step back. You know, to give you some independence.~

~So you want to give me more freedom? I guess you won't mind if I ask Alexander to accompany me to dinner on Friday night?~ She played close attention to Josh's reaction, and when he shrugged his shoulders as if he didn't care, she walked over to the phone and dialed Alexander's number. *If this doesn't get Josh to open up, I don't know what else to do.*

As much as he wanted to grab the phone away and take Jennifer into his arms, Josh couldn't risk pulling her heart back toward himself, knowing how much harder it'd be on her the next time he tried to distance himself. *Gisabella's right: the more I keep my distance, the easier it'll be on my wife.*

"Alexander, there's no need for you to go out of your way. I can meet you at the restaurant," Jennifer said into the receiver. "Fine, you can pick me up at the house. Thanks for agreeing to fill in for my boyfriend." Jennifer paused before saying into the phone, "No worries, none of my friends ever met him."

"What do you mean—is my boyfriend real?" Jennifer asked, rolling her eyes. "Of course he exists." After listening for a moment, she burst out laughing. "A spy? What kind of question is that?" She glanced back at Josh before turning away. "Seriously? You think he's wanted by the FBI!" She giggled. "What was that? Did you really just ask me if he's married? Enough with your silly questions—I'll see you Friday night."

She was silent for a moment before her cheeks turned pink as she broke into a smile. "I like you too… How do you expect me to believe that? You European men are always throwing around the 'love' word!" she teased. "Fine, you can say it as much as you want." Jennifer laughed flirtatiously. "See you Friday." She gently placed the receiver down with rosy cheeks, grinning widely, but when she turned around to face Josh, he was gone, and so was his energy.

She didn't see or hear from Josh until she was leaving for school the next morning. Her heart skipped a beat at the sight of him translucent across the room.

~Jennifer, I have to meet with Gisabella this afternoon, but I want to wait until you get home before I leave. You don't have any plans that I don't know about, do you?~

~Just the one you told me to make for Friday night!~ Jennifer baited, hoping for a reaction or sign of Josh's possessiveness, but when none came, her heart sank. *Something's way off!*

~Okay—see you later.~ Josh transported, making his escape before Jennifer picked up on his broken heart. *Shit! The locket!* If he wasn't careful, it might give away his true feelings. Either way, Jennifer's eyes mirrored his sadness. *What a selfish person I was to lock her into this temporary marriage without thinking of the hurt I'd be causing her.*

~Wait!~ Jennifer watched as Josh faded away without responding before she covered her eyes and burst into tears.

When Friday night came, Jennifer found herself alone, waiting in the driveway for Alexander. If not for her friends' insistence, she'd have begged off, but even then, there was no guarantee Josh would've spent time with her. *Maybe our marriage is over?* The thought sank her mood deeper into despair.

Please don't think our marriage is over, Josh silently begged. *Someday what I've sacrificed for you will make sense. My love, if there was any way it wouldn't damage your soul, I'd whisk you away to a place where the two of us could live on our own terms forevermore.* The words did nothing to ease Josh's soul as he watched Alexander warmly greet Jennifer.

"You look beautiful, Jennifer," Alexander complimented, kissing her cheek.

"You clean up well yourself," Jennifer replied, attempting to sound lighthearted. *Who am I kidding? Alexander looks hot!*

They arrived at the restaurant and were immediately escorted to where her friends were seated.

"Where has Jennifer been hiding you?" Mary's mouth dropped open as she said the words, earning a dazzling smile from Alexander.

"You must be Mary," Alexander greeted.

"I am, and this is my fiancé, Fred." Mary motioned to the blond boy next to her. "And this is Colleen and Elizabeth with their dates, James and Brad."

"It's a pleasure to finally meet you all!" Alexander pulled out Jennifer's chair. Once they were seated, he shared his menu, holding it up high enough to cover their faces, so he could suggest ordering an assortment of appetizers for the table as his treat.

When the waiter walked away, they raised their glasses in a celebratory toast to love and all the promises it held for the future. Conversation and laughter flowed, and when dessert menus were passed out, the table grew quiet as everyone ogled the choices.

"What do you mean you've left no room for dessert?" Alexander exclaimed then laughed at the way Jennifer was holding her belly in protest. "Ah, *cherie*, the meal isn't complete without a taste of something sweet." Alexander's eyes never left Jennifer's, even after he'd finished speaking. His actions attracted the attention of those seated around the table, in addition to Josh, who wished he was anywhere else but there.

"Well, kiss her already!" Mary demanded, with the others seconding the sentiment.

Alexander leaned in closer, bringing his lips close to Jennifer's ear. "I think we should give your friends a small sample so they believe we're dating. It'll save you from answering a lot of questions later. Squeeze my hand if you agree."

What harm can one quick kiss.... Jennifer was lost in her train of thoughts as Alexander slowly inched his lips toward hers and brushed them across her cheek. His hand smoothed her hair, coming to rest on the back of her neck. By the time his mouth was close enough to touch hers, Jennifer's heart fluttered as quickly as a hummingbird's wings. His ever-so-light kiss upon the corner of her mouth helped her relax, and before she realized what she was doing, her hands were caressing Alexander's face.

Lost in the moment, everything but Alexander's touch disappeared as she parted her lips and welcomed their first kiss. Soft and gentle, Alexander's mouth lingered on hers while he softly caressed his hand along her jaw. When his lips parted from hers, his thumb brushed her bottom lip; so sensual was his touch that she was enveloped in a moment of intoxication. As if unable to stop herself, much to her horror, she moaned with pleasure, causing loud cheering to ring out all about them and snapping her back to the present.

"You better be taking notes!" Colleen told her date.

"*Mon ange*," Alexander broke into Jennifer's thoughts.

"We should leave. I have to be up early, and you have lots to do to get ready for your opening," Jennifer said breathlessly while avoiding Alexander's gaze.

"Of course." Alexander lifted her hand to brush his lips across Jennifer's knuckles. "Jennifer and I must take our leave now. I hope to see you all again soon."

"I have a feeling we'll be seeing a lot more of *you*!" Mary added with a huge smile. "That was sure some kiss!"

"I'm afraid I've embarrassed my date," Alexander said sheepishly.

"Why? It was like watching a beautiful kiss out of a romance movie," Elizabeth expressed. "You know, the much-awaited, tender first kiss between the main characters."

"I'll see you all on Monday," Jennifer blurted and grabbed Alexander's hand, pulling him toward the exit while waving goodbye.

CHAPTER TWENTY-FIVE

The ride home was done in unspoken silence accept for Jennifer's blaring inner thoughts. *How could I let Alexander kiss me?! Worst of all, why did I kiss him back?! Maybe because I feel like my husband no longer wishes to be married to me! I wish I knew why Josh has pulled away, or why he's acting so distant.*

The mixture of thoughts created a pit in her stomach, and her heart ached at the thought of losing her already distant husband. *Please don't leave me, Josh,* she pleaded in her unblocked mind. *I love you with all my heart, but you're pushing me away, and I don't know why.*

"Jennifer," Alexander said when they reached her front door. "I know you're upset about our kiss, but I'm not. I've tried to deny my feelings for you because you claim to love another man, yet none of your friends know of him, nor do you mention him when you're with me. If he was so important to you, then you wouldn't be able to keep everything about your relationship up here." Alexander pointed to his head. "Knowing you the way I do, if you loved this man so much, you would've never kissed me back with such intensity."

"Alexander, I—" Jennifer began, but Alexander pressed his finger to her lips.

"Shhh, my darling. Think about what I said. Regardless of whatever you decide, I'll always remain your friend, and if tonight's kiss meant nothing to you, than I'd rather cherish this feeling a little while longer." Alexander kissed the top of her head and waited until she disappeared inside before he walked away.

Jennifer slowly climbed the steps up to the bedroom she shared with the man she loved, her heart full of pain and remorse. *Please be here; we need to talk.* When she opened the door to the room, it was empty except for Talos, who was stretched out on the bed sleeping. There was not one sign of Josh: no notes, no messages, nothing but a desolate, empty room they once shared.

Two nights later, Jennifer was awakened when the bed dipped. Opening her eyes, she found Josh sitting on the side of the bed, solid in form. He hadn't returned any of her messages or shown up even when she'd begged him to do so. Now the sight of his hunched-over back and drooping head reverberated the pain she'd caused by kissing another man. Sitting up, she embraced him and rested her face against his back as tears slowly escaped her eyes. They stayed like this for hours—or maybe it only minutes; she had no idea.

"You need to get some sleep," Josh finally spoke in a hoarse voice.

"Please don't leave," Jennifer whimpered, holding him a little tighter.

"How about I curl up with you and hold you until you fall asleep?" He removed his shoes and joined her in bed.

"It didn't mean anything," she tried to explain. "I'd give anything to take it back." She turned in Josh's arms and saw how red his eyes were, breaking her heart even more. "I miss us, and I miss talking to you and the way you used to love me. Please tell me what's going on," she begged, but he remained silent.

"I didn't kiss Alexander back out of love. I returned his kiss out of loneliness. You haven't held me like this in a long time, nor have we stayed awake all night talking for hours. It makes me wonder if you still love me."

"Of course I love you! You're the only person I could ever love—only you, Jennifer—my heart will always belong to you," Josh professed.

"Then why have you distanced yourself? Ever since I transported by myself, things have felt on and off. Worst of all, you pushed me into a friendship with another man! You tell me to attend parties with Alexander, even when I can see me doing so is killing you."

"It's complicated." Josh pushed back a tendril from his wife's face. "You curled your hair tonight, looks nice."

"What are you keeping from me? Are you seeing someone else? Do you want a divorce?" The implication of the words she'd spoken cut through her like a knife. *Sarnia?*

"No," Josh swallowed. "There are things I'm not at liberty to say. Please believe that I want to be with you every second of the day and hold you every night. You must trust me when I tell you that there'll never be anyone else in my life other than you."

"This has something to do with Gisabella, doesn't it? You always said your job came first, and this proves it more than ever. How naive I was to think I could change that part of you. Worst of all, the irony is that I *am* your job! Was that the real reason you married me?" Tears welled in her eyes, but she forced them away.

"I married you because I fell in love with you."

"But you no longer wish to sleep with me?"

"Nothing could be farther from the truth—I want you more than ever before."

"Then take me as if it's our last time together, just in case whatever my grandma is holding over you pulls you away forever."

It wasn't long before his hands slid under Jennifer's nightgown, seeking solitude in the feel of her breasts. "The kiss you gave Alexander was meaningless to me! You! Are! Mine!"

Josh grabbed the hem of her nightgown and yanked it over her head while Jennifer tugged at the buttons on his shirt. "I got this!" Josh jumped out of bed, removed all his clothes and was on Jennifer faster than a fireman.

"Love me," Jennifer begged with her arms stretched wide, each wrist encircled by one of Josh's hands. She was helpless to do anything but gaze up at the man positioned between her thighs. There was no escaping from Josh or the way her heart would always be his, never free to love another, even if Josh was forced to leave her.

"Need you so bad," Josh called out, crushing his mouth to Jennifer's. He was frenzied with desire as he his tongue sought entry into her mouth. Once inside, he reclaimed every bit of it, cleansing away every hint of Alexander's kiss. The feel of Jennifer's heated skin under his touch made him crazed with lust, making him harder than ever before.

"I must have you!" Using his legs, he separated hers, spreading them further apart with his feet until Jennifer lay spread eagle, panting and totally at his mercy.

"Lose yourself in me," Jennifer whispered, offering the man she loved solace from the pain she'd caused and whatever it was that had tormented him to this—his breaking point.

Jennifer's words were his undoing, and he answered by taking her with one deep thrust, causing his wife to moan and tighten around his hardness. He looked down into her watery eyes and stilled, giving her a chance to adjust to his size.

"So help me, if you don't continue, I'll scream!" she warned, earning a grin from Josh as he began his vigorous pace, sliding out before thrusting deep inside her. He held her in place splayed out like a starfish and completely at his mercy. "Oh my god! It's—too—much," she cried out between heady strokes.

"Give it up, baby!" Josh commanded through gritted teeth. "So help me, woman, if you don't come soon, I'm gonna explode!" His words did the trick, and soon his manhood was embraced in wave after wave of spasms as Jennifer's womanly nectar flowed, making it impossible for him to hold out any longer.

"Jennifer!" he cried out as hot, searing ripples of ecstasy shot up and down his shaft until his release filled his wife with his everlasting love.

"I love you," Jennifer whispered as she held on to him tightly, afraid Josh would disappear before her eyes. "Please stay the night."

"I'd love nothing more than to hold you all night, my love."

She didn't dare ask if this was the last night they'd have together. She didn't have to, because she could see the answer in his eyes. "When my life on earth is over, will we still have our happily ever after in heaven?"

"I give you my word of honor, nothing will ever change our forever after."

"Now I understand why you wrote our wedding vows."

"Your grandma wasn't too happy with me."

"Who cares—I get the feeling my grandma has caused enough problems between us to last several lifetimes."

"She doesn't see it that way. Gisabella's only doing what's best for every living being in each of the dimensions she oversees. Someday, you'll be doing the same."

"So help me, when I become high priestess, if she or anyone else tries to keep us apart, they'll be banished on the spot!"

"I guess that's a good enough reason for accepting your position." Josh chuckled before he rolled over, taking Jennifer with him. "I think that calls for a second round of lovemaking."

"I couldn't agree with you more."

When Jennifer awoke the next morning, she found the bed empty and Josh gone. After grabbing her robe, she headed into the bathroom and turned on the shower. They'd made love throughout the night while Josh was still solid, until she'd fallen asleep curled up next to him. A glance in the mirror at her knotted hair, swollen lips, and puffy eyes brought back the memories of his beautiful words of love, along with the hideous realization that last night was possibly the last time Josh would be allowed to make love to her. *Why? What possible reason would Gisabella have for tearing us apart?* Memories of her dinner with Alexander and her friends came to mind. *It must have something to do with Alexander!*

After taking a quick shower, she hurried back into the bedroom and looked around until her eyes landed on Talos. ~Tell me what you know!~ she demanded by way of messaging, while blocking her thoughts from anyone who might be listening.

~My lady, I have no idea what you're speaking of.~

~I happen to think otherwise. How else would you have known the page numbers in the High Priestess manual?~

~Lucky guess, I suppose.~ Talos began licking his paw.

~Look, if you hope to remain with me and keep your capabilities to change back into a panther, then you need to help me find out what's going on.~

-Fine, but only if I can read what's on page 3,089.-

-Deal!-

-I suggest you wait to look at it until Josh is called away to Gisabella's side.-

-That could take weeks!-

-Better to wait weeks than have her first-in-command protector find out what you're up to. Josh may love you with all his heart, but he's sworn to uphold the law.-

-It's not like they haven't both insisted I read the manual.-

-True, but I'm sure that was when you were reading it in Gisabella's realm. Think about it, princess, if the high priestess wanted you to read the manual so badly, she'd have suggested you bring it home with you to earth. Why else would you have felt the need to hide the manual from everyone but me?-

-Good point. Do you think Josh was telling the truth when he said we'd still be together once my lifetime here was over?-

-He and I may bicker, but there's no man I trust more than your husband.-

-I guess I can wait until it's safe enough to read the manual.- Jennifer resigned herself to waiting and went in search of her hairbrush and dryer.

CHAPTER TWENTY-SIX

*S*arnia walked down the desolate alleyway, ignoring the few down-and-out drunks who were slumped against the brick buildings hugging three-quarter-empty bottles as if their lives depended on it. If not for the fire of revenge coursing through her blood, she'd have been tempted to join them. Kicked to the curb by Josh, then fired by Gisabella years ago, she'd lost the only two things in existence that she loved. Being friendless, jobless, and homeless fueled Sarnia's desire to destroy each of the people who'd played a part in her recent string of bad luck.

Sarnia pulled the hood of her cloak over her bright red curls to avoid any unwanted attention. With only a couple more yards to go before reaching the entrance of her least favorite hangout, she passed by a group of boys. With her head down, she avoided eye contact and hurried her pace. A glance out of the corner of her eye proved there to be five or six boys, who looked like they were in their late teens or early twenties, dressed mostly in sweatshirts, jeans and sneakers. The smell of marijuana hung in the damp air like a dark cloud, thick as her foul mood. *They must be the ones responsible for the odor,* Sarnia surmised. With only a few more steps to go before she arrived at her destination, she heard their catcalls. *I wouldn't do that if I were you, boys!*

"Hey, sexy mama, where ya going? The party's over here," a young, dark-haired teen called out.

"A babe like you is welcome to join our little get together. C'mon, doll, walk those high heels and your sexy ass over here," another older boy yelled.

Sarnia was reaching for the door handle, doing her best to ignore them, when she felt a hand on her arm. Using her former protector training, she fired a bolt of energy so fierce in volume it sliced through the boy's skin, clear to the bone. To her dismay, all sorts of chaos immediately followed.

"Fucking bitch! Look what she did to me!" the boy cried out.

"Now look what you went and done. We were gonna be real nice to you, bitch, but you decided to play rough. Now you gotta pay the price. On your knees, slut!" an older boy with both arms tattooed commanded, pointing to the ground in front of him.

Sarnia turned around until she was facing the outspoken teen, who stood less than four feet away. "If I were you, I'd run home before your mommy needs to pull out her sewing kit to stitch you back together."

"Over here, bitch—my cock needs sucking," the much younger blond-haired teen taunted while reaching for his zipper.

"You wouldn't last ten seconds in my mouth, hardly worth my time," Sarnia mocked. "I bet you're still a virgin."

"Am not!" he answered, pulling out his dick as if to flaunt its hardened size.

"Go home, little boy, before you no longer have a dick," she warned nicely.

"I told you to get over here and suck my dick!"

Sarnia bit her lip to keep from grinning as she slowly sauntered toward the teen, stopping a foot away from him. "So you decided you want to be castrated?"

"*What?*" he asked in a voice laced with fear before he regained his composure. "Enough talk, whore, your only purpose is to service my cock!" He never saw the bolt of energy Sarnia sent flying toward his cock until it was too late.

"Who's next?" Sarnia asked sweetly before addressing the boy screaming and bawling his eyes out, "If I were you, I'd pick up your penis and go to the nearest hospital. Don't worry, they'll sew it back on. I suggest you beg the doctor to add a couple more inches because God sure didn't do you any favors. Talk about being short-changed!"

Ignoring them, she turned and casually walked back to the entrance before disappearing inside. Sarnia had another target in mind for tonight instead wasting her time playing with a bunch of little boys.

Once inside, she sashayed toward the bar, making sure to accentuate each sway of her hips enough to catch every man's attention, both living and spirit. She didn't have to wait long before being approached.

"What's your pleasure?" an older, silver-haired man asked with a smile that crinkled the corners of his eyes.

"Certainly not you, grandpa." Sarnia squeezed the hand resting on her arm until the man loosened his hold. She watched with disinterest as he walked away. *Where are you?* she wondered, doing her best to peer into all the darkly lit corners filled with tables. It wasn't until she reached the stools situated at the bar that Sarnia found whom she came to see.

"Is this seat taken?" she asked using her best seductress, Lauren Bacall kind of voice.

"I suggest you move along unless you want to share my foul mood," Richard answered, his eyes never leaving his glass of scotch.

"Good—looks like we have a lot in common." Sarnia balanced herself on the barstool next to him.

"Don't say you weren't warned."

"Not a chance." She gave her order to the bartender before turning back to the demoted protector who was partly responsible for her position of unemployment.

"Hey, I know you," Richard blurted, staring at the redhead he'd once called a "total knockout babe." "You're Josh's girlfriend." His eyes drifted up her black, thigh-high boots until he found four inches of naked skin that disappeared underneath an electric blue dress. He quickly diverted his eyes upward before he forgot why he'd sat in this bar for so many nights.

"Boy, do you have that all wrong! I finally got that jerk off my back!" she lied while ensuring her expression remained impassive. "I'd much rather have a man who knows his way around a woman's body than a jerk who's taken up residency in Gisabella's ass. I don't suppose you know of anyone who fits that description?"

"I thought you'd be furious with me after what happened at the meeting," Richard interjected. "After all, I'm partly to blame for you getting fired."

"I doubt you knew what you said was going to get me canned."

"No!" Richard shook his head. "Had I known, I would've never said anything."

"That's what I thought, Richard. Too bad you ended up demoted, while all Josh received from Gisabella was a slap on the wrist. I *guarantee* the two of them are as tight as ever!"

"You can say that again!" Richard downed his drink and ordered another round for Sarnia and himself.

"Thank you. Cheers!" Sarnia toasted with a brilliant smile. "I'm surprised to find you here—what are the odds?" She tossed her red mane over her shoulder provocatively and ran the tip of her tongue over her bottom lip.

"On the contrary, I hang out here often. Maybe you're stalking me," he joked.

"Well, word has it that you're a good lay." She skimmed her red lacquered nails up Richard's thigh, stopping just shy of his crotch. "I don't suppose you're in the mood to give me a sample?"

"I'll think about it," Richard answered, biting the inside of his cheek to keep a straight face. Sarnia's expression wasn't a laughing matter.

"Playing coy doesn't suit any man." Sarnia stood and downed her drink. "Thanks for the drink." Placing the glass on the bar, she turned to leave.

"Not so fast, kitten." Richard grasped Sarnia's wrist. "Josh warned me about you, and judging by the look in your eyes, I believe he was telling the truth."

"Let go of me before I send you to kingdom come!"

"I suggest you sit back down and enjoy another drink, unless you're prepared to take on the entire bar," he warned, pointing out how much attention they were attracting.

After a quick glance around, Sarnia took Richard's advice. "Fine, as long as you're buying!"

"I wouldn't have it any other way," he said with a twinkle in his eyes. "Bartender, another round over here." He motioned to the older man before turning his attention back to Sarnia. "I suggest you relax because we're going to be here a while."

"Who the hell do you think you are?" Her green eyes flared.

"I'm your new master," Richard said darkly, as though issuing a warning: his comment wasn't up for negotiation.

"My *what?!*"

"You heard me. A while ago I heard a story about a redhead who'd picked up a guy I used to know. His name was Byron. Funny thing about that—he was never heard from or seen again. So, it got me to thinking, what woman could have possibly taken down such a virile young protector in his prime? Funny thing about this story is the only one who seems to remember Byron and you leaving together went home shortly after you and Byron left. So, if I had to guess, I bet when you went back to the bar to clean up the loose ends, you missed the one witness who could identify you."

"I have no idea who and what you're jabbering about." Sarnia held her poker face in place, but she was unable to stop her right leg from bouncing on its own.

"Now who's playing coy?" Richard leaned in and took hold of the redhead's bottom lip between his teeth and tugged. "You are so tempting —but oh so—dangerous. The thing is, unlike Byron, I know better than to ever trust you."

"That makes two of us; I'll never trust you!"

"Good! I prefer it that way." He downed the rest of his drink. "Drink up; we're going back to my place." Without giving Sarnia any choice, he waited until she licked the rim of her glass clean before he grasped her hand and pulled her upright.

"Maybe I wanted another drink!"

"Do you know what the definition of 'master' is? The way I see it, Sarnia—you're jobless, homeless, and have no friends to turn to other than myself. I'm prepared to help you get back on your feet as long as you obey me. Be forewarned—one slip up and we're finished! Got it?!"

"Yes," Sarnia replied meekly.

"That's more like it." He placed a protective hand on Sarnia's back, guiding her out the front door, where he then transported her to his new home, located at opposite end of the dimension from Josh's apartment. Within seconds, they reappeared outside a log cabin hidden amongst pine trees and thorny bramble.

"Welcome to my home," Richard offered, taking Sarnia by the hand as he waved the other to turn off the unseen alarm. "Come inside, and I'll give you a tour."

"Quaint place," Sarnia voiced with disdain.

"Don't knock it. You'll be safe here, and no one will be able to locate you—in case anyone else figures out what you've done."

"I haven't admitted to doing anything." Sarnia roughly swiped her hair off her face and glowered.

"Have it your way. As soon as Byron shows up, I'll grant you your freedom. How does that sound?" Richard bargained, knowing that would never happen.

"Are you going to open the door to this dump or not?"

"Coming, dear," Richard chuckled as he reached past her and opened the door. Once he flicked on the lights, the log home was filled with a soft glow.

Sarnia was greeted by a two-story great room with floor-to-ceiling windows, wide-plank flooring, and walls made of logs with chinking visible between each. "This is a lot nicer than I thought it'd be. *Oh!*" Sarnia jumped in surprise. "What the hell is that?"

"He's some grizzly bear who picked the wrong day to show up at my door," Richard snorted with a dry smile. "I had him stuffed as a warning to all the other bears."

"Yeah, I bet that worked well." Her eyes traveled up the beautiful animal with the huge paws, shaggy coat, glass eyes, and very menacing teeth. "So, what did all these other animals do to you...." Sarnia's voice traveled off as her gaze landed on each one of the stuffed creatures. Some were mounted on the wall, while others looked like they were fishing. There was a silver fox with a mouse, a gray wolf pouncing on a white hare, hawks stuffed in mid-flight, mountain goats, deer, quail, buffalo, each staring back at her with fake eyes and fixed expressions.

"Nothing much, it's a hobby of mine."

"That's sick! You don't honestly expect me to stay here with all these animals you murdered?!"

"As a matter of fact, I do. I think the sooner you get it through your head that you're here as my slave, the better we'll get along."

"Your *slave*? Fuck you, Richard! You can take your offer of protection and shove it up your ass!" She started for the door, only to be frozen in place and unable to speak. All she could do was stare at Richard through unblinking eyes.

"I can leave you frozen in place for days if you'd like, or you can earn your freedom by promising to be more respectful. Which will it be?"

"Freedom," she mumbled through unmovable lips.

"Very good choice. Next time you disrespect me, I won't be so nice. Understand?" Richard asked, grasping Sarnia's chin, which rewarded him with a glimpse of fright from Gisabella's former number two elite protector. He released her chin and his spell, setting her free.

She stumbled forward and fell to her knees, gasping for air, but was careful not to lash out, as she was clearly at a disadvantage. "How did you become so powerful?"

"I was always this strong, but I've chosen to hide my abilities from everyone until the time is right," Richard boasted.

"What do you want with me?" She looked up at him through mascara-coated lashes from her kneeling position on the floor.

"Everything! I want to hear you beg for me to make love to you and hear you scream my name when I make you come."

"Surely you want more than sex from me," Sarnia's voice wavered.

"Sarnia, though you are my slave, I desire you to occupy my bed and share in my revenge against those who have belittled us. Do you think you can grow to love me enough to stand by my side and take on everyone who dares to stand in our way? If so, I will lay the world and more at your feet, but until such time that can you prove your loyalty to me, I'll make you beg and keep you humbled before me. Do I make myself clear?"

"Yes, Master," Sarnia forced out in a barely audible whisper, then crawled toward Richard on all fours until she was by his feet. Biting back tears, she lowered her head and kissed both of Richard's leather shoes.

"Very good, my pet. You may stand now and follow me into the bedroom," Richard instructed, holding out his hand to help her up. "I think it's time I get to see every bit of what I now own."

"Yes, Master." Sarnia gracefully rose with a hint of a smile and willingly followed Richard down the hallway leading to his bedroom.

CHAPTER TWENTY-SEVEN

*A*fter her last class, Jennifer wiggled on her coat and headed for the exit. Once through the door, she was greeted by a gust of brisk wind that whipped her hair to and fro, forcing her use one hand to hold it back to see where she was walking. The usual vibrant shades of crimson, amber, pumpkin and mustard fall leaves held no joy this year. For Jennifer, the happiness of each day had been ripped away two months ago, the last time she and Josh had made love. Though Josh was still around, their marriage had become one of two friends sharing a few conversations in between her classes and work.

Alexander, on the other hand, had become increasingly attentive, and the parties and charity fundraisers at which she'd posed as his date had taken up many of her weekends. From nighttime receptions and brunches at exclusive country clubs to other charity events and gatherings, Jennifer was thrust in the middle of those who loved the fast-track way of life: heads of corporations, movie stars, politicians. If they had a well-known name, they were there. Even though Alexander provided her with the necessary clothing so she'd fit in, the lifestyle was beginning to suffocate her.

With Alexander's new show opening in two days, Jennifer decided to wait before broaching the subject of taking a month or two off to get her head together. After all, Alexander had been a perfect gentleman after their dinner with her friends and their kiss. *That kiss!* It was the kind of sensual kiss that leaves a girl weak in the knees.

After Josh pulled back, she found it harder and harder to resist Alexander's sweet attention, but something felt off when it came to loving two men. Everything was made worse by the undeniable pull Jennifer felt toward Alexander that became stronger every day, almost too powerful to resist. *I bet all this has something to do with Gisabella!* Josh hadn't gone to meet with Gisabella, so she and Talos hadn't had time to read the manual, but now she was more sure than ever that it held the answer to what caused her husband to pull away.

When she arrived home, Jennifer found several boxes from Alexander had arrived. *More clothes! Ugh!* One thing the guy had was an eye for fashion and what designs and colors suited her best. A tinge of glee sparkled inside her knowing they contained what she'd be wearing to the opening night of Alexander's new exhibit. He had kept all his new pieces under lock and key and hadn't even spoken one word about them to her or anyone.

The first box contained the most elegant gown she'd ever seen; it was floor-length and the color of pale champagne. The top was covered in sequins and cream-colored flowers with leaf appliqués that continued past the beaded gold belt cinched at the waist and down the sheer overlay that covered folds of matching satin fabric.

~Well, what do you think?~ she asked Talos, holding the gown up against her.

The cat's eyes widened. ~My lady, there couldn't be a more breathtaking gown that'd suit you better. Why, it's as if it were made just for you, princess. Where are the shoes?~

~Oh, Talos, you always know the perfect thing to say. I swear, now that you've been stuck being a cat for months, you've mellowed.~

~Thanks a lot! I don't suppose Josh is going to Gisabella's soon?~

~I sure hope so. Not reading the manual is killing me! I know the answer as to why Josh has pulled back can be found in it!~

~Open the next box.~ Talos eyed the other two packages.

The next box contained matching heels, and the final, a floor-length cape the same color as the gown, which Jennifer twirled around in, showing it off to Talos.

~What, no jewelry?~

~Talos! This is already too much. If it wasn't Alexander's opening night, I'd ask him to take it back.~

~Then wear it for Josh's benefit. Maybe it will shake him up enough to visit your bed.~

~Do you really think so? Or are you just saying that to cheer me up?~

~Princess, every time Josh looks at you, his eyes betray his coolness. I think with a little bit of tormenting, you can get him crawling back to you on his knees.~

~Talos, I don't want to reduce my husband to his knees. I just wish to go back to the way things were.~

~Then wear the dress and pretend you're happy to be going out.~

Jennifer scowled at the feline before she went over to the mirror and held the gown up, then lifted her hair to see what it'd look like. ~Maybe I'll wear my hair up—what do you think?~

~I sure hope Alexander gives you some long earrings to match,~ Talos purred.

~I'm sure I can borrow something from my mom. Enough with the gifts from Alexander. I don't feel right taking them under false pretenses.~ Jennifer hung the gown up in the closet and dragged out her schoolbooks.

It was well close to midnight when Jennifer received a message from Josh saying he had a meeting with Gisabella and would be gone for hours, and warned her not to leave the house. She was careful not to give away their plan of reading the manual while he was gone.

Once Josh left, Jennifer wasted no time in retrieving it using the spell she'd learned to enlarge the ancient tome to its full size. Then she added the invisibility spell, just in case Josh returned earlier than expected. *It's not like he'll stop by in person to see me when he gets back!* The painful thought drove her harder to find the answer to what had caused Josh's distance.

~Okay, Talos, spill the beans—what page should I read first?~

~Depends what you want to know.~

~You know darn well I want to know why Josh is distancing himself while pushing me toward Alexander.~

~That's what I thought.~ Talos sighed and laid his paw on the cover of the ancient tome before issuing a warning: ~My lady, I must warn you that even if you read the manual, some circumstances, like destiny or fate, cannot be altered.~

~I understand, but I must know why Gisabella's forcing him to stay away.~

~You'll find what you're looking for on page 1,111.~

~Thank you, Talos.~ Jennifer took a deep breath before she flipped to the page only to find it totally blank. ~Are you sure this is the right page?~ Jennifer glanced at Talos, missing how his eyes glistened with a soft hue of golden light.

~My lady, look again. The information you desire is there before your eyes.~

Sure enough, when Jennifer glanced back, the page contained words she swore were not there a moment ago. With a shrug of her shoulders, she began to read.

Each High Priestess must fulfill their life's purpose and destiny to marry and have a child during their final lifetime on earth, with whomever has been written into their last life-path. Without such a fulfillment of marriage and a child born to them during their final lifetime, no transference of the High Priestess title can be achieved, forfeiting their family's lineage and all future titles.

Jennifer read the information a second time through blurred vision. *This must be why Josh has changed.*

~Princess, are you okay?~ Talos rubbed his head against her arm.

~Did you know I had to marry and have a child with someone alive on earth?~

~I suspected that was the case.~

Jennifer flipped to page 3,089. ~It's all yours; I need a few minutes alone.~ She turned the book toward Talos and headed for the bathroom.

What am I to do? No wonder so much has changed! Josh wanting me to spend time with Alexander and no longer sharing our bed. I knew it had something to do with his job, but I never thought it was because I was locked into some rule that required me to marry someone who was selected on my behalf. Well, now I know the "why" part in my grandma's plan.

"Your Excellency," Josh's greeting was frosty at best.

"Josh, how good it is to see you. I take it my granddaughter's doing well?" Gisabella motioned toward the couch. Once they were both seated, Josh turned toward her with a sour expression.

"She's doing as well as can be expected for a woman who has no clue why her husband has abandoned their shared bed."

"I'm sure when all this is over with, Jennifer will be thrilled to join you in heaven."

"Is there a reason for this meeting?" After he posed the question, the fact that Gisabella shifted in her seat gave him a nuance of pleasure.

"Why don't you try one of these?" Gisabella passed a plate of jam-filled cookies. "I picked them up from the bakery." Her voice was almost as shaky as her hands.

"No thanks." He refused to give his boss any outward indication of how torn up he felt inside.

"They're excellent." She took a bite. "Yum—so good."

"If I wanted a fucking cookie, I'd have taken one. Now what was so important that you felt the need to call me away from my job? One that, I might add, needs round the clock protection."

"I know you surrounded Jennifer with enough protection to keep even the most determined rogue spirit at bay."

"The only reason I showed up is because I needed to get into our honeymoon house to retrieve a few items Jennifer wishes to have."

"Like what?" Gisabella leaned back.

"Oh you know, her favorite blue sweater, a dress and some shoes. She mentioned a hair clip with sparkles too. Seeing as though I'll soon be banned from our house here, I'd like a few articles of clothing and a couple of books as well."

"Fine, you can head over there once we're done talking." Gisabella sighed. "Thank you for taking such great care of my granddaughter. You've made her very happy."

What does she mean? I can take anything but being removed as Jennifer's protector.

"I know I've asked a lot of you in the past, and each time, you've surpassed my expectations. Now, I need you to do so again."

"So help me, Gisabella, if you've changed your mind and expect me to walk away from my forever marriage to my wife, I'll hide her where no one will ever find us!"

"No—that's not what I was going to say. I simply wanted you to know that everything is in place for Alexander and Jennifer to wed next spring."

"I think he's a nice guy who'll make my wife happy until she transitions home, here to me."

"I thought you would approve of him. He can give Jennifer all the things on earth that you cannot."

"He's been very generous."

"I take it you've stopped being intimate with her? The last thing you should be doing is confusing the poor girl—it'd damage her soul if were to you do so."

"I understand." Bile rose to settle in his throat.

"Good. For the time being, all Jennifer's high priestess training and lessons are officially placed on hold."

"Given the circumstances, I concur with your decision." Josh leveled his gaze while waiting for Gisabella to continue.

"Why don't you go fetch the items you and Jennifer wanted, then head back to earth."

"Thank you, Your Excellency." After he accepted a brief hug from Gisabella, Josh headed toward the door then glanced back with a puzzled look. "Where has Merlin been these days?"

"Oh, you know, here and there."

"So he came back from his retreat?"

"He did, but then he had a few others he wanted to attend. You know him, I'm sure he'll be banging on my door soon."

"Of course he will." Josh hid his thoughts in case his boss decided to read them. *Sounds more like Merlin has dumped Gisabella!* "I'll keep you posted if anything happens."

After he left Gisabella's house, Josh hurried over to his and Jennifer's honeymoon house with the hope of having plenty of time alone to gather the things he needed.

Once he found the paperwork he was looking for in his desk, he headed upstairs to their bedroom, where he pulled out a couple of suitcases and loaded them with the items Jennifer wanted. He pulled out a few things from his closet. Josh was just about to zip up the cases when an image of Jennifer walking down the aisle toward him wearing her wedding dress with the large blue diamond around her neck filled his mind. *The necklace!* With that thought, he rummaged through Jennifer's jewelry armoire until he located the necklace hanging from the matching silk cord and stuffed it in his pocket. Then he zipped up the suitcases and transported back to earth.

Jennifer walked back into the bedroom with a renewed look of determination to find Talos lounging on Josh's pillow.

-You'd better not let Josh catch you!- Her warning heeded, Talos slinked his way to lie at the foot of the bed. -Do you know if there's a way to change a person's destiny?-

-Afraid not, princess. If I remember correctly, you can delay your fate, but never will you be able to outwit your destiny. Wouldn't it be better to resign yourself to accept your fate since you and Josh will be reunited as soon as your life here has ended?-

-How could I, knowing I'd be breaking Josh's heart? Alexander's a nice man and all, but to marry him? I'll never be able to recite wedding vows when my heart belongs to my forever husband.-

-Princess, you must face the fact that Josh must have known and accepted your life-path before the two of you were married. He's a strong man who'll do the right thing in letting you finish your required destiny.-

-Then I'll delay my destiny until Gisabella gives in and changes her mind!-

~My lady, if you do that, you'll risk losing Josh once you transition to heaven.~

Jennifer plopped down on the bed and covered her face with her hands. ~Then it's true—I'm trapped.~

~If it's any consolation, I'll be your cat the entire time and help Josh watch over you. Then, when the time comes, I'll transition home with you.~

Jennifer scooped Talos into her arms and held him tightly. ~I wish my life was over.~

~Mistress, you shouldn't say such things. I promise it won't be so bad. You've been programmed to fall in love with Alexander, and I've watched the way your eyes light up and your smile widens whenever he calls.~

~He is fun to talk to,~ she agreed.

~Once you admit you're falling for Alexander, things will be easier for you and for Josh.~

~What do you mean it'll be easier for Josh?~

~Trust me, you being in limbo isn't helping either of you.~

~Are you done with the manual?~ Jennifer released Talos and stood up, sending him rolling off her lap.

~You'd better put it back in hiding before Josh discovers it here.~

Once she reduced its size, she returned it to its hiding place. ~I suppose you're hungry?~ Jennifer led the way to the kitchen where she placed an opened can of tuna on the floor and took out the orange juice for herself.

She spent the remainder of the night trying to study while she waited to hear from Josh, but after ten p.m., she could no longer keep her eyes open.

Josh waited until Jennifer was asleep before he placed the items she had requested and others he'd selected on the loveseat with a short note. But he pocketed the diamond necklace.

Jennifer, You were asleep when I returned and I didn't have the heart to disturb you. I brought back the items you requested along with a few surprises I thought you'd like to have. I'll touch base with you before you leave for the gallery tomorrow night. I see he's sent you a gown, and if you don't mind, I'd love to see you before you leave, so I can admire how beautiful you look.

With my love, Josh

~Hey cat!~ Josh messaged, and when Talos opened his eyes, he continued, ~How is our girl doing?~

~She'll be fine as long as you continue to stay away like you're doing. You must know Jennifer is heartbroken and missing you terribly, but I can tell she's wavering on the edge of caring for Alexander. Not in the same way she loves you, but enough to move forward with her destiny.~

~I get what you're saying, but I'll be here to see her off tomorrow night. She's still my wife, and I refuse to completely abandon her without so much as a goodbye.~

~She'll be happy to see you tomorrow. Is there anything you want me to tell her?~

~Nah.~ Josh gazed longingly at Jennifer, whose hair was fanned out on her pillow. ~I guess I'd better go.~

~That'd be best.~ Talos closed his eyes and snuggled closer to Jennifer as Josh transported up above the house.

CHAPTER TWENTY-EIGHT

"Jennifer, why don't wear my good coat tonight?" Mrs. Parker suggested.

Could Mom's smile get any bigger? "No thanks, Mom, I'm wearing the one Alexander sent. It matches the gown and shoes he picked out." *I thought she didn't like artists? Geez, with the way her face is aglow, I'm surprise she isn't offering to let me wear her wedding dress tonight!*

"Alexander's coming in to say hi, right? I want to take a photo of the two of you in front of the fireplace—you look so sweet together. Maybe we could have his parents over for dinner!"

"Aren't our photos plastered all over the tabloids enough?

"Oh, Jennifer, that's not the same, and you know it!"

"Well, I'm sure you'll get your chance to capture the Kodak moment in," Jennifer glanced at her watch, "exactly one hour."

"Do you think he'll want to stay for dinner?" Mrs. Parker's eyes sparkled.

"Mom, there'll be a ton of food at the reception. Maybe we can all go out to dinner next week?" Jennifer offered when her lack of enthusiasm made her mother's excitement turn sour.

"Your dad and I'd love to go out on double date with the two of you."

"Okay, that's enough of your matchmaking; I need to get dressed."

Jennifer tried her best to hide her disappointment over not hearing from Josh, but the sympathetic look on her mother's face proved she hadn't succeeded.

"You've never gotten over *him*, have you?"

"No, and I doubt I ever will." There was no use denying she knew who her mother meant; after all, her family had met Josh at Sarah's wedding, and he'd made them breakfast the next morning—*approximately sixteen hours before our wedding.*

"Have you spoken with Josh lately?"

"He called a few weeks ago."

"Honey, I know you don't wish to hear this, but Alexander's much more stable and attentive than Josh has ever been. Sure, he was nice and all, but he only swooped in for the wedding, and he was gone again the next afternoon. Other than the few phone calls you've mentioned, he's never flown back to see you. I think it's time to let him go and move on with your life."

Jennifer couldn't stop the tears from welling in her eyes. "I know some things aren't destined to be, but I loved Josh with all my heart." It felt good to profess her love out loud.

"I'm sure you did. But I've seen the way Alexander looks at you and you at him. Don't throw away your chance at happiness with someone who loves you in hope of Josh coming back."

"I need to get ready," Jennifer said before dashing upstairs to the bedroom. *Great! Now my eyes are puffy.* She blotted them with a tissue and fixed her makeup, then slipped on the gown and heels from Alexander.

~Jennifer, you look like a princess,~ Talos messaged from his spot on the loveseat.

~Thank you.~

~Please don't be sad; I know if he can, Josh will stop by to see you.~

~I wish more than anything I was wearing this dress for him.~

~In a way you are, because no matter what the future holds, he'll always be nearby watching over you. Even if there comes a time you can no longer see him, you can be certain Josh will be by your side. I can promise he'll be the one who'll transition you home when your life here has finished.~

~Is it wrong to wish that time was now?~

~Please don't wish your experience here away, but instead, embrace each moment as if it were your last. There's much for you to learn, and before you know it, Josh and you will be reunited.~

Jennifer reached for the pearl necklace her mother lent her and clasped it in place, then donned the matching earrings. A glance at the clock showed Alexander would be there in fifteen minutes, lowering her hopes of seeing her husband.

~You look beautiful, Jennifer,~ Josh messaged from behind her while hiding his emotions as best he could. *For once being translucent is beneficial.* He ran his fingers through his hair, but it failed to calm his trepidation. *She belongs to someone else now, and there's not a damn thing I can do about it.*

Her eyes met Josh's, and her heart accelerated. ~Thank you,~ she messaged, doing her best not to make eye contact so he wouldn't see her tears.

~Baby, I want you to have a good time tonight. I'll be there watching over you, making sure to keep you safe—*always*.~ He left the last word tucked away in his thoughts.

The words from the manual haunted Jennifer as the truth played out before her eyes. ~You want me to be with Alexander for real?~

~Can't you tell this is killing me?! The last thing I want is to lose you, or see you with another man, but there will come a time I won't have any other choice.~

~So this is it? Whatever happened to fighting for our love?~

~Alexander can give you everything I can't! I see how happy he makes you and how alive you are around him. All I'm doing is holding you back from living the life you're supposed to live.~ Josh turned around and walked over to the window, staring out into the night without seeing.

~If you're trying to end our marriage, you better say so to my face! I deserve that much from the man I pledged my heart to forever!~ Jennifer pushed back, hoping to bring Josh to his senses. *There must be a way we can defy destiny!*

~Never!~ Josh whipped around, no longer able to hide his pain. ~Fuck Gisabella! She doesn't want you to find out that you're locked into a contract to marry someone here on earth! Worst of all, there's not a goddamn thing I can do to stop it because it's been written into your lifepath.~

~So you're finally admitting that to me.~

~What do you mean—*finally* admitting?~

~I know about the high priestess obligation to marry someone and to bear their child.~ She watched Josh pale.

~You mean you've known about the rule for a while? Great, Gisabella's gonna kill me when she finds out I told you.~

~Oh no she won't, not if she wants me to accept my position as high priestess! I knew she was manipulative, but this?~ Suddenly, Jennifer's expression transformed as recognition bloomed.

~What is it?~

~I remember the night you and Gisabella were fighting. The two of you were having a terrible argument when I came downstairs—and going back and forth accusing one another. Gisabella mentioned Sarnia, and I remember being stunned.~ Jennifer paused as if trying to visualize the scene. ~But it was you who spoke of my being forced to marry someone in eight years' time. I was so angry and shocked over how you and Gisabella conspired together to trick me; that's why I transported out of there.~

Jennifer lowered her gaze away from Josh's wild-eyed expression and swiped at her tears. After a few seconds, as if more of the memory snapped into focus, her eyes shot up. ~Gisabella lied to both of us, didn't she?~

~She didn't lie.~ He closed his eyes to escape the pain written all over Jennifer's face.

~So when you married me, you knew we'd only have eight years before I'd be forced to marry someone else? Why did you lie to me?~

~Please believe I had no choice but to agree to her terms. Yes, we should've had eight years together, but when Alexander showed up, all but sweeping you off your feet, I figured out he must be your destiny.~

~So you decided to give me up before our time together was over.~

~Jennifer, I know you too well not to recognize how torn you are between the living and the dead.~

~If that isn't the biggest cop-out I've ever heard—labeling yourself as dead. Weren't you the one who once said, "I'm as alive as you are, complete with organs and blood"?~

~That's just semantics. Either way, as far as anyone else is concerned, I don't exist in your world.~

~Is this why you haven't made love to me in weeks?~ Jennifer accused.

~You're falling in love with another man, and I see it written all over your face each time he calls, takes you to lunch, talks to you at work and so many other countless moments. I've watched the way your eyes light up when he's around. Think of my backing away now before you throw me to the curb as a form of self-preservation. Look, Alexander's a great guy, and as much as I'd like to think otherwise, he can make you happy. It'd sure be easier if Alexander was an asshole—so I'd have a reason to pull you away.~

~If you like Alexander so much, then you marry him!~

~I know this is hard for you to understand, but as your life-path moves forward, there'll be no way you can stop yourself from falling in love with him, no matter how much you love me. Even if we both do everything we can to stay together, your soul has been preprogrammed to be with him. Not only that, but the spell Gisabella has surely placed on you guarantees you'll follow your destiny.~

~What will happen to us?~ Jennifer's lips quivered.

~When I said my vows to you, I made sure I did so in a way that after your life has ended we can be together forever. Thankfully, you followed my lead. So, once your life here ends, I'll be the one waiting to transition you home forever. I can only hope when that time comes, that you'll still love me.~

~Mr. Smith, my love for you will never die! Mark my words, I will never give my entire heart to another, no matter what potion my grandma has cast. You alone own my heart and soul! Furthermore, nothing anyone does could ever take them away from you—not Alexander or anyone else!~ Jennifer's breath came in gasps as she tried not to break down.

Josh covered the space between them in two strides while densifying his energy, then pulled Jennifer into his embrace. ~Baby, my heart and soul will always be yours alone. I swear I love you as I have never loved before.~ His lips crushed hers passionately as he poured the past few torturous months into his kiss before he was forced to reluctantly pull back. ~Alexander will be here shortly. You'd better wipe your tears and touch up your makeup before your mother comes to check on your progress.~

~I wish I was staying home with you.~

A perplexed look flashed across Josh's face. ~Baby, you said you knew about your obligation to marry before you remembered overhearing Gisabella and myself arguing?~

~Umm, kind of...~ *Oh no! If I don't think of something to say, he'll figure out I have the book!* Jennifer tried to think of an explanation, but she wasn't fast enough.

~Talos, did you have anything to do with this?~ Josh glared in the cat's direction.

~It was my idea,~ Jennifer spoke up.

~What exactly was this idea you came up with?~

~Fine—if you must know, I brought some of my homework here.~

~What does school have to do with us?~ Josh paled as her meaning hit home. ~Holy fuck! Did you sneak home the High Priestess manual? You did, didn't you? Great, another reason for Gisabella to kill me.~

~She was the one who insisted I read the damn thing! Serves her right that I felt pressured into taking it with me. I was only catching up on my studies to make you both happy.~

~Maybe she won't find out it's here.~

~If my grandma so much as touches one hair on your head, I'll run to the Council and tell them everything I know.~

~Don't *ever* let her hear you say that, or we'll both be disintegrated.~

~I'd never really go to the Council; I'm just so angry! We haven't been given nearly enough time together.~

~Baby, no matter how much time we had together, it still wouldn't be long enough. Believe me when I say, if there was a way to hide you where no one could find us, I'd have found it.~

Before Josh could consider their options, Jennifer raised her lips to his. He returned her kiss, softly at first, until the thought of losing her grabbed hold of his heart, and his need for his wife consumed his senses. Brushing the pain aside, he slid his hands down Jennifer's body until they rested on her backside. Then he pulled her against his hardening ache that was longing to make love to her. ~God, how I need you!~

~Tonight, my love. Please, Josh, before destiny pulls us apart, I want to make love every moment we can. Promise me you won't push me away or let me go any sooner than we must.~ The feel of Josh's mouth on hers sent waves of unanswered desire coursing through her body.

~Jennifer, I want to more than anything, but I risk damaging your soul.~

~I promise you won't damage any part of me. I know my destiny lies in another's love, but for tonight, I only want to be with you. I can tell Alexander I've got a headache so he'll have his driver take me home early. I promise I won't stay any longer than I have to.~ She ran her hands up and down his biceps with a wicked smile meant only for him. ~The whole time, I'll be thinking of your naked body and all the pleasure I want to give you. This time, don't you dare try and pull away before I've had my fill of you.~

~I'd love nothing more! I promise to be here, my love. Besides, what's one more broken rule?~

~I'll be thinking of you the entire time,~ she promised.

~All the while, I'll be watching over you until you arrive safely home. Then the only danger you'll need to worry about is how little sleep you'll be getting.~

Before she could answer, there was a knock on the door.

"Alexander's here," Mrs. Parker called out.

"I'll be there in a few minutes, Mom."

~I'd better go. If you change your mind, I'll understand,~ Josh said, making sure to give Jennifer an out in case she fell deeper in love with his replacement between now and then.

~Not gonna happen!~

After one more kiss, Josh disappeared from the room, and Jennifer did her best to touch up her makeup before she grabbed her coat and headed downstairs.

With a cleansing breath, she tried to muster a smile as she headed in the direction of her mother's voice. *Maybe when she's done grilling Alexander, I won't have to worry about him sticking around—goodbye destiny!* The thought brightened her desolate mood.

"It's a shame my husband and I haven't had a chance to get together with your parents," Jennifer heard her mother say as she approached. *Oh mother—please don't encourage him.*

"I apologize, Mrs. Parker; it's entirely my fault. I should've made more of an effort to break away from my work. My parents are out of town, but you and Mr. Parker are welcome to join us this evening. Although, I'm afraid these events can be quite dull."

"Here I thought my daughter was deliberately keeping you all to herself, " Mrs. Parker retorted with a cool expression. "I suppose she told you how I feel about art. If so, I can see why you kept your distance. However, I believe there's a huge difference between the vagabonds who have no future, and the way you've managed to turn your love of art into a successful career. To be clear, I wholeheartedly approve of you and Jennifer's relationship."

Alexander looked up in time to see Jennifer heading down the steps. "If you'll excuse me, Mrs. Parker, I'd like to greet my date." He skirted around her and headed toward the staircase. "Jennifer, you take my breath away—that color gives your skin an iridescent glow, like you are standing in the moonlight."

Jennifer's expression softened. *Alexander's such a sweet man who doesn't deserve to have his heart crushed.* Smiling brightly, she reached out and accepted the rose he offered while admiring his elegant attire. "You weren't kidding when you said you'd be wearing a tuxedo." Jennifer gulped. *I love my husband, I love my husband...* She repeated the mantra over and over while making sure to block her thoughts.

"Alexander, you look very handsome." *Oh no, that came out too breathy. Agh, why is the pull to Alexander so strong? Because he's been written into your destiny, stupid!* "We should be going so we're on time. You know how Oscar gets—he'll have a cow if we're late!"

Jennifer turned to her mom and gave her a quick peck on the cheek. "Goodnight, Mom. I'll be home late, so don't wait up." *Actually, I plan on being home a whole lot earlier!*

In the driveway, Alexander's limo awaited to transport them to the city with Claude poised next to the opened door.

"Thank you, Claude," Jennifer greeted. Alexander assisted her with her gown as she climbed into the limo. Soon they were alone in the back seat and on their way.

"Maybe now you'll tell me about your new exhibit," she teased. "I can't believe you've kept your collection a secret from me all this time! At least give me a clue."

"Nope!" Alexander laughed at his date's sweet pout. "Darling, I want you to be surprised. I only hope you love the collection as much as I do."

"I think loving anything you've painted is a given. I'm so lucky to have such a handsome and talented escort."

"Be careful, Jennifer, or I may whisk you away and keep you all to myself."

"Sorry, but I have a curfew," she retorted, opting instead to change the subject. "Do you think there'll be a lot of people?"

"Oscar received over four hundred R.S.V.P.s."

"That many!" Jennifer squeaked. "Where will they all fit?"

"The gallery's a big place, and they won't all be there at once. Many will only stop by to say a quick hello, while others will stay for a while."

"I sometimes forget how famous you are." She wrung her hands together.

"*Mon ange*, there's no need to be nervous; I'll be by your side the entire night."

"Right, and I'll be there to make sure all the bimbos leave you alone."

"That was our original deal, but I'd rather hoped by now, you'd consider changing the parameters."

"Do you think the driver can turn up the heat?" Jennifer asked, rubbing her arms briskly to overemphasize her need. *Please don't ask me to be anything but your friend because I'm frightened I won't have the resolve to turn you down.* Once Alexander requested the heat be turned up, he peeled off his jacket and draped it across her lap.

"I don't wish you to catch a chill, especially on such an important night."

Josh frowned. *What does Alexander mean by an* important *night? Something doesn't sound right.* When Josh attempted to read the artist's thoughts, he couldn't break into them. *Something's up!* It was as if Alexander's thoughts were being protected by a steel barrier. *I swear this has Gisabella written all over it! She must've conjured some spell to keep me in the dark. But why?* An unbidden thought occurred to him. *For fuck's sake! He can't be asking Jennifer to marry him—it's too soon!*

"Your hands are like ice," Alexander exclaimed, grasping both of her hands between his to rub some warmth back into them. "Is that any better?"

"They're fine—I always have cold hands," Jennifer softened her rebuttal after she snatched them away. "Maybe we should go over the list of women I need to distract." Ever since the day they'd agreed on their arrangement, Alexander usually gave her a list of names with descriptions of the people he wished to avoid; ninety-five percent of them had been women. "I still don't understand how you've managed to stay single for so long when you have so many of the most beautiful women I've ever seen surrounding you."

"My sweet, do you not see that they do nothing for me? Those women are nothing but sparkling jewels, who, when examined up close, are only an imperfect imitation. *Ma cherie,* if I were still painting in my garage and broke, none of them would've given me the time of day. I learned the hard way not to trust many people's sincerity. You, on the other hand, have always been real with me. So much so, I know I can count on you to knock me down a peg or two if my ego gets too inflated."

"I don't know what you're talking about? I've never been able to deflate your ego." Her nervous laughter rang out, preventing any possibility of Alexander turning the moment into something serious. To her relief, Alexander began listing the people she needed to help distract.

"You already know Alisha. Tall, emaciated, model-thin, with hair extensions...."

As Alexander continued, Jennifer found herself staring at him. *Why does he have to be so handsome? Those soft, soulful eyes and inviting lips. I wonder if his kiss is as great as I remember? It was as if he'd poured all his artistry into it: sweet, soft and scrumptious. Oh my god, what's wrong with me?! Josh is the only man I ever want to kiss from now on! Mmm, but Alexander is sitting oh so close, and his magnetism is so strong. That's it! I'm weak! In fact, I must be the weakest person in the entire world. Damn it— spell or not, his mouth's so inviting.*

"Jennifer, are you okay?" Alexander asked.

"Um—yes, I—I was trying to picture the people you were talking about, though I'm afraid I zoned out somewhere after Alisha," she admitted, doing her best to hide her wayward thoughts behind her flushed cheeks. *What am I going to do now? I can't risk my future with Josh. I still love him. It's just that Alexander's alive in this dimension, and it's nice to hold hands and hear the sound of his voice. People greet us as a couple! Pretend or not, I like feel like I'm in a normal relationship—I mean friendship. No, no, no! No matter how I look at it—he's no Josh!*

"Darling, you can zone out anytime you want if you keep staring at me like that."

She found herself hypnotized by the sound of his velvety voice. So much so, she failed to stop him from tilting her chin up with his fingertips until her eyes met his.

"There's no reason to be shy with me. I know you better than you think."

When Alexander lowered his lips to hers, all Jennifer's plans to resist him melted away. She was hopelessly lost in his sweet, seductive kiss when his hand moved from her chin to the back of her neck, making it possible for him to deepen the kiss without her backing away. Alexander's tongue was in her mouth before it registered in her mind to stop him. All her thoughts evaporated as his kiss gave her so much pleasure that her body began reacting with need.

Oh, Jennifer, how could you have given in so easily? Josh thought as sharp pains lanced through his heart. *I can't watch this!* The realization that he'd agreed to stay on as Jennifer's protector was a rude awakening. *How did I think I could handle watching her fall in love with another man?*

Jennifer pushed Alexander away. "I'm sorry—I can't!"

"Please don't tell me you're still holding out for that stupid guy who's never around? *Mon ange*, you deserve far better than him. Besides, there's no ring on your finger, which to me means he wants you to remain on the market. Silly boy, he has no clue what a priceless treasure he has. Maybe when you see my new pieces, you'll know how deeply my feelings for you run."

"We'd better finish going through the list." Jennifer glanced down at her wedding rings that only she, Josh, Gisabella and Merlin could see before she raised her fingers to her fully kissed lips that were aching for more. *I pray Josh wasn't watching.* Her stomach roiled at the thought.

They'd just finished the list of names when their limo pulled up in front of the gallery, where they were greeted by roving spotlights and swarms of people. Most of the crowd was dressed in elegant gowns and tuxedos, flashing their diamonds and fur coats with their wealth on full display.

"Stay put, Jennifer. I'll come around to your side and help you out," Alexander instructed, removing his jacket from her lap. Once he pulled it on, he nodded to Claude to open the door. The moment he stepped out, Alexander was greeted by loud cheering, camera shutters clicking, and TV crews asking for much-awaited interviews. Jennifer noted how many women rushed forward with desperate looks, hoping they'd be the one to catch the famous artist's eye.

As much as she wanted to send Josh a message, there was no time, nor would she be able to find the words needed to make up for kissing Alexander—*again. Future husband or not, I must refrain from ever kissing him again,* she thought, squelching the reality that Josh had been right: she'd never be strong enough to fight her destiny or Gisabella's powerful magic. She dragged in a deep breath and, donning her poker face and fake smile, she accepted Alexander's hand as she stepped out of the limo.

CHAPTER TWENTY-NINE

"Over here, Alexander," a reporter shouted, his camera poised as if desperate to capture at least one newsworthy photo.

Blinded by the bright flashes and lights, Jennifer squeezed Alexander's hand while he waved the other, acknowledging each person who waved or shouted for his attention. She found it easy to be in awe of his ability to handle the huge crowd as if they were old friends and for making each person feel appreciated. The enormity of the crowd pushed away all thoughts of her conversation with Josh and her shared kiss with Alexander.

"Thank you for coming," Alexander greeted an older man who was leaning on a cane. "I'll see you inside." When the man's expression drooped, Alexander patted him on the shoulder. "Don't worry, I'll make sure the guards let you in, as long as you promise to find me later. I want to know what you think of the new pieces."

Jennifer felt the man's emotional response. *How did Alexander know he's not on the guest list?* Such a thoughtful gesture made her heart swell with pride. He was so kind and would've made a wonderful husband if she hadn't already given her heart away to the man she'd always love more.

Josh's temper rose with every minute they remained outside. *What the hell is wrong with Alexander? This mob is making it impossible to protect Jennifer!* Josh added another layer of white light protection on top of the previous two he'd conjured before they'd exited the limo. All he could do now was watch helplessly as his wife stood by Alexander's side as he greeted each of the fans, noticing how her shoulders lost a little more tension with each introduction.

"Are you getting too cold, *mon ange*?" Alexander asked, lifting his free hand to caress her cheek.

When she shook her head no, Alexander lowered his lips to hers in a public display of affection. *Push him away,* Jennifer commanded her limbs, but her hands had other ideas, moving up to rest on his shoulders as her lips parted, welcoming him into her mouth.

If Josh's emotions weren't so tangled up, he'd have found the spectators' reactions entertaining: the men cheered and laughed while a number of women shot daggered glares at Jennifer before storming off. When the kiss ended, he followed his wife and Alexander inside, where champagne flowed like the Nile, and caviar was served in enormous silver punch bowls. The show was opulence at its very best. Men in well-tailored suits escorting elegant women dripping with diamonds, each trying their best to outdo one another. Meanwhile, each was consumed with determining who in the room could advance their careers or which person could make them the most money. Conversations became nothing but a calculated risk, and they were betting alright, not on horses—but people.

The night dragged on as Josh endured several hours of watching Alexander moving in on Jennifer during the exclusive gala. *My job must come first,* he told himself. Jennifer seemed happy, and he knew it'd be wrong to message how much he loved her. It'd only confuse her and could push her into Alexander's arms faster. No matter how many lies he told himself, the ache in his soul kept expanding, becoming more unbearable by the second.

"Congratulations, Alexander," a blond man in a well-cut tuxedo greeted while holding out a freshly manicured hand.

"Daniel, how kind of you to stop by. How's your father been?"

"He's well, thanks," Daniel replied while glancing at Jennifer. "And who's this pretty little lady?"

Alexander hesitated before he introduced Jennifer.

"The pleasure is all mine," Daniel said, holding out his hand.

As much as she was dying to take the man, who seemed very arrogant, down a peg, or three, Jennifer held out her hand politely.

"If you'll excuse us, we need to speak to Oscar."

"We?" Daniel said with his eyes resting on Jennifer.

"Jennifer and I have been seeing each other for a while, and she works for Oscar. Please tell your father hello from me. Next time my parents are in town, I'm sure they'd love to set up a meeting."

"I'll pass along the word. It was a pleasure meeting you, Jennifer." Daniel extended his hand once more.

"Good night, Daniel." Jennifer pulled back her hand as soon as Daniel loosened his grip, then reached for her date's hand instead. "How do you know him?" she whispered when they were out of earshot.

"His father's a senator, but Daniel didn't take after him. Instead, he graduated from some ivy league school and became a lawyer. Word has it his father will be running for president, and he's forcing Daniel to run for his vacated senate seat," Alexander relayed before he held open his arms to greet the gallery owner.

"The show's a success!" Oscar gushed. "Of course—I never had any doubts about your work." Turning to Jennifer, Oscar's smile doubled in size. "What about you, young lady, what do you think of your boyfriend's opening night?"

"It's marvelous!" Jennifer beamed. "Oh no—don't look now, but number five on your list is walking over here. Excuse me, gentlemen," Jennifer said before heading off to intercept the woman before she could get close enough to sink her claws into Alexander.

"Oscar, while we have a moment alone, I wanted to ask if it'd be okay if I steal your employee for a little while?" Alexander asked. "I'd like to show Jennifer the special piece I painted?"

"You mean the one you've been working on for over a month? I can't help but feel slighted that my employee gets to see it before me."

"If all goes well tonight, it'll be on display in your gallery for all the world to see."

"Only to look at, huh?" Oscar teased. "In that case, you and Jennifer run along." Oscar lowered his voice, "Young lovers should always have private moments away from prying eyes."

"On that we agree, my friend!" Alexander patted Oscar on the back and headed to where Jennifer was busy talking to number five on his list. He came up to Jennifer from behind and planted a soft kiss on the back of her neck.

"Oh—*Alexander*, it's you," Jennifer stuttered, momentarily thinking it was Josh who'd kissed her. If Alexander suspected something was off, he hid it well.

"You don't mind if I steal my girlfriend?" Alexander asked while leading Jennifer away before the lady could protest. "I want to show you a piece I created." Upon Jennifer's approval, Alexander led the way to the elevator, where, once inside, he pressed the top floor button.

"Why isn't it with the collection?" Jennifer gulped. *Why am I so nervous? Maybe because he's kissed me a few times, and I failed to push him away. No more! I must make it clear that we'll never be anything but good friends. And certainly not the type with midnight booty calls!* The elevator crawled to a stop, and the door opened.

"It's over this way." Alexander made a quick right and headed down a long hallway with doors on either side.

"Are you sure it's alright to be up here?" Her voice came out shaky, and she wondered why Alexander hadn't noticed. Aware that Josh was surely watching helped ease her apprehension.

When they reached the last door on the right, Alexander pulled out a key and opened the door. A flick of the light switch illuminated a workroom full of artists' tools, blank canvases, tubes of oil paint, brushes, palettes, and a lonely stool positioned in front of a tall easel.

"Jennifer, I've been working on a special piece that I hope to make the centerpiece of my next collection. I have a series of paintings in mind that will tell a story of friendship—once new, at the beginning frail and unsure, deepening as time moves forward and their trust grows. I painted this final piece to show you how special you are to me."

Alexander walked to the large black velvet curtain and took hold of the braided cord, giving it a gentle tug. The falling folds of fabric floated to the floor, revealing a life-sized canvas of Jennifer standing in the room they were in, wearing the same dress she had on tonight.

Oh my God! Alexander painted this very moment! Oh no! Jennifer thought in horror when she noticed he painted himself into the picture, kneeling before her with a small box. Their painted faces depicted their rapture with each other, but her real expression was a far cry from the one captured on canvas. She was too stunned to move or speak—she could only stare in shock when Alexander knelt before her, mirroring the image in the painting.

"Jennifer, I know at first we agreed on a friendship with no fringe benefits, but I can no longer deny how deep my feelings for you have grown. I think the time has come to propose a new agreement between the two of us."

"I—" Jennifer tried to say something, but nothing came out.

"Please let me finish before I lose my nerve. I've known a lot of women during my lifetime, but none have made me feel the way you do. I couldn't be myself around them, and after a while, I pulled away from all hope of building a future with someone. Then I met you, the only person who's taken the time to get to know the real me and not try to force me into being someone I'm not. I know this is soon, but I promise I'll do everything in my power to make you happy. Jennifer, I don't want to live another day without you. Please say you'll marry me?" Alexander gazed up as if Jennifer was the answer to all his prayers.

"I—I'm sorry—I—I must go," Jennifer cried, fighting back the pain in her soul that was screaming—*yes—yes, I'll marry you*!

"I don't understand? What's wrong?"

"Nothing's wrong with you; that's the problem. Please let me go. Forget me, Alexander—I could never bring you happiness."

"What are you talking about? Everything about you makes me happy." He stood and grabbed hold of her arms to prevent her from bolting out the door. "Don't tell me you're still in love with that fool who has never shown his face to anyone but you! If so, please give me any other reason for turning me away. Tell me this hasn't all been a game to you, like all the others!"

"Don't ever think you were a game to me. I am falling in love with you, but I—I can't tell you why I must resist you. I'm sorry, I can't marry you."

"Jennifer, what are you afraid of? You're not making any sense. Tell me I didn't imagine the way you responded to my kisses," Alexander demanded.

When Jennifer said nothing, he lowered his mouth to hers with determination, willing her to respond like she had earlier. He kissed her hard, taking what he wanted, and when she gave in to his desire, separating her lips, he softened the kiss, teasing and enticing her. Using his artful French kiss, his tongue lingered in all the right places until he felt Jennifer's nails dig into his arms, demanding he give her more.

"Please," Jennifer begged against Alexander's soft lips with her eyes closed. "I need you." Her words were tumbling out of their own accord, but in her mind, it was her husband whom she was begging.

"I'll give you my heart and the desire you crave. I want to take you to my bed and make sweet love to you, but only once you agree to marry me. I couldn't bear it if you left me afterwards. Jennifer, please say yes," Alexander begged as his hand traveled to her breasts.

"No, please don't—I'm sorry, Alexander—I could have easily fallen in love with you if not for already being spoken for. Forget me; it's for the best." Jennifer watched the hurt register in Alexander's eyes, but it was too painful to witness. *How could I have done this to him?*

When he dropped his hands to his sides and turned his back, she raced out of the room, running as fast as she could down the hall. Once in the elevator, she pressed the lobby button several times, only to catch one last glimpse of Alexander's tear-soaked face as the doors shut.

What have I done? There was no time to think about the ramifications to her life-path or destiny, or how it would impact her job at the gallery as she fought to escape to a place where no one could find her.

Her heart pounded as the elevator made its slow descent to the lobby. *Hurry up!* Each second that ticked by, her stomach clenched, threatening to void the few hors d'oeuvres she'd eaten.

I pray Alexander isn't waiting in the lobby. Realizing how Alexander could have run down the steps in time to meet the elevator made her frantic. *Please let me escape without him making a scene in the lobby. I don't know if I'll be able to resist Alexander's offer if I see him again.*

What am I thinking?! I will not betray Josh no matter what spell has been cast upon my heart and soul. I loved Josh long before I knew about my destiny or the rule that says I must marry Alexander and birth the next heir to the high priestess throne! Josh is my one true soulmate, and I need to find him! There must be somewhere we can go where no one can find us.

When the elevator dinged at the lobby floor, Jennifer pressed the open door button, hurrying it along. Adrenaline coursed through her entire body, magnifying her nervous system's flight or fight response. Consumed with panic and her need to escape from Alexander, she was left with only one option—*run*!

Her legs were shaking when the doors began opening. She wildly scanned the room for any signs of Alexander, praying he hadn't been fast enough to catch up. The crowd had thinned, so it was easy for her to exit the elevator and run across the lobby to the front door.

"Jennifer!"

She hurried out the door without turning around to see who called her name. *Please don't come after me!*

The temperature had dropped, making her rapid puffs of shallow breaths appear like little fluffy cotton balls hanging in midair. The blaring sounds of horns, flashing lights and smells of the city further overwhelmed her oversensitive nervous system, making it a struggle to remain upright, let alone think straight.

She wrapped her arms around her shivering body. Even though the traffic was lighter than usual, she still had to wait a couple of moments for an opening in the many lanes of traffic before she was able to dart across.

~Jennifer, stop! Please wait for my help.~ Josh messaged, doing his best to control the situation, but Jennifer was too wild with fright to hear him.

"Jennifer, stop! Let me at least take you home," Alexander yelled out, chasing after her.

She quickly looked over her shoulder, but the only thing she saw was how full of despair his face appeared. Alexander was shouting, causing her to double her efforts, running as fast as she could in her heels. It was useless, Alexander would catch her before long.

Drivers honking, people shouting, and the alarms blaring in her thoughts mingled in the background, only to be replaced by something far louder. It took a few seconds for her to register what was happening, but by then, all she could do was cover her ears and scream. The horrific sound of screeching tires was all she heard.

No! Josh cried out before he became solid.

When everything went pitch black, the only thing that remained was the faint sound of Josh's voice. It lingered in her mind like a light in the distance, beckoning her to follow before so many destinies were altered, and the world as she knew it forever ceased to exist.

You've reached the end of Book 2 in the Destined To Be Lovers Saga.

CONNECT WITH SUZANNE NEMEC

Thank you for reading Book Two of my *Destined To Be Lovers Saga*. If you enjoyed it, please take time to leave a review on Amazon, Kindle, Goodreads, Barnes and Noble, or one of your other favorite online retailers.

I'm currently working on Book Three, and like most readers, I want to know what happens next with Josh and Jennifer too!

For more information on Josh and Jennifer, plus updates on future books, please stop by my website; www.suzannenemec.net. While you're there, don't forget to sign up to receive my newsletter.

Followers welcome here:

Reader Facebook page:
@Josh's Visionaries: Suzanne Nemec Reader Group
facebook.com/groups/suzannenemecreaders/

facebook.com/AuthorSuzanneNemec
twitter.com/SuzanneNemec
instagram.com/SuzanneNemecAuthor
pinterest.com/SuzanneNemecAuthor
bookbub.com/authors/suzanne-nemec
goodreads.com/SuzanneNemec

SHATTERED DESTINIES PLAYLIST

1. Louie Smith - Can't Live If Living Is Without You
2. Lady Gaga - The Cure
3. Kristin Chenoweth - I've Got a Crush on You
4. Ghostly Kisses - Spellbound
5. Charlie Puth - One Call Away
6. Fleetwood Mac - Tango in the Night
7. Michael Buble - God Only knows
8. Alex Lattimore - Ma Cherie Amour
9. Percy Sledge - When a Man Loves a Woman
10. Sam Smith - I'm Not the Only One
11. Jessica Simpson - When You Told Me You Loved Me
12. Little Mix - The Four Walls
13. Dami Im - Gladiator
14. Katy Perry - Unconditionally

ACKNOWLEDGMENTS

Thank you to all who have been a part of this journey. My husband, Michael, for the many lifetimes we've shared. My spirit guide, Josh, for putting up with me and for the countless validations I needed before I finally believed in you. My Reiki healer and psychic teacher, Dominique, for helping me stay healthy and sane through it all, while also putting up with Josh. Sandy Anastasi, for your wonderful coaching sessions and help in working with my snarky spirit guide. Medium Kelly Muslim, for bridging the final gap that gave me no choice but to finally believe. My new editor, Krista, for taking on this project. Angelina, for the great memes, critique and friendship. My author bff, Acacia, I'm so glad you're part of my life. Elizabeth, for showing up at my front door for my 60th! My beta readers, Laura, Melinda and Acacia, for being the first to read Book 2. My formatter/web designer, Alex, who amazingly puts up with my Virgo pickiness, no matter how many times I bug him. My family and friends who believed in me even when I sometimes doubted myself. And, to all who have read and taken the time to leave a review—I'm very grateful. Finally, to all those on the other side who have played such a large role in my life, thank you for the many signs you've given me and your help with this story.

LEARN MORE

If you would like to learn more about astrology, psychometry, gemstone properties, scrying, mediumship, and all other metaphysical studies, visit Sandy Anastasi, creator and author of the *Sandy Anastasi System-Psychic Development* series at: www.sandyanastasi.com.

CPSIA information can be obtained
at www.ICGtesting.com
Printed in the USA
LVHW041058010419
612520LV00004B/306

9 780999 041727